THE GIRL
ON THE HORSE

STEVE BAILEY

The Girl On The Horse

Copyright © Stephen R P Bailey 2019

Novels by the same author:

The Girl On The Horse

The Fourth Cart, which is a trilogy comprising:

- The Avenging Buddha
- No Tears For The Fallen
- The Tibetan Heist

PROLOGUE

Six years ago

As summer holidays go, Jennifer's was going about as perfect as she imagined was humanly possible, having had six weeks of absolute bliss away from school and exams. Charged by her parents with no responsibility other than to enjoy her freedom while it lasted, and to foster fond memories before the burdens of adulthood jaundiced her view on life, it was a duty she'd taken to heart, filling her days with copious amounts of physical activity and family picnics on the beach.

Horse riding, in particular, had featured high in Jennifer's growing stock of cherished memories, largely due to Surachai, a honey-skinned sarong-wearing stable-boy who habitually directed her riding sessions away from the stables at the British Club down through the woods to the beautiful white sands of Dongtan Beach.

Inevitably, the last day of Jennifer's holiday arrived far too soon and it came as no surprise to her mother that her eighteen-year-old daughter would choose to spend the last hours of daylight with Surachai, a boy of a similar age, at the beach, on horseback, away from prying eyes.

Riding in silence, side by side along the water's edge, Jennifer had been in a reflective mood for some time, content to allow her horse to amble at its own pace. Her mind had strayed far beyond the beach, for tomorrow she would have to pack her bags, say farewell to her family and set off for a new life; a life to be spent in an unfamiliar land, away from the people she loved. She looked across at Surachai, an eager grin beaming across his face, and realised she would also miss the boy deeply.

Perhaps misinterpreting the expression on Jennifer's face, Surachai enthusiastically asked, 'Do you want to race, Miss Jennifer?'

Jennifer heard the question, but it took a while for it to sink in, her mind trapped in a fog of self-doubt as she endlessly revisited the question as to whether taking up her hard-won place at university in England was the right thing to do or not. 'In a minute, maybe,' she responded in the local tongue. She returned to her reverie, thinking she could probably stay in this tropical paradise, if she so chose. Yet the idea of a life in Surithani's foreign enclave left her with a sense of dread as the atmosphere of the five-hundred strong community of predominantly British expats was profoundly claustrophobic.

Surachai was, apparently, not going to be put off. 'First one back to the beach hut wins?'

'Why not,' Jennifer responded nonchalantly. 'You're on.'

Catching her off guard, Surachai's horse bolted forward, opening up a ten-yard gap before Jennifer realised what had happened. Undaunted, and with a shriek of exhilaration, she gripped her horse's reins tightly, dug her heels in hard and gave chase. To her chagrin, it took over a hundred yards to catch up with the horse in front. 'You cheated,' she shouted across to Surachai as she drew level. 'You didn't say when to start.'

Surachai returned a sideways glance and laughed. 'Am I going too fast for you, Miss Jennifer? I can slow down to a girl's speed if you like.'

In mock indignation Jennifer retorted with a few choice expletives she'd recently overheard in a street market. The effect of her new vocabulary was rather more dramatic than she'd anticipated, for, within a split second, Surachai brought his horse to a grinding halt. Satisfyingly, she sped past and punched an arm in the air. 'I win,' she shouted in jubilation as she reached the communal beach hut.

Surachai looked shocked as his panting horse eventually drew alongside. 'Miss Jennifer,' he said, 'Who taught you such words? Not my aunt, I hope. They are very bad words for a lady to say.'

Jennifer swung her right leg over the saddle and slid off her horse. 'No, Surachai. It wasn't your aunt. Jum teaches me nothing improper, I promise you that. Don't worry, your family's honour remains intact. Now, let's tether the horses. I want to watch the sun set before I leave.'

Surachai jumped off his horse and, like the faithful servant he was, took the reins from Jennifer and led both horses into the small enclosed paddock in the shade of trees behind the hut. Leaving him to attend his charges, Jennifer sauntered towards the shoreline to admire the spectacle of the sun's sparkling, golden rays shimmering on the sea, stretching in a line to the horizon.

No other beach in the world came anywhere close to the serenity offered by Dongtan Beach. For, like the rest of country, it was entirely devoid of pollution and tourists. As the fiery orange ball in the sky finally touched the sea, Jennifer sat on the sand, hugged her knees and let out a heavy sigh.

Surachai squatted on his haunches a few feet to one side and said, 'Why do you look so unhappy, Miss Jennifer?'

Jennifer snorted. 'Why?' She waved a hand in a wide arc. 'Because of all this. Everything I hold dear is here around me; my childhood memories, my family, my friends, my hopes. This is my home, Surachai. But I have to go away tomorrow, and that breaks my heart.' She wiped away a stray tear.

'Why go away then?'

Jennifer sighed again. 'Because I have to.'

'I don't understand.'

'Nor do I, Surachai. Nor do I.' She looked over at the boy, saw the confusion on his face. 'I envy you. You have a future here. You have a good job at the British Club tending the horses. You'll get married someday, have kids, have grandchildren, and you'll still be here, in this paradise. You don't know how lucky you are.'

Surachai looked forlorn. 'But you can stay here, can't you, Miss Jennifer? You don't have to go; you can live with your parents. That's permitted, is it not?'

Jennifer shook her head. 'It's not as easy as that. I want a life. My own life. I want a career, a fulfilling career. I want to be someone, get somewhere, before I have kids.'

'I don't understand. You can marry, have kids here, can't you?'

Jennifer shook her head. 'No one living here would marry me. All the men bring wives with them on arrival. And their sons move on when they become adults.'

Surachai shuffled a few inches closer. 'I would marry you, Miss Jennifer. You can live with me. I would take care of you.'

Jennifer smiled at the boy. 'Oh, Surachai, that's so sweet of you, but you have no idea how difficult that would be.'

Surachai looked hurt. 'Am I not good enough for you, Miss Jennifer?'

Jennifer laid a hand on the boy's arm. 'I didn't say that, Surachai, and it's not what I was thinking. I shall be at university in England for the next three years, maybe even longer. I just don't know where my life is heading right now.'

'Then I shall wait for you, Miss Jennifer,' replied Surachai with sincerity. 'I shall wait for you, for ever.'

The compliment lifted Jennifer's spirits. She smiled and said, 'I may just hold you to that.' And then she drew closer to him, lent her head on his shoulder, nuzzled up and said, 'Hold me, please, Surachai,' as a torrent of tears rolled down her face.

It was unlikely that Jennifer Collins knew much about drone technology. But even if she did, it was unlikely she'd have believed a drone could be so advanced, so sophisticated, that it would allow an observer to feel as though he was standing right next to her, able to identify the finest of hairs on her arms, to hear her intimate whispers, to smell the fragrance of her hair, all without her knowledge.

Yet a few miles away from where Jennifer sat on the beach, that was exactly what an observer was doing. For half an hour he had watched as she'd galloped along the shoreline, her shoulder length brown hair flying in the breeze, her white cotton blouse wet from spray kicked up by the horses, her vocabulary vulgar when provoked. She had an admirable spirit, similar to a girl he'd known a long time ago. And as he listened, mesmerised, to the pouring out of her heart to the stable-boy, he realised just how endearing was her innocence.

He wiped a solitary tear from the corner of an eye. It was a scene all too familiar, one he'd enacted in his own youth, saying goodbye to a girl before setting sail to a distant, uncharted land. He closed his eyes and drew a deep breath. Even now, he could remember that moment, remember her scent as he hugged her, remember her whispered vow in his ear that she would wait for him.

As always, he could remember every second he'd ever spent with the girl who would become his wife. And the pain of her loss had never left him, despite the passing of forgotten millennia.

Chapter One

Hopes and dreams

The day had been exceptionally dull despite it being the middle of July. Grey clouds had loomed heavily for nigh on a week and there was talk of worse to come. For the residents of Lewes, the depressing weather was just one more thing to gripe about along with divisive politics, outrageous property prices, terrorist attacks and a host of other worldly troubles.

Yet there was no griping from Jennifer Collins. Not on this day, since it was turning out to be the best day of her life. For, just moments ago, whilst in the act of selecting a handful of fresh tomatoes in Tesco supermarket, she'd received a text message from Sussex University advising that her thesis had been accepted. Finally, after six years of a self-imposed, tortuous regime of study and research, her academic goal had been achieved. She was no longer just a graduate; she was now up there amongst the elite in her chosen subject.

With a sense of elation, she skipped along Cliffe High Street, swinging a plastic shopping bag in each hand, smiling broadly at strangers as they passed by, seeing nothing but beauty all around her, from the quaint hump-back bridge over the River Ouse, the famous Harvey's Brewery perched on the banks of the river, the antiquity of the town's medieval twittens, to the modern brickwork of a controversial new hotel rising from the ground. Nothing was going to spoil her happiness; of that she was determined.

Jennifer almost ran up School Hill, despite its steep gradient, grinning at anyone who caught her eye, unable to hide her glee, unable to calm the rush of endorphins pumping through her veins. Lewes was her favourite English town, and its picturesqueness only enhanced the wonderful feeling of euphoria that had taken its grip over her body.

Past the Law Courts, Jennifer gave a sidelong glance into Castle Gate, admiring, as usual, the remains from the bygone age of Norman castles, keeps and barbicans, and wondered how long she would be able to continue living in this beautiful, historic town. Things were bound to change now she was properly qualified. She may even have to relocate to take up a job. Although that, she thought, would be a shame.

Jennifer's flat was only a few steps past Castle Gate, on the other side of the High Street, above an estate agency. She opened the front door, climbed the stairs to the first floor, dumped her shopping bags on the kitchen table and called out, 'Sue? Are you in?'

A tired voice replied, 'I'm soaking in the bath.'

Jennifer found the bathroom door ajar, her blond-haired flatmate lying behind a mountain of foam bubbles, a nurse's uniform draped over the laundry basket, a pile of underwear in an untidy heap on the floor. 'Bad day, I'm guessing?'

'You wouldn't believe me if I showed you the video.'

'Is Alan coming around tonight still, or are you too knackered?'

'He'd better come. He's promised me a massage. I could marry the man just for the soothing effect his hands have on my neck muscles.'

Jennifer smiled. 'You're easily pleased. Is he staying the night?'

'Certainly not. I have my limits after a twelve-hour shift.'

'Of course.' Jennifer waited a few seconds before tentatively adding, 'What about food tonight?'

'Don't worry, Jen. I haven't forgotten it's my turn to cook. Anyway, Alan wouldn't come over without the promise of lasagne. Did you get the shopping?'

'It's on the kitchen table. Along with a couple of bottles of wine. My treat, I'm celebrating tonight.'

Sue poked her head up from behind the mountain of bubbles. 'Has Mike proposed?'

Jennifer cringed. 'No, he has not. And I'm not sure I'd want him to. He's been behaving very petty this last couple of months.'

'So, you're celebrating dumping him then?'

'No. Well, not quite yet, anyway. No, it's just that my thesis has been accepted.'

Sue lay her head back down. 'That's big news is it?'

'It means I have a title now. Doctor.'

Sue poked her head back up. 'And here's me, a nurse! People will talk, Jen, accuse us of playing Doctors and Nurses. Maybe I should get Alan to move in. No, cancel that thought, people will say he's the patient. Sounds like a threesome from a very dodgy video.'

Jennifer made a face. 'Do you ever think of anything other than sex?'

Sue put a finger to her lips. 'Hmm. Yes, there was a time once, about two years ago, for about three minutes. But I got over the experience without suffering too much trauma.'

Jennifer laughed. 'Right, well, I'm just popping along to the Brewers for a quick celebratory drink. I'll give you a hand with food preparation when I get back.' With that, she grabbed her keys and a couple of twenty-pound notes from her purse, scooted downstairs and out on to the pavement. Fifty yards away was the Brewers Arms, her usual drinking hole, reputedly also a favourite of Thomas Paine some two hundred years ago. She stepped inside, scanned the crowded bar looking for a familiar face, pushed through a throng of boozed-up office workers before spotting a group of scruffily-dressed, fellow post-graduate students from Sussex University huddled around a long wooden table in a far corner.

'Here she is,' one of the more studious looking of her friends called out as Jennifer drew close. 'Congratulations, Doctor Collins. Mike's just told us your excellent news.'

'Thank you, Jim,' responded Jennifer with a sweet smile. 'But I'll save the title for use on more formal occasions if you don't mind.' She squeezed past the back of a couple of chairs and made to sit on a bench facing into the room. 'Come on, you lot, budge up a bit.'

'What beats me, Jen,' continued Jim, as those around him shuffled on their seats, 'is why old Friswell has been holding back for so long. Your thesis should have been accepted months ago. I proof read it in April, it seemed perfect then.'

Jennifer looked forlornly down at the minute space that had opened up on the bench. 'That's as maybe, Jim, but I'm just glad it's been accepted. I can get on with life now, start a proper career, that's my main objective.' She sat down and, after a few seconds of wriggling, managed to get into a position as comfortable as was going to be possible. She turned to the young man sitting beside her, pointed at one of two glasses in front of him and said, 'Is that for me?'

The young man nodded. 'It is, yes. A Skinny Bitch, as normal. Sorry, but I wasn't too sure whether you would want something posher. It's not every day one gets awarded a doctorate.'

'It'll do. Thanks. And I don't do posh, Mike, you should know that by now.'

'Right,' replied Mike with a weak smile.

'Hey, Jennifer,' a bearded young man called out from further up the table. 'You're our resident expert on social anthropology, what's your take on it?'

Jennifer looked blank. 'I'm sorry, what subject are you talking about?'

'The UFO.'

Jennifer's look turned to one of puzzlement. 'Which UFO is that, Dom?'

The bearded man laughed. 'There's only one that I know of, Jen, the one that's heading our way at fifty million miles an hour.'

It took Jennifer a moment to realise what the man was talking about. Four months ago, NASA had reported their observation of a fast-moving object heading in the rough direction of Earth. Over the ensuing months NASA's daily updates had become a regular feature on news and current affair programs; not so much the technical aspects of the object, but rather the speculation of what it was. 'Oh, that one,' she replied at length. 'Sorry, Dom, I haven't been following the news today. I have to admit I lost interest in the story when I heard some nutter on the radio say he was in communication with it.' She paused a moment before adding, 'But the object heading our way is an asteroid isn't it, not a UFO?'

'Not any more, it isn't,' muttered Mike. 'Certainly not according to that tabloid rag Dominic reads. He's been boring us senseless for the last half hour about it. I think he seriously believes it marks the Second Coming; the Star of Bethlehem all over again.'

Jennifer looked bewildered. 'Sorry, but it's just a lump of rock isn't it, so NASA has been telling us.'

'That's just a cover up, so Dom says,' Mike continued. 'It can't be an asteroid, you know that, it's only recently entered our solar system and it's not following an orbital trajectory.'

'I'm no scientist, Mike, but there's no point speculating until it can be seen, surely?'

'There's still no clear image of it yet, true. Deliberately so, according to the Almighty Bearded One.'

Jennifer frowned. 'Dom can't be serious, can he? We've had the loonies parading their theories for weeks. He can't possibly be siding with any of their ridiculous speculations?'

Mike shrugged. 'I'm reserving judgement. But I'd certainly prefer a Second Coming to the Extinction Level Event that would follow an asteroid impact, or to the doom and destruction that would probably follow an alien invasion.'

Jennifer's jaw dropped. 'What? Not you too, Mike. You can't possibly be taking this rubbish serious.'

Mike shrugged. 'Why not? This latest turn of events doesn't auger well does it?'

Jennifer put her hand on Mike's arm. 'What are you talking about?'

Mike grunted. 'Haven't you heard the latest? Dom's been virtually glued to his mobile phone's screen all afternoon. Apparently, NASA says the thing has slowed down and changed direction. Instead of probably missing us by a long chalk, it now seems its intention is to come at us head on.'

Jennifer raised an eyebrow. 'Intention? How can a lump of rock have intention?'

Mike gave a sheepish smile. 'That's Dom's point in a nutshell. To slow down, to change direction, it must have intention. And to have intention, then it must either have a brain itself or is being steered by something with one. Whether it's being steered by God or by an alien, is what Dom's going on about. I think he would actually value your opinion on this issue, Jen. You know how he likes you, worships the ground you tread on. He's still smitten with you, you know that, even though it was you who broke up with him.'

Jennifer gave Mike an admonishing look. 'Don't be jealous.'

Mike shrugged again. 'I'm only saying the truth.'

'For goodness sake,' muttered Jennifer under her breath. She leant forward, caught Dom's eye and slipped into her lecturing voice, 'Dom, religion is a man-made concept. It serves a purpose, many purposes actually, and in troubled times delegating responsibility to a higher power provides comfort. Shooting stars, or whatever the Star of Bethlehem was, are works of nature, not the hand of God. And as for aliens, well, I certainly don't think we're alone in the universe, but I find it hard to accept the possibility of being visited by some being from another solar system because of the logistics involved with space travel. As NASA said initially, this is an anomaly and it will be resolved in due course. I don't see any point getting wound up about it until we have a better picture. Hubble is being turned in its direction in a couple of weeks, I believe. I'm happy to wait until then, you should too. Speculation does no one any good.'

Dom grimaced. 'So, basically, you're just going to ignore it?'

'I am indeed, Dom. I've decided to go off on a well-deserved holiday next week. I intend to relax, have a laugh, go swimming and enjoy the sun. I certainly won't be giving this asteroid, or whatever the hell it is, one second of my attention. You really should do the same.'

Dom slunk back into his chair, picked up his beer glass in defeat and downed the remains of its contents.

'Now,' said Jennifer loudly. 'I guess it's my shout as I'm the one with something to celebrate. What's everyone having?' Nine empty glasses were raised off the table. 'Right then, I make that six pints of bitter and three Skinny Bitches.' She stood up and headed towards the bar.

As Jennifer squeezed her way to the counter, a tall, balding, pale middle-aged man caught her attention. She turned in surprise and said, 'Tony, fancy seeing you here. I didn't think this was your territory.'

Professor Anthony Friswell smiled awkwardly and indicated the fresh-faced lad next to him. 'My son, Peter, he's driven down from Norwich to have a birthday drink with me.'

Jennifer looked surprised. 'Your birthday? Today?'

'It is.'

'Sorry, I didn't know. I'd have got you a card or something.'

Professor Friswell returned a false smile. 'Thanks, but I'm well past those type of sentiments.' He waited silently until Jennifer had placed her order with the barman before saying, 'Look, while you're here, may I talk shop for a minute?'

'Sure thing.'

'I assume you'll be staying on for a while, tutoring?'

Jennifer nodded. 'Probably. I put my name down to take a handful of undergraduate classes each week next term. I certainly haven't sought a position anywhere else yet, it's not an easy job market out there at the moment.'

'Of course,' replied Professor Friswell. 'Well, if it helps, I can give you three mornings a week as a research assistant, afternoons if you prefer, so it can fit around your tutoring. It doesn't pay too well, but at least we have funding in place.'

Jennifer was startled by the offer. 'Wow! Really? That would be great. Thank you, Tony, the money would come in handy. My landlord's been threatening to put the rent up.'

Professor Friswell returned a weak smile. 'See you next term then.' He pointed at the glasses mounting up on the bar in front of her. 'Do you want a hand with those?'

'That would be kind.'

The professor's son, Peter, interrupted. 'Allow me,' he said.

Jennifer grabbed two of the glasses and made her way back to her friends table, Peter in tow.

After two return trips, and a bit of banter with Peter along the way, Jennifer settled back down on the bench, picked up her Skinny Bitch and said, 'Cheers, everyone.'

Her friends raised their glasses in return. Mike, looking jaded, toyed with his glass. 'Who's your new admirer? A bit young, isn't he?'

'Peter? He's Tony Friswell's son. I just bumped into them both at the bar.'

'Oh, sorry, I didn't realise.'

Jennifer gave Mike a sideways glance. 'He's just offered me a job, part-time, of course.'

Mike looked shocked. 'Friswell did? That old lecher? Typical. You know where that's going to lead don't you?'

Jennifer looked affronted. 'Mike, that insinuation is not very nice.'

'Maybe not, but he's got a track record. It's the reason he's divorced.'

'I'm not naïve, you know.'

'I'm not saying you are, Jen, I'm just pointing out the obvious. He's done this before; offer a young woman a job and then try to take advantage of the situation. All I'm saying is watch out for him.'

'Don't worry,' responded Jennifer tersely. 'He won't be the first twat I've had to deal with. Or the last, I'm sure.'

Mike seemed to realise he'd overplayed his hand. 'Sorry for putting a downer on your evening. You should be celebrating. And what's this about a holiday?'

Jennifer brightened up. 'Well, I haven't seen much of my parents this last couple of years and I've missed out on seeing my brothers growing up. I want to spend a few weeks with them all, until university restarts in September.'

'Can I come with you?'

Jennifer laid a hand on Mike's arm. 'I'd love you to come, Mike, you know that. But it's impossible; you'd never get into the country. Surithani doesn't allow tourists.'

'Can't I apply for a visa to accompany you?'

'There's nowhere really to get a visa from, other than trying your luck with the consulate over here which, if rumours are true, is manned by a bad-tempered recluse stuck out in the middle of nowhere who repels any approach to his property with a pitchfork.'

'What about applying for a visa on arrival?'

'Well, technically, yes, you could try when you get there. However, you'd be stuck on the docks waiting for your case to go in front of the king himself. And he's not exactly known for being friendly towards foreigners.'

'It's worth a try isn't it?'

Jennifer sighed. 'That's easy to say, Mike, but you'd be regretting it if you did. It takes ages to get there. The closest airport is Singapore. From there it's by boat only, all the way. And I don't mean by scheduled ferry. You have to ask around the port, find a cargo boat that's heading that way and hitch a lift. The trip can take three days sometimes, especially if the only boat you can find is an old rice barge plying local waters. You get dropped off at the docks in Nakhon Thong and the only way out of the dockyard is through the Customs Hall, and if the Immigration Officers don't know your face you won't get past them. Waving a British passport cuts no ice either; you need a letter of authority signed by the king and if you haven't got one of those, you'll be going nowhere other than back to the boat you arrived on.'

Mike looked miffed. 'How do you get one of those letters of authority then?'

'Well, usually it's done by correspondence. The British Consular out there would process it for you, but he'll only do it for people who fall within strict guidelines, like my father who's a representative of a London based importer. Tourists are banned, as are the merely curious.'

Mike sniffed. 'Sounds very insular. Communism at its worse, I suppose, like North Korea. Can't think why you'd want to support such a regime.'

'Communism? With a king?' Jennifer snorted. 'Hardly. Surithani is a peoples' paradise precisely because the king looks after his people and refuses to let commercial enterprise exploit the country's resources. Can you imagine a country unspoilt by corporate greed or pollution? It's absolutely beautiful there, and the only way of keeping it like that is to squash tourism and industrialisation before they take hold.'

'So, it's backward, then?'

Jennifer flushed. 'And what's wrong with that?'

Fortunately for Mike, he must have recognised the danger signals for he sighed and said, 'Never mind, I doubt if I've got the time to spare anyway. I've still got a long way to go with my own thesis. I seem to have reached a low point, I've run out of ideas, I just thought a break might help restore my mojo.'

Jennifer placed a conciliatory hand back on Mike's arm. 'I'm sorry, really I am. I'd love to have company out there; it can be terribly dull at times. My parents behave like the worse type of British expat one hears about. They can appear very snobbish, stuck in their enclave with little to do except gossip and moan about their servants. It can be very claustrophobic at times.'

Mike spluttered on his beer. 'An enclave! Jesus, that doesn't sound good. What is it, a prisoner of war camp?' He brushed away a few drops of beer that had landed on his wrist.

Jennifer laughed. 'Not quite, but there is one there, in the foreign enclave. A prisoner of war camp, I mean. And it still gets used, quite regularly.'

'Oh my god. Really?'

'Yes, really. The king dislikes foreigners trying to invade his country. Anyone trying to do so will find themselves in prison until a ransom is paid.'

'A ransom? That's pure medieval.'

'Well, it teaches them a lesson, that's for sure.'

'You've got me worried for your safety now. This king sounds barbaric.'

'That's precisely what he is not. He may, effectively, be a dictator. But he's not despotic. He's loved, adored by the people; held in awe and worshipped. And he exercises his power with the Wisdom of Solomon. You just don't want to cross him, that's all.' She knocked back the contents of her glass. 'Now, sorry, but I have to get back to my flat. Sue's making her famous lasagne tonight and I've paid for most of the ingredients.' She stood up, bent down to give Mike an affectionate peck on the cheek and said, 'See you tomorrow, perhaps. Bye everyone.'

As Jennifer walked the fifty-yard stretch of pavement back to her flat, she pondered upon her friends' comments. 'That's all I need to get my career off to a flying start,' she muttered under her breath, 'a bloody alien invasion.'

Chapter Two

The Enclave

Dressed in denim shorts and a white cotton Tee-shirt, revealing a skin paled by lack of sunshine, Jennifer sat at a much-weathered teak table on the veranda of a sturdy wooden villa built by a wealthy spice trader a hundred years ago in a prime location in the heart of Surithani's foreign enclave. Contemplating an assortment of breakfast items on the table, she poured herself a cup of coffee and leant back to enjoy the fabulous view that had become etched in her psyche.

Ahead, beyond the garden and track that passed for a road, lay fields of rough grass, grazed by the occasional water buffalo, running down an incline to the gently flowing waters of the Patunam river, some two hundred feet wide and spanned by a five-arch stone bridge built by unknown hands in the ancient mists of time. Across the river lay the country's capital city, Nakhon Thong, as ancient in origin as the bridge, its buildings constructed of wood, its roads of a paved stone smoothed by hundreds of years of yoke-carrying street vendors hawking their wares on foot.

To her far left, a mile downriver, lay the docks, where the stone-built quayside had remained unchanged since the first European visitor, the Portuguese explorer Vasco da Gama, landed seeking trade and good fortune. On the opposite side of the docks, a great curved breakwater stretched a mile out into the gulf in an effort to tame the turbulent storms that often blew in from the distant South China Sea.

To her far right, four hundred yards up river she could just make out the tops of the stone walls that formed the foreign prisoner camp, beyond which lay rice fields and elephant-dwelling forests undisturbed by man.

Across the valley floor, way beyond the outskirts of the city, lay a mountain range, rising majestically from the plains to an impressive height of ten thousand feet. Legend dictated that its contours resembled a crouching tiger, and that the tiger protected a god asleep his winged chariot entombed beneath. And for that tiger, one of its front paws was formed by a protruding low promontory, no more than five hundred feet high, upon which perched a marble-hewn palace with a golden, jewel encrusted pagoda-style roof that sparkled as it caught the rays of the early morning tropical sun.

Above all else was peace and tranquillity, for there were no cars, no motorbikes, no noise from any combustion engine. All that could be heard was the sound of birdsong.

Jennifer sighed. A deep yet highly contented sigh. It was so good to be back in the home of her childhood. For the view evoked happy memories of a bygone innocence and a loving family. She could sit and stare at the comforting view for hours on end.

The sudden noise of a door shutting made her look around.

'Morning, Jen. Excellent weather, isn't it?'

'Morning, Mum. Yes, it's perfect, isn't it? It hasn't been much of a summer in England so far. I could do with a tan; I feel so ugly being this white.'

Judith Collins looked aghast. 'Ugly? Good heavens, girl, the locals will be in awe of you. You know how they feel about white-skinned farang.'

Jennifer smiled. Her mother hadn't changed one bit. 'That's as maybe, Mum, but I intend to go back bronzed. I want to be the envy of Lewes.'

Judith Collins sat down and helped herself to a plate of freshly cut fruit from a bowl at the centre of the teak table. 'Is fruit alright for you, dear, or shall I ask Jum to rustle you up something more substantial? Scrambled eggs on toast perhaps? It shouldn't be any trouble; she usually cooks eggs for the boys.'

'Fruit's fine thanks.' She leant forward and filled a plate with slices of mango and papaya.

'So, what plans do you have for the day then?'

'None whatsoever. And none for the next six weeks either.'

'Good.' Judith Collins seemed pleased with her daughter's response. 'You'll come horse-riding with Jill Somersby and myself this afternoon then? Marcus and Gerry are coming along, Jill's boys too.'

Jennifer reflected on the idea. 'Now there's a thought. I haven't done that for a while.'

'You used to love riding. You'll come then?'

'Of course I will, yes.' She paused for a moment, lost in thought. 'Is that stable-boy, Surachai, still working at the stables?'

'Young Surachai? Yes, he's in charge now; he has such an excellent rapport with the horses. Mind you, he's not so young now, and he's broadened out considerably.'

Jennifer smiled. 'He proposed to me once, about six years ago. On the beach, on my last day here before I left for university. I politely said I didn't know how long I'd be away for. He said he'd wait until I was ready for him.'

'Really? Well, you could do worse, Jen. He's grown into a real dish.'

Jennifer smiled vacantly. 'He was a nice boy.'

'We'll ask him to take us down to the beach. The path through the woods is beautiful at the moment and it'll be a fine gallop along the shoreline for you and the boys.'

Jennifer perked up. 'Now that does sound heavenly.'

'Indeed, it will be. I'll set it up for two-thirty.' With that, Judith Collins' top lip curled imperceptibly.

Jennifer stabbed a slice of mango with a fork and put it to her mouth, a little unsure of quite why her mother looked so pleased with herself.

Chapter Three

Surachai

Like most people on a holiday, Jennifer found that the days passed far too quickly. Surachai proved to be a hit, and not just with the horses. Her initial innocent ride through the woods with her mother and brothers soon led to more intimate walks along the beach hand-in-hand with the handsome bronzed youth she'd previously known as a boy. It was a tearful girl who woke up on her last full day in paradise, hugged her pillow and wondered where her future lay.

For an early September day in the heart of the so-called wet season, the weather appeared to be holding up remarkably well, and so a farewell party was hastily arranged for the beach. It really couldn't have been a more perfect afternoon; the sky was a brilliant blue, the sun hot without being scorching, the sea calm and crystal clear and, most fortunately, the odd squall, when it came, passed by far out to sea.

Jennifer was used to last days of a holiday on the beach; a chance for one last look at the view, one last walk along the shoreline, one last farewell to loved ones. Her life had been plagued with such days since she'd turned eighteen. Yet today was going to be the hardest of all, for she knew her heart would be broken.

Dressed in a skimpy red bikini, thoroughly disapproved of by her father, Jennifer stood absorbing the unspoilt beauty of the white sandy beach. Her break to visit parents and recharge batteries was finally drawing to an end. And these last few moments were the most important, for they would provide cherished memories that would offer a degree of comfort during the lonely, grey, miserable days she would have to endure during the upcoming English winter.

She swept a few loose strands of long brown hair back behind her ear and cast an appreciative eye over the small gathering of family and friends who had joined the party. Nine couples lay sprawled in the shade of a row of leafy trees on the edge of the beach, their children playing in the sand or paddling at the water's edge under the watchful eye of maids. It was a privileged lifestyle, one that compared well with the glory days of the British Raj in India. Slightly tragic, she thought, but nonetheless somewhat reassuring to know that life in Surithani's foreign enclave continued in complete and utter disregard for the outside world.

Coming out of her reverie, she became aware of a hand being waved in her direction from higher up the beach. 'Sorry, Daddy,' she called out. 'Did you say something? I was miles away.'

'I said how about a glass of champagne? The bottle's nicely chilled at the moment.'

'Thanks, Daddy. I'll be with you in a second, just got to finish this off.' She knelt down alongside her younger brother and placed a handful of sun-bleached shells on top of a sandcastle. 'There you go, Gerry,' she said. 'Now it's perfect.' She got to her feet and walked a few yards further up the beach towards a motley collection of rugs and raffia mats scattered on the shaded sands, on top of which sat a generous amount of food dishes, water bottles and cooler buckets.

Jennifer's mother lay stretched out on a recliner reading a magazine, her father sat upright on an adjacent rattan chair clutching two champagne flutes in his hands. She reached out for a glass and said, 'Thanks, Daddy.'

'You're most welcome.' He lifted his own glass in a toast and said, 'Here's to your very best health, Jen, and to a long and successful career. May you have the very best of luck with your new job.'

'Cheers,' responded Jennifer. 'I'll drink to that, but it's only a part-time job, just three mornings a week. And I'm not sure quite how secure it is. A few of my colleagues are jealous, I know. They could scupper my prospects yet.' She took a sip and said, 'Mmm, very nice. I could get used to that.'

'Well, if they do, scupper you, that is, you know there's always a home for you here.'

'But no job,' responded Jennifer.

James Collins lifted a finger into the air. 'Well, actually, there might be, Jen. Don't dismiss the idea but I understand there may be a position coming up shortly at the school. And in any case, in the long run, we'll all be retiring, there'll always be the odd opportunity arising.'

'Dead men's shoes? Thanks, Daddy, but I want to make my own way in life.'

James Collins sighed. 'I understand that, Jen. But England, I ask you, it's so damp and miserable. You know in your heart you'd prefer to settle down here.' For that, he received a slap on his thigh. 'Ouch!' He turned sharply to his wife. 'What was that for?'

'Don't start on her now, dear,' replied Judith Collins. 'Not on her last day.'

Jennifer knelt in front of her father and placed a hand on his knees. 'Exactly, Daddy. Enjoy the moment. I'll be back soon, I'm sure.'

'I'm sorry, Jen, it's just that I care about you. There are some pretty unpleasant things going on in the world at the moment, and I'm not happy that old phoney Anthony Shepherd is in charge. Call-Me-Tony will ruin the country with his wishy-washy woolly-minded liberal policies.'

Judith Collins tutted. 'You're just jealous of him because he's done better for himself than you.'

James Collins looked miffed. 'No, I'm not. It's just I know what he's really like, underneath all that waffle.'

Judith Collins sighed. 'Rubbish, dear. It's been well over thirty years since you left prep school. Tony's bound to have changed since then.'

'That's as maybe, but he's damaging the economy, allowing all those migrants in. There won't be many opportunities left for our young people soon. And that will damage Jennifer's prospects.'

Judith Collins put her magazine down and said to her husband 'You really don't need to worry, dear. Our beloved daughter has got her life planned out, isn't that so, Jen?'

'Exactly so,' replied Jennifer, but her mind had drifted from the problems of placating anxious parents entrenched in their middle-class values. Her attention had been well and truly caught by the sight of a magnificent white horse stepping out from the trees lining the path that led down through the woods. The rider, a young bronze-skinned lad, shirtless and wearing cotton sarong trousers smiled as

Jennifer waved in his direction.

James Collins looked over his shoulder. 'And that's another thing we need a conversation about, my dear girl,' he said turning back to face his daughter. 'You've spent most of this holiday having riding lessons. Is he the reason why?'

Jennifer stood up, stooped over and kissed her father on the forehead and said, 'None of your business, Daddy. And don't worry about me, I'll be back to visit whenever I can find time. Love you lots.' With that, she knocked back the remaining contents of the champagne flute and set the glass down on a nearby upturned wooden crate that was functioning as a table. 'Now, if you'll excuse me for a few moments, there's someone I need to say goodbye to.' She turned and walked to the water's edge and moments later the white horse came to a halt alongside her. The rider dismounted, engaged her in conversation and within a few seconds they set off together hand-in-hand ambling along the beach away from the others.

James Collins turned to his wife who appeared engrossed in her magazine. 'Is Jen serious about him?'

'Who, dear?'

'Him, of course,' said James Collins, pointing in the direction of the horse rider.

Judith Collins squinted in the direction her husband indicated. 'Surachai? He's just a boy.'

'He must be about the same age as Jen.'

'A year or so younger I believe, but he's not a man yet.'

'Boys have the same desires as men. Even stronger perhaps at that age, if I remember correctly.'

'No doubt,' responded Judith Collins dryly, 'but they don't offer much in the way of a future at that stage, do they?'

'Meaning what, that he's not good enough for our Jen because he's a stable boy?'

Judith Collins tutted. 'No, that's not what I meant at all, dear. He may well make a good match in a few years' time, but Jen's got a lot of learning to go through before then. And I don't mean academic learning. She's still only twenty-four years old. Give her five years or so to experience life more, then she'll be able to choose the right man. But bear in mind it won't necessarily be a local man; you'll just have to brace yourself for that calamity.'

James Collins squirmed in his seat. 'But Jen loves it here. She wants to settle down here, join us and the boys, doesn't she?'

'That's as maybe, but who here could possibly give her the mental stimulation she so craves.'

'I fear for her happiness, that's all.'

Judith Collins took her husband's hand in her own. 'So do I, dear. Desperately so. Give it time, though, hopefully something will work out.'

'I'd be heartbroken if she falls for a Chartered Accountant living in Bromley. I wouldn't go back for anything in the world.'

'Not even for grandchildren? Marcus is fourteen now, Gerry eight. It won't be too long before we're on our own.'

James Collins appeared to ponder the issue. 'As you say, hopefully something will work out.' He watched Jennifer and Surachai for a few moments then said, 'You have to admit, they make a beautiful looking couple, don't they? Where's my camera? I'm sure she'll love a picture. It'll make an adorable pin-up for her desk.'

Chapter Four

Invasion

The walk from the bottom to the top of the High Street in Lewes
was normally one that Jennifer enjoyed enormously. But not today.
Not on a gloomy, damp, drizzly morning in early February. And
certainly not when weighed down by two shopping bags full of cans
of food. For Jennifer, like everyone else in the country, was stocking
up with emergency rations. It was a totally anti-social response to a
national crisis, she was well aware, but nevertheless a response she
considered justified in the circumstances. That thing, that hideously
frightening machine hovering in the sky for the past two months, had
not only ruined Christmas but had made the whole world jittery.
Only yesterday Tony Shepherd, the Prime Minister, had pleaded for
the public to remain calm, to go about their daily business as though
nothing had happened, not to panic-buy and not to horde food. Idiot
man, she thought, as she reflected on the hour-long battle she had
just fought to get to the front of a supermarket queue. The Prime
Minister's message had caused exactly that which he had warned
against. Just like her father, she thought, it would have been so much
better to have said nothing.

Head bowed against the rain, she didn't even pay a cursory glance
towards the castle as she quickly passed by the entrance to the
precincts and came to a halt outside the front door to her flat. Feeling
cold, tired, hungry and downright miserable, she elbowed the bell
hoping Sue would be back from her night shift at Brighton General
Hospital and had not yet gone to bed.

'Oh, thank god,' Jennifer sighed as the door opened inwards off the street. 'Sorry, Sue, I hadn't the strength to search for my keys. My fingers are frozen.'

'No problem,' responded Sue, stepping aside to let Jennifer pass by. 'I was only watching the news.'

'At this hour of day?' asked Jennifer as she climbed the stairs. 'You've not even changed out of your uniform. Has anything serious happened?'

'Haven't you heard?'

'No, what?'

'They've made contact. The aliens, that is. Peace talks are in hand, so they say.'

'Thank god for that. Perhaps the Americans will now stop blowing the world to bits.'

'Even better,' said Sue as she took note of the contents of Jennifer's bags, 'we might be able to get back to a healthy diet.'

Jennifer staggered through her flat's interior front door, stumbled into the kitchen and heaved the bags on to the worktop. 'You have no idea what it's like in Tesco. The shelves are almost empty.'

Sue picked up one of the cans. 'Meat pie filling? Really?'

'Better than dog food. I reckon that's all there'll be left by the end of today.'

'Perhaps we should start foraging, like the chap on River Cottage that looks like my dad.'

Jennifer looked aghast. 'Foraging? In February? Are you nuts? It will be months before anything's ready to harvest. We'll be eating rat burger long before then.'

'Can't be more disgusting than some of this stuff,' responded Sue.

Jennifer rubbed her hands together and nodded towards the shopping bags. 'I'll unpack later. I need to warm up first.'

'Go and sit down, I'll make you a cuppa.'

Jennifer visibly sagged. 'Would you? You're an angel.'

'No problem. You can pay me back by cooking tonight, just so long as it doesn't involve any of this stuff. Alan said he'd pop in after he finishes work, so if you wouldn't mind stretching the rations a bit, I'd be eternally grateful.'

As Jennifer made her way into the sitting room, she shouted over her shoulder, 'Tinned mushroom soup followed by tinned saveloys with tinned potatoes and tinned carrots. Is that all right with you both? Either that or pot noodles all round. And before you ask, all the restaurants, cafes and takeaways in the town are now closed until further notice.' She collapsed on the sofa, picked up the television remote control and searched through the program menu. Seems there was little on the main channels other than continuous live discussion of the thing in the sky. Funny, she reflected, she'd always assumed an alien invasion might have been more ferocious.

Not that you'd call it an invasion. Not a proper one like in a Hollywood film. One solitary spaceship, that was all. And not that big either, certainly nowhere near as big as everyone had feared. A fat cigar-shaped ship, a mile in length, it had been calculated, a quarter of a mile wide and nearly as much in height, with a dark, menacing look. It had finally arrived in early December, after a long, slow, presumably cautious approach to Earth, and had appeared content circling the world's skies, presumably allowing the occupants time to study the planet's inhabitants and languages. After a fraught Christmas, ruined by even more panic buying than usual, and a nervous January as the human race waited on tenterhooks, the Americans could stand the tension no longer and mounted a pre-emptive strike. The ensuing battle had been painful, embarrassing and thoroughly belittling to behold as the combined air forces of the Western World were defeated in less than thirty minutes by just four starfighters, as the media had termed the sleek alien craft that flew from the bowels of the mothership. Thankfully, following the futile deployment of the nuclear option, retaliation had been mild and the Americans had stood down after accepting the complete annihilation of Mount Rushmore as a sufficient display of who had the biggest weapon.

Jennifer settled for the BBC news channel which, she hoped, would offer a more factual, less melodramatic version of events than the channel Sue had been watching. She had listened to far too many nutters in the last few months espousing their lunatic views on the origins and purpose of the aliens. She wanted the comfort of a serious reporter, like the BBC's current affairs editor Nick Ohlson, with his thick black-rimmed spectacles and middle-aged gravitas, to give her a sensible opinion.

Seconds after pressing the button on the remote, a picture of a starfighter hovering a few inches above the ground in St James's Park, London, appeared on the television screen. She looked at it in wonder whilst listening to the commentator reporting that, after landing a mere half hour ago, two menacing, near-humanoid beings had exited the vehicle, headed across Horse Guards Parade and entered 10 Downing Street.

Sue entered the room and handed Jennifer a mug of tea. 'Sorry there's no biscuits. Can't think why. Perhaps if they came in cans, we'd have some.'

Jennifer smiled. 'Thanks.' She placed the mug on a coffee table to her side, turned back to the television and gave an involuntary gasp. 'Oh my god!'

Sue jerked sharply. 'What? What's the matter?'

Jennifer's jaw dropped. She turned to face Sue, said nothing, and turned back to face the television screen. She stared, transfixed at the sight of a close-up shot of a collection of symbols on the side of the starfighter. Utterly bewildered, she muttered, 'But that's . . . that's impossible!'

'Are you alright, Jen? You look as though you've seen a ghost.'

Jennifer's face had indeed paled. 'I mean, well, it's meaningless.'

'Sorry, Jen, you've lost me. What exactly are you talking about?'

But Jennifer fell silent as the television camera paused on the symbols whilst the presenter pontificated on their possible meanings. He hoped, he was saying, they meant something like "Spirit of Adventure" or perhaps more appropriately "We come in peace" which would be more reassuring as an opening line for a first encounter.

How wrong he was, Jennifer mused, for she knew otherwise. But who would believe her?

Chapter Five

Saviour

Mitch, a young Ministry of Defence analyst, gazed out of his Whitehall office window in wonder at the sight of a hundred-foot long beast of alien technology, stationary though hovering a foot off the ground, on the eastern edge of St James's Park near Horse Guards Parade. He thought the squat, stubby-winged, flat-bottomed starfighter resembled Thunderbird 2, except that it was a greyish black colour instead of dark green. He also thought it possessed a haunted look, as though it had a disturbing history. For a few moments he allowed his imagination to play out a battle from which the pilot had fled, battle-scarred, a refugee defeated by a conquering army of marauding intergalactic warriors.

'Wishing it away won't help, you know.'

Mitch glanced over his shoulder at his office colleague who was glued to a computer screen. 'Sorry. Did you say something, Russ?'

'It's happened, Mitch. It's real. You can't make the bloody thing disappear by wishing it wasn't there.'

'I'm well aware of that, thank you.'

'Well come away from the window then, for Christ's sake. Someone might still be inside the damn thing. Your staring at it could freak them out. Then you'd be toast.'

Mitch crossed his arms, his forehead creasing. 'Why just the two of them? Why not a whole unit of star troopers? That's what I don't understand.' He glanced around again at his colleague but received nothing more than a shake of a head in response. 'Trillions of miles they must have travelled,' he continued unperturbed. 'And what do we see of them? Two humanoids, resembling nothing more startling than Samoan rugby team prop forwards, dressed in unflattering uniforms reminiscent of the Star Trek wardrobe from the nineteen sixties television series. Talk about a let-down. I was expecting octopus-like things, with loads of tentacles waving all over the place like the creature Will Smith captured in Independence Day. Or dolphins maybe, that would have been amusing, wouldn't it?' As Mitch's eyes wandered over the sleek machine that lay less than a hundred yards away, he wondered how the hell the world had got itself into such a precarious position in such a short time. It didn't make sense. It had to be a bad dream. If only he could shut his eyes, blank out from his mind the object hovering unnaturally above the grass where he'd often sit on a summer's day eating a lunchtime sandwich, then maybe he would wake up to find that it really had all been just a nightmare.

'Look, Mitch, why don't you do something positive?'

Mitch grunted. 'Like what? We've tried to nuke the buggers already. Fat lot of good that did, eh? We'll have radioactive particles raining down on us for years to come.'

'Hmm. Not the wisest of decisions was it?'

'At least it wasn't us that chose that route.'

Russ snapped at his colleague. 'Look, we're all in it together. Whether it's the Americans, Russians or Chinese that have a go, it doesn't really matter does it? It's just us against them.'

Mitch huffed and returned to his desk, reflecting on the dire fact that not far away, in 10 Downing Street, sat the Right Honourable Mr Anthony Shepherd, the youthful looking, forty-six-year-old Prime Minister, doing his best to negotiate a deal with a couple of slime balls from some swamp on a far off planet. He hoped to God that the alien emissaries that had landed in Washington, Moscow, Beijing and Paris at the same time as in London would be lenient. 'What do you reckon they'll want from us?'

'Nothing short of world domination is my guess,' responded Russ sharply. 'A big palace somewhere, lots of humans as servants, maybe they want us for food. Jesus, Mitch, how the hell would I know.'

'Sorry, I'm just . . . well, I'm just really pissed off.'

'Yeah, you, me and the rest of the world too. Look, just do something that doesn't distract me, will you?'

Mitch took a sudden interest in what his colleague was looking at so keenly on his computer screen. 'Why? What can you possibly be doing that could help the world?'

'Well . . .'

'Well? What do you mean by "well"? What's that supposed to mean?'

'I've got something really odd here.'

'You mean your computer is going to save the world? Pacman to the rescue!' He huffed again. 'Fat chance, Russ, get real.'

'Quit bitching will you and come and look at this.'

Dubiously, Mitch wandered over to his colleague's desk. 'What you got, then?'

'Watch this. I just typed in "Alien invasion, help" into search. I'll do it again, see what happens.'

Mitch watched as his colleague typed the words into the Ministry of Defence database search function, pressed enter and sat back waiting as the cursor blinked for a few seconds.

Mitch snorted in derision. 'You think the answer is in our records system? You've lost it, mate, you know that?'

After another ten seconds, a one-word message appeared: Saviour.

Mitch's jaw dropped. 'What the blazes is that?'

'Odd isn't it?'

'Decidedly, but what is it?'

'Well, I don't know. But watch this, it gets weirder.' Russ entered the cryptic word back into the search engine. A new message appeared: Access Denied.

'What the hell!'

'I need to try a higher-level security code. Trouble is, I don't think anyone in the building is in a fit state to bother with it. It could be important but, there again, probably not. Hard to say really.'

Mitch scratched his nose for a few seconds before his eyes lit up. 'Colonel Ben Travis. He'll know. He's an old mate from schooldays and owes me a few favours. I got him hitched up last weekend with this real tasty bit of skirt that he . . .'

Russ held up an admonishing hand. 'Need to know, Mitch. I really don't need to know about your sordid private life.'

'Right. I'll get on to it. Won't be long,' responded Mitch as he left the room. He was back within ten minutes accompanied by a youthful, tense looking Army Colonel in full armed combat gear, wearing a face as depressed as any imaginable.

'Russ, show the Colonel what you've got, will you?'

'Sure thing,' replied Russ. He went through the procedure for the twentieth time within the past hour.

The worry-lines on Colonel Travis's forehead managed to deepen further. 'May I?' he asked, as he indicated the keyboard. Russ stepped out of his chair allowing Colonel Travis room to sit. The Colonel exited the screen back to the menu, keyed in a new password and typed "Saviour" into the search engine. Access was denied again.

'Guess we'll never know then,' Russ mumbled.

'I'm not beaten yet,' muttered Colonel Travis. He returned to the menu and tried another password. Access Denied. 'That was the Prime Minister's personal access code. Please don't let on I know it.'

Mitch felt disappointed. 'That's it then?'

'Certainly not,' replied Colonel Travis with a curt smile. 'This has got me intrigued.'

'Has anyone got a security code higher than the Prime Minister?' asked Russ in an off-hand manner. 'What about the programmers?'

Colonel Travis flipped open his mobile phone, scrolled down the address menu and placed a call. 'Arthur, can you come over to Room 213 please. Yeah, right now, it's urgent.'

'A programmer?' asked Russ as Colonel Travis ended the call.

'Not just a programmer, but the best there is,' replied Colonel Travis. 'Arthur wrote almost everything on this system. He's been working here for donkey's years. If he doesn't know, then no one will.'

Arthur Tompkins, a plump, wild haired, late middle-aged man, arrived in less than seven minutes. He looked more dishevelled than usual, but those that knew him also knew that his shabby appearance did not reflect upon his abilities. 'What have you got for me, Colonel? Something delectable I hope.'

'It certainly beats us, Arthur. A fiver says it beats you too,' said Colonel Travis as he dug out a note from his wallet.

Arthur Tompkins rubbed his hands together in glee as he sat down in front of the computer. 'Your money's lost already, Colonel. So, what's your problem?'

'We need to know what Saviour is. Presumably it's a file.'

'Saviour, huh?' Arthur chuckled. 'We certainly need one of those. Did you see those two thugs step out of that machine hovering in the park?' He gave an involuntary shake. 'Talk about ugly. Do you think they'll want to breed with us?'

Mitch laughed. 'Let's just hope they prefer girls, not guys, eh?'

'Bleah!' replied Arthur, sticking his tongue out. 'Now then,' he said, as his fingers deftly flew over the keyboard. Row upon row of data appeared on screen. 'Wow, this is old stuff, been here since the ark. Transferred over from previous systems in let's see, two thousand, nineteen ninety-four, eighty-five, seventy-nine. No wonder you couldn't get into it, must have been written in the Jurassic period. Now then, yes . . . there you go!'

All four men stared at the screen as a line of words appeared on screen.

Project Saviour: In the event of alien invasion or other world catastrophe send alert on long range radio 280.5 kHz. Help will come, as it has before. Authority: President James A. Burford 25th July 1971.

Mitch was thoroughly perplexed. 'What the hell is this?' he muttered.

'Haven't the foggiest,' replied Arthur, as he prised the five-pound note from the Colonel's tight grip. 'I can't imagine why an American president's words are in our system. Unless the intelligence services put it there, of course.'

Mitch asked, 'Do you think it's valid?'

The programmer gave Mitch the sort of look that questioned his intelligence.

'Sorry, I wasn't thinking straight. Don't you think it's worth trying out, though?'

'Not my area,' replied Arthur with a shrug.

Mitch turned to Colonel Travis. 'What do you think, Ben? It's got to be worth a try, surely? We can't just sit back and wait for the worse.'

Colonel Travis nodded his agreement. 'There's a radio transmitter over the road in the office of the Department of Culture Media and Sport. Let's get over there quick before those bastards up in the sky decide to cut off our communications.'

Chapter Six

Contact

Colonel Travis was a man used to hostility from civilians. Gone were the days when a man dressed in British Army uniform commanded respect from the general public. He knew, nowadays, the sight of an army uniform was more likely to prompt a rant on the legitimacy of meddling in another country's affairs than any remark of respect. It was therefore with a heavy heart that, having tracked down a member of staff in the Whitehall office of the Department of Culture Media and Sport with sufficient skill to operate their radio, he found himself up against the notorious Civil Service strategy of non-cooperation with outsiders.

'We don't use the term longwave any more,' said the radio operator. 'It's purely an historic term.'

Colonel Travis struggled to keep his cool. 'So you keep saying.'

'And I'd have to patch in through the BBC omnidirectional aerial.'

'Just do it, for goodness sake!'

'It's not authorized, Colonel,' the radio operator replied. 'I can't just go using the BBC world service for your own personal requests.'

Colonel Travis leaned over the operator's desk and exploded with rage. 'For God's sake, do you really have no idea what's going out there? Just do it while there's still life left on this planet.'

'I take no responsibility for what happens. I can't just go broadcasting on a whim.'

In an attempt at intimidation, Colonel Travis laid his right hand on the top of the revolver holstered to his belt and said, 'Fine! I'll sign a form for you if that helps. I'll take full responsibility. Anything you like, but just do it right now or I'll blow your fucking brains out!'

The radio operator sneered. 'There's no need to be tetchy.'

'I'm trying to save the planet. Will you please stop playing these mind-fuck games with me?'

The radio operator reluctantly adjusted a knob, coughed delicately to clear his throat and spoke clearly into a microphone. 'This is London calling. Is anyone there? I say again, this is London calling. Is anyone there?' The radio operator waited for a few seconds before looking up at Colonel Travis. 'See, no one there.'

'Try again please.'

The radio operator did as he was told. Nothing happened. 'What did you expect?' he asked. 'A response? As I said, this channel is not used. No one would be monitoring it.'

Colonel Travis exchanged a glance with Mitch. 'It was worth a try, I guess.' After a few seconds of silence, he said, 'I suppose we should get back.' As he turned away from the radio operator, a loud blast came from a nearby loudspeaker.

A loud demanding voice bellowed, 'Identify yourselves, immediately!'

'Jesus H. Christ!' the radio operator hollered as he jumped out of his seat.

'I think not,' came an amused response through the loudspeaker.

Colonel Travis leant over the microphone. 'This is Colonel Travis of the British Army. Who am I talking to?'

'None of your damn business. What are you doing on this channel?'

'I'm hoping you can help us.'

'With what?'

Colonel Travis felt rather stupid. What he had to say seemed ridiculous. 'In case you hadn't noticed, we've been invaded by aliens. We need help.'

'And just why do you think I can help you?'

Colonel Travis felt his face flush. The conversation was heading nowhere. For all he knew he could be talking to a truck driver on a CB radio somewhere out on the M25 motorway. 'I found a message on our computer, left by President Burford back in nineteen seventy-one. It suggested help could be obtained by making radio contact on this channel.'

There was silence for a moment. 'President Burford? The

American president you mean?'

'Yes, sir.'

'He left you a message?'

'He did indeed, sir.'

'Did he leave you a name to contact?'

'Umm, unfortunately he did not, sir. No.'

There was a long silence before a response came. 'Matters are already in hand. The opposition is being taken out at sixteen hundred hours London time today.'

'One hour from now?'

'Correct.'

Colonel Travis was at a loss. 'But . . . who . . . Look, who are you? How can you fight against the aliens' superior technology? What's your plan?'

'Sorry, that information is on a need to know basis, Colonel. Stand down, it will be over soon.'

'Wait,' Colonel Travis pleaded. 'I need to know what you're going to do. I need to protect the Prime Minister. He's being held hostage in his office at the moment, supposedly in discussion with two of the aliens. We need him alive.'

Silence returned for a moment. 'I'll let you walk into the room ahead of me. You'll have a chance to shield your precious Prime Minister.'

'Sixteen hundred hours then.'

'What was your name again? You say you're a Colonel?'

'Travis, sir. Colonel Travis.'

'Well, Colonel Travis, I'll park next to the alien ship in St James's Park. Identify yourself upon my arrival. Get all civilians out of the area. I want a clear path to Downing Street, right up to where the bastards are sitting. Anyone in my way is likely to finish up as collateral damage.'

'Will do, sir. Over and out.'

Colonel Travis turned to Mitch and smiled. 'I think the cavalry may be on its way.'

Chapter Seven

Rescue

At three minutes before sixteen hundred hours GMT, a starfighter appeared at the western end of St James's Park flying silently and low amongst the trees, barely six inches above the ground. At the eastern end, Colonel Travis stood at the head of a hundred troops drafted in to protect the area between the park and Downing Street. As the starfighter drew nearer through the drizzly greyness, he heard a collective moan from the men behind him.

'Bollocks,' muttered Colonel Travis in the direction of an adjutant standing alongside. 'This doesn't look good. The bloody thing's exactly the same.' Nevertheless, he ran across to meet the machine as it drew to a halt.

Moments later a door to one side of the starfighter opened and an imposing giant of a man emerged, looking as though he'd just stepped off a Star Wars film set. Bronze-skinned, standing well over eight-foot-tall with a broad muscular frame, long white flowing hair, carrying what looked to be black helmet and sporting a black cape that trailed in his wake, he epitomised the definition of a warrior.

Colonel Travis took in the haunted look etched on the giant's face. He blinked at the apparition and muttered, 'Sweet Jesus,' as he saluted the man he hoped was the Saviour.

'Are you Travis?'

'Yes, sir. Colonel Travis. Welcome to London, sir.'

'No time for social pleasantries, son,' the warrior said, putting his helmet on as he continued walking without pause. 'Come on, lead the way. We have a tight schedule to maintain.'

'Yes, sir.' Colonel Travis snapped his arm down and ran to catch the warrior up. 'Follow me, sir.'

A few seconds later the warrior pulled his cape close and muttered, 'God almighty, this country's cold. Why the hell don't you settle somewhere warmer?'

Colonel Travis looked sideways at the warrior. 'I guess we wouldn't be British otherwise.'

'Mmm, guess so,' muttered the warrior. He pointed to the double line of soldiers ahead of him, spaced evenly every ten yards, rifles to their sides. 'I hope they haven't been noticed. This is supposed to be a surprise.'

'The room the aliens are in faces out the other way. We can't be observed here.'

'I hope not, or it could get messy. You say there are just two here?'

'Yes, sir. Just the two.'

The warrior grunted. 'You couldn't even disarm two hostiles? Christ, there really is no hope for you lot is there?'

'Sir, they are . . . erm . . . well, they are aliens, sir.' Colonel Travis tried to hold the warrior's glare. 'Their weapons are superior to ours.'

'That's as maybe, Colonel, but they're still made of flesh. Stick a knife in deep and they'll bleed to death, same as sticking a pig.'

Colonel Travis was taken aback. 'I'll try to remember that for next time, sir.'

The warrior placed a hand on Colonel Travis' shoulder. 'So, you want to see how to kick ass properly?'

The image of a swaggering John Wayne in an old black and white Western film briefly flitted through Colonel Travis' mind. He grinned and responded, 'I sure do, sir.'

'Right, follow me then.'

The warrior strode through the entrance hall of 10 Downing Street, mounted the soldier-lined stairs two at a time and came to a halt outside a large oak door where the trail of soldiers ran out. He stood to one side and said quietly, 'Open the door gently, you go in as though nothing's amiss but tell the Prime Minister to hit the floor. I'll come in on the count of three. Good luck, son, I hope you can save your man.'

'Sir,' responded Colonel Travis, 'The Prime Minister is on the left sitting at a desk surrounded by our three Chiefs of Staff. The two, erm, aliens are on the right, sitting in green armchairs.'

The warrior nodded his acknowledgement of the scene. 'Ready?'

'Here we go then,' said Colonel Travis. He pushed open the door, walked in casually and said calmly, 'Gentlemen, hit the deck please. Now!'

In unison, Colonel Travis and three Chiefs of Staff hurled themselves at an unsuspecting Prime Minister, dragging him from his chair to the hoped-for safety of the carpeted floor. Startled, the two aliens jumped out of their chairs and made to grab their weapons.

From the doorway, the warrior barked a few words in an unknown tongue that seemed to momentarily shock the two aliens into paralysis. With a snarl on his face, the warrior strode over to the aliens, grabbed the nearest by the lapels and struck him on the forehead with a jab so hard his head snapped backwards. He grabbed the other alien by the throat, lifted him off the floor and shook him violently like a dog might shake a rabbit in its mouth. Both aliens were dead by the time they hit the floor.

'What the hell?' came the muffled voice of the Prime Minister from under a pile of bodies.

'Sorry, sir,' replied Colonel Travis. 'We thought it best you didn't know.' He stood up and gallantly held his hand out to assist the Prime Minister to his feet.

'Dear God, you nearly crushed me to death,' muttered the Prime Minister as he adjusted his clothing and brushed carpet hair off his trousers. He indicated the two dead aliens and muttered, 'What the hell happened here?'

The warrior turned sharply on the Prime Minister and said, 'Listen to me. Over the last fifty years, you and your predecessors have been warned repeatedly not to broadcast this planet's presence by transmitting radio messages into space. You have also been warned about sending unmanned craft deep into space in the hope of contacting other civilisations. Understand this, there is no benevolent civilization out there waiting to befriend you. There is nothing but war and despair awaiting you. Believe me, I know these things. Stop your space exploration programs immediately or you'll end up with more hostile incursions.'

'Just a moment,' the Prime Minister interrupted. 'Who the hell are you?'

The warrior ignored the question and gestured to the two dead bodies. 'You were lucky on this occasion, but what about the next time? Maybe we won't be around to help out. Maybe it will be you lying on this floor instead with a broken neck.'

With that, the warrior stooped, took a purchase on each of the aliens' uniforms and marched out the door trailing their limp bodies along the floor.

The Prime Minister looked at his Chiefs of Staff and demanded, 'Will someone please explain to me what just happened?'

Chapter Eight

Keep calm and carry on

When the alien spaceship had first become visible to the naked eye, almost every television channel in the world fixated on the phenomena. News programs ran with the topic day and night, regurgitating the limited available facts and tapping into a general malaise that was developing within people who felt a sense of outrage that an alien spacecraft had somehow managed to creep up on them without due process of intervention by the authorities. Unsurprisingly, much vitriol was directed towards NASA for not making ordinary citizens aware of the emerging crisis. NASA, in their defence, maintained they'd been issuing press releases daily for three months on the subject of an unidentifiable object on a potential collision course with Earth, and that it really wasn't their fault the general public found it of little interest until the damned thing was right on top of them.

Few people had gone to work the day after first seeing the spaceship in the sky. Expecting the worst, families had huddled together on sofas, transfixed by the images on their television screens. As Armageddon threatened, the British public were told to Keep Calm and Carry On, a much-used and much-loved government slogan from another era of impending disaster. But as sure as day follows night, eventually dogs needed walking, children grew restless, shops needed deliveries and bosses telephoned absent staff threatening breach of contract. And so the world quietly returned to its daily routine, except that nothing could quite be the same again. Food was hoarded, bills weren't paid, apprehension mounted.

Cameras had followed the spaceship's journey around the world's skies until the vast majority of the viewing audience lost interest due to the ship's apparent inactivity. As the level of newsworthiness withered, television stations resumed normal timetables and reporters resorted to interviewing so-called specialists who claimed an ability to communicate with aliens through telepathy, to receive messages through their false teeth, or to have alien writing appear on misted shaving mirrors. As audience figures tailed off to inconsequential levels, reporters tried to renew the flagging public interest by suggesting alternative possibilities to alien invasion, thus giving airtime to an army of conspiracy theorists. No possibility was overlooked. Some thought the disturbingly human-looking visitors were our own species from the future travelling back in time to warn us of the errors of our ways. Others thought the visitors were our own species from the past, revisiting us to see how their colonisation program was working out. Others suggested the visitors were our own selves from a parallel universe who had somehow fallen through a crack in the space-time continuum.

By the time of the fracas in Downing Street, only one television crew had remained close at hand on stand-by. The action in St James's Park, when it came, was almost missed because of a union-scheduled tea break for the satellite communication-link workers in their van which was parked illegally in a bay marked "Police Operational Vehicles Only" in Horse Guards Road. Nevertheless, the BBC's six o'clock early evening television news broadcast showed the extraordinary image of the two aliens, presumably dead, being dragged by their collars across the road from Number 10 into the park and unceremoniously tossed on board their own craft like garbage sacks. The newly arrived starfighter quickly departed but had returned an hour later, manoeuvred over the top of the other craft and, like copulating insects, flew off, intertwined, out of sight within seconds.

Like most of the BBC's audience, Jennifer Collins had sat on her sofa watching the scenario unfold with fascination. Unconfirmed reports were cited of similar events occurring in Paris, Washington, Moscow and Beijing. The climax of the news report focused on the disappearance of the mothership; one moment it could be seen clearly in camera shot, the next moment completely gone. It had simply vanished. Clearly, a counter-attack against the aliens had been successfully mounted. But by whom the Prime Minister's office refused to say, as did the governments of France, America, Russia and China.

Unlike most of the BBC's audience though, Jennifer Collins was not shouting for joy, hugging family or drinking in celebration. Her mind was elsewhere, firmly entrenched in the world of academia. Having had her interest piqued by the alien symbols, she had been video-recording the momentous events of the day for possible future analysis and lectures. After the six o'clock news had finished, she pressed rewind on the remote control and watched again as the warrior strode across the park from Downing Street.

It had been a dramatic liberation, that much was certain. But admiration wasn't the reason Jennifer sat gawking at the television. What she was focusing on were the symbols on the second vehicle that had landed in the park. Flummoxed, she scratched her head and pondered the meaning of it all.

Jennifer Collins was not the only person who had been left flummoxed by the events that had unfolded in St James's Park that day. For, five miles south of Jennifer's flat in Lewes, ninety-six-year-old Alfred Fry sat in his armchair, stroking his Golden Retriever dog, who's head lay across his lap, and looking pensively at the ferry docked across the river.

Ever since the mothership, as it had been dubbed, had been caught on camera traversing the skies, Alfred Fry had been put in mind of an extraordinarily large vehicle he'd once seen in the Far East. It, too, had resembled a ship, with rows of portholes. But, exhausted, sick and in acute pain at the time, he had never quite been sure whether it had been an hallucination or not.

But after the evening news broadcast, Alfred Fry could certainly not be mistaken about the smaller craft that had been dubbed starfighters. The two filmed earlier in St James's Park were identical to the one in which he had once flown. Of that fact, he had no doubt. Seventy-odd years may have passed since that extraordinary flight, but he could recall every last detail of that vehicle and the journey, having relived it in his nightmares a thousand times since.

'What to do, Tess,' he said to his dog. 'What on earth should we do about it?'

Nodding off, Alfred Fry found himself back in a Malaysian jungle as an eighteen-year-old soldier, propped up against a tree, his left leg nowt but a bloodied stump, blown off below the knee, wanting to be left alone to die. But then this vision had arrived; a guardian angel, flying silently, just off the ground, in a wingless, open-top vehicle no bigger than a car. The angel had stepped out of his vehicle, raised a hand, quelled a barrage of Japanese bullets and calmness had reigned.

He woke with a start. As always after the recurring dream, he lowered a hand, rubbed his left leg and wriggled the toes on his left foot. 'My Saviour, Tess, that's who he was. And it looks as though he's shown his hand again.'

Chapter Nine

Conundrum

The days following the disappearance of the mothership were as traumatic for the general public as had been the days following its original arrival. The absence of the ship had actually created a mystery of far greater intensity than had its physical presence. NASA was confounded. Given that they had monitored the spaceship for three months as it came ever closer to Earth, there should be a trace of it leaving. But there was none. The conclusion was that, since there was no evidence that it had left, it must, therefore, still be close-by. Many questions nevertheless remained unanswered. How could the mothership disappear into thin air? Who had control of it? Where was it? How could it evade satellite detection?

The conspiracy theorists were invited back into television studios. Fingers were pointed at the CIA, NSA, FBI, NCIS, MI6, MI5 and a host of other agencies who were seen as possible keepers of technological secrets learned from superior beings, and therefore holders of the wherewithal to pull off such an audacious plot. DVD purchases of alien-attack films, especially *Men In Black*, rose to stratospheric levels as people searched for answers. The telephone lines of Russell T Davies, Stephen Moffat and a host of other *Dr Who* screenwriters burned red hot with inquiries from journalists wanting them to share their "inside knowledge".

Each country had its own demon to accuse of a cover-up. As days turned into weeks, theories got weirder. Without physical evidence of the mothership's destruction, no one would accept Earth's salvation had been brought about successfully. Nerves became increasingly frayed; people feared the ship might suddenly re-appear, its occupants stronger, bolder and more aggressive.

The more Jennifer Collins listened to the populist theories expounded on television of how the mothership's disappearance could have been pulled off, the more resolute she became that the symbols on the sides of the alien craft were important. One thing she was pretty sure of was that she was quite likely to be the only person in the western world who knew how those symbols translated. She also knew she really ought to tell someone about what she knew. But whom?

On the other hand, one thing Jennifer knew was that there was danger in raising one's head above the parapet and making sensational declarations, especially in public. She'd seen quite enough ridiculing of experts over these past few weeks to know that fact-based evidence was paramount to retaining one's credibility in the harsh light of the media's glare. She needed more information and, more importantly, clarity of contextual meaning. What, for example, was she actually alleging?

With a deep sigh she got up from the sofa for the first time in a couple of hours and went into the kitchen to pour herself a glass of chilled white wine. She didn't have enough facts to go on, of that she was sure, so if she did make an allegation public, she would almost certainly make an utter idiot of herself. With a resigned air, she decided there was no other course of action; she would simply have to go back to Surithani despite the dreaded, tortuous journey to get there. But it should be worth it for, in times of strife, who better to turn to than parents?

'Sue,' said Jennifer, returning to the sofa with her glass of wine. 'I need to go away for a while.'

'Oh yes? Where to?'

'Surithani. Same as last time.'

'Where is that, exactly?'

'Far away. South East Asia.'

'Ooh, sounds great. Can I come with you?'

'Sorry, no, you wouldn't be able to get a visa.'

Sue looked miffed. 'Why not?'

'Tourist visas aren't given out for that country.'

'What do you mean?'

'Tourists aren't allowed in.'

'How come you can get in?'

'My father works there. I spent my childhood there. I'm allowed to visit my parents whenever I like.'

'Is it warm there?'

'It's in the tropics. So, yes, it is.'

Sue looked hurt. 'But you can't take a friend with you?'

'You wouldn't like it. There are no pubs, no nightclubs. The foreign residents are kept in an enclave where there's little to do other than hang out at the British Club which is full of middle-aged women playing Bridge and gossiping. It's not like Magaluf.'

Sue folded her arms, looking grumpy. 'Why are you going there then?'

'Because I haven't seen my family for a while, I want to make sure they're okay.'

Sue gave Jennifer a glare.

'Alright, there's more to it than that, I admit. I miss the place. It's beautiful because it's completely unspoilt.' Jennifer paused to wipe away a tear. 'There's a boy there I'm in love with and I haven't seen him for five months.'

Sue unfolded her arms. 'What about Mike?'

Jennifer sighed. 'Mike's just a friend, I like him . . . usually . . . but he's a bit dull. I'm not sure I could ever actually fall in love with him.'

'Why this other boy then?'

'Well, he's a great horse-rider, we've spent hours galloping along the beach together. He's the one I dream about when I need cheering up.'

Sue snorted. 'You've kept that one quiet.'

'He's going to father my children. I just haven't told him yet.'

Sue gave Jennifer a look. 'Do you have any idea how freaky that sounds?'

Jennifer laughed. 'That didn't come out the way I meant it to.'

'So, what's his name? What does he look like, then?'

'Well, his name is Surachai. He's a year younger than me. He maintains the stable and horses at the British Club in the enclave. He's fun, he makes me laugh. He's had a crush on me for at least six years. Oh, and he's got the most gorgeous body imaginable.'

'Why have you never mentioned him before?'

'Because thinking of him hurts too much. I want to be with him, but I love the challenge of a career. Or at least I thought I did before

I joined Professor Friswell's staff. Oh, I don't know, Sue, I'm confused. I want to be here and there, both at the same time.' She reached across and held Sue's hand. 'Enough of me, will you be okay by yourself for a few weeks?'

'Sure,' replied Sue. 'Only, well, if you don't mind, I'd like to move in with Alan for a while.'

'That's fine. I didn't realise you'd been getting on quite so well. Is this going to be permanent?'

'Just while you're away, Jen, I know you need my share of the rent, and I know I've been here less than the full year I promised.'

'Really, it's okay.'

'I just want to see how we get on together. Alan and me, that is. Sorry, but I've been meaning to say something for the last few weeks. It's the commute, you see, it's not that easy. Alan lives in Kemp Town, it'll be so much easier for me, staying at his place, especially with night shifts.'

Jennifer smiled. 'Honestly, Sue, it's fine. I hope it works out well for you. And I won't expect any rent money next month. Don't feel guilty about it, life changes, I adapt quickly.'

Sue gave Jennifer a hug. 'Thanks, Jen. Come out for a drink with us when you get back, won't you? Tell us more about Surachai.'

'I will, I promise.'

Chapter Ten

Parental concern

Within the week, Jennifer Collins was back sipping coffee for breakfast at her parents' much-loved teak table on the veranda outside their villa. A few yards away, out across the front garden on the road, a woman in a sarong bargained harshly with a passing street hawker. Minutes later, the woman brought over a tray of expertly cut fresh pineapple, papaya and mango and set it down on the table. Jennifer thanked her and picked at the succulent fruit whilst looking at the glittering palace in the distance nestling above the city. It was one of those reassuring views that had remained unchanged throughout her life.

A voice called out from behind her, 'Morning, Jen. Sorry I didn't catch you last night. Bit of a lads do at the Club. I looked in about ten, but you were fast asleep. Didn't want to wake you.'

Jennifer turned her head in time to see her father stepping out on to the veranda. She gave him a warm smile and a peck on the cheek as he lowered his head to embrace her. 'Hi, Daddy,' she said. 'Sorry about the surprise nature of my visit. I came on a whim.'

'We're always pleased to see you, Jen. You know that.' James Collins pointed at the fruit and added, 'Is that fresh today?'

Jennifer nodded. 'Yes, Jum just haggled quite spectacularly for it. It might be few days before I get back into the swing of bargaining like that, I'm out of practice.'

James Collins tutted as he scooped several slices of fruit on to a plate. 'Now, Jen, don't go native on me, you know how indignant Jum will be if you try and take over her duties.'

'Ever the puritanical colonial master, eh, Daddy?'

'Ever the practical colonial master, if you don't mind. It's not you who has to pacify staff when they get upset by obstinate farang.'

Jennifer's face broke into a wide grin. 'I've missed our discussions on life.'

James Collins grunted. 'Well, I haven't.' He took his daughter's hand and gave it a squeeze. 'God, it's good to see you again, Jen. How long can you stay for?'

'A few weeks, I suppose. I don't really have a schedule.'

James Collins smiled. 'That's great. I really miss having you around. You'll come out in the evenings with your mother and me?'

'The usual social invitations? Dinner parties, musical soirées, Bridge evenings?'

'Of course, although now you'll no doubt be too busy fending off admirers to play Bridge.'

Jennifer playfully slapped her father's wrist. 'I have no time for admirers, as you put it, Daddy. I am not here in search of a husband.'

'You could do worse than settling down here, Jen. You couldn't get wild horses to drag me back to England. Society there sounds far too brutal now. The concept of kindness to one's fellow man has gone, from what I read.'

Jennifer looked off into the distance and sighed. 'I know, Daddy. I don't disagree, but I still feel there's more for me out there in life. I need to satiate that thirst before I can think of returning here full-time.'

James Collins adopted a serious expression. 'Don't leave it too long, will you? Don't get old and lonely.'

'I won't, Daddy, I promise. I just wish I could find a job that gave me the opportunity of having a foot in each camp, as it were.'

'Unfortunately, Jen, I don't think such a job exists.'

'It would help if there was an airport here. Travelling here by air would be so much quicker than having to catch a boat up from Singapore.'

'And if there was an airport here, this country wouldn't be the same, would it?'

'Maybe a helicopter pad? Just for me, that is?'

James Collins looked aghast. 'Good grief girl! What sort of job would pay for a helicopter ride from Singapore to here?'

Jennifer shrugged. 'Don't kill my dreams, Daddy.'

'Sorry, didn't mean to. Now then, what are you up to today? Going into town with your mother? Going to reacquaint yourself with the local culture?'

'It's a start, yes. But I need to undertake some research.'

'And there was I thinking you were on holiday.'

'It's called multi-tasking, Daddy. It's one thing we women are good at. I can work, rest and play all at the same time.'

The edge of James Collins' lip curled. 'Play? I thought you said you weren't interested in admirers?' He received a smack on the wrist for his efforts.

'Not that sort of play, Daddy. I was thinking of riding. I presume the British Club still has its stables and horses to hire?'

'Of course. And that handsome young man, Surachai, is still working with the horses. Your mother tells me he's turned into a real dish. I gather he's inundated with requests for riding lessons, but I'm sure he'll be delighted to . . .'

'Stop right there, Daddy. I won't have you matchmaking for me.'

James Collins pretended to look shocked. 'Jen! How could you? I wouldn't dream of such a thing.'

'Glad to hear it. Now, if you'll excuse me, I haven't unpacked yet. I'll catch you later.' She got up from the table and took a step towards the house.

James Collins stabbed a slice of papaya with a fork, grinned and said quietly to Jennifer's departing back, 'He's twenty-three years old, lean, muscular, still rides shirtless and, so the rumour goes amongst the ladies, shares similar attributes with his charges.'

'I heard that, Daddy,' shouted Jennifer over her shoulder. 'Soap. Mouth. Wash. That's all I'll say on the matter.'

James Collins' face broke into a wide smile.

Chapter Eleven

A technophobic society

While Jennifer's father was at work, and her mother organising an event at the British Club, she made herself comfortable on her parents' veranda with a glass of freshly squeezed orange juice, turned on her computer tablet and scrolled through old files searching for essays she'd written as an undergraduate. One in particular she sought. One that had been part of a special interest module in which students had been encouraged to compile a paper on a subject of their own choice. She had, quite naturally, based hers on a topic dear to her heart - The Kingdom Of Surithani: How has it survived the onslaught of technological development?

Ignoring the desire to cringe, Jennifer read the words of an innocent nineteen-year-old:

> *Although almost the size of England, the Kingdom of Surithani is home to a population of a little over four million people. No more than fifty thousand people live in Nakhon Thong, the country's only city. Most people live up-country, farming the fertile plains. It is a country in which many would be considered financially poor by European standards, yet no one lives in poverty. Orphans, the elderly, sick and the disabled are cared for by a legion of saffron robed Buddhist monks who form the backbone of each and every community. Above all others is the peoples' beloved king, Taksin the Great, who commands a structure of regional governors to administer his own personal brand of feudalism. Benign in his rule, a stickler for tradition, he has admirably demonstrated that he is a man incapable of being corrupted by western culture.*

The Kingdom of Surithani has experienced none of the social breakdowns experienced in the West as the human race has interacted with advances in technology, science, agriculture, construction and consumerism. The inhabitants of Surithani live the simple lives of farmers, fishermen, traders and servants, in wooden houses that have seen little change in design for hundreds of years. Yet the locals are the friendliest, happiest, most content people one could ever meet. There is full employment; no one suffers the social ostracism that can be brought about by unemployment. Family and religion are the cornerstones of society. No one lives in despair. No one has a lock affixed to their front door. No elderly person lives in fear of feral children or teenagers terrorising the neighbourhood.

Paradoxically, the country is a socialist's dream. The Crown is the sole freeholder of land; residents lease their land from the Crown, mostly at a peppercorn rent. Those who commit crime stand to lose their land rights. Services such as water and electricity, which is generated by solar power, are provided free by the Crown. The Crown is also the sole exporter, and buys all surpluses of rice, silk, spices and minerals, adds a tariff and sells it on at a premium to foreign buying agents. The export tariff provides the funds to pay for government administration and for temples to feed, clothe, house and nurse the disadvantaged. No native inhabitant has ever been required to pay a penny in tax of any description or pay for healthcare, education or a pension.

The country has never had an army; not one single soldier has ever been employed since the Kingdom was founded three thousand five hundred and forty-seven years ago. And with no visible means of defence, Surithani has all too often been considered a soft target. Over the centuries, many a European government has misguidedly dispatched a military force to make an impression on the king and his country, to win better trading terms or simply to plunder the gold and precious stones on display in the temples. Yet the country's borders have never been breached by an invading army, and each and every predatory empire-builder has been turned away confounded and, invariably, deeply humiliated.

Relatively few natives of Surithani have seen a farang, the local word for a Caucasian. The foreign population, of which there are no more than five hundred, and nearly all British, consist mainly of buying agents and agricultural experts, either current or retired, along with their families, and, although a few are scattered around the country working on projects, most of them are confined to a six square mile enclave comprising the port, warehouses, residential homes, a school, a prison camp, a church, a park, woodlands and a beach. Resident foreigners are allowed to visit the city for shopping, and to visit areas covered by work permits, but if they stray beyond those limits without due permission then they are likely to be hauled in front of the king to beg for clemency or to face exile.

The western world appears to have had little impact upon this secretive, spiritual country for which time seems to have forgotten.

Jennifer lowered her tablet and took a refreshing sip of juice. It was all coming back to her. She had sketched out the framework of her paper within a few hours of it being set by her lecturer. From that moment on, she had just needed to fulfil the minimum requirement of ten thousand words. She'd achieved that through describing real-life experiences in the country to support her views outlined under each chapter heading, along with a conclusion on the last page; one that would explain the anomaly of the continued existence of a thriving, ancient society in the modern world.

But that was where she had come unstuck. Since the birth of the country, the monarchy had managed to keep the crown, maintain civil unity and prevent foreign incursion. The king was a huge man, physically strong, had a powerful presence and would be feared by many. Yet without a single soldier, and no obvious military weapon at his command, was the sheer force of his personality enough to achieve peace and harmony?

Jennifer remembered how, at the time, she'd felt a fraud for not finding a satisfactory answer to the anomaly. In the end, she had settled for "good diplomacy". It had been a weak answer, but the least controversial of her conjectures. A couple of alternatives had been widely abstract and would have made her the laughing stock of her colleagues had she given voice to them. Now, with the knowledge of the symbols she'd recently seen on television, she wasn't so sure of their absurdity.

She picked up her tablet and continued to read:

For more than three thousand five hundred years the country has lived in peace, its borders never once having been penetrated by foreign invaders. And the king, Taksin the Great, the beloved ruler, a god amongst his people, presides over the country's administration with a fervent benevolence. With no tax, no poverty, no armed forces, and an uncountable number of temples and shrines, it is a country considered by its occasional visitor to be a social and spiritual paradise.

A political philosophy akin to that of the European Green Party movement is prevalent in Surithani. Combustion engines are banned, as are all petrochemical industry activities and non-biodegradable products. Logging, mineral extraction, property development and any other exploitation of the country's natural resources is not allowed by anyone other than the Crown.

Because of the king's technophobic tendency, any new technology or foreign manufactured product has to be approved by him personally before it can be imported into the country. Whether this has benefited the country economically or not is debatable, but his refusal to allow the importation of pollution-inducing products and processes has kept the countryside in an enviably pristine condition.

Jennifer put the tablet down sharply. Technology! That's what had been missing from her reasoning on the recent alien invasion. Alien technology had to be more advanced than that found on Earth. Yet alien technology had been trumped. But by what? Superior technology perhaps? But then if so, who could possibly have technology more superior than that displayed by intergalactic-travelling aliens?

Chapter Twelve

The British Club

'Hi, Mum.'

Judith Collins, a bunch of white orchids in one hand, abruptly turned around to see her daughter coming through the British Club front door. 'Oh, hi, Jen. Have you come to give me a hand after all? I'm nearly done here in the hall, but the bar area still needs brightening up. There's only Jane and myself on duty today. Mary can't make it; she's down with some dreaded lurgy. And Angela's having to sort out her laundry by herself, her girl's off sick again. That's three times this month. I keep saying she needs to replace her with a more mature woman.'

'Mum, sorry, but I need to use the records office. I need to do some research.'

'I see. Oh well, never mind. I'm sure we'll manage. Will you join us for lunch in the bar? Say one o'clock?'

'Yes, thank you. That would be nice. Catch you later,' replied Jennifer, as she brushed past her mother on the way down the hall and up the stairs of the magnificent Victorian villa which had been built by a wealthy trader and left on his death for the benefit of the community. In the grounds lay a swimming pool, a couple of tennis courts, stables, a paddock, a bowling lawn, a children's play area, a gymnasium, and formal gardens which catered for an annual fête and occasional tea party. Inside, the downstairs reception rooms had been turned into a bar-cum-dining area, an activities room where Bridge was played most afternoons and evenings, a well-stocked lending library, a billiards room, a reading room where members could

borrow out-of-date international newspapers and magazines which
had been brought up from Singapore, and a sitting room where the
ladies would take afternoon tea, catch up with gossip and complain
about their servants. Upstairs, one room was dedicated for use as the
manager's office, another as a staff room, one for use by the consular
for official duties, one for records and archives, and a spare room for
any particular meeting or function that could not be fitted around the
use of the ground floor. It was to the records and archives room that
Jennifer headed. It contained a treasure trove of diaries, journals,
corporate records, maps, news sheets, documents and letters left
behind by generations of traders and their families who had found no
room for such detritus as they packed for their final voyage back to
the home country.

Jennifer smiled. The room contained row upon row of floor-to-
ceiling height shelving, jam-packed with papers and books in no
particular order. She was in heaven. She wandered around the room,
getting her bearings, picking up odd items that took her fancy,
formulating a strategy to cater for her task. She could spare a week or
so. Maybe more. It wasn't like she had a proper job to rush back to,
especially since she'd made arrangements for her part-time lecturing
work to be covered while she was away. This undertaking was far
more worthy of her attention.

It wasn't long before she pulled out a notebook and pen from her
bag and jotted down notes of eighteenth century eye-witness
accounts from seafarers of monsters forcing ships to turn and flee; of
invasion fleets marooned for weeks in the gulf, trapped by a devil fog
and unable to make headway; of invading armies surrendering as
soon as they stepped ashore; of ships that disappeared in broad
daylight.

Jennifer spent a brief lunch break with her mother, sufficient time
to appear sociable but short enough not to tire of trivial local gossip.
Then she was back delving into ancient reports of bewildering
shipping events. Bewildering, that was, for the people of the time.
For Jennifer, however, maybe less so. In the right context, there may
have been quite logical and feasible explanations. Nevertheless, her
dreams that night were haunted by tales of monsters lurking in
Surithani's territorial waters.

It was three days before Jennifer chanced her luck with twentieth
century writings. It was another two days before she came across a

ribboned bundle of papers in a folder marked as belonging to "Mr Jonathan Trepte, British Consular 1959 to 1967", at the front of which was a faded colour photograph of a large number of men marching out of the huge wooden doors of the foreign prisoner camp. Intrigued, she undid the ribbon, picked up a typed report headed "Attempted American invasion of Surithani, November 1964" and began to read of the exploits of a certain Captain John Triscott. The more she delved into the detail of the event and subsequent correspondence, the more thrilled she became.

Chapter Thirteen

November 1964:

As dawn broke, the golden, jewel encrusted palace roof sparkled in the early morning rays of tropical sunlight. Below, at the base of the mountain that gave shelter to Nakhon Thong, the capital of Surithani, the city's inhabitants had long been awake. Well-worn stone-paved streets, wending their way amongst ancient wooden buildings, were full of the cries of market traders and yoke-carrying vendors hawking their wares.

Away from the bustling city that had changed little since ancient times, peace and tranquillity reigned in the plains, for there was no noise from any combustion engine. For the sarong-wearing workers on their way to nearby rice fields, and for saffron-robed monks offering blessings outside their temple gates in exchange for food, little could be heard other than the sound of birdsong and the gentle splash of oar from canoes traversing the waters of the Patunam river that coursed their way down to the harbour, into the gulf and out to the distant South China Sea.

Five miles offshore, a periscope broke the surface of the gulf's deep-blue tropical water as an American submarine crept smoothly and silently across the maritime border. Below the waterline, down in the belly of the USS Chesapeake, Captain John Triscott swivelled the periscope three hundred and sixty degrees and saw no hint of a naval presence. Other than an occasional fishing boat, nothing stirred on the surface of the water between him and the enormous breakwater that protected the entrance to Nakhon Thong's port. And the mountain behind the breakwater showed no sign of fortification. A pacifists' nirvana, is how the country had been described to him by his hawkish superiors. He grinned. It would be easy, so damn easy, to head straight into port and mount a surprise raid on the city. And if he could do that, then Charlie could too. So it was high time the idiot pacifists learned the hard way what "vulnerability to communist attack" really meant.

'Take note,' said Captain Triscott. 'Invading this country would be a walkover. Fortunately for them, our mission stops short way before that.'

'How far do you want to push it?' replied Jake Henderson, the Executive Officer.

'All the way, Jake, all the way. There's a breakwater at the base of the mountain, sticks well out into the sea. Let's get past that, right into the harbour mouth. We need to show these dimwits exactly what threat Charlie poses. Without our help that is.'

Jake laughed. 'Uncle Sam to the rescue again, huh?'

'Too right . . .' Abruptly, Captain Triscott tensed. 'Hang on, there's movement near the port. It's, it's . . .' he fell silent, transfixed for a few seconds before continuing, 'Jesus, would you look at that. What the hell is it?' He stood back from the periscope, rubbed his eyes and gestured towards his Executive Officer. 'Take a look, Jake. Tell me my eyes aren't deceiving me.'

The Executive Officer complied. Within a couple of seconds he responded, 'It's a fog bank, Skip.'

Captain Triscott tutted. 'Yeah, I worked that one out for myself. But check out it's speed. It wasn't there a minute ago. And it's coming from inland towards us, if you hadn't noticed. It will be above us in less than a minute if it continues at that rate.'

The Executive Officer shrugged. 'It's just fog, Skip.'

Captain Triscott shook his head. 'You think so? It's a beautiful day up there, and we're in the tropics in case you've forgotten. Why would fog occur? And why would it aim for us.'

A bewildered looking Executive Officer replied, 'Aim for us?'

Captain Triscott gestured for his Executive Officer to move aside. 'Aim is what I said, is what I meant. There's something weird about that fog.' He turned from the periscope and shouted, 'What you got on radar?'

The radar operative responded, 'Whatever it is, sir, it's got a solid centre.'

'You mean there's something in the middle of it? A ship?'

'Don't think so, sir. The mass appears to be above the waterline.'

'An aeroplane then?'

'Don't think so, sir. Wrong profile.'

'But you just said it's above the waterline.'

'I did, yes, sir. I'm just saying its profile is not of a known aeroplane or ship.'

Captain Triscott resumed his position at the periscope. 'Well, it looks like a simple fog bank to me, but it's covered a couple of miles in the last thirty seconds. And if there is an aeroplane in there, it hasn't broken free. How can fog travel at the speed of an aeroplane?' He turned around and muttered something unintelligible towards his Executive Officer then, on turning back, swore, 'Shit! It's right on top of us now.' He stood back, let his Executive Officer have another look.

'Do you want to contact the Bennington, Skip, let them know what's going on?'

'Not yet,' replied Captain Triscott. 'We're supposed to be on reconnaissance duties. We stay silent, just observe.'

The Executive Officer stood back from the periscope and nodded. 'You want to sit it out?'

Captain Triscott grunted. 'Too damn right I do. Surithani's a poxy, undefended little country. There's no army, no navy, no air force that we know about. God knows how they got through the war without being taken over by the Japs. We're in no danger from anyone down here, even if we are in their waters. It's not as though they can do anything about our presence.'

The Executive Officer nodded. 'If you say so, Skip.'

'I do.' Captain Triscott stared hard at the Executive Officer's back as the man moved away. 'We stay on mission. Last thing we want is for Charlie to take over Surithani, we need to encourage them to see things our way.' As he stepped towards the periscope something jarred the boat, sending it rocking. 'What the hell was that?' he shouted, stumbling into the radar operative's chair. 'Damage report!' he screamed as the boat rocked again. 'What the hell is happening out there?'

It was thirty seconds before the Executive Officer responded. 'We're ascending, Skip. Something's pulling us up.'

'Don't be stupid, Jake,' shouted Captain Triscott. 'Nothing on

Earth could do that.' He nevertheless grabbed the periscope, turned it a few degrees and yelped as his eyes took in the sight of what looked like the underside of a gigantic black metal bird hovering in the fog with its talons wrapped around the boat. Seconds later the submarine was pulled clean out of the water and he stood up straight, ashen faced.

'What's up, Skip?'

'No one move,' shouted Captain Triscott. 'Stay calm.' He stood in fearful silence as a strange sensation took possession of his body, as though he was flying through the air. A fleeting image came to his mind of a salmon trapped in the deathly clutches of a fish eagle.

For four very tense minutes, Captain Triscott awaited his fate, trying to make sense of the impossibility of what he'd seen. Nothing could lift a submarine, there was no crane in the world powerful enough to pluck a three-thousand-ton object from the sea. And as for the notion of flying, maybe the submarine was simply dangling in air since no aeroplane could possibly fly carrying such a weight. The stomach-churning feeling of flying abruptly stopped and changed to one of being lowered as though he was going down in an elevator. Unnerved, he grabbed the radio operative's shoulder for support but stumbled as the submarine rocked before coming to a rest. A minute passed before he ventured to look in the periscope. What he saw did not bring him reassurance. 'I'm going up top,' he muttered.

Moments later Captain Triscott stood atop the conning tower, taking in the view of rice fields to one side of the submarine, a stone-paved road to the other, a wide river that ran alongside the road, and a mountain range set further in the distance. The submarine, he realised to his horror, was sitting in what appeared to be nothing more than a couple feet of water.

'We're inland,' the Executive Officer gasped from behind. 'In a ditch.'

'You don't say.'

'How the hell did we get here?'

'More's the point, Jake, how the hell do we get out. We're stuck fast.'

'Shall I get on the radio, Skip, see if I can make contact with anyone?'

'And say what?'

'Well . . .'

'Exactly. Get the men off the boat, Jake. It's going to be hell down there soon in this heat.'

'Right. You want the men armed?'

Captain Triscott shook his head. 'We're on foreign soil. Secure the boat as much as you can, switch off power, leave anything threatening on board, but get the men to bring out as much water and food as they can carry. Let's see if we can get down on to dry land without breaking any bones.'

Two hours later, Captain Triscott and his crew of sixty-six men stood, bemused, in a huddled group on the stone-paved road, pondering their predicament. To their discomfort, a group of peasant women had stopped to gawk at the sight of the stranded submarine and to giggle at the bunch of fretful looking foreigners.

'We'll be the laughing stock of the whole world if this gets out,' muttered Captain Triscott as he wiped sweat from his forehead. 'Christ knows what we can do . . .'

'Sir,' a shout came from the outer edge of the group of submariners. 'Sir, there's someone coming.'

The men parted, allowing Captain Triscott to see a wooden cart, pulled by a water buffalo, heading their way at a leisurely pace. The driver, a wizened old man dressed in a sarong, his bare chest exposing brown wrinkled skin, waved in his direction. Some minutes later the driver brought the cart to a halt a few feet from where Captain Triscott was standing.

'You come me,' the old man said in Pidgin English. 'See King.'

'And you are . . .?' asked Captain Triscott.

'You come me, see King,' the old man repeated, gesturing to Captain Triscott and the men behind him. 'King angry, very angry. You come now.'

Captain Triscott wiped his forehead. 'I guess we've no choice.' He nodded at the old man. 'Okay, let's go.'

The old man steered the water buffalo in a half circle and set off back the way he had come, singing in an appallingly flat key as he drove away. The Executive Officer gave his captain a look of disdain and said, 'This is the king's emissary? He's taking the piss, isn't he?'

'Actually, Jake,' Captain Triscott responded, 'I think we're being taught a lesson. Take a look at the old man's cargo. It's a dung cart.'

After an hour's trek, signs of civilisation appeared. A stone bridge arching its way over the river came into view, on the other side of which lay a small city of wooden houses nestling at the base of the mountain range. In the distance, further down river, could be seen the tops of cranes and ship funnels.

'That must be Nakhon Thong over there,' said Captain Triscott to his Executive Officer as he wiped his brow. 'The port can only be a couple of miles from here. Perhaps the old man is going to take us there, put us on a ship.' But to his dismay, the cart driver halted outside what appeared to be an ancient stone-walled fortress with a large wooden gate serving as the entrance.

'King come. You look,' said the old man pointing towards the distant mountain.

Captain Triscott squinted into the sun. The old man seemed to be pointing towards a promontory jutting out from the mountain, on which sat a golden roofed palace. Beautiful as it was, he wasn't sure what he was supposed to be looking for.

The Executive Officer nudged his captain. 'In the air, Skip.'

Captain Triscott raised his eyes, scanned the skies. Sure enough, a fast-moving object was flying in their direction. He blinked. Blinked again, trying to focus on what type of aeroplane it could be. Certainly not one he'd ever seen before, for it had no wings, nor propeller. He thought it looked more like a car with a glass domed canopy and no wheels. And virtually no noise, he observed, as it effortlessly came to a halt a few yards away, hovering a foot off the ground. The canopy drew back and the pilot stepped out; a giant of a man at least seven foot in height, broad, muscular, dressed in black from head to foot and a look of fury set hard on his face. Although the pilot was an intimidating sight, oddly, he noticed, the cart driver seemed indifferent, merely cajoling his buffalo to continue its journey, as though the appearance of this giant and his flying vehicle was a routine event.

'Damn you Americans,' the pilot swore as he strode aggressively towards Captain Triscott. 'Your arrogance is astonishing. What right do you think you have to enter my territorial waters? Your leaders insist on establishing international maritime treaties, yet your military don't observe the rules. Damn you all, I've a good mind to flail the lot of you.'

Captain Triscott stood to attention and saluted. 'Captain Triscott, United States Navy. I apologise profusely for our unwarranted incursion, sir. We offer our unconditional surrender to you but, under the Geneva Convention, I request . . .'

The ensuing explosion of expletives from the pilot's mouth shook Captain Triscott to the core. He waited for the man to pause for breath before saying, 'I can only apologise again, sir. Unreservedly so.'

'Apologise?' the pilot spluttered. 'What good are apologies? You're only apologising because you got caught.'

Captain Triscott frowned. 'Er, well, yes, sir. I can't deny that.'

The pilot stood fuming for a moment, looked as though he'd like to hit something, or someone, before saying, 'Right, this is what's going to happen. Your action amounts to a declaration of war. This building,' he gestured to the fort-like structure behind the Americans, 'is the foreign prisoner camp. You will stay here until further notice, and don't try to escape or I'll have you locked up in dungeons. Provisions will be brought to you and I'll have the British Consular make contact with you since there's no other diplomatic official stationed here.' With that, the pilot moved forward, yanked open one of the gates, waited for Captain Triscott and his men to enter and slammed it shut.

'Well, that went well,' muttered Captain Triscott as he took in the sight of the camp that resembled a barracks with a square in the middle surrounded by long rows of buildings extending some hundred yards in each direction. 'Right then men, let's see what facilities this delightful residence offers.'

Whilst Captain Triscott and his crew were becoming acquainted with their new surroundings, news of the capture of the submarine was relayed by the British Consular to the US Navy, along with a demand for payment for its release. It came as no surprise that the US Navy chose to respond with a show of force, and promptly despatched the USS Bennington to investigate. What did come as a surprise, though, was that as the aircraft carrier crossed into Surithani's territorial waters all radio contact with the ship was lost.

Perplexed, the US Navy despatched a small flotilla of ships, including another aircraft carrier, with orders to find out what had happened to the USS Bennington and to engage in hostilities if necessary. However, to the incredulity of observers on an accompanying fast patrol boat, the USS Connecticut disappeared from radar on being engulfed by a fog bank.

After a week of humiliation by an American press outraged at the loss of a submarine, two aircraft carriers and their combined crews of over six thousand men, the presidential office wisely decided to change tactics from aggression to diplomacy.

Former army general James A. Burford, the incumbent President of the United States was not having a good day. In fact, he could not recall ever having had a worse day during his long and turbulent time in office. As he sat alone awaiting his audience with His Supreme Highness King Taksin The Great, in a grand palatial room, surrounded by exquisite works of art, he felt like a disobedient schoolboy awaiting the wrath of an angry headmaster rather than being the most powerful man in the world awaiting an audience with the leader of a country assessed by his intelligence services as being backward and inconsequential.

He checked his watch, anxiously shifted a large black carrier bag sitting at his feet, and stifled a sigh. It had been fifteen minutes since he had been shown into the room by a palace aide; left for fifteen minutes to contemplate life, presumably. Perhaps the impoliteness was deliberate, an attempt to increase his humiliation.

As it happened, contemplation came easy to him today. For four weeks he'd done little else other than contemplate how events could go so badly wrong; the capture and ransom of a submarine; the row that had erupted when the Soviets publicly offered five million dollars to buy the submarine; the disappearance of the USS Bennington and the USS Connecticut; the outrage in the press against his administration for perceived incompetence.

And then there'd been that eerie fog bank that had surrounded the USS Ulysses Grant, the ship on which he'd arrived just two hours ago, with the extraordinary appearance of a monstrous, hundred-foot-high talking head at its centre. Quite what the head had been, and how he had managed to reason with it to allow safe passage into harbour, were matters still quite beyond him.

He vented another sigh as he refocused his mind on the reason he'd travelled halfway around the world to this little-known country. It was to beg; to beg for clemency. Begging was a demeaning act for someone holding his office, of that he had no doubt, but he could see no option. It was his own fault; he should never have let matters get this far. A long time ago, at the height of the war, a wise old politician in London had warned him about Taksin's technology, that it was vastly superior to anything existing on the planet. He should have taken heed.

A noise from the corner of the room caught his attention. He looked around and saw a giant of a man, dressed head to foot in black, anger etched all over his face, striding purposefully in his direction. He rose out of his chair quickly, bowed his head in supplication and said, 'Your majesty, I cannot apologise enough for the illegal violation of your sovereign territory and the injury to your good name and distress to you the defamation in our press must have caused.' It took the President ten seconds before he risked looking up from the floor. Taksin stood no more than a yard away, towering over him, his large fists furiously clenching at his side, his enraged eyes glaring down. For the first time in ages James A. Burford felt vulnerable, felt the frailty of his seventy-five-year-old bones, felt the despair that must have been reflected in his face. He held Taksin's glare and said, 'Please, your majesty, I beg for forgiveness. I accept complete responsibility for this fiasco. I blame no one else and I will accept any punishment you deem appropriate.'

It took a further ten seconds before the giant's body appeared to relax. 'Sit down,' Taksin muttered. 'Before you faint.'

The President all but collapsed into a nearby chair. 'Thank you, your majesty.'

'May I offer you refreshment?'

'A glass of cool water would be much appreciated.'

'Of course,' Taksin replied and withdrew a hand-sized contraption from a pocket and depressed a button. Moments later a servant boy appeared in the corner of the room, carrying a tray on which two glasses and a jug of iced water were visible. The boy crossed the room and lowered the tray in front of Taksin, who poured a generous measure of water into a glass and passed it to an ashen-faced President. 'I should apologise, Mr President. At times, I forget how intimidating I can appear.'

President Burford knocked back the entire glass of water in one gulp. 'Intimidating is the word, your majesty. I thought you were going to throw a punch. It's been a few years since I've been in a brawl. I'm not sure I would have come out of it with much credit.'

Taksin snorted. 'Wars would occur less often if politicians had to fight it out amongst themselves instead of putting soldiers on a battlefield.'

'I won't deny that, your majesty. I would just hope in that situation I wouldn't be up against you. I can think of few men who would dare challenge you. You have a most impressive physique.'

Taksin broke into a smile. 'More water? Something stronger perhaps? I have a decent brandy at hand.'

President Burford held out his empty glass. 'Another water would be fine, thank you. I'll save the brandy until later if you don't mind.'

Taksin poured another glass of water. 'Now,' he said, as he cast a curious look at the carrier bag on the floor, 'I imagine you've come to plead for the return of your ships and men?'

President Burford nodded. 'Indeed, I have, your majesty. I have belatedly come to the view that you possess powers far greater than my own country. So great, in fact, that I believe my country probably only exists in its present form because of your benevolence.'

'I see. Pity you hadn't realised that before that submarine was sent here.'

'Indeed so, your majesty.'

'Did you authorise it? The submarine incursion, that is?'

'No, I did not,' President Burford replied. 'I have to admit our military are known for being rather aggressive. They were simply testing your defences, seeing how vulnerable you may be to invasion. The influence of communism in this area is a major concern to them. The submarine captain's orders certainly came from high up the command chain, but without my knowledge. The mistake is costing us dearly.'

Taksin appeared to reflect on the matter. 'Am I to assume you are here to make an offer for the release of your men and ships then?'

'Well, yes and no.'

'I see,' Taksin responded. 'Or rather I don't.'

President Burford sighed. 'Your majesty. I could sit here and continue to apologise for the rest of my life, but with regard to financial recompense, it is my belief that offering money would mar our relationship, that your ethics are far above the immorality associated with ransom demands.'

Taksin raised an eyebrow. 'I see. So that means . . .?'

'It means, your majesty,' interrupted President Burford, 'that you could demand anything you wished. Human life is sacrosanct. No amount of money is worth more than a man's life. I couldn't possibly place a figure on the head of six thousand men. What would I say to their families if I failed to reach a bargain?'

Taksin crossed his arms. 'Where exactly is this conversation going?'

President Burford reached for the bag at his feet, removed a cooler box from within it, hoisted it up on to his lap. 'The level of your technology is way beyond our own. Devastatingly so. You could attack and destroy the United States of America at your whim. Yet you don't, and you haven't in the past. Nor have you done so with any other country in the world. I assume your laissez-faire attitude is because you wish to see us develop without interference. So, what I offer you in exchange for my men is this.' He put his hand in the cooler box, rummaged amongst the ice, pulled out a small oblong package and offered it to Taksin.

Taksin stared at the offering in astonishment. 'And what is this?' he asked.

'It's a Hershey Bar, your majesty. It may only be a bar of chocolate, but it typifies America. It typifies the American spirit, the American dream. I offer it to you as a symbol of my country. It is yours for the taking, to destroy or leave to flourish.'

Taksin stared at the offering in apparent shock. 'A bar of chocolate? You offer a bar of chocolate in exchange for your men and boats?'

'I certainly do. And before you ask whether the budget for it was approved by Congress, I can reveal it cost ten cents which came out of my own pocket.'

Taksin guffawed. Yet he took the offering, peeled back the covering, broke a couple of segments, slipped one into his mouth and offered the other to President Burford. 'To tell you the truth, I don't really care for chocolate.'

President Burford took the other segment and laughed as he popped it into his mouth. 'To be honest, neither do I.'

Taksin sighed and said, 'Do me a favour, will you? Promise you won't mention this to a sole. I wouldn't want anyone to think I'd gone soft.'

'That is a promise I will happily keep, your majesty. I doubt whether anyone would consider the Hershey Bar trick a wise move. It could well have backfired with disastrous consequences.'

Taksin smiled. 'Indeed, it could. I hope never to witness it again. My reaction is unlikely to be quite so conciliatory.'

'May I ask when you'll free my men?'

'You can collect the submarine crew immediately. March them down to the docks, by which time the submarine will be there awaiting them. The missing boats will be free once the boat you arrived on and the submarine are back in international waters.'

'Thank you, your majesty. May I ask for one thing though? May I have a way of communicating with you direct?'

Taksin frowned. 'That's not something I would welcome. There's a consulate in England, any messages can be passed on from there.'

'We know of the consulate, your majesty. We tried it last week, but the gatekeeper is a curmudgeonly bastard who refused to talk to my representative and threatened to pelt him with rotten vegetables.'

Taksin laughed. 'Did he? I'm not surprised, he's only following orders.'

'It would help enormously if there was a less fallible means of communication. Like a simple telephone number? For emergencies only perhaps.'

Taksin got up and crossed the room to a table. He came back with a scrap of paper and a pen. 'Here, this is a radio frequency I monitor. A radio operative will know how to send a signal. For dire emergencies only, though. And I mean dire, such as impending world catastrophes.'

President Burford pocketed the piece of paper. 'Thank you, your majesty. Now, if I may, I shall take my leave of you.'

And so, at the end of the submarine crew's fifth week of incarceration, the gate to the foreign prisoner camp was flung wide open and a furious looking President Burford stormed in to the compound. Minutes later, the crew marched out, heads held high and in silence, their president in the lead.

To President Burford's annoyance, a camera flashed, capturing for posterity his moment of abject humility.

Chapter Fourteen

A favour

Sitting around the family dining table that evening, a thoughtful Jennifer turned to her father during dessert and said, 'Daddy, am I right in thinking you used to go to school with Anthony Shepherd?'

'You mean Call-Me-Tony? Yes, I did. We were both at Ascham, in Eastbourne. The prep school, that is. I just managed to get out before the developers moved in.'

'Do you know him well? Well enough to ask a favour?'

James Collins put his fork and spoon down. 'Tony was in the year below me. I wouldn't say we were friends, but we did play in the same school cricket team together in my last year, so I suppose we got to know each other reasonably well. I would imagine we'd still be on nodding terms. Why? What are you up to?'

'Nothing much, but I need to speak to him. Would you write me an introductory letter?'

James Collins' face fell. 'Good grief, Jen. He's Prime Minister now. I'm not sure he'd welcome the intrusion. What's so important?'

'Oh, um, National Security, Daddy,' said Jennifer whilst putting on a serious face. 'I couldn't possibly tell you.'

'Are you after a job on his staff?'

Jennifer smiled sweetly at her father. 'Maybe. But first I'd like to ask him a couple of questions. For my research, that is.'

James Collins sat back, ignoring the last spoonful of mango and sticky rice on his dessert plate. 'Yes, this research of yours, Jen. What exactly is it for? You haven't explained it properly to us yet.'

'Just academic stuff, it wouldn't interest you. Honestly.'

Jennifer's mother took the opportunity of joining in. 'Is it a book dear? Have you secured a deal with a publisher?'

'No, Mum, I haven't. Sorry, it really is just academic research.'

'And Call-Me-Tony can help?'

'His answers are central to my conclusion, Daddy. I'd be lost without his input.'

'But you've got a doctorate already, Jen. What greater academic achievement is there?'

'Well, there's a Nobel Prize, but I'd settle for a well-paid job. I'm running short of funds.'

James Collins looked into his daughter's eyes and sighed. 'Oh, very well. Fortunately, we're too far away for him to berate me.'

Jennifer rose off her chair, came around the table and gave her father a hug and kiss. 'Thanks, Daddy.'

'You're very welcome,' he sighed. 'But does this mean you're leaving us again?'

Jennifer nodded. 'Yes, but not for a while. I'd like a few days of rest to get my head clear. And it's high time I went horse riding again. It's been ages since I last went down to the beach.'

James Collins placed an arm around his daughter, gave a gentle squeeze and said, 'That's my girl.'

Chapter Fifteen

Breakthrough

Dressed smart as a pin, in a brand new grey trouser suit, Jennifer Collins had sat for what seemed an eternity on a black leather sofa in a reception area on the first floor of 10 Downing Street, in silence, tightly gripping a file in her hands and clutching a briefcase between her feet, under the watchful gaze of a burly security guard. She couldn't remember ever feeling quite so uncomfortable, not just because she was attired in something more formal than a pair of jeans for once, but also because she felt a complete fraud.

Within seconds of having been asked to sit and wait, she had the daunting feeling of impending failure, certain that her father's letter, requesting a moment of the Prime Minister's time to pass on a personal message from an old school friend, would be exposed for the lie that it was. Just as she had argued herself into thinking she was wasting everyone's time, convinced she would be dismissed as a loony, a door opened and the elegantly suave figure of Anthony Shepherd appeared. In his mid-forties, well known for having a young family of three teenage daughters, he looked as though he'd aged ten years since the day his beaming smile had won him a general election a year ago.

'Jennifer,' said the Prime Minister, extending a hand. 'Nice to meet you.'

Jennifer jumped up and clumsily offered her hand. 'You too, sir. Thank you for seeing me, sir.'

'Please call me Tony.'

'Yes, sir.'

The Prime Minister gave Jennifer a look that suggested no one else had ever felt disposed to be so intimate, especially on first introductions. 'Now then, it's been a long time since I've heard your father's name. I'm intrigued to know what he could possible want to say to me.'

Jennifer gulped. 'Well, to tell you the truth, sir, the letter was merely a ruse to get a moment of your time.'

The Prime Minister laughed. 'You're not the first person to pull that trick. Come on then, for the sake of old times, I'll give you two minutes as you're bearing such a charming smile.'

'Thank you, sir. I only have a couple of short questions to ask. The first is, are you trying to locate the people that rescued us from the aliens?'

The Prime Minister's face fell. 'I couldn't possibly comment on that, I'm afraid, Jennifer.'

Jennifer nodded her understanding. She hadn't really expected anything different. 'Have you located them yet?'

The Prime Minister appeared uneasy. 'I'm sorry, Jennifer, but may I ask the purpose of these questions?'

Jennifer took a deep breath. 'Well, sir. It's just, well, you know the symbols on the spacecraft? Well, I can translate them.'

The Prime Minister's head and shoulders sagged. 'Oh, no, Jennifer, not you as well? Do you have any idea of the number of phone calls, letters and emails we're receiving from people who claim to have intimate knowledge of the aliens and the planet they came from?'

'I'm not here to talk about the aliens that invaded us, sir. I'm here to tell you where one of our rescuers lives.'

The Prime Minister sighed deeply. 'And we've had just as many people claiming that our rescuers were also aliens and are living in the house next door to them. Please, Jennifer, don't delude yourself. Go home, we've got a lot on our plate at the moment. Now, please pass on my regards to your father, but I must say goodbye.' The Prime Minister turned and walked away.

In an effort to seize the moment, Jennifer raised her voice at the Prime Minister's retreating back, 'President Burford knew one of them. I have proof they met.'

The Prime Minister stopped abruptly and spun around on his heels. 'What did you say?'

'I said, sir, that President James Burford knew one of our rescuers.'

The Prime Minister froze. 'That's classified information. Who told you that, Jennifer? If there's been a breach of security, the police will need to interview you.'

Jennifer's mouth dropped. 'Erm, I don't know anything about a security breach, sir. And I haven't talked to anyone about the matter either. I got the information from an old newspaper.'

The Prime Minister looked incredulous. 'I beg your pardon?'

'There was a military incident back in the sixties. President Burford stepped in and saved the day through diplomacy. That's when he came face-to-face with one of our rescuers.'

'What newspaper? What on earth are you talking about?'

Jennifer flipped through the file she'd been carrying and held it out open at a copy of a cutting from the Singapore Times. 'It's all in here, sir. I specialise in social anthropology. I've been inadvertently researching one of our rescuers and his habitat for several years.'

The Prime Minister snatched the file from Jennifer and began reading. He stood, mesmerized, as he read the newspaper cutting before flipping back to the first page and working forwards through the file. After a few minutes he sat down and stared vacantly ahead as though his mind was far away.

After a full thirty seconds had passed, Jennifer sat down alongside the Prime Minister and asked kindly, 'Sir? Are you alright, sir?'

The Prime Minister broke his reverie. 'Sorry, Jennifer,' he said at length. 'I shouldn't have snapped at you just then.'

'That's okay, sir. It's understandable in the circumstances. If I may explain, about my work?'

'There's no need, Jennifer.' He tapped the file. 'No need at all. I get it. You've solved a big problem I've been working on. Thank you.'

'You're welcome, sir.' She fell silent while the Prime Minister continued to sit beside her, lost in thought.

It was a while before the Prime Minister spoke. 'Jennifer, look, what you've got here, in this file, I trust you realize its explosive nature. How many others know about it?'

'No one else, sir.'

'Not even your father?'

Jennifer returned a grin. 'Especially not my father, sir. I love him dearly, but the expatriate community in Surithani have little to do with their days other than trade gossip. He wouldn't be able to hold his tongue on the matter.'

The Prime Minister took a deep look into Jennifer's eyes. 'Do you have any idea what will happen if this gets into the press?'

Jennifer held the Prime Minister's stare. 'I can guess, sir. The consequences could be a calamity of far worse proportions than we experienced a few weeks ago.'

'You understand the seriousness of the issue then?'

'I believe I do, sir. It would be like provoking an unfettered grizzly bear with a pointed stick. The subsequent mess would not be a pretty sight.'

'And we need the bear to remain friendly.'

'We do indeed, sir. I think we're only alive and living in freedom because of the grace of that bear.'

The Prime Minister nodded. 'You've given me what I've been looking for. It's the breakthrough I've been waiting for.'

'Use it wisely, sir.'

The Prime Minister caught Jennifer's eye. 'I intend to,' he replied. 'I want to talk to our rescuers, to ask if we can join forces, share their technology, be better prepared for the next invasion, god forbid that it may happen again. Will you help me?'

'Of course I will, sir.'

'Good. I need to start straight away. Are you up to talking through your findings to the Joint Chiefs of Staff?'

The unexpected request made Jennifer's throat go dry. She nodded her assent.

'To be frank,' the Prime Minister continued, 'they're in denial. They can't accept someone has bettered them in a fight. They can't accept that the billions of pounds they spend on conventional weapons systems each year is a complete waste of money when it comes to defending our world from extra-terrestrial attack. And they've been looking in the wrong direction for answers. They need refocusing. They need a jolt of reality. You've found the one thing they've been missing. Unfortunately, they won't thank you for it, although that's their problem, not yours, to be fair. Fancy doing a presentation for them?'

Jennifer was shocked. It took her a moment to compose herself. 'I'd be honoured, sir.'

'Good. I have to warn you, though, they're a pretty mean bunch of male chauvinists. They'll be sceptical of both you and your report. If they're true to form, they'll try to run you down personally and discredit your findings.'

Jennifer drew a deep breath and replied, 'I'm used to it, sir. Some of my university colleagues have derived great enjoyment from tearing apart my ideas in the past.'

The Prime Minister looked relieved. 'Thank you, Jennifer. Would you mind waiting a few moments? I'll get someone to bring you a cup of tea while I set up an urgent meeting.'

'That's fine, sir.'

The Prime Minister stood up, turned to Jennifer, said, 'And please, call me Tony.'

Chapter Sixteen

Cantankerous old men

Jennifer Collins sat back down on the sofa in 10 Downing Street and waited patiently for another half an hour, wondering what she'd got herself into. A presentation to the Joint Chiefs of Staff? That was pretty mind-blowing. Was she crazy? She wondered what on earth possessed her to agree to it. She played out a scene in her head, about how to conduct the presentation; should she sit down, stand at a podium, use a white board? Her mind soon became scrambled, not helped by the security guard's habit of staring daggers at her every couple of minutes.

Finally, a door opened and a beaming Prime Minister reappeared. 'Sorry about the wait,' he said. 'Whitehall's a large place, it takes time for people to get through security. Mind you, I have to say most of the delay around here is all about posturing, as you'll find out in due course, I'm sure.'

Somewhat perplexed, Jennifer gave the Prime Minister an enquiring look. 'Sir?'

'Politics, Jennifer. People like to make themselves look grand around here. Important people are always late. Come on, you'll see. I'm hoping you can knock some sense into three very obstinate old men.'

Jennifer was rather taken aback. 'That should be fun. And there was I, worried you thought I was a crank.'

A thin smile broke on the Prime Minister face. 'Come on, follow me. I want to introduce you to three men who will surely think you are.'

'Really?' responded Jennifer, setting off at a trot behind the Prime Minister as he headed down a panelled corridor. 'Is this a wise idea then, sir?'

'It's a necessity, I'm afraid, Jennifer. Your report raises some very important issues. More importantly, the Chiefs of Staff haven't raised them, so you're coming in like a breath of fresh air to this debate. I want you to explain your reasoning to the Chiefs, even if it rattles them.' He paused a moment, then said, 'Actually, make that particularly if it rattles them.'

Jennifer was momentarily flustered. 'If you say so, sir.'

'I do. There's a lot at stake here, a different approach is needed to what I've been hearing from those around me recently. I've always had full confidence in the Chiefs of Staff, but the events of the last few weeks are way outside their experience and I'm not sure whether their advice is the right way to move forward. You see, one thing you have to understand, Jennifer, is that they feel particularly raw over the alien attack. Their egos are bruised. They were utterly helpless when faced with that spaceship and the aliens' visit here to make their demands. They feel neutered. You're bound to get their backs up, so be prepared for the flak.'

'Thanks a bunch, sir.' To this response, Jennifer noticed a grin appear on the Prime Minister's face. 'Sir, I don't wish to be rude, but why am I get the feeling you're looking forward to me getting my comeuppance.'

The Prime Minister came to a halt in front of a large oak door, chuckled and said, 'I remember your father as a prefect. He once made me run around and around the school playing field, as a punishment for some misdemeanour I forget, until I eventually threw up. I always wanted my revenge. As his daughter, you'll do in his place.'

Jennifer's eyes bulged. 'You're kidding me?'

'Nope. By the way, how's your timetable for the next few months?'

'Erm, I can be flexible. I'm only working part-time at university. Why?'

The Prime Minister laid his hand on the oak door's handle and said, 'Excellent, because I may well have a job for you.'

As the Prime Minister opened the door and stepped into a brightly lit room of white furniture and pale shades of decoration, three men in military uniforms rose from their seats. 'Good afternoon, gentlemen,' said the Prime Minister. 'Allow me to introduce Dr Jennifer Collins.' The Prime Minister gestured across a round table in the centre of the room and said, 'Dr Collins, may I present Admiral John Dickins, head of the navy, General Bob Wilson, head of the army, and Air Chief Marshall Gordon Grantham, head of the air force.'

Jennifer cheerfully wished the three grey-haired men a good afternoon. For respectable gentlemen, their grunts fell somewhat short of a socially acceptable response. Feeling somewhat chided, her face flushed crimson red as she hastily sat down. In a more relaxed atmosphere, she would have liked to have made a biting comment about their similarity to Statler and Waldorf, the grumpy curmudgeons in the Muppets.

'Now,' the Prime Minister continued, 'I'll get straight down to the matter in hand, if I may. I've called this meeting in response to the events that took place in my office five weeks ago. The facts are this. Firstly, out of nowhere comes this mysterious Saviour character, who promptly disposes of the threat of those two thugs in my office. Secondly, the Saviour's vehicle looked remarkably similar to that of the aliens. Thirdly, at exactly the same time, President Santerre is rescued from a similar fate in Paris. Fifteen minutes later it's the same story with President Franks in Washington and President Asimov in Moscow. A further fifteen minutes later a rescue occurs in Beijing, by which time we hear from NASA that the mothership has disappeared out of the skies. Those are the facts. So, what is our assessment of it all?'

General Wilson leaned forward fractionally and said, 'Well, as I've said already on this matter . . .'

The Prime Minister raised a hand. 'Sorry, Bob, that was a rhetorical question. My assessment is that there were three people involved in the rescue. One rescued me, one rescued President Santerre and one dealt with the mothership. Those three missions occurred at precisely the same time.'

'But there could be hundreds involved,' responded General Wilson.

'I beg to differ on that point, Bob.'

A grizzly General Bob Wilson crossed his arms and said, 'We don't know how many men it takes to neutralize a spaceship that size.'

'True, I accept that,' responded the Prime Minister. 'But if there were higher numbers of men involved, then it would be reasonable to expect three more of them would have been allocated to take out the enemy in Washington, Moscow and Beijing at the same time as the missions in Paris and here in London. Our rescuers left themselves exposed during the period it took to finish up here and get to the other cities. It simply isn't logical that there were more than three involved.'

'That's a matter of conjecture, sir,' Admiral Dickins chipped in. 'They may have had restricted resources, like only three vehicles to fly.'

'Again, that's true, John,' responded the Prime Minister curtly. 'But I'm staking my money on three men rather than just three vehicles.'

Admiral Dickins shrugged defensively.

Air Marshall Grantham piped up, 'You're saying they flew from London to Washington in fifteen minutes? Washington to Beijing in a similar time? Like hell they did.'

The Prime Minister gave the Air Marshall a mean look. 'Why not?'

The Air Marshall shrugged.

The Prime Minister sighed. 'It is my conclusion that there were three rescuers involved. Furthermore, I reckon they were lying in wait, ready to pounce on the enemy in their own good time. That scenario is evidenced by the radio conversation Colonel Travis had with one of the rescuers an hour before the strike. I also believe these men have been here for a long time. Certainly since nineteen seventy-one, when President Burford seems to have got to know about them.'

'When you say men,' said General Wilson, 'you really mean aliens, right?'

'Yes, Bob, I do. But let's refer to them as men, please. They rescued us. They don't deserve to be insulted by us referring to them in derogatory terms.'

'Actually,' General Wilson continued, 'what I was getting at is that I know you think the rescuers are alien, but that might not be correct.'

The Prime Minister rubbed his forehead. 'So, your answer is what exactly?'

General Wilson shrugged. 'Your rescuer had a Caucasian look to him. Travis says he spoke English fluently and had a grasp of our idioms. I'd say chances are he's human.'

'But we don't have the technology,' replied the Prime Minister.

'I'm not suggesting we do,' General Wilson countered. 'Maybe our rescuer managed to capture one of those alien starfighters.'

'In which case, wouldn't he be telling the world about it? Relishing in the glory of it?'

'Not necessarily, he could be biding his time. Maybe he's learning more about alien technology, waiting until he's got a strong loyal army behind him. Then he'll pounce, take over the world on his terms.'

'So, you're saying you agree with some of the dafter conspiracy theories?'

'Not at all. I'm just trying to keep an open mind.'

'So open, in fact, that we're getting nowhere in our progress?'

General Wilson stared daggers at the Prime Minister. The heated atmosphere pervaded for a few moments before Air Marshall Grantham intervened to avert another flare-up. 'Any ideas on President Burford's memo yet, sir?'

'No, Gordon, not yet,' said the Prime Minister. 'But I'm confident we will get to the bottom of it in due course.'

Jennifer had been sitting in stunned silence, desperately trying to absorb the information bouncing across the table. On hearing the familiar name, her ears pricked up. 'Excuse me,' she interjected. 'Did you just say something about a memo from President Burford?'

The Prime Minister caught Jennifer's eye and grinned. 'I did indeed, Jennifer. He left us a message buried in the depths of a Ministry of Defence computer telling us how to make radio contact with our rescuers.'

'Oh,' she responded, and lapsed back into silence.

The Prime Minister turned away from Jennifer and continued, 'Anyway, the point is, I want to know who these three rescuers are, where they live, when they came here, why they came here, how friendly they are, can we trust them. In effect, everything possible about them.'

General Wilson sneered. 'And just how do we go about that, sir? Put an ad in The Times?'

The Prime Minister turned to Jennifer, beamed and said, 'Your area of expertise, I believe.'

Three sets of defiant eyes glared at Jennifer as she squirmed in her seat. Her face flushed as she realised she had been caught off-guard, had nearly missed her cue. She cleared her throat and said, 'Everyone leaves a trace on their environment. No one can live without interacting with others in some way. These three men are no different. The longer they've been living here on planet Earth, the greater the traces. We've just got to look for those traces.'

'Like where exactly?' General Wilson demanded.

'Well, we start with their technology,' responded Jennifer. 'I imagine we should look hard at areas where, historically, strange phenomena have been reported.'

General Wilson guffawed. 'Are you suggesting we investigate the Bermuda Triangle?'

'Yes,' replied Jennifer with a serious look on her face. 'Well, places like that, certainly.'

'Young lady,' responded General Wilson harshly, 'you are certifiable.'

The Prime Minister slammed a fist on the table. 'I can assure you, Bob, that she is not. Dr Collins is a respected lecturer in the Anthropology Department at the University of Sussex. She is highly qualified in this area and her father is a personal friend of mine from my schooldays, so I won't tolerate any rudeness towards her.' He waited a few seconds before turning to Jennifer and saying, 'Sorry, Jennifer, please continue.'

Jennifer locked eyes with General Wilson, tried to imagine she was addressing a stroppy student in class. 'What our ancestors thought of as mysterious, magic or acts of a deity, are more likely to be explained away as everyday events misunderstood by them because of their lack of scientific knowledge. Air Marshall Grantham scoffed just now at the thought of being able to travel from Washington to Tokyo in fifteen minutes. I'm sure he'd have been happy if that journey had taken, say, eight hours but, because the fifteen-minute time-frame is outside the parameters of his experience with technology, he dismissed it. That is exactly the same attitude that our ancestors would have displayed. They would have put the phenomena of a flying machine down to witchcraft.'

General Wilson had a contemptuous look on his face. 'You seriously think you'll find aliens in the Bermuda Triangle?'

The Prime Minister pointed a threatening finger at the general.

'Sorry, Dr Collins, let me rephrase that,' General Wilson continued, 'Do you think these men live in the Bermuda Triangle?'

'Not necessarily there, General,' replied Jennifer cautiously. 'But somewhere like it, certainly. You'll find these men living in an area where odd phenomena have been recorded down the centuries.'

General Wilson rolled his eyes.

The Prime Minister looked at Jennifer encouragingly.

'General,' said Jennifer cautiously, 'Do you recall the incident involving a couple of American naval ships and a submarine that were held to ransom by Surithani back in nineteen sixty-four?'

General Wilson rubbed his chin. 'Vaguely. I think I've read about it somewhere in the distant past. What of it?'

'The incident started when an American submarine invaded Surithani's territorial waters. You may recall that the crew later said the submarine had been scooped out of the sea by a monster bird and placed into a lake some five miles inland, leaving them stranded?'

General Wilson tapped a pen against the table top. 'Stories of monsters are easily dismissed. Fear breeds mass hysteria amongst men, especially at sea.'

Jennifer, well into her stride, was not going to be put off. 'An American ship was sent to locate the submarine. It slipped into a bank of fog as it encroached upon Surithani's territorial waters. When the fog lifted, the ship had disappeared from view, leaving no trace on radar either. Another ship was sent in to find out what had happened to the first. The same thing happened to it. By this time, the Americans had gone into panic mode. The American navy made all sorts of idle threats via the press and, in response, the King of Surithani let it be known that he was putting the submarine and the two ships up for sale. There was, reputedly, an offer of five million dollars from the Russians.'

General Wilson shrugged. 'So, the King's got a big mouth, but he saw reason in the end, if I remember correctly. He knew he was up against stronger forces and came to his senses.'

Jennifer gasped and sat back, astonished. 'You just don't get it, do you?'

'What's there to get?'

'Surithani has no army, no navy and no air force. Never has. There is no indication the country has ever had any military weapons.'

'So? Proves my point doesn't it?'

Jennifer shook her head in despair. 'I don't believe I'm hearing this.'

The Prime Minister laid a calming hand on Jennifer's arm. 'You'll have to spell it out to them.'

Jennifer drew in a deep lungful of air. 'The Americans sent in their most powerful forces, yet what happened? They were neutralised. Surithani possesses a much stronger power, and just because the Americans couldn't see it, they refused to accept it could exist.'

'What exactly are you suggesting?' General Wilson snapped.

'I'm not suggesting anything, General, I'm telling you a fact.'

'Which is?'

'The American military could not win a fight against Surithani. No matter what the Americans threw at the apparent defenceless country, failure was a certainty from the outset. The Americans were overwhelmed by superior technology.'

'But you just said Surithani has no weapons.'

Jennifer clapped her hands slowly, three times. 'Exactly, General.'

'How could Surithani possibly be responsible for defeating the Americans then?'

'You've finally got there, General.'

General Wilson looked to his fellow chiefs. 'I'm lost. Help me out here, guys.'

Admiral Dickins held a finger up. 'I think, Bob, that our learned doctor is suggesting superior technology defeated the Americans. She's suggesting that Surithani has the ability to pluck a submarine from the sea, to make a ship disappear into thin air.'

'That's impossible, and you damn well know it.'

The Admiral shrugged. 'It happened back then, Bob, so it must be possible. If the scenario came from a Star Trek film, we would accept it without question. Think about the ship disappearances for a moment. You're experimenting with stealth technology yourself, projecting the rear view of a tank on to its front to make it appear invisible. Something like that happened perhaps, or maybe the ships were still there but frozen in time. If I remember this event correctly, I believe there was a significant disparity over the ships' clocks when they reappeared. Several days' disparity, that is.'

'That's science fiction nonsense,' muttered General Wilson.

The Admiral tweaked an earlobe. 'I think not, Bob. Don't forget the alien spaceship disappeared from our sight and from radar just a few weeks ago.'

'For God's sake, John, don't tell me you're falling for this rubbish?'

The Admiral frowned at his colleague. 'I think you should be more respectful to Dr Collins, Bob. May I remind you how that debacle ended in nineteen sixty-four? If my memory serves me correct, the President of the United States went to the King of Surithani on bended knees to beg for release of the submarine and the two ships along with several thousand personnel. I don't recall a ransom being paid, or the ships being sold, so it was a politician who sorted the mess out, not the military.'

'What's your point?'

'Do you know who the President of the United States was at the time?'

'Erm, that would have been . . . erm . . . damn, it was Burford, wasn't it?'

The Prime Minister intervened. 'Now do you see where Jennifer is heading?'

General Wilson let out a snort of laughter. 'Excuse me, Dr Collins, but are you saying that an alien, living in Surithani, was responsible for that crisis in nineteen sixty-four?'

Jennifer shook her head emphatically. 'Absolutely not, General. What I'm saying is the American military was responsible for the crisis, as you put it. Their ships strayed into a foreign country's territorial waters. No doubt they were testing defences, seeing how far they could push their luck. I think the Americans had the misfortune to pitch their might against vastly superior alien technology. And I believe that technology was controlled by one of our very own rescuers who was eventually persuaded by President Burford to back down from further confrontation.'

General Wilson's eyes widened. 'Then . . . who is it?'

Jennifer took a deep breath. 'I believe one of three men in question, one of our rescuers, to be the King of Surithani.'

General Wilson howled with laughter. 'How can you possibly make an accusation like that?'

Jennifer sat back and crossed her arms defensively. 'Well, I grew up in Surithani, my father has worked there for twenty years. I've seen the king occasionally, at parties put on by the handful of

Europeans who are permitted to live there, or when he attends festivals. He's a very tall, very powerful looking man, well capable of the physical demands the rescue would have required.'

General Wilson cupped his face in his hands and rubbed his eyes. 'Is this getting us anywhere?'

The Prime Minister leant forward and said, 'I am going to ask Jennifer to head up a team of historians, analysts, linguists, all sorts of specialist people, to explore mysterious phenomena arising over the last three thousand five hundred and fifty-one years.'

General Wilson lowered his hands and threw the Prime Minister a querulous look. 'Why that specific length of time?'

A smirk appeared on Jennifer's face. 'In Surithani, the calendar year now stands at three thousand five hundred and fifty-one. The country's timeline starts from the day the king came to power.'

'What?'

Jennifer smiled. She had them on the run now. 'We only know of the current monarch, General. There is no mention in the history books of a predecessor.'

General Wilson's mouth dropped open, as did Air Marshall Grantham's.

'That's insane!' Admiral Dickins commented.

'There has only ever been a King Taksin the Great,' Jennifer continued. 'No other name has ever surfaced. Not even King Taksin the first, second, third and so on. There's no mention anywhere in the history books of a coronation ceremony or of a royal funeral. All I can determine from diplomatic correspondence, personal diaries, letters from businessmen and the like, over the last five centuries of trading with the country is that the king always looks remarkably youthful for his age. What age he is, I have no idea. I can only extrapolate backwards to year zero, some three thousand five hundred and fifty-one years ago.'

'I was right,' muttered General Wilson, 'you really are barking mad.'

'He'd actually be older than that of course,' Jennifer continued. 'Considerably older since, presumably, it took him several centuries to get here from another solar system.'

General Wilson laughed. 'You're not serious about this are you?'

'Bob,' said the Prime Minister quietly, 'our three rescuers have been able to hide well, blend in without causing ripples, precisely because of our tendency to disbelieve things beyond our experience. We must open our eyes and look harder.'

'Well I simply don't believe it,' General Wilson bellowed. 'It's a load of claptrap.'

The Prime Minister shuffled uncomfortably in his chair. 'Do you have any other theory to explain where three aliens have been hiding themselves on this planet? Remember, Bob, the best place to hide a tree is in the middle of a forest.'

'You mean out in the open, amongst the rest of the population?' asked Admiral Dickins. 'I agree, best place to hide.'

'Well I don't agree,' General Wilson spat back. 'I'd want to see a lot of hard evidence before I started making accusations that someone was an alien. Especially a king, even if he rules a tin-pot, third world country like Surithani.'

The Prime Minister fixed the general with a glare and said, 'I have the utmost faith that Dr Collins will demonstrate King Taksin of Surithani possesses technology so powerful that it couldn't possibly have originated on this planet.'

'And then what?' asked General Wilson. 'Will you confront him?'

'Yes, that's exactly what I intend to do,' the Prime Minister countered. 'I will seek an audience with him, show him our findings. I want him to help us.'

General Wilson looked astonished. 'To help us? With what?'

'I want him to give us that spaceship, teach us how to fly it, teach us his technology. I want us to be able to defend the planet next time we're invaded. I didn't enjoy the experience of being held ransom by a couple of thugs and I do not want a repeat of that drama. But if there is to be a next time, I want us to be prepared. I want us to be in control. I want us to be able to defend Planet Earth with our own people. I do not want to be reliant on the goodwill of aliens for our defence, no matter how friendly they may be.'

General Wilson smiled for the first time during the meeting. 'That's the first sensible suggestion I've heard in ages, sir.'

'Thank you, Bob.'

'But I'm still not convinced about their identity.'

The Prime Minister's head sagged. He turned to Jennifer and pleaded, 'Will you tell them about your discovery please.'

Jennifer steeled herself. 'Of course. But if anyone laughs, I'm walking right out of here.'

'No one will laugh, Jennifer,' replied the Prime Minister, in a comforting manner. 'I promise you that. It would be the last thing they ever did in my presence.'

Jennifer acknowledged the seriousness in the Prime Minister's eyes. She made eye contact with each of the Chiefs of Staff then said, 'I assume you noted that the spacecraft had symbols on the side?'

'Of course we did.'

'Have you had the symbols translated yet?'

General Wilson frowned. 'We've got people working on it.'

'I can save their time.'

General Wilson sighed. 'Oh God, don't tell me you're able to communicate with aliens. We've had hundreds claiming that already.'

'I'm sure you have, General,' replied Jennifer. 'But I'm not claiming that. However, I sure as hell know their alphabet and numerical system.' She reached for her briefcase and removed a file containing a handful of loose leave pages and a DVD. 'My pet project for the last six years has been to build up a dictionary and a phrase book of the Surithani language. To my knowledge, it's never been done before, very few foreigners bother trying to learn Surithani since it is tonal.' She held out a couple of the loose-leaf sheets and said, 'This is the alphabet used in Surithani. There are forty-four consonants and thirty-seven vowels or vowel clusters. And this is their numbering system, these characters being the basic numbers one to ten.'

General Wilson took the sheets and glanced down the list of characters and frowned. 'So, according to this alphabet, what do the symbols translate as?'

Jennifer passed over another page. 'The characters on the mothership were FCN 13674 BEH. The two smaller craft that touched down in St James's Park were FCN 1469352 CAW and FCN 1457168 CAW.'

General Wilson studied the page a while before nodding. 'Fleet registration numbers,' he said.

'Or manufacturer's registration numbers perhaps,' Jennifer added. 'You'll notice the closeness of the numbers from the two vehicles visiting St James's Park.'

'Not unexpected, given the circumstances.'

'But you must see their significance?'

General Wilson shook his head. 'I'm sure it must mean

something.'

'Our rescuers must have come from the same world.'

General Wilson considered the comment. 'Why not from a nearby planet or another solar system? There could be interplanetary trade in ships, for all we know.'

'Point taken, General,' replied Jennifer. 'But we can assume they were neighbours, in relative terms, that is.'

'Granted. And the significance is?'

'Although they are neighbours, they obviously dislike each other. Our rescuers didn't bat an eyelid in killing the invaders in cold blood. Which side are the good guys, as opposed to bad guys, we don't know for sure. But what it does mean is that we have something in common.'

'And that's significant?'

'It is if you want to make a military alliance, General. Think of Churchill and Stalin, there's no way they would have tolerated each other without Hitler in between them.'

General Wilson gave a genuine smile. 'For an academic, Dr Collins, that's a remarkably perceptive analogy.'

'Right then, Jennifer,' said the Prime Minister joining in with other smiles around the table, 'it looks like you've got yourself a new job, heading up a special task force to track down and identify our three rescuers. Can you start tomorrow if I square it with your university? You'll be given an office here in Whitehall, a rent-free apartment close by and as many staff as you need.'

Jennifer was bowled over. This was her break. Her first proper job away from academia. She broke into a smile. 'I'd be delighted, sir.'

Chapter Seventeen

Mysteries

Jennifer Collins placed a glass of water to the side of a podium, laid a handful of notes down in front of her and looked out at the audience of fifteen academics who had been drafted in to her task force.

'Ladies and gentlemen, may I have your attention, please. For those who have only just arrived this morning and not yet met me, my name is Jennifer Collins. The reason I'm here is because a few days ago the Prime Minister charged me with the task of identifying three men who came to our rescue six weeks ago and eliminated the threat to this world posed by beings from a distant planet; three men who share similar technology as those who invaded us. The reason you are here is because you have specialist knowledge and considerable experience in social anthropology, and I am confident that it will be your expertise that will identify those three men. You have kindly accepted the Prime Minister's personal invitation to come here on a rather vaguely worded assignment, and I shall do my best to explain the briefing in more detail in the next few minutes.' She paused for a sip of water, during which time everyone in the room put a hand in the air. She indicated to a handsome young man with shaggy hair seated at the back, a familiar face she recognised from a seminar she'd attended a year or so ago. 'Yes, Duncan.'

'Pleased to see you again, Jennifer,' responded Dr Duncan Montgomery in a broad Scottish accent. 'Your introduction raises a dozen or more questions in my mind. Will you be able to answer them all, or are we operating on a need-to-know basis here?'

Jennifer was well prepared for the question; it was an issue she had wrestled with herself. 'Let me say this to all of you right here and now; I need to know. I need to know in order to present honest findings to the Prime Minister, because the world's survival may well depend upon it. That means I will not tolerate the withholding of information from me by any person or organisation in this country. By extension, that means I will not accept anyone withholding information from you either. We are a team and you have been chosen for your integrity as well as your skills. Nothing will be kept secret from you by me. I will share everything I have with you, and I expect a reciprocal arrangement from yourselves. Having said that, I'm sure I needn't remind you of the sanctions that will come into force if any information is leaked into the public domain. I understand you have all signed the Official Secrets Act on arriving here today. I would like to stress the seriousness of that undertaking.'

'Aye, point taken,' replied Dr Montgomery. 'So, to be candid, we're tracking down aliens, are we?'

'Indeed we are, but I would be grateful if you would refer to them simply as "men". The reasons for that will become clear in a minute. Now, if I may, I will answer all your questions in good time, but I would first like to give you some background information, as this may clear up some of your concerns.'

Jennifer was pleased to see the raised hands being lowered. 'The Prime Minister has asked me to compile a dossier of mysterious happenings that have arisen during man's recorded history. By this, I mean events and sightings that were documented at the time but could not be explained by reference to the known technology. You will all know of the theories being expounded in the media that our rescuers were already living here on this planet. I too believe that to be the case, so does the Prime Minister. So, our goal is to identify precisely who those rescuers are and where they live. It is my belief that the rescuers live among us. I also believe that it would be impossible for them to do so without interacting with their community, and without putting on the occasional display of technology beyond man's comprehension. This team has been put together to find such incidents and, from studying those incidents, to build up a picture of where we should be looking.' She paused to take another sip of water. Dr Montgomery had his hand up in the air again. 'Yes, Duncan?'

'You mean Chariots of the Gods stuff?'

Jennifer gave a nod. 'Indeed, yes, but we must be wary of latching on to subjects that may bring ridicule from the powers above. The Bermuda Triangle is certainly a subject I think best avoided as I believe it belongs in the same category as the Loch Ness Monster. And before you object to that, Duncan,' she added tongue in cheek, 'I offer my sincerest apologies to the Scottish Tourism Authority.'

'Damn! That's my starting point blown out of the water.'

Jennifer grinned. 'That's okay, Duncan, I'll give you another starter. I grew up in the small South East Asian Kingdom of Surithani. It's reclusive, ancient and backward by comparison to western European standards. Combustion engines are banned, as are most technological advancements. But I'd like to share with you some odd occurrences which should give you an indication of the type of research we shall be carrying out.' Jennifer picked up another sheaf of papers and took a step to the side of the podium. 'The reigning monarch is King Taksin the Great. I've had the honour of being in his presence a few times in the past. He's very tall, seven foot at least, a very powerful looking man, very handsome with classic South East Asian features and, judging by his looks alone, no one would place his age above forty. Yet there is no documentary evidence of any royal coronation or funeral ceremony ever having taken place in that country. I have testimonies from Europeans who have lived there for fifty years stating that it has always been the same man on the throne. Old records I found in the British Club archives over there also show those same sentiments have been expressed by many other Europeans down the centuries. Now, given that the country's timeline started from the day the king was crowned, and that Surithani's calendar year now stands at three thousand five hundred and fifty-one, something is out of kilter.'

Dr Simon Langdale, a middle-aged, wild haired man sitting at the back of the room raised a hand and interjected, 'Excuse me, Jennifer, but are you seriously saying that the King of Surithani is three thousand years old?'

Jennifer nodded. 'Yes indeed, Simon, but if I'm right, he'd be much older. Very much older, given that it would have taken him an awful long time to travel here.'

A greying woman, well into her sixties, in the front row asked, 'But you say he still manages to look young?'

Jennifer looked to see where the comment came from, and smiled as she saw another familiar face. 'Yes, indeed, Deidrie. He certainly does. His complexion is extraordinarily youthful.'

Professor Deidrie Saunders pulled a face and said, 'Well, I'd certainly like to know what moisturiser he uses.'

'So would I,' responded Jennifer. 'Unlike his majesty, I'm beginning to develop crow's feet and I'm not yet twenty-five.' The resultant laughter seemed to bring a more relaxed atmosphere to the room. She waited a moment for the noise to die down. 'Diaries from early European traders talk of a giant head over a hundred feet high appearing out of a fog bank, demanding that ships-of-war turn away from Surithani's territorial waters or face their doom. The sight of such a monstrous phenomenon must have been frightening and probably succeeded in its task. Today, however, we might be less frightened if we understood it was, say, not an actual monster but just an enlarged holographic projection of a man's head. I'd also like to mention that Surithani has never had an army or navy, there has never been any observable presence of weapons, yet the Dutch, French, English, Spanish, Portuguese, Chinese, Burmese, Japanese and Americans have all failed in their attempts at invasion over the last five centuries. And they've failed spectacularly badly, I have to stress, whether they've employed vast overland armies or fleets of warships, they've all been defeated by unseen forces. But I won't say any more about Surithani for now, as I have a large dossier already full of data and theories for which I shall ask you to professionally scrutinize in due course. But I hope I've given you a flavour of the sort of mysteries that I'm looking for.' She noted a hand in the air. 'Yes, Duncan?'

'How about the Dogon Tribe in Mali with their visitations of alien mermaids thousands of years ago?'

Jennifer replied in a dismissive tone, 'I'd put their claims in the same category the Loch Ness Monster, but worth a look at, I suppose.'

Professor Deidrie Saunders threw a despairing look towards her Scottish colleague sitting at the back of the room before asking, 'Any other sensible leads?'

Jennifer shook her head. 'Unfortunately not. Surithani is the only lead we have at the moment, and we only have that because I've been researching the country for six years for my own academic interests. But I believe we'll find other leads if we look at the history of the rest of the world.' Dr Montgomery's hand was in the air again, trying to get her attention. 'Yes, Duncan?'

'If you're looking for three men who are compatriots, would it not be likely that they all live in Surithani?'

Jennifer rubbed the back of her neck and took a moment to compose her answer. 'Yes, that's logical, and I've considered that point at length. But I don't think it's the case. I know of no one being close to the king, and certainly not of two people being on intimate terms with him. He heads the country alone as a benevolent dictator. His power is not shared. He has no close advisers. He cuts a somewhat solitary, lonesome figure. He comes over as melancholic, and a man not entirely at peace with himself, as though burdened by the weight of the world's troubles on his shoulders. He's not the sharing, caring type. I don't think he could tolerate anyone else's presence as a permanent fixture. It's just conjecture, I know, but with a character like that I believe his two compatriots would be compelled to live somewhere else.'

Professor Saunders responded, 'You make him sound as though he may be hiding something.'

'Yes, I do, don't I. I hadn't looked at it that way. You may have a valid point there.'

'Any other character traits to help build a profile?'

'Well, bear in mind it's quite likely that these three men are refugees from a faraway solar system, or perhaps even a different galaxy, and maybe they were the only ones that came here. It must have taken them hundreds of years to get here and that must have been an extraordinarily solitary experience. It would take a certain type to be able to endure that kind of journey.'

'But they were, I assume, refugees,' Professor Saunders interjected. 'And we all know that refugees will endure hell to get away from whatever is causing them grief.'

'Yes, Deidrie, I agree. But bear in mind, also, that we don't know the reason why they came here, and what, if anything they have fled from.'

Professor Saunders looked a little shocked. 'Are you saying you don't know whether they are the good guys or the bad guys?'

'Correct, Deidrie, and I know how important that could be to building an objective profile. All I can say is that I simply cannot believe Taksin to be one of the bad guys. After all, he's acted as a fair-minded and benevolent ruler for over three thousand years.'

'But,' continued Professor Saunders, 'assuming he has superior technology, he must have the ability to intervene in wars and prevent wholesale slaughter. He could have stopped Hitler, for example, but obviously didn't. I find nothing benevolent about that position.'

'I understand where you're coming from, Deidrie. But if he's going to intervene like that, where should he stop? Would you have him halting the armies of the Romans, of Genghis Khan, of the British Empire? Ultimately, he would have had to conquer, and rule by domination, the whole world in order to subdue man's aggression. That is not his character, I believe he has followed a non-interventionist policy; he has let us develop our own path.'

'Except for Surithani,' Professor Saunders objected. 'That hasn't developed much at all, from what you say.'

'Yes, indeed. Except for Surithani. He controls that with a very firm hand.'

'And why would he make an exception of that, if it's otherwise out of character, as you would put it?'

Jennifer considered the matter for a moment. 'That's a very interesting point, Deidrie. Maybe it's just because he wants to control his own backyard.'

'Or has something to hide?'

Jennifer nodded. 'Yes. I can't fault your logic, Deidrie, but let's move on for now. I believe there is one, or maybe two, other areas in the world that should capture our attention. Unfortunately, I have no idea where those areas are, so that's something we need to work out between ourselves in the next few hours, how best to tackle that issue. Finally, may I just point out the urgency of this task. The Prime Minister is looking for solid results inside of three months. One thing that wasn't mentioned in your introductory letters is that, in addition to your engagement fee, there will be a ten-thousand-pound bonus for each and every one of you if we succeed within that three-month schedule. Now then, that's quite enough from me. Let's get some coffee and then I'll take your questions.'

Chapter Eighteen

An old soldier's tale

On a warm but overcast May morning, eight weeks into her research program, Jennifer felt a buzz of anticipation as she turned her silver blue Honda Civic car into the steeply rising Bay Vue Road in Newhaven. Halfway up the hill she pulled over and parked amongst a row of cars. She picked up her bag and a file from the passenger seat, climbed out of the car, locked it and walked back to the dusty, unmade track that served as Hillcrest Road, hoping that a parking ticket was not warranted. Looking professionally smart in a new grey trouser suit, she made her way eighty yards along the track to a bungalow, rang the bell, stood back and swept a loose strand of hair away from her face.

'Good morning,' she said in her politest tone as the door opened to reveal a plump, grey-haired woman who looked to be in her early sixties. 'I'm Dr Jennifer Collins. I've come to see Mr Alfred Fry. I trust I've got the right address?'

'Oh, yes, come in, luv. He's in the living room, ready and waiting. He's been looking forward to meeting you so much. He's put his best gear on and even managed a shave. I'm Maureen, by the way. Alf's daughter. Maureen Gent.'

'Thank you, Mrs Gent,' replied Jennifer, as she shook hands, 'but it really wasn't necessary to go to any trouble.'

Maureen chuckled. 'Oh, don't worry about that, luv, you're the most exciting thing that's happened to him since a kiss-o-gram girl arrived at his ninetieth birthday party a few years ago. He still talks about that with a twinkle in his eye.'

'Right,' replied Jennifer, slightly bemused. 'I hope he isn't expecting quite such a high level of excitement today.'

'So do I, luv,' said Maureen with sincerity. 'It wouldn't be good for his heart. His blood pressure is getting far too high, so the doctor says.' She opened a door leading off the hallway and said, 'He's in here.'

Jennifer put on her sweetest smile as she stepped into a living room that looked as though it had stayed exactly the same since the nineteen sixties. It may have been clean and tidy, but the brown carpet, yellow floral wallpaper and green covered armchairs were from an era she had no empathy with. The only redeeming feature was a wonderful panoramic view out the window across a bay to a glimmer of a chalk cliff in the distance.

'Dad? Your visitor is here.'

'Good morning,' said Jennifer to an old, bald headed, liver-spotted gentleman rising from an armchair. 'Please don't get up on my account.'

'That's alright, lass,' said Alfred Fry as he offered his hand. 'The doctor says I must keep moving.'

'Tea, luv?' asked Maureen.

Jennifer turned her head and responded, 'Yes, please. Milk, no sugar.'

'I'll bring it in, in a sec. Then I'll leave you to it. I'll be in the kitchen making up Dad's meals for the week.' She turned to her father and said, 'I'll keep Tess in the kitchen with me, Dad, we don't want Dr Collins' getting dog hair on her nice suit, do we?'

'Thank you,' Jennifer called out to Mrs Gent as she departed the room. She sat down in an armchair opposite the nonagenarian and said, 'Thank you for replying to my advert in the newspaper.'

'You're welcome.'

'To be honest, we haven't had many replies. You're fairly unique, in terms of attracting responses, that is.'

'Aye, I'm not surprised, lass. It was a slightly odd advertisement that was.' He picked up a newspaper lying on an adjacent coffee table and flipped through a few pages. 'Here we go, "The BBC seek your reminiscences of royal palaces in South East Asia, especially Laos, Cambodia, Thailand, Surithani and Myanmar, for a forthcoming documentary." A half page advertisement to boot, you must have been keen to get it noticed. And it must have cost you an arm and a leg, I noticed it appeared in at least six other national papers last week.' He placed the newspaper back down on the table and gave Jennifer a meaningful glare.

Jennifer shrugged. 'We had an important message to convey, Mr Fry. The cost was somewhat inconsequential. I'm just glad you spotted it.'

Alfred Fry rubbed his chin for a while. 'To tell you the truth, it didn't surprise me. I've been expecting something of that nature to appear for a while now. I've been keeping an eye out, reading the papers in the library every day, listening to news bulletins on the radio, watching endless current affairs programs on television.'

Jennifer felt her heart racing. 'I see. You must have an important memory of your time out there, then?'

Alfred Fry frowned. 'Maybe.'

Rather cagily, Jennifer ventured, 'You said on the telephone yesterday that you spent some time in Surithani during the war?'

'I did.'

'And you have memories of the inside of the royal palace in Nakhon Thong?'

'No, I don't.'

Jennifer was taken aback. 'But your response to the advert inferred you did.'

'Your inference, young lady, not mine.'

'I'm sorry, I thought . . .'

'Underneath.'

Jennifer blinked hard. 'I beg your pardon.'

'My memory is of being underneath the palace.'

Jennifer gasped. 'Underneath?'

The old man grinned. 'I thought that might grab your attention.'

Jennifer scrabbled in her bag and pulled out a tape recorder. 'Do you mind if I record this interview.'

The old man crossed his arms. 'That depends, young lady.'

Jennifer gave the old man a quizzical look. 'On what, may I ask?'

The old man fixed his eyes on Jennifer. 'Do you really work for the BBC?'

Jennifer shook her head. 'Personally, no. Although I can get someone high up in the BBC to verify my credentials, if that concerns you.'

'Are you a journalist?'

'No, Mr Fry, I am not.'

'A novelist? Are you writing a book?'

'As I explained on the telephone to you yesterday, this interview is being held in the strictest confidence.'

'Yes, I recall you saying as much. But your advertisement mentions a documentary. This interview can't be confidential if you're intending to broadcast a documentary on television, can it?'

'Erm . . .'

'Are you saying the advertisement was a cover story?'

'Um . . .'

The old man sat back in his chair and fell quiet. By the expression on his face, he appeared to be enjoying Jennifer's discomfort.

On hearing a door opening behind her, Jennifer turned around to see Mrs Gent enter carrying a tray on which sat a cup and mug of tea and a plate with four biscuits.

'There you go, luv. Now don't let Dad eat all those biscuits by himself. Doctor's orders.'

'Thank you,' replied Jennifer and waited for the woman to leave the room before turning her attention back to the old man. 'You said, in your response to the advert, that you resided in the foreign prisoner camp for six months or so?'

'I did, yes.'

'As a guest, you said?'

'Correct.'

'That must have been unusual. You had the freedom to wander around?'

'We were restricted to the foreign enclave. We were allowed in to the British Club and could visit Dongtan Beach whenever we wanted. We had to stay at the camp because there was no other accommodation. No hotel, for instance.'

Jennifer threw the old man a smile. 'I know. I grew up there myself. My father got a position as a buying agent when I was three years old. I spent my childhood there. It's a beautiful country, isn't it?'

'It is indeed.'

Jennifer relaxed back in the armchair and said, 'My favourite view from my parents' house is watching the evening sun glow on the palace. Those soft, end-of-day rays produce the most heart-warming array of colours as they catch the gold on the palace roof, don't you think?'

'Young lady,' replied Alfred Fry tersely. 'I may be ninety-seven years old at the end of this month, but I am not stupid. Nor has my memory gone. If you have lived in Nakhon Thong, as you claim, then you will know that the side of the mountain on which the palace sits faces south-east. The palace roof sparkles with the morning sun, not the evening sun. Not that there's what you'd call an evening sun anyway, as it sets promptly at six in the afternoon, as everywhere else in the tropics. You seem to be testing my authenticity and I don't take kindly to that. I think it's about time you revealed who you really are.'

Jennifer took a deep breath and replied, 'I am here on classified government affairs.'

The old man leaned forward and said quietly, 'Listen here young lady, he . . . he saved my life. He is the reason I am here today, alive and able to enjoy the company of my daughter, my two grandchildren and my three great-grandchildren. I am not going to betray him. I am not going to sell him out, to see him exposed and hounded by the media. He deserves his freedom and he will have my loyalty to the end of my days.'

Jennifer's jaw dropped. She quickly rummaged in her bag, brought out a tablet computer, logged into her Skype account and pressed a number. 'Barbara? I need to speak to Tony. Urgently.'

'Right now?' came the response.

'Yes, right now please.'

'He's in a meeting with the Chiefs of Staff, I'm afraid. He asked not to be disturbed unless all hell broke loose.'

'That's what I'm hoping to avoid.'

'Do you want me to interrupt him?'

'Please, Barbara. Sorry, but I need him to vouch for me right now.'

Jennifer waited patiently for a moment before she saw a familiar figure come into view on the screen. 'Sir, sorry to bother you, I'm with Mr Alfred Fry, formerly a private in the British Army during the Second World War. He spent part of the war in Surithani and I need to hear his story. Could you have a word with him please, verify my credentials?' She crossed the room and knelt beside the old man, put the tablet in his hands and helped him adjust the screen until he could see the Prime Minister's face.

'Good grief,' the old man spluttered.

'Good morning to you, Mr Fry. I assume you know who I am?'

'Aye, laddie. I do.'

'Dr Collins is working on an assignment for me. It's classified, I'm afraid, so I can't go into detail, but it is absolutely vital for you to be completely candid with her. She needs you to talk about your time in Surithani. I can vouch for her integrity. Her father, who lives in Surithani, is a personal friend of mine, and I can assure you she has the best interest of both this country and Surithani at heart.'

'Yes, sir. I understand.'

'One moment please, Mr Fry,' the Prime Minister continued. 'I have someone else here who would like a word.'

The face of the Prime Minister disappeared and another appeared.

Alfred Fry spluttered. 'Good god!'

General Bob Wilson laughed. 'Not quite, soldier,' he said. 'I take it you know who I am?'

'I do indeed, sir. I've seen you being interviewed on the television quite a lot recently.'

'Then, as the Head of the British Armed Forces, can I ask you to please talk candidly to Dr Collins. Whatever you did or saw in Surithani, we need to know about it.'

'Yes, sir.'

Jennifer put the tablet back in her bag.

Alfred Fry puffed out his cheeks and blew hard. 'Well, lass, you certainly have some interesting friends in your address book.'

Jennifer took a sip of tea and turned the tape recorder on. 'I understand from your military records that you were in Singapore in nineteen forty-one?'

'Aye, that's right. I arrived there in March nineteen forty-one as a fresh-faced eighteen-year-old, but after a month I was sent to the air base at Kota Bhara.'

Jennifer frowned. 'Sorry, where's that exactly?'

'Northern Malaya. On the eastern side of the peninsular. The RAF had a base there, we were sent to boost its defence. It was one of the first places to be hit by the Japanese, on the eighth of December later that year.'

'You escaped the Japanese?' Jennifer interjected. 'I thought they took no prisoners? Not until the surrender of Singapore, anyway.'

'Aye, that was their creed; no prisoners. They were cruel. Very cruel indeed. But I wasn't captured. As soon as the first shots were fired, me and two mates were dispatched to protect a group of English ladies and their children taking shelter at a nearby school. One of the ladies, a teacher, insisted that the only safe option was to head north into Surithani. She told us she'd lived in Nakhon Thong a few years beforehand, and that we would find sanctuary there. The ladies agreed to go; they were terrified at the thought of being taken prison by the Japanese. We weren't sure though; our orders didn't say anything about leaving the school let alone leaving the country. Still, we'd been told to protect the ladies and, since we were little more than kids ourselves, we didn't feel we could disobey an adult. Especially not the woman who was determined to leave for Surithani, she wouldn't take no as an answer from anyone. So we decided to escort them away to safety.'

'You fled to Surithani?'

'Aye, but it wasn't a simple exercise. There were nine women and seventeen children to look after and we had no choice but to walk. Through the fields and jungle that is. We kept off the roads, hid by day and walked by night. It was hellishly hot. Some of the younger children had to be carried. Everyone was hungry, desperate for water. Foolishly, we'd fled without provisions, save for a few water bottles. After the eleventh day, we got spotted by a lone patrol of three Japanese soldiers, on bicycles of all things. There was a shoot-out, we managed to kill them, but not before they had lobbed a grenade in my direction. I was knocked unconscious and woke an hour later to find one of my mates carrying me over his shoulders. I screamed then, as loud as I've ever done in my life; I was in absolute bloody agony. I'd lost the lower part of my left leg, from just below the knee. My mates had used my belt as a tourniquet, but the stub of my leg was banging against my mate as he walked and, sweet Jesus, I can still remember that pain as we speak.'

Jennifer took a quick glance at the old man's left leg. The prosthetic must be a good one, she thought. It was certainly a good shape and filled his trousers well, and his socks and shoes. Odd, she thought, it was something she hadn't noticed when he'd risen to greet her.

'My injury slowed us down to a crawling pace,' Alfred Fry continued. 'I was reduced to limping my way along on two sticks fashioned from tree branches. We barely covered five miles each day for the next week or so, and it wasn't long before I reached the end of my tether. I simply could not go on an inch further. My body had given up. I just lay down on the ground, hungry, dehydrated, in pain and knowing I was at death's door. But I didn't care; death would have been a relief.'

Jennifer waited patiently while the old man wiped his eyes with his hands and composed himself.

'Maud Comyns. That was her name. The teacher who had lived in Nakhon Thong before the war. She came back to me at that moment and told us that we were within a mile of the border. It might as well have been a hundred miles for all I cared. I simply had no energy left to go on any more. I took comfort, though, that we had succeeded, that the women and children would be safe in a matter of minutes. She asked for a gun. It seemed an odd request, but she insisted she took one of our guns. She said it was needed to announce our arrival, to let him know we were there. I hadn't a clue what she was talking about, but she was such a forceful woman we didn't argue.'

Jennifer placed a hand over her gaping mouth as she realised the significance of the woman's intention.

'Aye, lass. I can see by the look in your eye you understand, don't you?'

Jennifer nodded. 'I believe there's a force-field around the country that can detect the presence of weapons. If Maud Comyns could identify the border, all she would have to do was to fire the gun at it from a safe distance and all hell would be let loose. He would know there was a potential invasion underway and would investigate immediately. Maud must have known about the forcefield, though god knows how.'

'Well, I don't know what a forcefield is, lass, but something certainly brought him to us quickly.'

'So, you managed to stagger the border after all?'

'No, I didn't. As I said, I was finished. Completely finished, I just wanted to die. But my mates wouldn't leave me. I protested, told them to go on without me, but they weren't having any of that talk. They propped me up against the base of a tree, put a rifle in my hands and said they would stay with me to the end. No matter what, they said.'

Jennifer rummaged in her bag for a packet of tissues, opened them and passed them to the old man whose face was streaming with tears.

'We were there for maybe an hour before we became aware that we weren't alone. Back along the way we'd come, there was movement amongst the dense undergrowth. We gripped our rifles, ready for an onslaught. But then this vision appeared. This thing, a flying vehicle, I can only describe it as looking like a sports car with a glass canopy, without the wheels, flying about six feet above the ground. It came to a halt right next to us, sank nearer to ground level, hovering silently, and this giant of a man stepped off it. He stood in front of us, put his hand out in front and this bubble-thing projected outwards. Like a soap bubble, only bigger, much, much bigger. At that moment, I thought we were done for, as dozens of Japanese soldiers broke cover and fired at us. But he just stood there, calmly, as hundreds of rounds of ammunition came our way. But none of the bullets penetrated the bubble. I thought I was hallucinating. I thought he must be an angel.'

Jennifer dabbed at the corner of her own eyes with a tissue.

'Ignoring the gunfire, he told my mates to pick me up off the ground and place me on a seat in his flying-car, then told them to hop on too and made them ditch their rifles. He jumped on, turned the flying-car around and sped away in the direction the others had gone. A minute later we caught up with them, sitting next to what looked like a really strange bulbous aeroplane with no wings. All the ladies and children were there, sitting in a group on the ground, crying and consoling each other whilst being tended to by a couple of servant boys he'd brought with him, handing out water in drinking vessels. Maud rushed over to us with a flask of water. Never has plain water tasted so good, I can tell you. She thanked him profusely for saving the three of us, but I got the impression he wasn't best pleased, he sounded a bit resentful about it, as though he'd had to put himself out.'

Jennifer sniggered as the old man paused to drink his tea. 'Yes, I can imagine. He doesn't like to interfere, and I don't think he likes to show his caring side.'

'Aye, that became quite obvious a little later. He bundled us into the aeroplane-thing, stowed away his flying-car, and flew like the clappers to Nakhon Thong. We were there in a matter of minutes, it was terrifying to look out the windows and see the land passing at such a dizzying speed, but not half as bad as the terror of what we'd left behind. We touched down close to the foreign prisoner camp and stepped out from the aeroplane-thing to be greeted by a handful of locals, bearing food as well as more water. We sat gorging ourselves on sticky rice, dried meat and fruit, while Maud walked around asking about wounds or illness. When she came to me, she squatted down, gave my bloodied stump a brief inspection, sniffed it and recoiled sharply.'

Jennifer asked, 'Did you have gangrene setting in?'

'I believe so. Not that it would have meant much to me at that age. Remember, half an hour before then, I'd been preparing myself to die. As far as I was concerned, the respite was only temporary. I was in my prime. I wasn't sure that I wanted to live without the ability to walk. But then the impossible happened again. Maud talked to him, begged him to help me, pleaded with him not to leave me crippled. She had such fire in her, that woman, forceful with anyone, even a king. He was livid. I recall he said something quite sharp about her demands. She simply crossed her arms, glared at him and said something back equally sharp about how easy it would be for him to heal my wounds. I thought they were talking about cleaning and sealing my stump. I was about to say "don't bother" when he relented with a few choice words. At that point, Maud smiled graciously and walked off to attend to a sick child.'

The old man fell silent. Jennifer waited patiently but, noticing a faraway look in his eyes, asked, 'Are you alright, Mr Fry? Do you want a break?'

Alfred Fry snuffled and wiped a finger across the bottom of his nose. 'No, I'm okay, thanks. It's just memories haunting me.' He paused a moment then said, 'Where was I?'

'You were saying Maud Comyns convinced him to attend to your leg.'

'Oh, yes. Well, he asked my mates to carry me back on to the aeroplane-thing. Seconds later, we were back up in the air and flying down the middle of the valley. We could see the river below, the palace off to the right, part-way up the mountainside, and then came the gulf. That's where we slowed down, turned around and flew right into the mountain. And I mean right into it. One second it was broad daylight, next second we were in pitch-black darkness on the inside of it. And then an artificial light came on and we pressed our faces against the windows to get a better look at something that was extraordinarily large. We appeared to be in an enormous cavern, to one side of which sat this monstrous thing. God knows what it was. It looked metallic; a cold, dark, unnatural creature. But it was so big we couldn't see all of it as one thing. There were portholes in its side, I remember that, or certainly what looked like portholes, so I guess it was a ship of sorts, but if it was then it was the biggest ship that's ever been built. After a few minutes we rose higher and higher and entered the ship through an open gate.' He paused and rubbed his temples.

Jennifer took the opportunity of posing a question, 'What length do you think this ship was?'

Alfred Fry scratched the back of his neck. 'At least a mile, I should think, probably much more. Two miles, more like. I reckon we must have travelled so far inside the mountain that we were back in line with the palace. Does that make sense to you?'

Jennifer let out a contented sigh. The old legend of the god asleep his winged chariot beneath the tiger sprang to mind. His arrival on Earth. His ship. And the cavern; he must have blasted out the rock, used the spoil to create the breakwater, the harbour and its docks. A huge engineering project. It would all have been witnessed. And the tale would have been passed down from one generation to the next, gradually falling into legend. A legend that was over three thousand years old. For an anthropologist, the story fitted perfectly. 'Yes, it does. Thank you, Mr Fry. Please continue.'

'Well, we came to a halt and he asked my mates to pick me up and follow him into the bowels of the ship. We walked through well-lit corridors, down a couple of floors in a lift, went past things the like of which I had never seen before nor since. It was certainly a well-equipped and luxurious ship, perhaps more akin to a modern cruise liner. And then he touched a panel on a corridor wall and a door opened to a room which had an unmistakable medical look to it, like a hospital operating theatre. He told me to strip completely and wash in a shower cubicle which air-dried me once finished, then he got my mates to lift me up and place me into what I'd call a tight-fitting glass coffin. He closed the lid and the sound of a jet of gas was the last thing I remember.'

Jennifer asked, 'An anaesthetic gas?'

'Presumably so. My mates told me afterwards that he spent a few minutes pushing buttons on a nearby machine and poured a luminous blue liquid into the glass coffin, then left them alone with me for an hour, telling them not to touch anything in case I grew a tail and came out furry. They weren't sure what he meant at the time, but he certainly scared the living daylights out of them. All I remember is waking to find the coffin-lid open and there he was, standing over me, coaxing me to consciousness. I was a bit groggy but was able to sit up, swing my legs over the side and he handed me fresh clean clothes as I climbed out. It was as I was putting on the shoes that I froze in utter bewilderment. My left leg was there again.'

Jennifer gasped. 'I beg your pardon?'

Alfred Fry held Jennifer's stare for a few seconds before saying, 'My left leg. It had regrown.'

Jennifer felt stunned. 'What? Are you sure?'

Alfred Fry snorted. 'Of course I'm sure, lass. Still got it, haven't I?'

Jennifer watched in fascination as Alfred Fry lifted the bottom of his trousers to reveal pink flesh. 'But that's . . .?'

'Impossible? Yes, one would think so. But it happened. In which case, I guess it's not so impossible.'

'Hang on,' said Jennifer. 'You were probably delirious after the incident with the grenade. Maybe the injury wasn't as bad as you thought? Perhaps he'd been able to patch you up?'

'Aye lass, that's what went through my mind at first. But not my mates, there was fear in their eyes. Absolute fear. It was several hours before they talked to me again. They were far more traumatized by the experience than I was. They said they'd watched it grow back, inch by inch.'

Jennifer crossed her arms and leant back in her armchair. 'Forgive me for being sceptical about this, but . . .'

'That's to be expected, lass, if you've never come across it before.'

Jennifer frowned, 'I'm sorry,' she said, 'is that supposed to mean something?'

'Well, to return to my story, we left the operating room in bewildered silence and he flew us out of the cavern in the smaller flying-car and back to the foreign prisoner camp. He dumped us without a word and flew off quickly, presumably fearing Maud may harass him again. When we did come across her, she inspected my leg, nodded her approval and commented upon the neatness of the heal line. She gave me the impression I wasn't her first patient to have gone through such a procedure.'

'Did she say so?'

'No, not as such. But it would explain why she had bullied him about helping me, saying she didn't want to leave me crippled.'

Jennifer rose from her armchair and crossed the room to the window. There was so much of the old man's story she wanted to believe; the wingless aeroplanes, the cavern, the enormous ship, the advanced medical knowledge. So much dovetailed with her own thoughts and hopes, but how could she possibly accept them as the truth? 'You have a lovely view from here, Mr Fry.'

'Aye, lass, I do, but it was even better before they built those blooming high-rise flats down below. I could see the river and the harbour before then. I used to love watching the ferries come in and out, that's why I bought the house. Those flats have ruined the whole nature of the harbour.'

Jennifer gazed out at the small wedge-shaped piece of cliff in the distance. 'Is that the start of the Severn Sisters over there?'

'The cliffs? No, lass. That's Seaford Head. You need to go passed Seaford to Cuckmere Haven for the Severn Sisters to start.'

Jennifer nodded, her mind imagining a life in Surithani seventy-five years ago. 'Did you ever report what happened to you? To your commanding officer, I mean?'

Alfred Fry guffawed. 'Are you joking? The reaction then would be about the same as it would be today. I'd have been dismissed as a loony or an attention seeker.'

'What about the rescue of Maud Comyns and her entourage? Did you report that?'

'No.'

The denial came as a surprise to Jennifer. 'Really? Why not? You and your two mates sounded pretty heroic, rescuing women and children from the clutches of the Japanese soldiers, protecting them, helping them through the jungle to safety, your mates refusing to abandon you. You said you were only a teenager at the time, that's pretty brave stuff for kids that age especially without an officer present.' She turned from the window to see the old man was in tears again. She went back to the armchair to find the tissues.

Alfred Fry took a tissue and wiped away his tears. 'We thought it best to say nothing. We didn't want to make a fuss. We thought if we reported on our mission, then someone in Records might question Maud and the others, you know, seeking independent verification of our stories. We didn't want anyone saying anything about my leg.'

'You just blanked it from your mind?'

'Aye. Or rather, no. We kept schtum, of course. But those weeks in the jungle, they weren't good. I still get nightmares. Some things you just can't blank, no matter how much you try. Fortunately, the rest of the war wasn't so bad for me and my mates; we managed to get posted well behind the front line as we went into Europe, mainly transporting provisions. Mind you, I always reckoned that was because we weren't fully trusted. We were a rarity, returning from the Far East after the Japs had taken over. I was convinced at the time that some people thought we'd been turned, that we must be spies for the Japs.'

'Just a second,' Jennifer interjected. 'You came back to England in the middle of the war? How on earth did you manage that?'

'That was Maud's work.'

'Maud Comyns again? Who was this woman?'

Alfred Fry chuckled. 'She was some woman, that one. We'd been there for the best part of six months. Bored stiff, we were, and resigned to staying put for the duration. The women were quite happy with their lot though. They knew they'd been lucky to escape, knew there was no chance of being reunited with their husbands until it was all over. The best they could do was to get word out that they and their kids were safe, and simply wait the war out. But for the three of us, safety wasn't the issue. We were restless, bored of the company of old women and children, and itching to fight for our country. Lazing about the camp, growing vegetables, tending chickens and milking cows at the nearby farm, catching fish in the river or relaxing down on the beach was not our idea of contributing to the war effort; the women and kids could do that well enough without our help. Maud could see that, so she asked him to return us.'

Jennifer blinked hard. 'I beg your pardon?'

'Maud went to see him at the palace. She did so quite regularly, it was the only way to get messages in and out the country. Again, quite how she knew he could do it was lost on me, but she would visit the palace occasionally with communication requests, letters home, that sort of thing.'

Jennifer was caught off guard, she hadn't seen that one coming. 'Letters home? To England in the middle of the war? How?'

'That, as I say, I don't know, although letters coming back to us were always addressed to us via the Surithani consulate in England. And, yes, before you ask, delivery was prompt, far too prompt for the letters to have gone by sea. We'd often get letters that had been franked just a couple of days beforehand.'

'So, the army was aware of where you were?'

'Aye, yes, they were, and they were probably quite happy for us to stay in Surithani, since there was no way for them to collect us.'

'He took you back?'

'Aye, he did. In one of those blasted aeroplane things of his. After six months in the camp, we said our farewells and were whisked off to Blighty one day just before lunch. Twenty-five minutes it took. Six thousand miles in twenty-five hair-raising minutes. I think he was upset, angry perhaps at Maud for twisting his arm again, for he flew like a madman that day. Straight up, vertical, until everything outside turned pitch dark, flipped us over, flew upside down for a few minutes before shooting back down to England. I suppose it was fortunate that our stomachs were empty that morning, what with the excitement and anxiety of leaving. Strangely, the last few minutes were quite tranquil and slow as he came to a halt in the gardens of a large country mansion. We couldn't get out that aeroplane-thing fast enough, and collapsed on the ground with shaking legs. He didn't even say goodbye as he took off in the dawn light. Next thing we knew, a very tall young man was helping us to our feet and requesting us to jump on to a horse driven wagon.'

'Do you remember where these gardens were, where the house was?'

The old man shook his head slowly. 'No, sorry, I don't. All I remember is being driven down a long tree lined track away from the mansion, at the end of which was a huge wooden gate set between turrets in a stone wall, like you might find in an old castle.'

'You mean a portcullis gate?'

'Yes, I think I do. I remember the young man knocked on the door to one of the turrets and this grumpy old bloke came out dressed in his nightgown. When the wooden gate opened there was, to our surprise, an army jeep waiting for us to the side of a narrow country lane.'

'You were expected?'

'I think he must have had it cleared in advance with Churchill.'

'Churchill? Winston Churchill, you mean? Are you serious?'

'Aye, I am. We were taken to see the great man himself straight away in another mansion. About six or seven o'clock in the morning this was. He was still in bed in his pyjamas, sitting up, mind you, reading papers.'

'And he knew about you, where you'd come from?'

'Indeed, he did. He asked about living conditions in the camp, asked how the women's spirits were, asked if there were any other foreigners there, in the enclave, that sort of thing. And, of course, he asked about our journey.'

'You told him?'

'Well, no, not really, we didn't think he'd believe us. We just mumbled, said it was a bit of an unusual flight, a bit disorientating, something like that.'

'And he accepted that?'

'He stared at us in silence for a few seconds then said something like "Disorientated, yes, that and travel sickness will probably mean you will never be able to render a full account of your flight here, is that not so?" We hastily agreed, and were summarily dismissed.'

'A cover up? Churchill knew, and didn't want you telling anyone else?'

'I believe so, yes.'

'Wow!' Jennifer rubbed her chin thoughtfully. 'I hadn't expected that.'

'And that's about it, I suppose,' said Alfred Fry. 'The end, as it were. Life got back to normal after that. I don't think I can add any more.'

'Just one point, if I may. Do you know where the mansion was, the one with Churchill that is?'

'No, sorry. But it wasn't far from the house with the portcullis. About twenty minutes or so by jeep, I reckon. All I remember of it was that it was a big red brick house with good views over a wide valley stretching to the horizon.'

Jennifer rose and crossed the room to the window again. After a few moments looking out across the bay, she turned and said, 'I'm sorry, Mr Fry, your story is wonderful, but I still have difficulty believing that part about your leg.'

Alfred Fry leaned over and picked up an old photograph album lying on the coffee table. 'Come over and look at this, lass.' He turned the pages quickly until he came to his days in the army. 'This is me, in Singapore.'

Jennifer came alongside the old man's armchair, leant over to see closer and smiled. 'You were a handsome lad.'

'I was, and a daft one at that age. Just a second, let me find the right picture for you. I hid it under one of these others somewhere. Ah, yes, this one,' he said as he eased a large picture out of its faded white sticky corners, revealing a smaller photo behind. 'That's it,' he said. 'My two mates and me on a beach just after we arrived in Singapore. Take a look at that.'

Jennifer looked at the picture of three lads in army shorts sitting on a sandy beach. 'Well, your left leg is displaying a very revealing image of a mermaid, that's for sure. I didn't know mermaids possessed such big, erm, features.'

'Aye, as I said, I was daft at that age. I got that tattoo during my first week out there. I got drunk on my first night in town and woke up the next morning with her on my leg. I was mortified at the time. I had no recollection of having it done or how much it cost. And it stung like crazy for two weeks. Still, that's what eighteen-year-old kids do away from home, isn't it? Now, if you'll excuse me, I will roll my trouser leg up.'

As Jennifer watched more and more flesh being revealed her mouth dropped lower and lower. The only part of the tattoo she could see consisted of a woman's head just above the knee cap, a jagged neckline but nothing below the knee, not even the merest remnant of an ink stain. 'But she's gone!'

'She has indeed. She went with the old leg.'

At that moment, the door opened and Maureen walked in. 'Oh, for goodness sake, Dad. You aren't boring Dr Collins with that old yarn, are you?'

Jennifer noticed the old man discretely close the photograph album. She responded, 'Oh yes? What old yarn would that be?'

'Well,' Maureen continued, 'the one about why he never got the tattoo of the woman on his leg finished, of course. Mind you, he tells everyone a different story.'

'Really?'

'Yes, he does. His favourite tale is that a bomb dropped on the tattoo studio, putting an end to the tattooist. I'm not sure he ever saw any action like that. Personally, I think he flunked it, couldn't cope with the pain and ran off before the tattooist could finish.'

Jennifer gave the old man a smile. 'So, Mr Fry, you never got the tattoo finished?'

'Of course not,' replied the old man resolutely. 'Half way through, I realized there was a platoon of samurai-wielding Japanese soldiers marching down the street. I paid the man the agreed price then ran out into the street to defend the honour of the regiment. The tattooist had closed the shop by the time I got back.' He gave Jennifer a sly wink.

'There you go, luv,' said Maureen. 'More yarn than a haberdashery.'

'Well I enjoyed listening to his war stories immensely.'

Mrs Gent looked surprised but pleased. 'Really? Well, if you want more, you're welcome to come back in a fortnight. It's his ninety-seventh birthday then. We're having a lunch party down at the Hope Inn on Friday week.'

'That's kind of you, Mrs Gent. But I fear my workload is rather heavy at the moment. However, I do have a friend in the army who I'm sure would be only too pleased to pop in and pay his respects to an old soldier. Once he's listened to your story,' said Jennifer, holding up the tape recorder, 'I'm sure he'll be minded to add a footnote to your military records.'

The old man's eyes lit up. 'Really?'

'Yes, really, Mr Fry. Don't underestimate your contribution to the lives of Maud Comyns and her entourage. You and your mates were heroes to them. That should be recognized in the finest of army traditions, and my army friend can make that happen.'

The old man reached for another tissue.

Chapter Nineteen

The sentinel

There was a light-hearted buzz in the room as Jennifer Collins squeezed past members of her team to get to the podium. 'Ladies and gentlemen,' she said loudly. 'May I have your attention please?' She waited patiently for voices to die down, but the morning's re-appearance of Professor Deidrie Saunders and Dr Duncan Montgomery after a two week long trip together to the Caribbean, now sporting tans and guilty looks was fuelling no end of gossip.

Some unseen wag at the back of the room shouted out, 'Make them take a lie detector test!'

Jennifer cracked a smile and retorted, 'I may well do that. But first I want to hear their version of events, give them enough rope to hang themselves.'

A fresh round of chuckles broke out and Dr Duncan Montgomery shook his head in denial. 'Not guilty, your honour,' he said. 'I was just doing my duty.'

The chuckles turned to hoots of laughter. Jennifer raised her hand. 'Please,' she said. 'We will hear everything. I promise you that.'

Gradually the room settled.

'Deidrie, I think you'd better come up here quickly and put everyone's mind to rest.'

Professor Saunders got out of her chair and took a couple of steps forward until she was at Jennifer's side. She stared over her thick black-rimmed glasses, as she had done a thousand times to rooms full of unruly students, and said in a serious tone, 'Duncan is thirty years my junior. Regrettably, he did nothing improper on our trip.'

The audience gave a collective moan of disappointment.

'But I live in hope,' added Professor Saunders to a fresh round of laughter. 'Now then, let me introduce you to the island of Cunera.' She placed a laptop computer on to the podium, connected a lead, fiddled with the controls and before long a map of the Caribbean appeared on a screen behind her. 'Nine weeks ago, at our introduction, Dr Collins said nothing was off limits although the Bermuda Triangle was best avoided.' She pressed a button and a fresh image appeared. 'The Bermuda Triangle, as can be seen on this map, extends from the southernmost tip of the Florida peninsular, down to Puerto Rico and up to Bermuda. The Lesser Antilles, where we've just come from, is actually outside that triangle, although I imagine some may wish to argue the point. Anyway, our attention was drawn to one of the islands in the Northern Lesser Antilles because it was one of those places in the world where attempts to colonise it have been thwarted.'

Jennifer caught Professor Saunders' attention and asked, 'I thought the Caribbean islands were fiercely fought over for centuries by both pirates and European armies?'

'And you'd be quite correct, Dr Collins. But there is something on this particular island that prevents that.'

Jennifer looked pleased. 'Oh good,' she responded.

'Anyway, Cunera Island,' continued Professor Saunders as she switched to another screenshot, an aerial photograph taken some distance from the island, 'named after the Dutch Saint Cunera, of course, lies between the Northern Lesser Antilles islands of Saba and St Eustatius. It has three mountains, one each to the north, the east and the west, which run straight down to the sea, forming an impenetrable barrier of jagged rocks. The centre is extraordinarily green, fed by an almost abundant supply of fresh water coming down from the mist covered mountain peaks. Along the southern shore is a five-mile long beach, mainly sand, allowing access to the island. Access, however, is restricted. There are an indigenous people living on the island, a population of about one thousand we believe, and they trade with neighbouring islands, but there is no colonial presence, no visitors allowed.'

Jennifer put her hand up again. 'When you say no visitors allowed, you mean no tourists?'

'No outsider whatsoever. We tried to get there by boat from both its neighbouring islands, but no one would take us anywhere near it, no matter what price we offered.'

'Sounds a familiar set up,' said Jennifer.

'Indeed. Whilst on Saba we managed to interview a few of the Cunera fishermen who were on a trading visit. They told us, through an interpreter of course, that their island was protected by a mighty and ferocious sentinel.'

Jennifer frowned. 'A sentinel? That's an odd choice of word, Deidrie. You don't mean a king or a god?'

'No, I don't. We weren't particularly comfortable with the word, but it's the best we could come up with. We certainly spent a lot of time on its translation, but the fishermen were quite emphatic. They have a democratically elected non-hereditary chieftain and no gods. The sentinel is not the chieftain. They said some of their people work for him, such as preparing meals and cleaning, for which he pays them in gold and they make the gold into jewellery for trading with the Saba and St Eustatius islanders. In turn, he watches over them, protects them. And his name is Narai, by the way.'

'Narai,' Jennifer repeated as she wrote the name down. 'Did you ask the fishermen how long this protection racket has been going on for?'

'For ever, of course; since they first settled there anyway. Mind you, they couldn't be precise about how long their people had actually been living on the island.'

'Do they have records? Written records?'

'No, unfortunately they don't. They're too primitive.'

'Could you make a guess?'

'Well, what was really noticeable was that they looked so very different in comparison with the natives of Saba and St Eustatius. We thought they might be descended from Arawak Indians or even from the Ciboney who've been traced on Saba back as far as eleven seventy-five BC. We thought a DNA test would be in order to try and determine their origins.'

'You got DNA samples from them?'

'We paid two fishermen for mouth swabs, yes.'

'What did you pay them?'

'A goat each. Adult females,' responded Professor Saunders as a few sniggers broke out from the audience. 'We bought them on Saba for a hundred American dollars each.'

'Have you received the DNA results yet?'

Professor Saunders broke into a broad grin. 'We have indeed. Would anyone care to guess?' She waited a few moments before adding, 'Five pounds for the correct answer? No Duncan, put your hand down. You know already.'

Jennifer laughed. 'Alright Deidrie, enough! Put us out of our misery.'

'Genetically, they match the indigenous population of Surithani.'

The silence in the room was overwhelming. Even Jennifer was stunned.

'Mind you,' continued Professor Saunders, 'that's a highly qualified result. There are only three Surithani samples in the DNA database.'

Jennifer asked, 'Are you saying they migrated from Surithani in the dim and distant past? By boat?'

'No, I'm not. I doubt very much that is what happened. It would have been an extraordinary achievement. More likely they were taken there, to populate an otherwise deserted island, to provide workers for this sentinel of theirs.'

'Oh, Christ,' muttered Jennifer as her head dropped into her hands.

'My thoughts exactly, Dr Collins. You described Taksin's reign of Surithani as benign. Presumably he was involved in the original migration of some of his people to Cunera, although whether this relocation was by force or not remains unknown. Another point to consider is that with such a small population, fresh blood would need to be added to the gene pool regularly to avoid the risk of genetic disorders arising. The DNA samples we tested showed no sign of European or African connections as one would find in the DNA of the natives of neighbouring islands. I know you indicated that Taksin doesn't like to interfere with man's progression, but it seems to me there must have been, and probably continues to be, some genetic interference to keep those islanders pure and genetically free of disorder. It raises the subject of genetic engineering, even experimentation.'

'Okay, Deidrie, thank you,' Jennifer cut in. 'I don't think we'll find the answer to that type of question without some frank discussion with the people involved.'

'Shall I move on?'

'Yes, please. Sorry for interrupting. You said earlier that something on the island prevents invasion. Would that be this sentinel of theirs?'

Professor Saunders turned her laptop off and came around to the front of the podium. 'This sentinel is a giant. By that I mean a very tall and muscular man, well over eight-foot-tall and built like a bull. He appears to be aggressive, often moody, and frequently wanders the shore in a morose state, angrily hurling rocks into the sea. If any boat gets close to the shoreline, they come under his attack. And when I say rocks, I mean boulders not pebbles. We heard stories from local fishermen on both the neighbouring islands of how this giant rages at them if they inadvertently stray too close.'

'You say he's angry?'

'So it would appear.'

'Any thoughts on that?'

'Other than speculation? No, none. But I imagine being stuck on a near-deserted island, trillions of miles away from home, with only yourself for company probably has something to do with it. Boredom? Frustration? Missing his wife? Who knows?'

Jennifer looked up from writing notes. 'You believe this sentinel has kept the island free of colonisation? Colonisation by Europeans, that is.'

'Indeed yes. We have proof of it. The island gets its first mention in 1632 when a group of shipwrecked Englishmen were washed ashore on the nearby island of Saba. They noted its presence but didn't attempt to reach it. The Dutch West Indian Company came along in 1640, but their landing party was seen off by the giant. In the following decade, several more landings were attempted by the Dutch. All failed of course, quite spectacularly. Credit has to go to Duncan for burying himself for a week in the depths of the Dutch National Archives in The Hague. He stumbled across a journal kept by the seafarer Abel Janszoon Tasman, in which there are a couple of delightful colour sketches of his landing party being beaten to pulp by the giant. Interestingly, notes accompanying the sketches say that musket shot had no effect on the giant, other than that they made him even madder with rage.'

'Another bulletproof man?'

'Quite, Dr Collins. It made me think of Private Alfred Fry's story. Of Taksin not being affected by Japanese soldiers' bullets in the jungle.'

'Can we see the sketches?'

'No. Well, yes, but not here. Duncan was not permitted to take a photograph or a photostat. We didn't wish to explain our need for it. I'm going to have to ask you to resolve the problem of identification with the museum authorities.'

Jennifer looked confused. 'Sorry?'

'The giant, Dr Collins. The sketches show not only is he tall but he's got long white flowing hair and a face that looks as though it's suffered a lifetime of misery. Just like the description we have from Colonel Travis of the saviour in St James's Park. The Colonel needs to go to The Hague to see the sketches, to identify our Saviour.'

Jennifer drew in a sharp intake of breath, let out a smile.

It was a bright warm afternoon in late May when Jennifer took a seat on a wooden bench outside the front of the building that housed the Nationaal Archief in The Hague. She looked around furtively, trying to guess which of the dozens of men coming and going was her appointee. It didn't help that none of them appeared to be looking for her. She checked her watch. One minute to three o'clock. He should appear any second now, she thought, as she adjusted the rose protruding from the button hole of her suit jacket. Or maybe he missed his flight, or got held up at the airport. As her eyes looked up, a clean-shaven man in a stylish black suit appeared out of nowhere and sat down close beside her, somewhat startling her.

'Dr Jennifer Collins I presume?'

'Colonel Ben Travis?'

Colonel Travis nodded. 'Bit cloak-and-dagger this, isn't it?'

Jennifer broke into a wry smile. 'Sorry, I've no experience arranging a secret rendezvous. It's the best I could do under the circumstances.'

'Well, I'm here. Guess that's all that matters. I've seen you around, haven't I? Inside Downing Street, I think, on occasion?'

'I couldn't possibly say.'

'No, I suppose not.' Colonel Travis fell silent a moment, his eyes boring into Jennifer. 'So,' he said at length, 'how can I help you?'

'Umm, well, first, may I ask what orders you've been given?'

Colonel Travis scratched the back of his head. 'To tell you the truth, Dr Collins, very little. This morning I was told by General Wilson, in person, to change out of uniform, fly over here and report to you, whereupon you would give me unspecified instructions. He made the point I was to follow your instructions strictly and to ask no questions.'

'He didn't say why I wanted to see you?'

'No, ma'am. He said he'd get sacked if he told me. He sounded serious about that, deadly serious. I imagine not many people have that power, to sack a Chief of Staff, that is, so someone pretty damn high up is pulling the strings today. Guess I should comply, if I want to keep my job too.'

Jennifer gave no reply.

'Guess your lack of response confirms that.' Colonel Travis wiped a little saliva from the corner of his mouth. 'Well, I'm all yours Dr Collins.'

Jennifer rummaged in her bag and extracted a badge. 'Please clip this on.'

Colonel Travis took the badge and gave it a cursory look. 'Dr Duncan Montgomery?'

'You'll be him for the next half hour.'

'And why not,' responded Colonel Travis as he clipped the badge to his jacket.

Jennifer held the colonel's gaze and said, 'I want to show you a few pages of a sketch book inside this building. It's an old book, a cherished item in the Dutch national archives so we can't just borrow it like from a library. There are access restrictions too, which I've managed to overcome, but we can't look at it without being under the watchful eye of a security guard. We need to be very circumspect as the guard is likely to give a report on us to his boss.'

'Is that your way of saying you don't want them to know a British army colonel is in their building?'

'Yes, partly. I would therefore be grateful if you could act in a non-military fashion. Perhaps you could slouch a little, rather than standing ram-rod straight, not call people sir or ma'am, that sort of thing.'

Colonel Travis relaxed his body and crossed his legs. 'Difficult, but I'll give it a go.'

'Thank you. Now, I don't want the security guard to know exactly what it is I'm interested in, so I shall be randomly showing you pages most of which I have no interest in. If you do see something of interest, please don't speak, don't make any indication that it has caught your eye. Do you understand?'

Colonel Travis looked bewildered. 'Umm, yes. Or rather no. I don't know what there could possibly be in this building that would be of any interest to me.'

Jennifer raised an eyebrow.

'Sorry, I forgot. My orders, of course.'

'Ready to go in?'

'I take it you'll be asking me questions when we come out?'

Jennifer shook her head as she stood up. 'Sorry, no. I'm not allowed to ask questions either.'

Colonel Travis looked startled. 'What? Why not?'

'Oh, you know, the usual bullshit; National Security, conflict of interests between politicians and the military, secrecy, take your pick.'

'This is madness,' said Colonel Travis as he followed in Jennifer's footsteps.

Jennifer strode into the building and headed for Enquiries where she explained that she and her colleague, Dr Duncan Montgomery, had an appointment to view a book, as arranged with the curator of the Netherlands Antilles archives. Minutes later, she and Colonel Travis were following a surly uniformed security guard up a flight of stairs and into a small room furnished with nothing more than a table and four chairs along with a lectern upon which a book was resting on a cushion. The guard came to a halt to the side of the lectern, removed two pairs of white gloves from a pocket and handed one each to Jennifer and Colonel Travis.

Jennifer opened the sketch book and pointed to a drawing of an eighteenth-century schooner lying anchored off a sandy beach. Colonel Travis leaned forward and pretended to be absorbed by what he saw. After ten seconds he turned to Jennifer and gave an exaggerated nod. She turned over a few pages to a drawing of what appeared to be a band of sailors enjoying a meal around a camp fire. Again, Colonel Travis waited a ten second period before turning to Jennifer and giving an exaggerated nod. The procedure was repeated four more times before Jennifer turned to a drawing of a band of Dutch soldiers in the throes of a hand-to-hand fight with a demonic looking giant of a man. Several soldiers were lying injured on the ground, others were firing their muskets at point-blank range, a couple were fending off the giant's flaying arms.

Colonel Travis' eyebrows furrowed and Jennifer gave him a few extra seconds before turning the page to reveal a portrait of the giant, his white mane trailing over his shoulders, his face tortured as though wracked in pain, suffering and anger. Colonel Travis' jaw dropped momentarily before he recovered his composure. After ten seconds he turned to Jennifer with an expression of discomfort etched on his face. Jennifer abruptly turned to another random page and signalled with her eyes for Colonel Travis to resume looking at the book. Three minutes later she thanked the guard and they left the building.

Outside, back sitting on the same bench as earlier, Colonel Travis sighed deeply and said, 'I can't ask you any questions?'

'Well, you could, but I won't be able to answer them. Sorry.'

'Do you not have any questions for me?'

Jennifer stared at the colonel but didn't answer.

Colonel Travis rubbed his temples and spoke quietly, 'General Wilson told me to comply with everything you requested, to answer all your questions fully, honestly and with an open mind. My problem is, he didn't tell me how I should respond if you don't ask me a question.'

'Life can be difficult at times.'

'It sure can, Dr Collins. Especially when national security issues arise.'

'I see.'

Colonel Travis took a moment to compose himself. 'That face, of the giant, with its haunted look. It's like the face of a battle-weary soldier, one who has seen far too much blood and death. Like a soldier who can't live with his past.'

'Ah-ah.'

'So, about that question, Dr Collins.'

'What question is that, Colonel?'

'The one you can't ask me. Are you sure you can't verbalise it?'

Jennifer remained tight-lipped.

Colonel Travis sat in thought for ten seconds, then said very quietly. 'Back in February, on a particularly miserable afternoon, I found myself in St James's Park having a conversation with a stranger. He said he was cold, pulled close a long cape he was wearing and said something like "Christ, this weather's dreadful, why do you live here? Why not settle somewhere warm?" At the time, I thought his use of the word "settle" was an odd choice. I thought maybe it was just his lack of familiarity with the English language. Now, well, maybe not. Thinking about it, it's a word a refugee might use. And a refugee who suffers from the cold is likely to choose a warm place to live in. The Caribbean would fit that purpose, wouldn't it?'

Jennifer nodded. 'I guess it would.'

'That stranger did the world a great service that day, Dr Collins. I trust he will be granted the utmost respect.' He got up, turned to her and said, 'Don't be a stranger next time our paths cross. A coffee sometime perhaps?'

Jennifer returned a smile. Colonel Travis was indeed a handsome man, but the thought of him morphing into General Wilson as he grew older was rather off-putting. 'Sorry,' she responded. 'I'm not allowed to answer your questions.'

Colonel Travis laughed heartily as he walked away.

Chapter Twenty

An adrenalin junkie

Carrying a warm takeaway pizza box, Jennifer Collins hesitantly pushed opened the front door to her flat above the estate agency in the High Street, Lewes, bent down and scooped up a couple of dozen envelopes and fast food leaflets lying on the doormat. Now mid-June, it suddenly occurred to her it had been over two months since her last visit. The place felt cold, bleak, uncared for. She poked her head into the living room and bedrooms, noticed a layer of dust had settled on surfaces. In a dejected mood, she walked into the kitchen, placed the post and the pizza box on the table, opened the fridge in the hope of finding something alcoholic inside. She was in luck, for sitting next to a half-full container of milk was a decent, uncorked bottle of Chablis. She withdrew the milk carton, upended it in the sink, recoiled in revulsion at the sight of its yogurty contents, reached for a glass off a shelf and a cork screw from a drawer.

It was late in the evening, well past nine o'clock and Jennifer was feeling hungry, in need of a hug and in a state of flux over her future. Before she'd left London at the end of a particularly hard day's work, her colleague Dr Simon Langdale had handed her a thick heavy file, saying he believed it was the final bit of the jigsaw. She had thanked him, asked no questions and had ignored the file on the train journey back home. Home? That particular thought struck a raw nerve. The flat had served as her home for six years and she'd enjoyed every minute of living there. But tonight was different. After three months living in a swanky government-paid apartment close to Whitehall, spending each day in the company of intelligent people fulfilling an important assignment, her life in Lewes no longer felt as rosy as she once thought it had been. If what her colleague had said was true, then what? End of assignment? Contract terminated? Back to part-time lecturing at Sussex University? For the entire sixty-minute train journey from Victoria Station she'd stared out the window, her thoughts bleak, her mind unable to provide any answer to her problems.

She knocked back half a glass of Chablis in one gulp, sat down and made a start on the pizza. After the second slice had been consumed, and with her hunger pangs satiated, she licked her fingers and made a start on the post. Unpaid gas, electric and water bills loomed large in the collection. Those would have to wait for the morning. Junk mail was binned without reading. Then she turned her attention to an envelope addressed in pen, in a style of writing she vaguely recognised. It was a card, a Valentine's Day card, though posted in May, from Mike with the briefest of messages "Any hope?" It had been a while since she'd thought of Mike, even longer since she'd last seen or heard from him. With a heavy sigh, she threw it in the bin along with the junk mail.

She dug out her colleague's report from her bag, picked up another slice of pizza, and read the summary:

In 1105, Henry Beauclec, fourth son of William the Conqueror and King of England, took control of the Duchy of Normandy following the defeat of his brother Robert at the battle of Tinchebray. Shortly after this battle, the King fell seriously ill with diphtheria during which time the lymph nodes in his neck swelled to such an extent that the blockage prevented him from breathing. As his face turned blue with asphyxiation, his aides watched in vain as death began to take its grip. Except that the king didn't die at that time, for Sir Prasert de Thame, an extraordinarily tall, athletic young man who had recently being knighted after excelling himself on the battlefield, stepped forward and, with a razor-sharp knife, neatly and expertly slit the king's throat.

Although this was not the first ever recorded tracheotomy, having been described by the Egyptians in 3600 BC and used on at least one occasion by Alexander the Great, it was far from common practice. Knowledge of the procedure would have been limited to a handful of scholars, with experience limited to the occasional trial on a goat. Yet somehow a twelfth century knight managed to acquire the wherewithal to undertake this most delicate of operations with remarkable competency, for the king neither succumbed to infection nor was his carotid artery damaged.

Once off his sick bed, a greatly appreciative king rewarded Sir Prasert de Thame by bestowing upon him one thousand acres of land in Kent in a secluded valley close to the Sussex border along with the feudal title of Lord of the Manor of Holtye. Upon this land, Sir Prasert built himself a manor house worthy of his position and, with an apparent limitless supply of gold, embraced the finest traditions of wining and dining the elite of society, along with catering for their exotic tastes. In the 1120s and 1130s, Holtye Manor became de rigueur for lavish and somewhat outrageous parties.

In 1156, Sir Prasert began the construction of a twenty-foot high parapetted wall that would surround his lands, with access facilitated through a large portcullis gate. At the time, this action was considered to be in defiance of convention since Lords of the Manor were expected to apply for letters patent to fortify their property and Sir Prasert had not applied for a licence to crenellate. Sir Prasert's actions were almost certainly a response to the Plantagenet's tendency to tax their vassals in an outrageously punitive fashion, yet in building the crenellated wall he signalled his outright hostile opposition to the monarchy. This was a dangerous move in the Plantagenet era. Yet Sir Prasert survived. So did his wall, for it proved to be impregnable; not only to the king's tax collectors but to the king's soldiers as well.

There have been numerous attempts by tax-collecting monarchs, or those merely suspicious of privacy, to gain access to the estate of Holtye Manor. There have been military sieges of Holtye Manor recorded during the reign of almost every king from John to Henry VIII, all of which failed dismally since the wall proved impervious to cannon fire. Storming the wall proved impractical too, since any soldier who touched it by hand, grappling hook, or through leaning a scaling ladder against it, appears to have received an incapacitating electric shock. Witness accounts of sieges tell of Sir Prasert manning the battlements alone, taunting soldiers, pouring vile concoctions down upon their heads, blasting siege towers, battering rams and trebuchets to smithereens, laughing at his would-be invaders and, in an act of utter disrespect, mooning his attackers.

In the twentieth century, requests for access from officers of HM Revenue & Customs, English Heritage, Ministry of War and Sevenoaks District Council have all been defied vexatiously. Visitation to the estate is by invite only, and local legend dictates that the gateman's job is only offered to those of a grumpy, rude and curmudgeonly character. Correspondence files found at HM Revenue & Customs and Sevenoaks District Council certainly appear to support this legend.

Throughout the centuries since the battle of Tinchebray, the name Sir Prasert de Thame has appeared at intervals not just in London society, but in Paris and Cadiz as well. The name is invariably associated with tales of an athletic, eager, sociable, knowledgeable young man in search of excitement and adventure. There is scarcely a war in medieval and modern European history without some tale of audacious bravery involving Sir Prasert's name. From studying Sir Prasert's courageous actions, three behavioural characteristics become clear. Firstly, his so-called acts of bravery would, in terms of a human life, be more aptly described as foolhardy, reckless and even suicidal in nature. Secondly, he appears to seek enjoyment, or even inner fulfilment, rather than blood. Thirdly, although he has a penchant for youthful bravado, he has shown remarkable restraint in displaying it, leading one to speculate that perhaps a higher influence may be restraining him, rationing him to small but regular indulgences.

The name of Sir Prasert de Thame is also associated with art, for it is said that Holtye Manor contains a collection of the most exquisite sculpture, jewellery and artwork from the ancient Egyptian, Greek, Roman, Mayan, Viking, Norman, Saxon and medieval periods. So exquisite, in fact, that one would think the objects had been acquired during the era in which they were made and carefully preserved ever since. Soldiers, of course, are well known for bringing home keepsakes. Perhaps this scenario offers an explanation as to how the items came to be obtained in such good condition.

The current manor house is rumoured to have been designed by Richard Jupp in 1785. Visitors have described it as not being a particularly grand house and certainly not a palatial one. It does, however, apparently serve the display of art collections well.

English Heritage is particularly dismayed at being denied access to the house to survey for purposes of listed building assessment, and to the grounds to evaluate the treasures of untouched ancient woodland. HM Revenue & Customs have frequently pursued estate valuations for death duty purposes but access has always been refused on the grounds that they could offer no proof that an occupant had died. The Ministry of War tried to gain access in 1940 to take over the house, especially because of its proximity to Biggin Hill, but were firmly rebuffed at the gate.

To this day the de Thame family still possess the land and title. Or, to be correct, Sir Prasert still does, for there are no parish or national records to indicate that Sir Prasert has ever been associated with any birth, marriage or death.

It is likely that Holtye Manor and its occupant will continue to successfully defy access to government authorities, for what possible sanctions could be applied to a man who has no need of public services?

In 1920, following the creation of the League Of Nations, the King of Surithani was reluctantly persuaded to allow the establishment of consulates in his country. Several European countries invested much money in doing so, presumably in the expectation of gaining an insight into that secretive country. However, their efforts were largely in vain since they soon discovered that their activities were restricted to the confines of the Foreign Enclave, travel within the country not permitted and visitors robustly denied admittance.

In a show of diplomatic reciprocation, the King of Surithani agreed to establish a consulate in England through which communication could be facilitated efficiently since Surithani has never been a member of the Universal Postal Union. For this purpose, the King nominated Holtye Manor to be his Consulate with Sir Prasert de Thame as his Consular. Access to Sir Prasert is therefore most likely to be achievable only through an approach first to the King of Surithani.

Jennifer spluttered on a mouthful of wine she'd been playfully rolling around her tongue. She hadn't been expecting that last comment. She coughed a couple of times to clear her throat. Her colleague had been correct, Sir Prasert de Thame was indeed the last piece of the jigsaw. Satisfyingly, the location of Holtye Manor dovetailed nicely with Private Alfred Fry's story about being met by a young man on landing in England and being taken to a nearby house to see Churchill. It had to have been Chartwell, near Brasted, that he had been taken to, only a few miles away from Holtye Manor. And most pleasing of all it yielded the answer to the question of why the manner of Private Alfred Fry's arrival, in a strange flying machine in the middle of a war, had not caused the young man any consternation.

So, that was it. Job finished. It had taken her team three months of arduous work to complete their findings. But they had succeeded. They had their three names, the three most likely candidates for the roles of Earth's saviours a few months back; Taksin, Narai and Prasert. Odd really, she thought, as she mentally summarised their profiles as being a technophobic dictator, a deranged desert island castaway and an adrenalin junkie. Not exactly what she'd hoped for, but then who was she to say what was to be expected from alien refugees? And at the last count there were over eight hundred pages of research, mostly copies of historical documents, which would now need to be bound up in a dossier and presented to the Prime Minister personally and confidentially. But that task could wait until tomorrow.

She poured herself another glass of wine, upending the bottle to catch the last few drops. She stretched her arm out and placed the empty bottle on the draining board, giving it a look of disgust as though it had been responsible for her moroseness. She needed a holiday, that was all. And she could afford one now with the ten-thousand-pound bonus she and her team would be getting, each, for completing the assignment.

As Jennifer rose from her chair, she wished the bonus had been higher. Much, much higher. High enough to fund a new life, one that didn't involve cold empty flats and the drudgery of teaching inattentive students. She knocked back the last of the wine in one swig, went to the bathroom, cleaned her teeth, stripped off and fell into her empty bed. She pulled a spare pillow close to her body, wrapped her arms around it and, with a holiday in mind, yearned for Surachai.

Chapter Twenty-One

The head in the fog

Early morning, some three weeks after the presentation of her team's findings to the Prime Minister, Jennifer Collins found herself on board HMS Portland staring vacantly out of a porthole as the frigate sailed north from Singapore towards the Kingdom of Surithani. As the familiar coastline appeared on the horizon, her heart sunk. For, on the verge of betraying the country she loved, self-doubt and self-criticism ate away at her soul.

On a table in the middle of her cabin lay one of the only two copies of the six-inch thick dossier her team had prepared. She knew its contents well, and since leaving Singapore she'd whiled away the hours revisiting her summary, rehearsing how a conversation with Taksin may go, becoming quite sick with anguish over how her remarks may be perceived. Although she had intentionally avoided direct accusation in her report, relying heavily upon insinuation instead, she just hoped to god that her words wouldn't be considered insulting.

She turned her head from the porthole and faced the dossier. It had been one of the most fascinating journeys she'd ever been on, compiling snippets of information that had been gleaned from an array of libraries around Europe. Astonishingly, her team had found hundreds of unusual tales amongst memoirs and diaries of seafarers and tradesmen who had visited Surithani over the centuries. Not just English accounts either, but Dutch, French and Portuguese too. The eyewitness accounts of Taksin's powers and longevity were compelling evidence in itself. As were the myriad of sketches in the diaries of sea monsters and giant heads appearing in banks of fog that had scared sailors witless. All in all, she wondered why no one had confronted Taksin before on the matter. Perhaps they had. Perhaps that even explained some of the oddities that her team had stumbled across, like a Leonardo Da Vinci sketch of the Earth that included extraordinarily accurate details of Australia, a continent that not only hadn't been discovered at the time the great Italian artist lived but which must have been glimpsed by the artist from space in order for him to gain the right perspective.

The cabin door opened without Jennifer being aware. The Prime Minister stood in the doorway for a few seconds before asking, 'Are you alright, Jennifer? You look a little peaky. Sea-sickness?'

Jennifer gave a deep sigh, the hundredth since she and the Prime Minister had left Singapore. 'No, sir. It's just that I can't help wondering whether we're doing the right thing.'

'Nerves playing up?'

Jennifer shook her head slowly. 'It's not that, sir. It's just that Taksin is so respected, so revered by his people. I can't help feeling we're about to commit a dreadful mistake, one that could destroy him and his country. I'd never forgive myself for that. This land was the home of my youth.' She made a light snorting noise. 'As Madonna once sang, this used to be my playground.'

The Prime Minister took a while before replying, 'Sometimes sacrifices are necessary. Of a lifestyle that is, rather than a life. If Taksin really is as ancient as we suspect, he'll have the wisdom to understand that.'

A voice came from behind the Prime Minister. 'Excuse me, sir. The captain would like to talk to you.' The Prime Minister nodded at the deckhand, motioned to Jennifer, and the three of them set off for the bridge.

A minute later, Jennifer and the Prime Minister walked on to the bridge. 'Yes, Captain?' asked the Prime Minister.

'This is about as far as we can go, sir,' said the salt-and-pepper bearded Captain Mandrake. 'At our current rate, we'll be in international waters for only another minute or so. What do you want me to do?'

'Don't cross the five-mile line,' responded Jennifer with a sense of urgency. 'Make it look like we're intending to breach territorial waters, but veer off at the last second. Get as close as you can. And I mean close, like a hundred yards or less if you can.'

Captain Mandrake scratched the back of his head. 'With all due respect, Miss, these waters are known to be dangerous. Many strange things have happened here in the past.'

Jennifer couldn't resist a smile at the irony of the captain's comment. 'Old wives' tales, Captain. No more than that.'

'I beg to differ with you, Miss. Many ships have gone down in this region. Survivors tell of a freak fog, giants, monsters, voices from god. I'm not saying I believe in such things, but it's only armed ships that have ever gone down. Non-armed trade ships usually have no trouble passing. We're on a frigate, a heavily armed and expensive frigate at that, if you haven't noticed. I'd hate to be responsible for losing it.'

Jennifer caught the eye of the Prime Minister who, in turn, clapped a hand on the captain's shoulder and said, 'You'll have my pardon in writing, if we go down that is, but I think we'll be okay. Please just do precisely as Dr Collins asks of you.'

The captain frowned. 'If you say so, sir. But I'm going to make a detailed entry in the log.'

The Prime Minister nodded. 'Of course.'

'Fog bank to port,' a voice shouted from behind a computer screen. 'Four miles and closing fast, sir. And I mean fast.'

'Hard to starboard,' Captain Mandrake ordered.

Jennifer steadied herself as the ship lurched. 'How close are we to the five-mile line, Captain?' she asked.

'Five hundred yards, less maybe.'

'We mustn't cross it,' Jennifer snapped. 'It's imperative we don't cross it by an inch. We mustn't violate Surithani's maritime law.'

The captain caught Jennifer's eye. 'Don't worry, Miss. We won't.'

'Fog bank three miles. Christ, that thing's moving like fury.'

Another voice shouted, 'Four hundred yards to the line, Captain.'

'Ten degrees to starboard.'

'Fog bank two miles.'

'Three hundred yards to the line.'

'Maintain current bearing,' shouted Captain Mandrake. 'Keep your distance from the line.'

Seconds later, the fog bank collided with the ship. Jennifer watched in fascination as layers of it spilled over the deck, enveloping the ship, just as it had done in the John Carpenter film with its eponymous title. Within seconds she couldn't see the ship's brow.

'Dear God, what the hell is that stuff?' Captain Mandrake asked as folds of the fog drifted together to form the outline of a gigantic head, rising some hundred feet high above the deck. 'Jesus Christ, it looks like the Face of Boe.'

Jennifer gave Captain Mandrake a wry smile.

'We've stopped sir,' shouted a midshipman. 'All engines have stopped. We're not moving in the water. We're making no headway.'

'That's impossible,' responded Captain Mandrake. 'We can't just stop dead in the water. Not without being thrown off our feet.'

Jennifer caught the Prime Minister's eye and smiled warmly. This was impressive, she mused. And what a frightening picture the head in the fog made. No wonder sailors of previous centuries thought these waters were cursed and inhabited by monsters.

The mouth of the giant head opened and bellowed in a thunderous roar, 'Turn back!' Jennifer clapped her hands over her ears, as did most of the crew. 'Turn back or perish!'

Captain Mandrake gulped and looked to Jennifer and the Prime Minister. 'What do you want me to do now?'

'Nothing,' replied Jennifer. 'And say nothing either, none of you. Let me do the talking.' She opened the bridge door, stepped outside, steeled herself for a confrontation and said loudly in the direction of the head, 'We are friendly.'

'You have no right here. Turn back!'

The Prime Minister joined Jennifer and shouted, 'We are in international waters. We have a right to be here.'

'You have invaded my seas.'

'No! You're wrong,' shouted Jennifer defiantly. 'Check your bearings. We are more than a hundred yards outside your territorial waters.'

'What . . .?'

'Check your monitors, we are at least a hundred yards short of your territorial line.'

The head fell silent for a moment. The Prime Minister looked quizzically at Jennifer and whispered, 'You do realise you're arguing with a lump of fog, don't you?'

Jennifer shrugged her shoulders. 'It speaks. It seemed the sensible thing to do.'

'But what's this about monitors?'

'Just a guess,' replied Jennifer with a smile. 'But if you hadn't noticed, it's just a holographic projection with an electronically amplified voice. There must be someone, somewhere, monitoring us.'

The mouth of the giant head opened again. 'Who are you?'

The Prime Minister took a deep breath and replied in a composed voice, 'I am the Prime Minister of the United Kingdom of Great Britain and Northern Ireland. I come in peace. I seek an audience with His Majesty King Taksin the Great.'

The reply came in a mighty bellow, 'You dare to come in a ship of war!'

'We have no other safe form of transport,' responded Jennifer. 'There is too much terrorism in the world these days. International seas are dangerous, full of pirates. The Prime Minister has to travel with an armed escort.'

'That is not my problem. You have not been invited here.'

Jennifer rubbed her chin in thought. It wasn't often she got to spar verbally with a hundred-foot high head of fog. 'You're not on the telephone. How am I supposed to contact you to arrange an invitation?'

'What . . .?'

'We humbly request an audience with His Majesty King Taksin,' she continued. 'We apologize for arriving unexpectedly, but we had no time to observe the normal etiquette of sending a letter via the consular. We need to see His Majesty on a matter of the utmost diplomatic urgency.'

'I . . . I . . . just a minute.'

The Prime Minister sniggered. 'I think you're doing rather well,' he whispered. 'You seem to have got it confused.'

Jennifer whispered back, 'I don't think anyone else has stood up to it before, sir. Maybe the doomed ships would have survived if only the captains had talked to it sensibly.'

'The ship of war must stay where it is. You and your Prime Minister may continue your journey.'

'How?'

'I don't know,' came a sharp retort. 'There must be a smaller vessel on board your warship. Get one of the crew to sail it to shore. Come unarmed, weapons are not allowed to be taken into the country.'

'That's interesting,' the Prime Minister whispered, 'the voice seems to have lost its grandeur.'

Jennifer agreed. The booming voice had indeed lost its ferocious tone. It had become domestic, tetchy even. 'I'm sorry,' she replied to the head of fog, 'but the Prime Minister's security team won't let him travel unarmed.'

'Oh, for goodness sake . . .'

The Prime Minister shook his head in bewilderment. 'This is surreal,' he said.

'I will guide you in to port. Your ship will be impounded and will remain out of action until permission is granted to leave.'

Jennifer and the Prime Minister returned inside the bridge and closed the door.

'That really was quite extraordinary, Dr Collins,' Captain Mandrake exclaimed. 'Is that what you do for a living? Talk to monsters?'

'I'm a career woman working in a very male dominated organisation,' replied Jennifer. 'Coping with inflated male egos comes as second nature to me.'

Captain Mandrake winced. 'We're not all like that, are we?'

'Ask your wife,' responded Jennifer dryly.

Captain Mandrake inclined his head in a cursory bow. 'Point taken.' He then turned to the Prime Minister and asked, 'What next, sir?'

'Well, you heard what was said, we're going to be guided in, apparently, although I'm not quite sure what that means.'

'We're moving, sir,' said a midshipman.

Jennifer glanced out the window. The fog above the deck-line was fast dispersing and, from what she could make of the coastline in the distance, the ship was indeed moving, though at a rate far faster than she imagined the engines were capable of achieving.

'We're being carried,' said Captain Mandrake. 'We're being carried on a bed of fog. But that's impossible . . .'

'Obviously not,' Jennifer retorted.

'But we have no control of the ship.'

'No, we don't,' replied Jennifer. 'But someone does, and I think you'll find that, whoever is in control, they'll do an excellent job of it.'

Chapter Twenty-Two

Royal audience

HMS Portland came to a halt at the mouth of the Patunam River, a stone's throw from Nakhon Thong's ancient docks. Jennifer, leaning on a railing, observing the goings-on at the docks, turned to the Prime Minister and muttered, 'This happened to Admiral Dupetit-Thouars' fleet in 1881.'

A look of puzzlement fell over the Prime Minister's face. 'I beg your pardon?'

'The French tried to invade this city in February 1881. A fleet of eight ships led by Admiral Dupetit-Thouars managed to get this far, but no more. Reportedly, the crew found themselves trapped, unable to make headway in any direction.'

'Completely stuck?'

'Yep. Apparently, they dropped a small, four-manned vessel into the water, but were unable to row anywhere. Even a swimmer couldn't get beyond the length of his dive. The Admiral wrote in his log of a cursed fog bank that hung around the base of his ships and of an apparent undercurrent that prevented his boat making headway. The French soldiers on board could see people coming and going on the dockside over there, just as we can now. They could even communicate if they shouted loud enough. But they were well and truly stranded for two weeks. I gather they tried to fire their cannons at the city only to find the shot backfired, as though it had bounced off an invisible wall. They became the laughing stock of non-French merchants in the dock area, especially the English who displayed little sympathy for their plight and positively delighted in their discomfort.

The French were left alone, right here in the middle of the river, to suffer the indignation of complete powerlessness.'

'Wow. How did it end?'

'Eventually, the Admiral ordered the white flag of surrender to be raised and they were allowed to retreat, although I believe a fortune in restitution was demanded by the king before they were allowed free.'

'So, the French weren't sunk out at sea, then?'

'No, they weren't. Odd that, now you come to mention it, sir.' Jennifer pondered a moment. 'I think the Admiral's fleet was allowed into port, yet no further, deliberately, to humiliate him and the French in general. It would have served as a good lesson for colonialists.'

The Prime Minister appeared reflective. 'Do you think we will be able to get ashore from here? Or are we trapped as well?'

In response, Jennifer pointed to a small wooden craft making its way from the dockside towards them. 'That's a Customs boat by the look of the flag it's flying. I think this'll be our lift ashore. Let's grab our bags and go meet it.'

'Right.' The Prime Minister popped his head into the bridge and said to Captain Mandrake, 'I would be obliged if you'd wait for my return. Maybe later today, or tomorrow morning, depending on how things turn out. Having said that, I doubt if you could leave if you tried. I'll sort that problem out, somehow.'

Captain Mandrake nodded. 'Aye, sir, as you wish.'

'Right, so how do we get down to sea level from here to get on board that little boat heading it's way here?'

Captain Mandrake smiled. 'Follow me.'

Twenty minutes later, Jennifer stood alongside the Prime Minister on the dockside looking back at HMS Portland. She gave a wave towards the bridge, as if to convey the message that they'd landed safely.

'Well, what now?' asked the Prime Minister. 'This is your territory, Jennifer. You'd better take the lead.'

Jennifer led the way into the Customs hall, a large wooden structured building of a bygone age. A handful of uniformed officials loitered, talking, joking, smoking. She went up to them, talked for a moment in their native language and received a nod of approval. She returned to the Prime Minister's side and said, 'We have clearance, let's go.'

'Really? No passport checks? No visa stamps? Don't they want to check what's in our bags?'

Jennifer shook her head. 'No, we've been cleared in advance. What's more, they were expecting us. Come on.'

'That's it? Cleared, just like that?' The Prime Minister scratched the back of his head as he set off in Jennifer's wake. 'To be honest, I have to say I'm rather disappointed. I was expecting a lot of aggravation, what with the stories you've told me of foreigners not being allowed into the country. This is too easy. Far too easy. What happened to security? What's stopping any foreigner simply marching through, guns blazing, intent on taking over the place?'

Jennifer pointed at a large wide gateway, towards which they were headed. It was surrounded by pictures depicting a variety of weapons and the word "No" in several languages. 'This gate is the only way in or out of the dockside area. Try going through it with anything more dangerous than nail-clippers and you'll be in for a nasty surprise. I witnessed it in operation once, when I was about ten years old, down here visiting my father at work one day. Some smart-ass deck-hand tried to walk through with a flick-knife concealed in his jacket pocket. Poor sod, I recall a blinding flash and I looked over in time to see him being thrown backwards with a thrust so powerful his body careered into that desk over there,' she said, pointing to a desk at least twenty feet away.

'Dead?'

Jennifer shook her head slowly. 'No, he survived. It took a couple of hours before he was himself again.'

The Prime Minister patted his trouser pockets, as though checking for elicit weapons, before stepping forward and passing through the gateway. 'We could do with one of these at Heathrow,' he mused, 'it would cut the queues at security quite nicely.'

Jennifer drew in a sharp breath. 'I thought you championed Health and Safety?'

The Prime Minister chuckled. 'I could be persuaded on the merits of a more time-efficient system, I'm sure.'

As they emerged from the Customs Hall, Jennifer strode over to a stationary three-wheel cycle rickshaw with attached covered passenger seat, the only one in sight. She spoke to the driver who, until then, had been snoozing in the back, and delved into her purse for some coins.

The Prime Minister viewed the rickshaw with disdain. 'Are there no proper taxis available?'

'Nope. No petrol driven vehicle of any description in the entire country. Taksin won't allow them. He says they cause pollution, laziness, death and injury, destruction of communities and a general cultural malaise. He cites all the other capital cities in the world as good examples of why he doesn't want cars here. Bicycles are about as far as he'll go with modern transport. He says bikes are healthy, they keep the riders fit.'

The Prime Minister had been staring at the sinewy frame of the rickshaw driver. 'He has a point. But what about transportation of goods around the country? Is everything done by manpower?'

'Almost. There's a good river and canal system for canoes, although most communities rely on whatever produce they can grow in their own neighbourhood.'

'Sounds a bit antiquated.'

'It may do, sir, but the country has a charm that more progressive countries lack. The indigenous people I've spoken to who've had experience of other countries say they're quite happy with the way things are here.'

The Prime Minister climbed into the rickshaw's passenger seat and put his briefcase on his knees for lack of space on the floor. 'Sounds like a paradise for members of the Green Party. Not sure it's for me though. Still, whilst in Rome and all that. Let's go. I haven't travelled in anything quite like this since my pre-university backpacking days.'

Jennifer climbed up and sat alongside the Prime Minister, pointed out the palace in the distance, on the other side of the river, perched on top of a promontory jutting out from the mountain, with its golden, jewel encrusted pagoda-style roof. 'That's where we're headed. It's only a couple of miles from here by road, shouldn't take us any more than thirty minutes if the city's roads aren't too crowded.'

The rickshaw set off along the flagstone road that took them across the stone bridge spanning the river and on into the ancient city. The landmarks and sights they passed possessed a welcome familiarity for Jennifer, but for the Prime Minister they were reminiscent of a period drama set in medieval days. The city's narrow streets were lined with wooden shop-houses; hawkers carried their wares in baskets hanging from bamboo yokes; traders shouted for attention above the bubbling melee of the crowd. People mingled between market stalls, picking up fish, meat, fruit and vegetables, examining them, haggling over prices. Yet nowhere was there to be seen the merest glimpse of any concrete, tarmacadam or motorised vehicle.

The rickshaw driver came to a halt at the base of a long flight of steps that rose steeply up the mountainside to the palace.

'Nearly there,' said Jennifer by way of encouragement.

The Prime Minister's mouth fell open a fraction. 'You mean we've got to go up these steps?'

'Of course.'

'No road up around the side perhaps, for the rickshaw to take us?'

'Nope. Bit too steep for a bicycle anyway.'

'Dear God, I'll never make it.' The Prime Minister wiped a bead of sweat off his forehead and asked, 'How many steps are there?'

'Fifteen hundred, I believe.'

'And we're expected to walk up?'

'Not if you don't want to, although it's considered a pilgrimage to do so. The country's finest and most important temple is up there in the palace courtyard. There's an easier way if you'd prefer.' Jennifer pointed to a wooden hut to one side of the steps. 'You can ride up on a cable-drawn chairlift. It's there for the old and infirm to use.'

The Prime Minister gave Jennifer a sideways glance. 'And under which of those categories do you classify me?'

Jennifer laughed. 'Ooh, that's a difficult choice.'

The Prime Minister frowned as he stepped into a small sofa sized gondola. 'Well, while you're making up your mind about that, you can demonstrate how this contraption works. I'll use it, you can walk. The exercise will do you good.'

Jennifer took a sharp intake of breath and jumped into the gondola alongside the Prime Minister. 'Oh, no you don't. You're not going without me.'

'Feeling old all of a sudden?'

'Not at all. I'm a lady. This is a lady's prerogative. I'm coming too, so budge up.'

The rickety chairlift gave them a tortuous journey up to the palace courtyard where they alighted onto a huge open-aired marble-floored square a hundred and fifty yards long in each direction. At the back of the square, a wide flight of steps led up to the palace entrance. To the left-hand side of the square lay government office buildings, to the right a golden spired Buddhist temple. The fourth side, past the opening to the steps, ran a four-foot high protective wall beyond which lay a stupendous panoramic view of the city and countryside. In the centre of the courtyard stood a magnificent fountain, featuring statues of mythological beasts spouting water from their mouths.

The Prime Minister momentarily stood speechless as he took in the beauty and magnificence of the gold roofed palace with its frontage of marble columns. The masonry work was immaculate; blocks of marble and stone used in the building's construction appeared seamless. 'This architecture is spectacular, Jennifer. Truly spectacular. And how old is it?'

'Building started in Year Zero, according to legend. Three thousand five hundred and fifty-one years ago, I suppose.'

'Wow. It's got to be one of the wonders of the ancient world, then.'

'Well, yes and no, I guess. Given what we suspect, I think the technology used here was pretty advanced compared to, say, the pyramids, and therefore not really such a wonder.'

'Do you think he helped them out?'

'Helped the Egyptians, you mean?' Jennifer reflected on the idea for a moment before replying, 'I doubt it. I don't think he's ever expressed any desire to help out mankind in its evolutionary progress.'

The Prime Minister turned around to look at the view over the city, across the river, the harbour and estuary to the south, forests to the north and east. 'This is breath-taking, Jennifer. Truly breath-taking. This place has such a natural, unsullied feel to it. There's no concrete, no high-rise buildings, no motorways.'

'Getting to like it? Appreciating the benefits of a country that has not been industrialised?'

The Prime Minister nodded. 'And you and your parents live here?'

'I did when I was young. I visit my parents as often as possible. Their house is over there,' she said, pointing in the distance. 'In the foreign enclave, set back a few hundred yards beyond the bridge. There's an area of about six square miles reserved just for foreigners. It contains some beautiful old villas, including the British Club. In the middle there's an enormous landscaped park and a path which leads through woods down to an unspoilt sandy beach.'

'You must show me later. It sounds divine.'

'We could go there by horse. Do you ride?'

'I haven't done so for a few years now.' The Prime Minister fell silent for a few moments, taking in the beauty of the view. 'I can see why you love it here. Why aren't you living here now?'

'Well, I'd love to settle here, sometime, but I can't see myself finding any satisfying work. The job market's rather restricted, and restrictive, as you can imagine. It would be great to be able to live here at the weekends but work somewhere else during the week, like London where life is a bit more vibrant. As you can imagine, I'm not sure how I'm going to resolve that issue.'

'I can certainly see it would be a tourist paradise here. Couldn't you try to set something up in that industry? A scuba-diving school, for instance, or as a tour guide?'

'Ah, that's where a problem arises, sir. Tourism destroys exactly that which people want to come and see. Take this courtyard. Right now there are barely more than, what, a dozen people going about their business? Can you imagine what it would be like with thousands of tourists visiting each day, dressed in their shabby clothes, armed with cameras, their bored children jumping into the fountain, their rubbish left scattered on the ground, stalls everywhere selling cheap plastic souvenirs? You must have visited St Mark's Square in Venice, the loss of dignity to that site would be suffered the same way here.'

The Prime Minister sighed. 'Enough, Jennifer. The thought is depressing.'

They crossed the square and climbed the short flight of steps up to the palace and in through the huge wooden doors of its entrance. Inside, the air was cool, a welcome relief to the tropical heat outside. They walked along a wide marble paved hallway, its sides hung with huge paintings of local settings and prominent people, towards a line of benches that served as a waiting area.

The Prime Minister froze, his jaw dropped, his eyes staring at one of the paintings which depicted a scene of ancient street life in the city with the palace on the mountainside in the background. He beckoned Jennifer back. 'Did you see this?'

'What's that?'

The Prime Minister drew closer to the painting. 'Look at this signature. My wife is an art aficionado. She's dragged me into practically every gallery in Europe. I know this artist's style. And his signature. I can't believe it. It's . . . well, it looks like a Caravaggio.'

'Really?'

'Yes . . . but it can't be, he never came out this way.'

'To your knowledge, maybe. But . . .'

'But? What do you mean "but"? Caravaggio never had the time, money or opportunity to come out this way. Anyway, it's far too early in the history of sea exploration for him to have got out here.'

'I don't doubt that, sir, but you're forgetting who his patron would have been. If he did indeed come out this way, he might not have come by sea.'

The Prime Minister's mouth closed with a snap. His eyes scanned several other paintings. 'Oh my god, they're all done by leading European artists from the Renaissance period.'

Jennifer coughed to get the Prime Minister's attention. 'Time to button it, I think, sir, we've got company.' She nodded towards a uniformed palace worker who was walking towards them. She greeted the official, explained that they had come for an audience with Taksin and were subsequently guided past the benches, up a flight of marble stairs, through what appeared to be a royal reception room and into a more comfortable, private room, though no less regal in its appearance. The official gestured for Jennifer and the Prime Minister to sit at an oblong teak conference table, the four legs of which were carved as dragons. As Jennifer ran her hand over the magnificent creatures, the official walked to the far end of the room and disappeared through a small doorway. She twiddled her thumbs for a few moments before saying, 'I guess we just wait.'

The Prime Minister responded, 'I suppose so. By the way, do I bow, shake hands or what?'

'Don't do anything, other than stand up. He doesn't expect foreigners to prostrate themselves on the floor like the locals do. He's not keen on contact either, so don't offer your hand unless he does so first.'

In the ensuing minutes Jennifer sat in awe, absorbing the sights of gold ornaments and more works of art on the walls. She gestured to a bank of what looked like computer monitors and screens in a corner and said, 'Have you seen those?'

The Prime Minister nodded.

'Given this country is so low-tech, it makes me wonder exactly what need there is for such . . .' She ceased talking on realising someone had entered the room.

Jennifer rose from her chair and turned to see a very tall, handsome man of classic south east Asian features, dressed in black, striding purposefully towards her. It was Taksin, an immensely dominant figure at a shade over seven feet tall, with the broad, muscular frame of a champion athlete. As he came to a halt, towering over her she craned her neck upwards and said, 'Your Majesty, may I present Mr Anthony Shepherd, the Prime Minister of the United Kingdom.'

Despite Jennifer's advice, the Prime Minister nodded his head in respect. 'I can't thank you enough for granting me this audience, your majesty.'

'You are welcome,' responded Taksin coolly. He turned to Jennifer and asked, 'And you are?'

'Jennifer Collins, Your Majesty.'

Taksin stared down at Jennifer and gave her a quizzical look. 'Your face is familiar to me, is it not?'

'Quite possibly, your majesty. I grew up here. I have attended a few consular parties at which you were present.'

'But not for some years I think?'

'I was fourteen the last time I attended such an occasion, sir.'

Taksin continued to stare down at Jennifer. 'I have seen you in more recent occasions than that.'

'Erm, not that I remember, sir.'

Taksin's jaw dropped slightly. 'Of course,' he whispered, 'The girl on the horse.'

'I beg your pardon, sir?'

Taksin looked lost in thought for a moment. 'Sorry, I meant nothing.'

Jennifer looked perplexed.

Taksin snapped out of an apparent reverie. 'Sorry, of course, you must be the daughter of James Collins.'

Jennifer was startled. 'I didn't realise you knew my father, sir.'

'I meet every foreigner who seeks permission to live in my land.'

'Of course, sir.' For a few uncomfortable moments, Jennifer endured the intense stare from Taksin, feeling as though her very soul was being scrutinized.

At length, Taksin diverted his eyes to the Prime Minister and said,

'Please sit down. Would you care for refreshment?'

'Yes please,' the Prime Minister answered as he took his seat. 'A glass of cold water if I may, I'm not used to the humidity of the tropics.'

Taksin turned to Jennifer, 'And yourself?'

'Thank you, sir,' said Jennifer. 'Water will be fine.' She watched in fascination as Taksin removed a small gadget from his trouser pocket, pressed a button and spoke a few words. Of course, she thought, a communication device. It would explain how knowledge of their expected arrival had reached the immigration officers at the port so quickly.

Taksin sat down, turned to the Prime Minister and said, 'You arrive in an unconventional manner. What is it you seek?'

The Prime Minister crossed his arms. 'Well, your majesty, to be honest, I'm not sure how to start this conversation. I have to admit I've come on a very delicate mission.'

If the Prime Minister had expected a kindly response, one which may have helped to put him at ease, he was disappointed, for Taksin appeared to be a man not given to indulge in social pleasantries.

'Yes, sir,' the Prime Minister continued, as a bead of sweat broke out on his forehead. 'First of all, if I may be so bold, I would beg you make me a promise.'

Taksin frowned. 'You make demands of me?'

The Prime Minister appeared unnerved by Taksin's ice-cold glare. Several more beads of sweat broke out on his forehead. 'No, sir, not at all. I apologize for phrasing that rather undiplomatically. I should have expressed myself better.' He threw Jennifer a sideways look.

'Sir, your majesty,' said Jennifer. 'The Prime Minister and myself would like to talk to you for a while, if we may. What we want to discuss is of a particularly sensitive nature, and I know it may make you angry. Please believe me, your majesty, we have no wish to cause you any grief, but I think it is unavoidable. And we fully accept that you may punish us quite severely for what we are about to say. All we want is the chance to say our piece before you terminate this interview. Please, your majesty, all we are asking for is a full and frank discussion; it would be tragic if we failed to make our point before you wreak punishment upon us. That's all the Prime Minister wants, a promise to let him speak his mind.'

Taksin held Jennifer's gaze for a full ten seconds before turning to face the Prime Minister and replying tersely, 'Very well. Make your point.'

The Prime Minister sighed. 'Thank you, your majesty.' The arrival of a servant boy carrying a tray of glasses allowed the Prime Minister a few seconds to gather his thoughts as he waited for the boy to cross the room. Gratefully accepting a glass, he took a sip of cool water before continuing, 'First of all, I would like to thank you and your two compatriots, Prasert and Narai, for saving my life.'

Taksin blinked hard. 'I beg your pardon?'

'Five months ago, I was being held to ransom in my office by two very unpleasant thugs from another planet. One of your compatriots freed me from that situation; Narai I believe it must have been. I would like to thank you for staging that rescue mission. I would also like to offer thanks on behalf of the whole planet for freeing us from a most unpleasant fate.'

Taksin looked bewildered. 'I'm lost. Have I missed something?'

'I don't think so, your majesty,' replied the Prime Minister, as he reached for his briefcase on the floor. 'I have brought with me the results of some research Jennifer has been undertaking these last few months. She's compiled a catalogue of historical events in which you and your two compatriots have exposed yourselves as being so superior to us humans, especially with the display of technology beyond our comprehension, that our only conclusion is that you must have come from another planet.'

Taksin crossed his arms and scowled. 'Is this some sort of perverse joke?'

'Not at all, your majesty,' replied the Prime Minister, as he slid a thick file across the table top.

Taksin looked down at the file with an expression of revulsion. He gingerly turned the cover sheet and glanced at the first page. His eyebrows furrowed as he began to read. At length, Taksin said, 'This is outrageous. Why have you produced this . . . this file of contemptible rubbish?'

The Prime Minister gulped. 'I simply wish to demonstrate to you, your majesty, that we know who you really are. The evidence stacks up, so I'm hoping you will not deny it. There have been eye-witness accounts of mysterious goings-on, documented by sailors, businessmen and diplomats over several hundred years. Ships disappear in your seas, only to reappear thousands of miles away;

armies of thousands are unable to penetrate invisible force-fields protecting your borders; your country has never been invaded, despite numerous attempts, but you have no army, no visible defence system. Yet it's all explainable if you accept the fact that vastly superior technology is being utilised to protect you and this country. And that superior technology can only possibly have come from a civilization far more advanced than our own.'

Taksin gestured dismissively at Jennifer's report. 'And just exactly what do you intend to do with this file?'

'There is one other copy, being held under close security back in London. It will be released to the press if I fail to return from here safely.'

Taksin guffawed. 'Blackmail? You're planning to blackmail me with this trash?'

'I hope not to, your majesty. I do not care for the practice of blackmail.'

'I'm glad to hear it,' responded Taksin with a healthy dose of sarcasm. 'But why threaten me with it? It hardly inspires trust.'

'Needs must, is all I can say. I need to deploy every weapon at my disposal at the moment. I hope your knowledge of the existence of this report will help.'

'Hah! How do you reckon on that?'

'By being candid with me, your majesty. By not treating me as a lesser person just because I'm human. Your technology may be superior to our own, and you may know more about the universe than I could ever do, but I want to talk to you man to man, as an equal. That can only be achieved if we start with the truth. I am hoping for some mutual respect between us in order to progress this conversation.'

Taksin fell silent as he spent a few more moments flipping through the voluminous pages of the report in front of him. After a while he looked up and caught the Prime Minister's eye. 'You know if you gave this report to the press, I'd be so angry I'd blast your entire western world back to the dark ages, back to a world without electricity, without oil, without mechanical engines, with no means of communication beyond the horizon. I'd destroy your libraries, your computers, your schools, your governments. It would take me seconds to achieve that outcome, but a thousand years for your species to recover.'

The Prime Minister's face paled, but he recovered fast. 'But you won't, will you, your majesty, because you are too humane.'

Taksin gave a false smile, lent back on his chair and responded dryly, 'Don't bet on it.'

After a few tense moments, Taksin appeared to relax. 'Come on, what do you really want? I'm sure you haven't come here with the sole aim of antagonizing me.'

The Prime Minister took a deep breath. 'Narai lectured me quite harshly on the dangers awaiting us in space. I have a duty to protect not just my country but the whole planet as well. I have experienced at first hand just how ill-equipped we are to defend ourselves, and it troubles me deeply. If there is another invasion, I want to be able to fight back, to counter-attack with similar weapons and know-how. I can't allow the responsibility of this planet's defence to rest solely on the shoulders of the three of you. What if you're overwhelmed by sheer numbers next time? It doesn't make sense for the three of you to take on all-comers alone, unaided. What I want, your majesty, is your cooperation. Give us the spaceship that arrived five months ago, teach us how to fly it, teach us how to use your technology so that we can fight alongside you next time.'

Taksin spluttered. 'Are you mad? There's no way you humans could cope with the complexity of the equipment.'

The Prime Minister grimaced. 'I think you look down on us too harshly, your majesty. We are able to explore space ourselves now.'

'Yes, thank you, I'm well aware of that, you humans are littering the outer atmosphere with discarded machinery, it makes travelling close to this planet extraordinarily dangerous. And you use such antiquated technology. You're still using fossil fuel for powered flight for heaven's sake.'

'We just need a boost. A steer in the right direction.'

'You're not ready for it. And in any case, it would take years to train you.'

'Then give us those years, I beg you, your majesty.'

'Certainly not, I've got better things to do with my time. But even if I did, you'd turn the technology against your own kind. And don't say you wouldn't, it's the history of your species. Every time you invent something you find a way to use it to kill your neighbours more efficiently.'

The Prime Minister hung his head low. 'That's true, your majesty.

I can't deny it. But I didn't say this task would be without its difficulties.'

Taksin grunted. 'Difficulties? That's some understatement. Within seconds of mastering the use of my equipment you'd be blasting some enemy country to smithereens.'

'Then we must devise controls to prevent that.'

Taksin gasped. 'This cannot be. What you ask for is madness, sheer folly. It would be like giving guns to a tribe of primitives in the depths of a jungle. One swig of their favourite alcoholic brew and they'd all be dead. Every man on Earth harbours grudges against his neighbour, or has material ambitions that can only be satisfied by stealing from others. My technology would cause untold misery. There'd be endless wars; there'd be mass destruction on an unprecedented scale. There'd be millions killed, billions even. I will not have that on my conscience, I simply won't allow it. It . . .'

'Forgive me, your majesty,' the Prime Minister interrupted. 'But may I backtrack a bit, please? All I'm seeking is a joint venture operation in which we supply the men and you supply the equipment and teaching. It would be a limited venture, strictly limited to the military. I have no intention of letting your technology drift into the public domain. You will have full control over operations at all times. You will have full authority over every person operating on the ship. My men will obey you; they will not try to deceive you; they will not try to take control of the technology. My vision is for a ship controlled by you, but manned by my men. Any operation will be strictly limited to fighting invaders from outer space. Please, your majesty, you must realize that a force of three against an invading army is far too weak. You could easily be outnumbered in a battle.'

Taksin snarled, 'We can manage very well on our own, thank you.'

'But wouldn't it be easier to have a helping hand? What about those starfighters? There must have been at least five of them that came out of that mothership, as well as your own. Don't you think it makes sense, in a war, to have some of my men flying those spares? Five extra starfighters may make that vital difference, surely?'

Taksin fell silent as though assessing the Prime Minister's comments. After a few seconds he responded, 'I'm sorry, it just wouldn't work.'

'I beg to differ, your majesty.'

Taksin turned to face Jennifer. 'And you, Jennifer Collins, a child of this country, do you think this joint venture is a good idea?'

'Erm, yes, sir, actually, I do'

Taksin looked genuinely shocked. 'You do. Really?'

'Yes, sir. Really. I'm just a human being, a very frightened one. I don't have the benefit of your knowledge of the universe. What happened five months ago scared me senseless. The thought of it occurring again, and losing, is just too terrifying to contemplate. I have hopes for the future, hopes for a family. Those hopes are in doubt without security, without protection against the threat of invasion.'

Taksin looked at Jennifer in apparent dismay. 'Why are you here, Jennifer, why are you involved with this? You have family here. And I thought you'd found happiness here.'

Jennifer frowned, unsure what Taksin was getting at. 'I love this country, sir. I love it that my parents are here. I love the simplicity of life here. I love . . . well, I would love to live here. I'm here to defend my dreams.'

Taksin leaned forward on to the table, rubbed his temples. 'I have watched over this planet for more than three thousand years. I have been its protection from invasion. That is not going to change.'

'You say that, sir, but . . .'

Taksin slammed a fist on the table. 'Enough!' He stood up and strode through a nearby doorway that led out on to a balcony.

The Prime Minister sat in silence a moment until Jennifer caught his eye, indicated the balcony and nodded her head. The Prime Minister rose from his chair and followed in Taksin's footsteps. He found Taksin leaning over the balcony peering down at beautifully laid out gardens and a nearby open-air pool, surrounded by marble columns, where a dozen youths were playing in the water.

Without looking at the Prime Minister, Taksin said, 'If I'd known today would work out like this, I'd have blown your ship out of the water. Much less hassle in the long run.'

'I'm sorry to cause you such grief.'

'No, you're not.'

'That's true.'

Taksin sighed. 'You ask the impossible of me. This journey you wish to take, you have no idea where it goes. I do.'

'I see it as part of man's development. It will come to us eventually, in time. This way, it just comes a little earlier. I understand your concern, your majesty, it must be similar to a father worried about his children growing up, not wanting them to try out dangerous things like driving a car.'

Taksin shook his head. 'If it were only that simple.'

'I sense I have overstayed my welcome, your majesty. We will go now. '

Taksin nodded his head.

'With your permission,' the Prime Minister continued. 'I would like to stay here for a couple of days. Jennifer has recommended I visit the British Club, meet the Consular, maybe go horse riding through the woods down to the beach. I'd also like to say hello to Jennifer's father; we were at school together.'

'Really? That's a coincidence.'

'Not really. Jennifer is academically well qualified in social anthropology. She used her father's connection to get to see me in the first place, a few months ago, to tell me she could read the symbols on the spacecraft.'

'I see.' Taksin gave a weak smile. 'Yes, of course. This country had no alphabet when I arrived, it seemed easiest to adopt my own. And this joint venture you're after, this is her doing too, then?'

'No, sir, it's my idea, but she guides me, tempers my thoughts. She's very good at human relations, how we react and relate to each other.'

Taksin nodded.

'May I return here the day after tomorrow?'

'To argue more?'

'No, your majesty. To say farewell, although I would ask you kindly to think about my proposition in the meantime.'

'I will, I'm sure. I doubt my head will stop spinning for the next week.'

'Just one last thing before I go. Do you and your compatriots operate democratically?'

Taksin looked puzzled. 'In what way?'

'I'd like to ask the other two for their views on this matter. Will they concur with you? Is it worth me visiting them? What if they both said yes?'

'I'll ask them, save you a journey. Narai's not easy to reach, nor is he easy to talk to. But I'm afraid they'll both say the same as me.'

'Well, if you don't object to asking them. I'd really like to canvass their support.'

'I'll talk to them once you've gone, but I'm sure their opinion will be the same as mine. I'll let you know their thoughts on your return.'

The Prime Minister pointed to the boys playing below. 'They look as they're having fun. Are they yours?'

'Mine? You mean am I the father?'

'I . . . erm . . . I don't mean to be rude, your majesty, but . . . '

'But, Prime Minister?' Taksin bristled. 'You're wondering if an alien can breed with humans?'

The Prime Minister's face flushed. 'No, your majesty, I wouldn't have put it so indelicately. The problem is, there are so many personal questions I'd like to ask you, but, well, I'm worried they may cause a degree of bad feeling.'

Taksin took a moment to respond, as though he was counting to ten. 'You said earlier you'd prefer to be candid with me. I would like our . . . relationship . . . no matter how short, to continue on those terms. However, that's just between the two of us. For others, not of your status, I expect a certain respectful distance to be maintained. I would not expect lesser mortals to pose questions that may be considered impertinent.'

The Prime Minister nodded. 'Thank you, your majesty.'

'As to your question, no, they are not my children. They're novice monks from the temple next door, they have access out here to the pool and gardens. It gives them some light relief from their studying. And it's always heart-warming to see youth at play.'

The Prime Minister reached into his jacket and took out his wallet. He flipped it open, removed a photograph of three smiling girls and held it up for Taksin to see. 'My children, your majesty.'

'Very cute. What are their names?'

'Jane, Jasmine and Justine.'

'You're a lucky man.'

'Yes I am. I just have one problem, your majesty. I've been suffering sleepless nights recently. I wake up in a cold sweat, dreaming that we've been invaded again, that the whole planet has been taken over by hideous creatures that enslave us and use us to satisfy their whims. In my dream, I find I have to shoot my daughters to stop the misery. Before shooting my wife and myself, that is. Tell me, your majesty, how am I to convince my girls that they are safe in their beds at night? That I can protect them? What about those boys down there playing so carefree? Who will protect them if we are invaded again and you lose the war? Will those boys be used too?'

Taksin's mouth dropped as if he'd been kicked in the guts. 'That comment, Prime Minister, was unbecoming of you.'

'Yes. Yes, it was. I apologize for it profusely, although it was said in much sincerity.'

Taksin sighed. 'I'm beginning to regret risking my neck to save you lot.'

'No you don't, your majesty. There's a compassionate, caring, humanitarian side to you. I think you want what's best for this planet, presumably because you're a refugee from your own world and you know what suffering entails. I'll take my leave now, if I may, your majesty, but please think on it. I'm sure you've got what it takes to put my plan into action, to overcome the prejudice you're bound to face, and to ultimately build a fighting force that will protect this planet from future invasion.'

'I'll see you the day after tomorrow, Prime Minister,' said Taksin with a warm smile. 'But I really don't think my position will have changed one jot. I'll get someone to escort you out,' he said, and depressed a button on his ever-present communicator. 'And by the way, you should check your genetic history before calling me an alien.'

With eyes agog and jaw dropped, the Prime Minister turned to leave, only to find Jennifer standing in the doorway, a similar look of astonishment on her own face.

Chapter Twenty-Three

The girl on the horse

'I need a word with Surachai, sir. Do you mind?'

'Not at all. Go right on.'

Jennifer dug her heels into her horse's side, overtook the Prime Minister's horse and trotted off to join Surachai who was some way ahead.

The Prime Minister turned to Judith Collins whose horse was alongside his own and asked, 'Are they an item?'

'I do hope so,' replied Judith Collins. 'She's been keen on him for a year now, but doesn't get the opportunity to see him very often. It hurts her deeply to leave him here and go off back to England. So, given that she's working over there rather than here, I'm really not sure where they stand at the moment.'

'You approve of him?'

'Oh yes, very much so. He's a dish, isn't he? He's often seen riding, or mucking out the horses, with his shirt off. He gets all us middle-aged women in quite a flutter.'

'I wasn't really thinking of his physical attributes.'

Judith Collins caught the Prime Minister's eye. 'I know you weren't, Tony. I was being light about it. James and I are keen to be grandparents. The more babies she has, the happier we'll be. But life's not easy for her at the moment. She says she wants a worthwhile career as well as having kids. Unfortunately, although her heart might be here in this country, there's no chance of getting any meaningful job here.'

'Couldn't she take Surachai to England?'

Judith Collins caught the Prime Minister's eye again. 'And what would he do? He speaks about ten words of broken English, possesses no British school qualifications, has no friends there. She would be out at work all day; he'd be left at home with nothing to do. That's a recipe for disaster. I'm sure he'd make a great father and be helpful around the house, but he'd be bored senseless, and he'd feel emasculated. I don't think their relationship would survive if they tried it that way around.'

The Prime Minister steered his horse around a low hanging branch before responding, 'Life can be tough, can't it?'

'It certainly can. I can feel her desperation at times. As her mother. That pains me deeply.'

They fell silent for a moment, content to enjoy the passing scenery as the horses made their way through the woods towards Dongtan Beach.

Judith Collins asked, 'How long will you be staying?'

'I'm really not sure, to be honest,' replied the Prime Minister. 'Yesterday afternoon and today have been wonderful in your company, Judith. I'd love to stay longer, but I have a lot of commitments, as you can imagine. I think I should be off in the morning.'

'And Jennifer? Will you be taking her back with you?'

'That, I really can't say. She's mentioned she hopes to have a holiday here, since she's come all this way.'

'Tony, please tell me something. Why are you both here?'

The Prime Minister grimaced. 'You've been very kind to me Judith, making me welcome at your house, feeding me, James letting me borrow these clothes from his wardrobe, inviting me to stay overnight. I'd love to be able to give you an honest answer, but that won't be possible. Please don't think ill of me for that.'

Judith Collins seemed to reflect on the matter at some length. 'When she was here last, about four months ago, she spent a lot of time researching material in the British Club's archives, then twisted James' arm to write a letter of introduction to you. Whatever she felt necessary to talk to you about, presumably she got her message across?'

The Prime Minister nodded. 'She did, yes.'

'I see. And that's why you're here now, why there's a great big warship sitting out there in the middle of the river mouth?'

The Prime Minister nodded again. 'I can't deny it.'

'You know we're not stupid out here. It may be hot, but our brains aren't addled. We might live as though we're stuck in a time-warp, pretending we're still in the heyday of the British Empire, but we do know something about what's going on in the world. We also know a lot more about this country than we let on. Some things are just never discussed.'

'I see.'

'I hope so, Tony. What I'm trying to say is that we love this country, all of us living out here, we would not want it to change in any way. We are all fiercely loyal to this country. I trust you are not planning to upset things.'

The Prime Minister's rode a few paces in silence, gathering his thoughts. 'What Jennifer came to see me about, she meant well by it. In doing so, she has managed to control the situation, managed to prevent the development of what might otherwise have been an ugly scenario. She has worked hard to make sure that the situation is dealt with whilst, as you put it, nothing gets upset. Your daughter is very much fighting on the side of this country.'

'Thank you for that, Tony. Now, enough of such seriousness, we're nearly at the beach. I'm sorry, but I think you'll have to put up with my company for the rest of this ride. I expect my daughter will be lost to us for the afternoon.'

'That's fine by me, Judith. She deserves a break. And I'm more than happy to be in your company. This is the most beautiful day I've had in years.'

As the path opened up to a sandy beach, two horses could be seen with their heads in a water trough in a shady corral alongside a wooden hut. 'We'll dismount here, Tony. Give the horses a break. This is our communal beach hut, well stocked with deckchairs and parasols if you wish to relax. However, I suggest we just stay a few minutes, walk to the water's edge and then go back to my house for a cup of tea. I think it would be far more romantic for those two if we left them alone. I wouldn't want them to feel that they're obligated to us in any way.'

The Prime Minister pointed at the shoreline ahead where Jennifer was strolling hand in hand with Surachai. 'Look at them. Do you really think we'll feature in their thoughts this afternoon?'

Judith Collins laughed. 'You're quite right, Tony. I'd almost forgotten what it's like to be young and so in love.'

Not for the first time, Jennifer was being closely observed as she strolled along the beach hand in hand with Surachai, as she stopped to look into his eyes, to hug, to kiss. Taksin stood in silence, fixated by the three-dimensional life-size image of the scene unfolding on the beach, listening to Jennifer explain how she had to go away, again, to a faraway land, that she would miss him dearly, that a small part of her heart would always have his name engraved on it. It was a touching scene, one that he had no right to overhear, one in which he felt an intruder. As he watched Jennifer give Surachai a final farewell kiss, he pressed a button on his ever-present communicator gripped tightly in his hand, and looked longingly at a frozen image of the couple in a desperate embrace.

Chapter Twenty-Four

Game on

'So, there was young Shepherd, standing butt naked, staring out the window into matron's room across the yard when I came in to his room to tell him it was time for lights out. Well, I'll leave the rest of the scene to your imagination, but for such disrespectful behaviour towards a member of staff I gave him the choice of detention or a run around the sports field. Maybe I should have given him a third option of a cold shower.'

News of the Prime Minister's impromptu visit to the enclave had spread quickly amongst its residents. Jennifer's plan for a quiet evening meal at the British Club with just the Prime Minister, her parents and her brothers along with the Consular and his wife, had soon dissolved into social disaster as the bar rapidly filled with nosy people determined to eavesdrop on their conversation. Unfortunately, the attention of such a large crowd, and the presence of an esteemed guest, had gone to her father's head. So, as James Collins laughed loudly at a brash memory of his days as a prep school prefect, Jennifer was left to suffer the righteous indignation of several onlookers. She elbowed her father and said, 'For goodness sake, Daddy. Must you be so crude?'

'What?' replied James Collins, picking up his beer glass and downing more than half its contents in three consecutive gulps.

The Prime Minister laid a calming hand on Jennifer's arm. 'Don't worry about it,' he said. 'I've had worse said about me. But in my defence, may I just clarify a couple of things. Firstly, I was only eleven years old at the time. Secondly, matron that term was a rather young and pretty Norwegian girl, not the stereotype middle-aged battle-axe.'

'That's as maybe, sir. But I think my father has had a drop too much beer tonight. I apologise profusely on his behalf. He'll feel sorry himself in the morning when he's sobered up, I'm sure.'

'Really, don't worry about it. It's a small price to pay for having such a wonderful day. I can't thank you enough for the trip down to the beach. It really was beautiful. And that steak and kidney pie was one of the tastiest I've ever had.'

'I'll let the staff know. They always excel with the food here; it all comes fresh from the local farm we have . . .'

'Good God,' James Collins exclaimed, slamming his beer glass down on the table and standing up promptly along with everyone else who had been seated.

Until that moment, the room had been abuzz with chatter. But Jennifer suddenly realised a silence had descended. She looked around sharply and saw the large frame of Taksin striding across the room towards them.

'I do apologize for disturbing your party,' said Taksin. 'But I was hoping to have a private word with the Prime Minister.'

'Of course, your majesty,' replied the Prime Minister.

'And Jennifer too, please.'

'Yes, your majesty,' replied Jennifer. She turned to a man standing a couple of places to one side and said, 'May we use your room, Bob?'

'Certainly,' replied Robert Harbolt. He put his hand in his jacket pocket and pulled out a set of keys. 'The smaller key is for the drinks cabinet. Please help yourself; the supplies are all on a UK government expense account.'

Grateful for the chance to escape, Jennifer left the bar, accompanied by Taksin and the Prime Minister, stepped into the reception hall and went up the stairs to the Consular's room. She headed straight for the drinks cabinet, unlocked it and said, 'May I offer you a drink, your majesty? A brandy perhaps?' She picked up a bottle and held it out for Taksin to see. 'This bottle looks a pretty good vintage.'

'Yes, that would be most welcome. And I'm sorry for the intrusion. I trust I haven't spoiled your evening meal?'

The Prime Minister shook his head. 'Not at all, your majesty. We finished eating a while ago. We were just chatting idly.'

'Good.' Taksin took a seat in a black leather armchair and waited for his glass of brandy. He took a large sip, leaned back and said to Jennifer, 'This joint venture you mentioned yesterday, may I ask what your role in it would be? If it came about, that is.'

Jennifer was slightly bewildered. She took a seat and replied, 'Um, well, actually, that hasn't been discussed. I'm not even sure there would be a role available for me to take up.'

'Would you like a role, if it were to go ahead?'

'Um, I'm not sure, sir. It would depend what it involved. I had hoped to stay here for a few weeks' holiday, with your permission of course, rather than heading back to England straight away.'

'Am I right in thinking you wish to stay here? Permanently, that is, rather than just a holiday?'

'Yes, sir. Absolutely,' responded Jennifer with unequivocal conviction. 'Nothing would give me greater pleasure. However, there's no job for me here and I couldn't possibly expect my father to pay for my life. I need a well-paid job. Unfortunately, that's more likely to be in England than here.'

'I see.' Taksin fell silent and stared into the contents of his brandy glass.

The uncomfortable silence prompted the Prime Minister to ask, 'Have you by any chance talked to your compatriots?'

Taksin looked up. 'I have indeed.'

A look of excitement momentarily flickered across the Prime Minister's face. 'Oh yes?'

'To my complete disbelief, Prasert was all for it. One hundred percent. No doubts whatsoever in his mind. I suppose that's only to be expected, young people are so impetuous, aren't they?'

The Prime Minister, brandy glass to his mouth, spluttered. 'Young? You have a funny definition of young, sir. He must be several thousand years old.'

Taksin nodded in acknowledgement. 'Well, young compared to his father and me.'

'His father?'

'Narai.'

'Narai is Prasert's father? I didn't know that.'

'There's no way you would. You couldn't get such diametrically opposed characters.'

'May I ask what Narai said?'

'Narai is sitting on the fence. He's an old soldier. He says having trained men to fly the spare starfighters makes strategic sense, but he's as concerned as I am when it comes to the risk of exposing your species to such a jump in technology.'

'And yourself, your majesty. Are you still dead against it?'

'I am, yes.'

'That's a draw, then, is it? One and a half votes each way. I don't suppose you could find it in your heart to give a little, say five percentage points, to tip the voting in our favour?'

Taksin grunted. 'Certainly not.'

'Oh.' Disappointment showed on the Prime Minister's face. 'I would hope that, in time, your estimation of us improves somewhat.'

Taksin frowned. 'That remains to be seen.' He took another sip of brandy and said, 'When were you hoping to start this preposterous venture?'

The Prime Minister reacted as though his heart had skipped a beat. 'As soon as possible, sir.'

'Immediately?'

'That would be up to you, sir.'

'Very well.' Taksin took another large gulp of brandy. 'Before we go any further, I have one important issue to discuss.'

The Prime Minister looked expectantly. 'Yes?'

But Taksin turned away from the Prime Minister and focused his attention on Jennifer. 'A joint venture such as the one under discussion involves a huge amount of planning, meetings, negotiation, cajoling, healing rifts between parties, pandering to bruised egos, that sort of thing, and it needs a key person at the centre to make it all happen. I really don't have the stomach for that, far too much politics for my liking. Same goes for Narai, he's too bad-tempered for that sort of thing. Prasert is a bit too, well, he was just a boy when we left, he's never had a proper job, never had to get a grip with responsibilities, I don't think he'd be the right candidate. So, Jennifer, I would like you to undertake that job. You are one of the few people who have a foot in both camps as it were. You understand the workings of this country and, by implication, of what I stand for and what my concerns are with the human race. You also understand the workings of the Western World and of the peculiarities of man. I want you to be my liaison officer. I want you in attendance at every meeting I have with the Prime Minister and the military chiefs who will, I'm sure, want to run the show by themselves. Don't get me wrong, Jennifer, I don't want you to spy for me. I want you there as yourself, in your own right and with your own mind, unencumbered by any concern over allegiance. I will listen to what you have to say, I won't necessarily agree with you, but the fact that the words are spoken by you, a child of this country, will make all the difference to me. At times, you may be put upon by people who want to pursue their own agenda and think you have my ear, and I trust in those circumstances you will tell me the truth as you see it rather than telling me what you may think I want to hear. I don't wish this to sound sad, Jennifer, but all the humans I encounter want something from me. I trust few humans and certainly none I would confide in. I can't think of anyone else who would come remotely close to being up for the job.'

Jennifer rubbed the end of her nose. 'Thank you, sir,' she responded. 'But I'm not sure if I'm free to make such a commitment. Technically, I'm still under contract working for the Prime Minister.'

Taksin continued to focus his attention on Jennifer. 'If I understand correctly, Jennifer, your assignment was to identify and locate myself, Narai and Prasert. I don't mean to be unkind, but if this venture goes ahead, I think you'll find your position with the Prime Minister is redundant. Furthermore, I can't imagine any military chief freely offering you a seat next to them at a table. They would feel no need for your input.'

Jennifer blanched. 'I hadn't thought ahead that far.'

'And of course, I don't expect you to take on this job for free. Since we shall be dealing with the military, you will need military authority yourself and I propose conveying upon you the rank of a naval Commander, at Prasert's suggestion. He said if that rank was good enough for Mr Bond it should be good enough for you. I'm not sure who Mr Bond is, or what Prasert meant by that remark, but he wanted me to convey it to you, said you'd appreciate it. I trust he wasn't being flippant?'

Jennifer covered her mouth as she sniggered.

Taksin frowned. 'It appears he was. I'm sorry about that, Jennifer. But I'm not surprised, my nephew has never taken anything serious. He enjoys winding me up, calls I'm an old fogey.'

'Prasert is your nephew?'

'He is, yes. By marriage that is. My wife was the younger sister of Narai's wife.'

Jennifer noted the use of the past tense, said, 'Oh.'

'Anyway, I shall pay a salary commensurate with what that position would command in England, but the employment contract will be established in this country so earnings will be paid into your bank account here without the imposition of any tax. You will be granted permanent residence in this country, in your own name, along with a passport and a house of your own choosing. And you'll have a generous expense account to cover whatever expenditure you incur in discharging your duties.'

Jennifer turned to the Prime Minister. 'Sir?'

The Prime Minister shrugged and said, 'That sounded like a job offer no one in their right mind would refuse.'

Jennifer, dumbfounded, turned to Taksin and said, 'Thank you, your majesty, I accept.'

Taksin nodded. 'Good. Then we have a deal, Prime Minister.'

The Prime Minister's body noticeably relaxed. 'Thank you, your majesty.'

'No doubt you have some questions?'

'Indeed yes. May I ask how many craft there are, sir, within the mothership? And what level of strength the ship actually is?'

'The mothership, as you call it, is what I suppose you may call an intergalactic battleship. It's in good condition with a very good weapons system. It's probably only ten thousand years old. That's relatively new,' responded Taksin on seeing the Prime Minister's face drop, 'you must bear in mind it would have taken at least four thousand years to get here. It was state of the art last time I was on home ground. Ships can be hundreds of thousands of years old. They're built of sturdy materials.'

'And those smaller jets? What we call starfighters, may I ask how many of those there are on board?'

Taksin grunted. 'One hundred and fifty. Mind you, a few of them are in a bad state and unusable except for spare parts. I guess at least a hundred are useable.'

The Prime Minister's eyes lit up. 'That many? Dear god, I couldn't have hoped for that much. But why weren't they all put to use against us? We only observed a handful.'

'The mothership was short staffed. There were only twenty-five personnel on board. They'd come under heavy fighting before fleeing here, taken a battering and I suppose they didn't want to expose themselves too much.'

'How many crew would you normally expect?'

Taksin rubbed his chin. 'That depends on the mission. The mothership can accommodate a thousand starfighters and perhaps a hundred thousand military personnel. Over and above that, the crew would normally contain a couple of hundred in technical support and maintenance. Catering and cleaning staff depend on the size of the military presence. The mothership can certainly house those numbers comfortably, there are easily that many cabins.'

The Prime Minister shook his head in wonderment. 'A hundred thousand personnel. That's extraordinary, we had no idea it had such capacity.'

Taksin took another sip of brandy and swirled the remnants in his glass for a while as he collected his thoughts. 'In addition, there must be ten thousand spacesuits on board. Each is capable of self-propulsion, capable of several days' travel. You'd die of thirst before the fuel reserves ran out. The military and scientists are the main users of the suits, exploring new planets, clearing enemy on the ground, that sort of thing.'

'Any other craft?'

'Well, there are a few odds and sods, a few troop buses, provision carriers, mining equipment. And there are four executive jets. They're smaller than the starfighters, but much more practical for flying around within the confines of a planet's atmosphere. I guess you should get your own personal one. It will certainly make your life more convenient travelling around fast and easily.'

'Thank you, sir.' The Prime Minister developed a faraway look in his eyes, as though he was seeing himself whizzing around the world in his own private spacecraft.

'You too, Jennifer. You'll need transport to and from your new home. And let me stress I do not expect you to work longer than a normal nine to five job, with weekends off, national holidays and six weeks' annual holiday allowance. And I imagine you'll be back here frequently, if for no other reason than engaging in more horse-riding lessons.'

Jennifer gave a little gasp.

'You will have to monitor your own hours, Jennifer, and I won't impose on your free time. If a meeting is required, and you're otherwise engaged, like having a day at home, then the meeting will have to wait. Same goes for me. You would be wise to appreciate that point, Prime Minister.'

The Prime Minister nodded.

'Good communications will be essential, Jennifer. I'll provide you with something better than the mobile telephone you no doubt use at present, so that you can contact me, Narai and Prasert direct.' Taksin looked up at a clock on the wall. 'Anyway, it's ten o'clock now, you must be tired, Prime Minister. Do you intend to stay here the night again, or would you like to sleep in your own bed? If we left now, we could land right outside Downing Street within thirty minutes. You could be tucked up in bed before eleven.'

The Prime Minister's face lit up. 'Are you serious?'

'I certainly am.'

'But the exposure? Radar? People seeing us?'

Taksin chuckled. 'Well, they're going to have to get used to that pretty soon, aren't they?'

'Your majesty, a flight home tonight would make me extraordinarily happy.'

'Right, let's go then. Better say farewell to your party first. Jennifer, I assume you'll want to return as well? No doubt you'll have some domestic matters to sort out. If you need to come back during the next few weeks, to bring your clothes and furniture back here, Prasert will be only too willing to give you a lift. He's been itching to get into the air for years; we've held him back somewhat since radar was invented.'

'Yes, sir. If you'll excuse me, I'll go and say goodbye to my family.'

'You'll find me out on the road.'

Five minutes later, Jennifer and the Prime Minister left the building and walked down to the bottom of the British Club's drive where they came across a starfighter silently hovering above the road. They stepped inside with a mixture of excitement and nervousness, and the Prime Minister took a sharp intake of breath as Taksin pressed a button and the door closed behind them. To each side of a central passageway lay two rows of spacious seats, three deep, with a table and monitor in front of each seat, whilst at the front a stairwell rose upwards.

'It seats twelve comfortably, as you can see. There's a kitchen and food storage compartments at the back. Upstairs, there are bed pods, bathrooms, cupboards full of spacesuits and tools, along with a decompression cubicle. Do you want a quick tour?'

Jennifer and the Prime Minister replied simultaneously, 'Yes, please.'

After a three-minute guided tour, Taksin opened the door to a spacious cockpit and gestured to two seats, each to the side of a central commanding seat. 'My seat's in the middle, help yourself to the others.'

As the Prime Minister settled into a seat he said, 'This is remarkably comfortable, sir. From my own experience, I can say our own cockpits are rather restrictive.'

'These starfighters are sometimes flown for months on end,' replied Taksin. 'Not just for a few hours like your antiquated jet-fighters. Comfort is a high requirement. Now then, I just need to plot a route. I plan to head up into the outer atmosphere, under a veil so my starting position can't be traced, down towards the southern ice cap, curve around the Pacific side of South America, across Panama and then straight for London. We'll be flying at about fifty thousand miles an hour and I'm curious to know what your radar technicians will make of it. I assume the whole world is more aware of the possibility of an attack these days. Do you think I'd better let them know we're coming?'

The Prime Minister seemed to reflect on the issue for a moment and said, 'Actually, it would be an interesting exercise to see precisely what they would do.'

'What's the procedure in England?' asked Taksin. 'If a radar operative does spot us, presumably he'll send word up the chain of command for someone to make a decision on any action to be taken. Who would make that decision? Yourself?'

'That's the way it should work, yes. If they can contact me, that is. Not many people know where I am at the moment.'

Taksin grunted. 'Let's say they could communicate with you. Do you reckon the information would filter through within thirty minutes? Personally, I reckon with the antiquated copper wiring communication systems you use it will take them several hours, if not days.'

The Prime Minister bristled. 'Really? You'll wager a bet on this, sir?'

Taksin chortled. 'Indeed, I will. It will prove my point about how backward you lot are. A bet, then. What would be appropriate in the circumstances?'

The Prime Minister turned to Jennifer. 'What do you reckon?'

Jennifer tutted. 'Men! Honestly, I have no idea. A beer perhaps?'

Taksin stuck his hand out to shake on the deal. 'A beer it is, then. The challenge is on.'

Jennifer shook her head in dismay. 'Boys will be boys,' she muttered.

Taksin threw Jennifer a quick smile, twiddled a few buttons and an image of Downing Street appeared on screen 'Now then, let's just lock in the coordinates. I suppose we'd better land in the park, your back garden looks a trifle small.' A few seconds later, the image on screen changed to the hallway of number 10.

The Prime Minister looked aghast. 'Good god, is this live?'

'Of course.'

'But . . . have you bugged my office?'

'No, not at all,' said Taksin impassively. 'The image is being beamed by a sensor I've just flown into the building. We can see and hear what's going on in there, but I doubt you've got the technology to trace the bug's presence.'

'A real fly on the wall,' responded the Prime Minister as a deep frown appeared on his forehead. 'Pretty spectacular drone technology, I must say. However, I have to say I'm a little concerned about the security issues at stake here.'

Taksin shrugged. 'I don't use it to spy. Not in the sense you use the word. I have no desire to watch and listen to your every word, I can assure you I'm not interested in petty politics. But in moments like this, it can be fun, I have to admit.'

The Prime Minister caught the smirk on Taksin's face. 'This is quite upsetting news, your majesty. I trust you won't use your technology inappropriately in our newly founded venture.'

'Perish the thought,' replied Taksin, straight faced. 'By the way, I'd rather you didn't call me "your majesty" in front of other people. I assume we'll be setting up something like a starship command committee, made up of the three of us and your military leaders, in which case I should like to be referred to as Admiral Taksin. Same for the others, General Narai and Admiral Prasert.'

'As you wish, Admiral.' The Prime Minister reflected for a

moment. 'Yes, that fits nicely.'

'Now then,' said Taksin, pointing to the screen. 'Who's in charge?'

'On the right, there. Colonel Travis.'

'Right, let's contact him.' Taksin pressed a button on a panel to his left. A telephone rang near to Colonel Travis. 'Tell him you'll be arriving in exactly thirty minutes. Don't tell him how you're arriving, or the bet's off.'

The Prime Minister rose to the challenge as he saw Colonel Travis pick up the phone.

'Travis? It's Tony. I've changed my plans; I shall be returning in precisely thirty minutes. Please maintain contact, I may need to discuss a few things. I suggest you put on your headset. I'll be speaking to you soon.'

'Yes, sir.'

'Right, here we go, then.' Taksin pressed the cloaking button, pushed forward on a lever, and the starfighter accelerated upwards into the night air. Seconds later it was streaming towards the heavens at several thousand miles per hour.

The Prime Minister's jaw dropped. 'Dear god, Admiral. This is unbelievable. The journey is so smooth, but how come there's no g-force effect?'

'It's the gravity-equalisation system. It keeps the gravitational force inside the craft at a constant level.'

'How fast can this starfighter go?'

'Half a million miles an hour easily, though I'd only want to do that in open space. It's far too hazardous near a planet, what with satellites and space stations floating around. We could certainly get to the moon well within an hour. I'll take it slowly through the outer atmosphere. Don't want to bump into any of the rubbish you've left lying around.'

As soon as Taksin reached the outer atmosphere he released the cloaking button. 'We can be spotted on radar now. I'll follow a slightly erratic pattern in terms of speed and direction. I don't want anyone to think we're just a meteor. Two days from now you may hear about it from your Colonel Travis.'

The Prime Minister smiled, but shook his head.

Within seconds of de-cloaking. NASA went into a panic, the word "incoming" being screamed by dozens of operators sitting in front of monitors all around the world. As the starfighter was tracked, alarms were raised as it headed towards North America followed by a sigh of relief as its course veered off across the North Atlantic. With a new trajectory determined, it was only minutes before NASA relayed the information to 10 Downing Street.

On Taksin's screen, they watched keenly as a door behind Colonel Travis was flung open and a frantic messenger relayed the news to him.

'I'm impressed,' said Taksin as he looked up from the monitor. 'But what will your Colonel Travis do now? He doesn't look too sure of himself.'

'May I speak with him again?'

'Of course, just press this blue button. Be careful what you say though,' Taksin grinned, 'I won't have you cheating.'

The Prime Minister put on an indignant look. 'I am an Englishman, sir. I do not cheat, especially not when such a serious bet is at stake. I just want to reconfirm our arrival time.' The Prime Minister depressed the blue button and watched Colonel Travis press a button on his earpiece. 'Travis, I shall be arriving in twelve minutes and thirty seconds. Do you read me?'

'Yes sir . . . but,' Colonel Travis picked up a scrap of paper he'd just been writing on. 'I'm assuming you're on an aircraft, sir. May I ask which one you're on, sir?'

'Never mind that, Travis, just clear an area in St James's Park for me to land, will you?'

'Of course, sir.' Colonel Travis rose from his chair and walked out of the office.

'Time's getting tight,' said Taksin. 'You're going to lose the bet.'

'I'm not beaten yet, Admiral. I know Colonel Travis, he's pretty astute.'

Jennifer tutted for the umpteenth time of the flight. 'Honestly, it's like being back in the school playground.'

'This is serious stuff, Jennifer,' said Taksin as he fiddled with a dial. The face of Colonel Travis reappeared on the screen as he made his way to the park, barking orders at people he met on his way.

'Seven minutes left, Prime Minister, care to admit defeat yet?'

'Certainly not,' replied the Prime Minister, and depressed the blue button again. 'Travis? I shall be there in exactly six minutes and fifty seconds. I hope there's a warm welcome party waiting for me. Have you told Beth I'll be home soon? I'm tired and want to go straight to bed.'

'Yes, sir, your wife knows you'll be here soon. Sir, can I ask you something?'

'Certainly, Travis.'

'Are you able to communicate with the pilot of your craft?'

'Of course I can. I'm sitting next to him. He can hear you, same as me.'

'May I speak direct to your pilot, sir?'

'Of course.'

'Mr Pilot, sir. If you're the gentleman I spoke to in this same park in February, then I welcome you back.'

Taksin grimaced. 'That wasn't me, Colonel Travis. But a close enough guess, I suppose.'

'Very well, sir. Thank you for giving our Prime Minister a lift home. However, your speed is worrying us, sir. Would you mind slowing down to below the speed of sound whilst still over the sea? We don't want your sonic boom to break all the windows in London.'

Taksin groaned. 'I hear you Colonel Travis. Just one problem though, you've cost me a beer and I don't possess any English money.'

'Sorry about that, sir,' replied Colonel Travis with a noticeable sense of relief in his voice. 'I'd be more than happy to make good your loss.'

'I'll hold you to that, Colonel. You really don't know how much that beer has cost me.'

'I can guess, sir. Our Prime Minister always drives a hard bargain.'

'He does indeed. Speed down to five hundred miles an hour. We'll be a bit late because of it, say ten minutes from now.'

'Thank you, sir.'

Eleven minutes later Taksin landed the starfighter in the park to the obvious panic of several hundred onlookers who had hoped they'd seen the last of that particular type of craft. To their astonishment, Colonel Travis ran towards the jet accompanied by several guards to form a welcoming party. To the onlookers' relief, the Prime Minister appeared and waved to the crowd.

'Take this, Jennifer,' said Taksin, handing over an object similar to the communications device she'd seen him use in the palace. 'You can read the numbers, I assume?'

Jennifer flipped open the communicator, looked at the digits displayed and smiled. 'Of course I can, sir.'

'Good. Press 1 to contact me, 2 for Narai and 3 for Prasert. Press the red button to cancel or end the call.'

'I'll call you the day after tomorrow, Admiral, is that okay?'

'That's fine.' With that, Taksin closed the door and the starfighter departed swiftly straight up into the air.

Colonel Travis stepped forward to greet the Prime Minister and said, 'Are you alright, sir? I was concerned you may have been abducted.'

'Of course I'm alright, Colonel,' responded the Prime Minister jovially. 'And that was not an abduction. Quite the opposite. More of an ambush, really.'

'Then . . .?'

'Sorry Colonel, but I'm really tired. I know it's light here, but it's the middle of the night as far as my body clock is concerned. I'm going straight to bed. Can you contact Captain Mandrake aboard HMS Portland and tell him I won't be returning to the ship and that he's to leave without me? Ask him to sail for Singapore and catch an airplane back here fast; I have a new mission for him.' He turned to Jennifer and said, 'I can't thank you enough for the last few days work, Jennifer. I'll catch up with you tomorrow, late morning perhaps.'

'Bye, sir.'

Colonel Travis looked alarmed. 'But the press, sir. They'll want some sort of comment from you about your . . . erm . . . mode of arrival.'

'Let them speculate,' said the Prime Minister as he strode off.

Colonel Travis turned to Jennifer. 'Dr Collins?'

'As the man said, let them speculate.' And with nothing on her mind except sleep, she walked off to her Whitehall apartment with a contented look on her face.

Chapter Twenty-Five

Unease

Jennifer had never felt at ease in General Wilson's company. Today was no different as she sat in a Downing Street office, looking across the table at him sitting there with a grim look set hard on his face, his arms crossed, scowling as he listened to the Prime Minister go over the plan for what she reckoned must have been at least the third time in the last half an hour.

'I still have grave doubts, sir,' said General Wilson. 'We really don't know what we're letting ourselves in for. We don't know where this will lead. It could be our downfall.'

Jennifer turned to face the Prime Minister. He looked agitated. Highly agitated. Not a good state to be in, she thought, for the meeting with Taksin which was scheduled to start in the next few minutes.

'Bob, look,' the Prime Minister appealed. 'We've gone over this already. We have no choice. We need their technology and their weapons. We can't simply take it away from them; they would retaliate ruthlessly. We do this my way, peacefully, with respect and with as much courtesy as we can muster.'

'Well . . . okay . . . Guess I have no choice.'

'No, you don't, Bob, so please get with the program. Now, if we're all sitting comfortably, we'll contact Admiral Taksin.' The Prime Minister caught Jennifer's eye. 'If you would, please, Jennifer?'

Jennifer hoped the grandstanding would now stop. Why, she wondered, did men fight so much over petty things, always trying to score points over each other? She picked up the communicator given to her by Taksin a couple of days ago and, somewhat reluctantly, pressed the button translating as "1" on its small keyboard. A few seconds later she heard a voice on the other end. 'Good morning, Admiral,' she said. 'I'm with the Prime Minister and Joint Chiefs of Staff. How do you wish us to proceed?'

'Please place the communicator down on the floor, close to a wall that's free from furniture,' came Taksin's response.

Jennifer did as she was instructed, and chairs and tables were quickly repositioned to accommodate Taksin's request. Moments later, a ten-foot square image of a familiar room appeared in front of her against the wall, or rather the image replaced the wall, for she felt she would be able to step through it if she so chose. And it was a real room she was looking into, not just a pixilated picture of a room as one would see on a television screen. It was as though she was simply looking into the room next door with the intervening wall removed.

It took Jennifer a few seconds to realise the image was of the room in the palace in which she and the Prime Minister had met Taksin a few days ago. Quite how that palace room could seem no further away than the room next door, she could not begin to comprehend, but was pleased that her brain had accepted the reality of the situation without further ado.

Taksin walked into view, stood right up close to the point where the wall must have been, looming over all present, and said, 'Good morning, Jennifer. I trust this form of communication doesn't startle you?'

'Not at all,' she responded. She turned to see the Prime Minister sitting mouth agape, eyes bulging wide. It was the same with the three Chiefs of Staff. 'Though I can't answer for them.'

'Forgive me for not stepping forward any further,' Taksin continued unabated, 'but the sensation can leave one feeling a little queasy. It's not to be recommended.'

Jennifer grinned. She imagined jumping six thousand miles in one step probably would indeed make one queasy, if not worse. Far worse. 'I'll take your word for it, sir.'

Taksin caught Jennifer's eye. 'Would you care to make the introductions, please?'

'Of course, sir,' she replied, and stood to one side. 'Admiral Taksin, may I introduce you to the Chiefs of Staff; General Bob Wilson, Admiral John Dickins and Air Chief Marshall Gordon

Grantham.'

'Good morning to you all, gentlemen,' said Taksin. He turned his attention to the Prime Minister whose mouth was still hanging open. 'May I start this conversation?'

The Prime Minister put his hand to his mouth, coughed sharply. 'Of course, Admiral.'

'Thank you,' he said, as Jennifer returned to her seat. 'Firstly, I want to request a degree of privacy in this venture. I don't think it necessary for my private address, or those of my two compatriots, to become public knowledge.'

Despite a lingering paleness to the Prime Minister's face, he seemed to have regained sufficient control to respond, 'Other than the five of us present here, there are fifteen others who worked with Jennifer on her investigation who know your true identity. I have strictly forbidden disclosure by everyone in the know. Everyone has signed the Official Secrets Act and they're all under dire threat of prosecution, imprisonment, dismissal from employment and loss of pension if they dare break their word.'

Taksin seemed pleased. 'Good. Thank you. Now, second point, just to confirm our arrangement. Over the next couple of years, I will train a sufficient number of your forces to fly the mothership and the hundred-odd starfighters it was carrying, and to teach your scientists and mechanics the technology involved in any necessary machine maintenance. For the moment, I'd like to keep this venture on a small scale. By which I mean I wish to restrict the number of people involved, and I wish to keep this venture open to British forces only. No Americans, Russians, Chinese or other nations involved. Agreed?'

'Certainly,' the Prime Minister answered.

'Thirdly, as far as a command structure is concerned, I'd like to propose we set up a committee at the top comprising eight people; that is Narai, Prasert, Jennifer and myself as full time members, along with the three Chiefs of Staff and your good self while you continue in your current employment positions. The name Star Fleet Council has been suggested by Prasert and Star Fleet Council will be responsible for establishing rules, regulations, strategy and policy. I trust you find that acceptable.'

The Chiefs of Staff nodded, as though giving their consent, although Jennifer thought they still looked far too shell-shocked to understand what was going on around them.

'Under Star Fleet Council will come Star Fleet Command,' Taksin continued, 'whose objective will be the practical implementation and undertaking of operations. The structure of that, gentlemen, I shall leave entirely to your good selves.'

'Thank you, sir,' responded the Prime Minister.

'Very well, let's begin. I plan to bring the mothership to your country on Thursday. That's three days from now. Is that too soon for you?'

'No, Admiral,' responded the Prime Minister without hesitation. 'That's just fine. We've earmarked our biggest station, Brize Norton in Oxfordshire, for the operation.'

'Good. What about men?'

'We'll start sending men there immediately. How many will you want?'

'Start with, say, five hundred. We'll need about two hundred pilots to double up on the starfighters, presumably supplied from your Royal Air Force. As for the mothership, it's a bit like running a large maritime ship, so I suggest your Royal Navy should supply the crew, maybe a hundred or so technicians. You'll also need a hundred or so staff for catering, cleaning, security and manning the social and recreational operations.'

'Admiral, if I may,' General Wilson intervened. 'There's a lot to take in here, and you're going at rather a fast pace. Do you mind if we bring in our ADCs and secretaries to take notes?'

Taksin nodded his assent. 'By all means, General.'

Jennifer stepped out of the office for a moment and was followed back in by a group of nine officers, each carrying a chair, notepad and a pen. Introductions were made swiftly, but no explanations offered.

'Perhaps I should recap,' said Taksin helpfully.

'Yes please,' replied the Prime Minister.

'Well then, gentlemen, I'm sure you all remember the spaceship that invaded this planet five months ago. Following the Prime Minister's request, I shall bring it over to your country in three days' time, along with one hundred and nine fully-functional starfighters of the type you had the unfortunate pleasure of encountering in your skies.'

'Excuse me?' blurted Colonel Travis. He looked sideways at his boss, General Wilson, in apparent disbelief. The other officers wore the same look of astonishment on their faces.

Taksin looked on curiously. 'I take it you haven't been briefed?'

'They certainly have not,' interjected the Prime Minister with a firm air of authority. 'As I mentioned before, Admiral, this operation has been undertaken in the utmost secrecy. Until this very minute, only the Joint Chiefs of Staff and Jennifer have been privy to what's going on.'

Taksin nodded, apparently pleased. 'Thank you. That is indeed encouraging. However, I think it now pertinent to let everyone know what is planned.'

'As you wish, Admiral. It's your call.'

Taksin looked direct at Colonel Travis. 'To continue. This Thursday, myself and my two colleagues, General Narai and Admiral Prasert, will be flying the spaceship over to Brize Norton. There, we shall be undertaking a program to teach you about the technology involved and how to fly the craft. Any questions?'

'Yes, sir,' responded Colonel Travis. 'Is this for real?'

'A good question,' retorted Taksin. 'I'm afraid so. It is very real indeed. My colleagues and I fear this planet is in grave danger of being attacked again from outer space. We were lucky five months ago. Your primitive technology lulled the attackers into a false sense of security, which we were able to exploit. Next time, we may not have the element of surprise. Therefore, it makes sense to have more machines and more men at our disposal. Consequently, I have agreed with the Prime Minister to spend the next two years devoted to this project.'

Looks of disbelief and worry rebounded around the room. It was Colonel Travis who ventured to put their fears into words. 'Admiral, sir, may I be candid?'

'Colonel Travis,' the Prime Minister snapped. 'Kindly be respectful in whatever you have to say.'

'I will, sir. But if we are to work together, there are a few issues that need to be addressed.'

'That's alright, Colonel,' responded Taksin. 'I'm sure I can guess what's going through your mind. Please continue. Be frank, let's clear the air. There's much to do in the coming weeks, it will need cooperation and that can only be achieved through mutual trust.'

'Am I right in thinking that you are one of the gentlemen who saved the world five months ago, by ridding us of the alien attackers?'

'Correct.'

'And the technology you used in the attack, it was the same as theirs?'

'It was.'

'Your technology is not from this planet?'

'No, it is not.'

'But your own spacecraft didn't arrive here at the same time as the attack five months ago?'

Taksin pondered a moment. 'That is correct.'

Colonel Travis took a deep breath and said, 'Am I right in thinking you've been here on Earth a long time then?'

'I'm not sure that's relevant,' interjected the Prime Minister.

'That's alright, Prime Minister,' responded Taksin. 'I'm happy to answer that question. Yes, Colonel, we have been here a long time.'

'May I ask how long?'

Taksin frowned. 'Does it matter?'

'Colonel Travis,' the Prime Minister interrupted. 'Your questions are becoming too personal and inappropriate.'

'Begging your pardon, sir. It wasn't my intention to get personal. You want military personnel involved in this project; it's going to be my job to get them to cooperate willingly. To achieve that, they'll need confidence, and that can only come with truth.'

The Prime Minister snapped, 'I'm relying on you to command your troops, Colonel Travis.'

'Yes, sir. But with all due respect, sir, they'll be looking to me to give them answers, to convince them that they're not making a huge mistake.'

'Mistake?' barked the Prime Minister furiously. 'What do you mean mistake?'

'Well, sir. The Americans lost a lot of men five months ago. My troops may not feel like working with . . . well, they may fear being so close . . .'

'What exactly are you saying?' demanded the Prime Minister.

Taksin chose to interrupt. 'Colonel Travis, are you saying your men may fear working with an alien? That my intentions may be different, that I may double-cross you, take over the world? Eat you, even?'

Colonel Travis' cheeks turned a rosy shade of pink. 'I'm sorry, sir. I wasn't going to put the point in such a manner, I didn't mean to offend.'

'No offence taken, Colonel. As I said earlier, we need to clear the air about certain matters. Jennifer, will you please tell everyone how long you've proved my two colleagues and I have been on this planet.'

All eyes turned to Jennifer. 'Our records indicate well over three thousand years.'

'Jesus wept!' Colonel Travis hissed.

'And during that time, do your records indicate any desire, or action, on our behalf to try to take over the world?'

'None whatsoever, sir.'

'And do your records indicate any wish on our part to interfere with the development of your species, to alter the course of events, to get involved with world politics.'

'Again, none whatsoever. Quite the opposite in fact.'

'Indeed. All we have ever wanted was to be left alone. Perhaps you would kindly confirm that this project was your Prime Minister's idea, that I wanted no part of it, that I did not wish to expose myself or my technology.'

Jennifer sighed. 'It certainly has been hard work getting your agreement.'

'Thank you. Now, Colonel Travis, I am here because a bunch of thugs from a distant planet stumbled into this quiet little haven we both share. I wish they hadn't and I wish I wasn't here right now talking to you. But the fact is we need each other's help if we want to continue living here as free men.'

Colonel Travis stuttered, 'I sincerely apologize, sir.'

'No need, Colonel. Now, is there anything more you need to know about me to gain the confidence of your men?'

'I hope not, sir.'

'Good. Let's continue, there's much to plan for my arrival on Thursday. Now then, Jennifer, would you handle the media please? They will need briefing about the imminent re-appearance of the mothership. You'll need to convey that it is not a threat this time, and that they should expect to see it in the skies as a matter of routine . . .'

Chapter Twenty-Six

Disbelief

'Ten-shun!'

The command, though shouted, was barely audible above the chaotic racket emanating from two hundred pilots that had been hastily gathered, without explanation, in one of Brize Norton's briefing rooms. It took a second shout before the men came to order.

Jennifer, dressed in a dark blue one-piece military uniform, cut a figure of administrative efficiency as she strolled into the room, clipboard under an arm, two steps behind a swaggering Group Captain Jack Tyson.

'At ease, gentlemen,' said Group Captain Tyson. He waited politely whilst Jennifer found herself a seat. 'For those that don't know her, may I introduce Commander Jennifer Collins, sitting right behind me.'

Jennifer smiled and gave a brief wave of a hand.

'Now then,' Group Captain Tyson continued, 'From tomorrow onwards, those that remain on this base will not fly a Typhoon or Tornado again. Not ever. Unless, that is, they voluntarily choose to do so in their spare time at an air show.'

'What the heck?' came the incredulous chorus.

'Anyone who has a passion for those old junk-buckets can leave the room right now and return to their base. You won't have much of a future though.'

'Hey, don't diss my kite,' shouted someone from the rear of the room.

'Why not?' shouted Group Captain Tyson. 'It's outdated. It's an antique, a museum piece.'

'Since when? It's state of the art. You know that, sir.'

'Well it isn't any more.'

'Since when?'

'Since today. That's official.'

'What are you saying, sir?'

'I'm saying the Typhoon's technology is obsolete. You've been brought to this base to learn to fly a completely new type of craft with technology far more advanced than currently available. A hundred of you are the country's elite fast-jet pilots, the other hundred are pretty darned good at flying too, so you should all learn fast. But this is a voluntary call-up. If you don't like it, you can walk away right now.'

'Hey, come on, sir. That's not being nice.'

Group Captain Tyson was known for his roughness. A smirk spread over his lips. 'From tomorrow, you'll be flying fighters around the Earth at fifty thousand miles an hour, and that's their near-stall speed.'

'Hah!' Several guffaws came from the back of the room. 'Come on, sir, get real. What's this meeting really about?'

'I just told you.'

'Yeah, right.'

'You'll also be flying these new fighters to the moon. They take under an hour to get there, so I'm told.'

'He's lost it,' someone heckled from the side. 'That's two hundred and fifty thousand miles you're talking about, sir. You can't fly that in an hour.'

'You can from tomorrow. Actually, I'm told the new fighters can fly at five hundred thousand miles an hour, on a long stretch that is.'

'That's impossible, sir. Come on, what's really going on?'

'I'm telling you the truth.'

'He's flipped,' came the retort.

The general mood in the room was as Jennifer had feared; disbelief and incredulity. Group Captain Tyson turned and looked at her questioningly. She stood up, drew alongside him and said to the audience, 'Who here was involved in the scuffle with that alien spaceship five months ago?'

The room fell silent. Half the audience raised their hands. 'Who here tried to chase one of those starfighters using a Typhoon or

Tornado?' The same hands raised again. 'Right, so who now maintains your current technology is not obsolete?'

The silence shattered. Two hundred voices erupted at once. One man stood up, motioned for calmness and asked, 'Commander, are you suggesting we've got our hands on one of those alien craft?'

'No, I'm not,' responded Jennifer. 'We've actually got over a hundred of them in good working order.'

'Holy shit!'

Jennifer allowed a grin. 'You said it.'

'Where from, Commander?'

'The mothership from five months ago, it's coming over here tomorrow morning. One hundred and nine starfighters are on board along with a handful of other craft. Group Captain Tyson says you're the best pilots the RAF has. He's selected you for training, should you volunteer.'

'Who's training us? ET or Mr Spock?' The comment caused an outbreak of laughter.

Jennifer tensed. 'Let's be clear on one thing gentlemen,' she responded. 'Derisory comments about the men who are going to train you will not be tolerated.'

'Men? Humans you mean?'

'Whatever you think of them personally, we shall nevertheless refer to them as men at all times.'

'You really mean aliens, then? We're going to be taught by aliens?'

Jennifer nodded.

The room exploded again. 'Hey, you can't be serious. You expect us to be friendly with some ass-hole alien?'

'I do. And you will be friendly. If not, you're out.'

'What do you mean out?'

'I mean out that door. Back to your old base. No involvement in our space program, no future.'

'Commander, please,' said Group Captain Tyson. 'Maybe you should take this a bit slower. It's rather a lot for the men to take in.'

Jennifer nodded and took a deep breath. 'You are going to be trained by alien friendlies. They've done a deal with the Prime Minister. They're going to put up the technology and training, we're going to provide the manpower.'

'Shit!' came a response from the room. 'Are you having us on?'

'No, I am not. Not a bit of it. These friendlies are concerned there may be another attack sometime in the not-so-distant future. They've agreed that Planet Earth would be more secure if its defence rested on more than just the three of them.'

'Three of them?' came the response from another pilot. 'That all? Where did they come from?'

'That's no concern of yours.'

'Like hell it isn't, Commander, with all due respect. Did they arrive with the mothership five months ago? That lot didn't seem too friendly.'

'No, they did not. These three were here already.'

'What do you mean here already?'

'I mean that they've lived here for a long time.'

'Spies? Is that why they're here already? Did they signal the others to come and get us?'

'On the contrary,' responded Jennifer in a raised voice. 'They took out the others. That's why the mothership simply disappeared five months ago. These three friendlies saved our backsides.'

The room settled into a general murmur. 'Commander?' a shout came from the back. 'How long have these aliens been living here?'

'Over three thousand years.'

The room erupted in uproar. 'Are you telling us there have been three aliens living on this planet for three thousand years? Jesus, man, are we talking Predator here or what?'

'Gentlemen, please.' Jennifer signalled for her audience to calm down. 'Let's get one thing straight right from the beginning. Our three friendlies do not hunt humans, nor have they ever sought world domination. They've lived here as, well, as refugees. We treat them with respect, they're as much entitled to their way of life as we are. That is something you must accept if you want to be in on this project.'

Low grumblings resounded throughout the room.

'Now, any other questions?' asked Jennifer. No one raised a hand. 'No? Good. Just one last thing. Keep this quiet for twenty-four hours. Talk amongst yourselves in here for a while with Group Captain Tyson if you like, but once you leave this room you will not discuss it with anyone else. Is that understood?'

The grumblings grew louder. As Jennifer made to leave, Group Captain Tyson whispered, 'Sorry, Commander, but I warned you it might not go down too well.'

Jennifer's heart had sunk by the time she'd left the room. The movie industry had never cast aliens in a good light. If it had, then perhaps her job would have been made easier.

Chapter Twenty-Seven

Morale boost

The call came over the tannoy at Brize Norton early the next morning, 'All personnel will report to Hanger C by eight hundred hours for an address by the Prime Minister.'

Jennifer looked up from her breakfast and grinned at the balding, bespectacled, middle aged man sitting on the other side of the table. He seemed agitated. She checked her watch. 'Calm down, Nick, there's only half an hour to go now.'

The BBC's current affairs editor, Nick Ohlson sighed. 'So, at last, this is it. The world finally gets to find out what this big secret is.'

'I guess so,' responded Jennifer. Five hundred service personnel had descended upon the air base within the past forty-eight hours. Many still didn't know what was being planned, and the BBC certainly weren't included amongst those who had been deemed to need to know. Rumours had spread like wildfire, none were confirmed, none were denied.

'Come on, Commander. You've been holding out on me for two days now. Does it matter anymore?'

'Sorry, Nick. Orders are orders. The Prime Minister wants to tell you, along with the rest of the world, himself. Anyway, you simply wouldn't believe me if I told you. Finish your scrambled eggs, this morning's going to be busy, it's going to be historic.'

Nick Ohlson's eyebrows raised. 'Yes?'

Jennifer grinned. 'Come on, let's make sure your camera crew is ready and set up in a good spot.'

By ten past eight, five hundred personnel had gathered in Hanger

C and were waiting in trepidation for the promised address.

The Prime Minister stepped up onto a makeshift platform and gave his audience a warm smile. 'Ladies and gentlemen, good morning to you. Thank you for your patience over the last day or so, I'm sure you're all deeply curious as to why you've been brought together here in Brize Norton. Well, you're about to find out. In thirty minutes from now, you are going to witness what I believe Hollywood has dubbed First Encounter.'

A gasp of astonishment rose from those members of the audience who had not been briefed.

'Yes, you heard right,' the Prime Minister continued. 'First Encounter, straight out of a science fiction script, I know. We all recall with horror the events of five months ago, when a lone ship armed by barbaric marauders from outer space arrived here with the intention of taking over the world. Fortunately for us, they were dealt with by friends of this planet. Now, today, those same friends are coming here to undertake a transfer of technology. They will lend us the mothership they captured, they will teach us how to fly it, they will teach us how to use its powerful weapons. Next time this planet is invaded we will be prepared; we will defend ourselves on an equal footing. We will engage the enemy and they will flee from our might. And you, the elite of the British armed services, will be the saviours of the world.'

The response was silence. Baffled faces stared at each other, as though questioning the Prime Minister's sanity. Nick Ohlson turned to Jennifer and said, 'That was rather theatrical for this time of morning. He's not serious, is he?'

Jennifer nodded in response. 'He is, yes.'

And with that came a solitary handclap from a member of the BBC team standing nearby, which gradually developed into a crescendo of rapturous applause and cheering.

After a minute of basking in the spotlight in front of his euphoric audience, the Prime Minister raised his hand and begged for silence. 'On a serious note, ladies and gentlemen, we have set up a new command unit, Star Fleet Command, which will draw from the strengths and skills of all military services. Above that will be Star Fleet Council, a committee comprising myself, Commander Jennifer Collins, the Chiefs of Staff and three new faces whom we will be welcoming shortly. Let me make this clear to you, those three new faces, Admiral Taksin, General Narai and Admiral Prasert, no one is to antagonize them, no one is to disobey their order. I will not tolerate any inappropriate talk of them either. They are our friends. They are here to teach us, to help us. We need their knowledge if we are to survive as a species on this planet, I will not stand for any bigotry, so be very careful of loose talk. If you upset any of our new friends, you will be thrown out of this base harshly and promptly. I hope I make myself clear on that matter.' He paused a few seconds to let the sombre tone of his warning sink in. 'Now then, we have an historic moment coming up in a few minutes. Let's get formed up outside to greet the arrival of our three new friends.'

Jennifer turned her head to find Nick Ohlson gaping in disbelief. She gave him a smile, unable to hide her amusement.

'Are you telling me that we've got control of that spaceship?' he said. 'The one that attacked us a few months ago?'

'We do, yes,' replied Jennifer in a very matter of fact tone. 'Why?'

'And it's coming here?'

'In a few minutes, yes. And you're on the VIP list, so you'll be amongst the first to board it.'

Nick Ohlson wiped his forehead with a handkerchief. 'Dear god. I think I'm going to throw up.'

Chapter Twenty-Eight

First contact

Jennifer Collins stood at the head of five hundred personnel on the edge of Brize Norton's airstrip, alongside the Prime Minister and Chiefs of Staff, all gawking at an ever-increasing expanse of dark billowing cloud drifting in from the east. This was it, no going back now. Mankind was about to take a giant leap forward. She turned her head to one side, noticed the Prime Minister staring at her, a desperate, pleading expression on his face as if seeking reassurance. She too had wondered a hundred times already that morning whether they were doing the right thing or not. She could not have given an appropriate response, if asked. Instead, she turned her gaze towards the control tower and spoke into her mouthpiece, 'How's it going up there? Anything on radar yet?'

'Not yet, Commander,' came the response. 'I have visual on that billowing cloud but nothing on . . . Holy shit! Where the hell did that spring from?'

'What can you see?' asked Jennifer.

'I don't know, but it's huge, it's . . . That's impossible, it can't just appear like that, out of the blue, like magic.'

Jennifer snorted. 'I did tell you to expect the unimaginable.'

'You did, I remember, but this thing wasn't there ten seconds ago, Commander. What the hell is it anyway?'

'It's a ship, of course. A spaceship,' responded Jennifer, wondering why it had been deemed not necessary to inform the Control Tower in advance of what precisely was arriving that morning. Through her earpiece, she heard the Control Tower suddenly explode with the sound of a booming voice. 'Control Tower, do you read me?' came a voice.

'Yes, sir, I read you,' Jennifer heard the Controller reply. 'Loud and clear. A little too loud, if I may say so.'

'Sorry,' came the response. 'I wasn't sure of your equipment's abilities. I'll adjust the volume. How's this?'

'Easier on the ears, sir, thank you.'

'Right, we're approaching you now. Ready to land in five minutes.'

'Yes, sir. Five minutes, over and out.' The Controller grabbed a microphone and said, 'Did you hear that, Commander Collins?'

'Couldn't miss it,' responded Jennifer. 'My ears are still ringing.' She felt a hand grip her elbow and turned to see the Prime Minister staring into the distance. She followed his gaze and saw the cloud ahead of them dissipating, giving birth to a monstrous, black spaceship.

'Oh, dear god,' the Prime Minister moaned.

To the other side of the Prime Minister, General Wilson shook his head in despair and muttered, 'I just hope to god they really are friendly.'

'It's too late for that, Bob,' replied the Prime Minister. 'It's sink or swim from now on.'

General Wilson grunted. 'You know what happened in that film, Mars Attacks? Bastards obliterated everyone waiting to welcome them, all because of a misunderstanding when some wishy-washy liberal leftie let loose a dove as a sign of peace.'

The Prime Minister gave General Wilson a sharp look. 'You really are a bundle of joy to work with, Bob.'

General Wilson shrugged. 'Just saying, that's all.'

Jennifer tried to put the image of annihilation out of her mind and focussed her attention on the spaceship as it came down slowly, carefully and precisely, its front end resting just a hundred yards away.

'That's one goddam big ship,' muttered General Wilson as he craned his neck upwards at the three-thousand-foot-high structure that towered above him. 'And ugly as hell.'

'It sure is, Bob,' replied the Prime Minister. 'Let's hope the contents are prettier.'

'Well, Admiral Taksin's certainly prettier than those thugs that came out of it back in February.'

'I meant the equipment and decor, Bob.'

'Oh, sorry, sir.'

Jennifer waited in patient silence for several minutes. Eventually, a groaning and hissing sound issued from the black beast and a massive door in its belly opened outwards and downwards to rest on the ground. Seconds later a bank of what looked like fog rolled down the ramp and three huge figures, dressed in long black robes, glided down, seemingly floating on air.

'Wow,' General Wilson murmured. 'Now that's what I call an entrance.'

In unison, Jennifer, the Prime Minister and the Chiefs of Staff walked forward to greet the three figures heading their way. Introductions were undertaken briskly and a formal military salute took place.

'Well, gentlemen,' said Jennifer at length, 'we're at your service.'

'Then let's get the program started,' replied Taksin. 'I'll escort you and your VIP party on a quick tour. Narai will oversee security and Prasert will take the heads of the support teams around the ship. After the tour I'll get on with training the fighter pilots straight away.'

'Great. Sounds like a plan,' replied Jennifer. She signalled to a group of some two dozen dignitaries behind her and they set off towards the ship. As she walked up the ramp, stared into the bowels of the ship, an ice-cold shiver went through her body. It was a scene similar to any number of terrifying alien films she'd watched; a central shaft towered upwards for three hundred feet with thousands of wires and ducting pipes draping down the sides like spaghetti, unfathomable vehicles and equipment lay strewn around the deck. 'You know something,' she muttered to no one in particular. 'I don't think I've ever been so frightened in my life.'

All of a sudden, a large hand appeared out of nowhere and grabbed Jennifer's shoulder. As if following a film script, she shrieked and jumped forward a couple of steps.

'Sorry, Jennifer,' came a voice from behind. 'I couldn't resist it. You looked petrified just now.'

Jennifer turned to find Prasert with a very broad grin on his face. 'You have a very strange sense of humour, Admiral.'

Taksin tutted and said, 'Ignore him, Jennifer, I told you he's a joker, he likes winding people up.'

'Well he's certainly succeeded,' replied Jennifer, giving Prasert an admonishing glare. 'Honestly, that scared the living daylights out of me.'

Prasert beamed back at Jennifer, gestured for her to lead on, and said, creepily, 'Won't you come into my parlour, little girl?'

Jennifer shook her head. 'You first, Admiral, I want to keep an eye on you, from behind.'

As Prasert stepped past Jennifer, he gave her an admiring look and said, 'Lucky me.'

The malevolent look Jennifer had intended to give him quickly morphed into a grin. For a seven-foot-tall alien, he really was quite cute.

'Try to ignore him,' said Taksin as he too stepped past Jennifer. 'You'll only encourage him.'

Moments later they drew to a halt at what looked like a row of lifts and Jennifer watched Prasert press a button on a wall panel. She gave the symbol on it no more than a cursory glance and said, 'That's something that'll get everyone lost. No one will have any idea which button to press anywhere.'

'Leave it to Prasert,' responded Taksin. 'He'll get new symbols applied throughout the ship. If nothing else it'll give him something constructive to do. Come, let me take you up to the operational decks.'

The lift was spacious, allowing all of the VIP party to fit in comfortably. As she watched Taksin depress a button, the doors closed and she took a steadying breath, for this seemed to be the point of no return. Deck after deck passed as they ascended. She caught the merest glimpse of corridors, rooms and equipment, the function of which she had not the slightest notion. 'It's like a scene straight out of a movie,' she commented. 'The engineering is exquisite. It's so vast, its mind blowing. How long does it take to build one of these, sir?'

'That depends entirely on the quality of the workforce,' replied Taksin. 'With good tradesmen, about twenty years, I suppose, with about ten thousand highly skilled workers. You don't want to rush construction and you don't want it built by the cheapest contractor. They've got to withstand a lot of punishment. The ship needs to be built carefully and to exacting standards.'

'Could we replicate it?'

'I doubt it. You need a special dry-dock to build ships this big, and there's only one I know of in existence. Anyway, some of the technology involved is too advanced. Take gravity-equalisation, for instance, we'll teach your scientists the basics, but to fine tune the mechanics is a tall order. We're not experts in everything. Anyway, some of the construction materials aren't found on this planet.'

'But there's hope?'

Taksin raised an eyebrow. 'You want more than one of these?'

'It's a thought, sir, just a passing thought.'

'A case of trying to run before you can walk, I should say.'

Jennifer acknowledged the point. 'You're quite correct, sir. You must keep our aspirations in check.'

Taksin nodded his agreement. 'I intend to.'

The lift stopped and the VIP party stepped out on to the flight control deck. 'Wow,' was all Jennifer could think of saying as she took in the sleek, stylish, futuristic look of the deck. 'This is unbelievable.'

Taksin took his cloak off, draped it over a chair, wandered over to a control panel and pressed a button. Seconds later a wall screen opened to reveal what appeared to be a gigantic window granting a view of the surrounding countryside. 'You'll find the view from space even more extraordinary,' he commented.

'When can we go?'

Taksin grimaced. 'All in good time, Jennifer. First, there are endless hours of learning the basics. I'm afraid you'll have to wait a while.'

'Weeks? Months?'

Taksin shook his head. 'Let's see how things progress. No promises.'

A prominent chair caught her eye. It looked to be the focal point of the control panels. 'Is that the captain's chair?'

'It is indeed.'

'May I?'

'Of course,' responded Taksin with a smile.

Jennifer lowered herself gingerly into the sumptuous chair and stretched her arms. 'I guess this is how Jim Kirk feels.'

The comment was lost on Taksin, although Prasert and the rest of the VIP group chuckled. 'The ship needs a name, Jennifer,' said Taksin. 'Would you care to do the honours?'

Jennifer sought the Prime Minister's eye. 'Do you mind, sir?'

'Not at all, Jennifer,' replied the Prime Minister. 'Ships are traditionally named by women. So, go on, go ahead.'

'Press and hold this orange button,' said Taksin. 'It's the tannoy system for the entire ship. It can be heard outside, as well, if you press the yellow button next to it at the same time.'

Jennifer composed herself. 'Do you mind a bit of theatrics?'

'Not at all,' Taksin beamed. 'It even seems appropriate.'

Jennifer pressed the orange and yellow buttons simultaneously. 'Ladies and gentlemen, may I have your attention please,' her voice boomed around the ship. 'This is Commander Jennifer Collins speaking. It is with the greatest honour that I name this ship Endeavour. May God bless all those who serve on board her.'

Taksin smiled as a roar of approval came from the room. 'You seemed to enjoy that,' he said.

'I've just lived out a fantasy. Not many people get to do that.'

'I'll leave you now, in the capable hands of Narai,' said Taksin. 'He'll take you around the crew sleeping quarters and on to the canteen and other operational areas. I'll go down and fetch the pilots. I'm sure they'll be itching to get started.'

Chapter Twenty-Nine

Training

Standing at the head of his squadron of two hundred pilots, Group Captain Tyson was fast becoming restless. Forty-five minutes had passed since the ship had arrived and he was at a complete loss as to what was supposed to be happening. Everyone else had gone aboard, even the cleaning and catering staff. Yet he and his men had been left standing on the airstrip and the day was warming up fast. With frustration mounting, he passed a few choice remarks amongst those nearest him.

'Watch it, sir,' one of his men said. 'Someone's coming.'

Group Captain Tyson turned to see an extremely tall handsome man dressed top-to-toe in plain black uniform striding purposefully from the ship in his direction. He crossed his arms and grimaced.

As the man approached, he asked, 'I assume you are Group Captain Tyson?'

Group Captain Tyson's eyes scanned the man's outfit, searching for any recognizable insignia. There was none. 'That's me,' he offered in response.

'I shall be instructing you and the other pilots on how to fly the starfighters.'

Group Captain Tyson looked startled. 'Really? But I thought . . . I mean, I thought our instructor was going to be . . .' He cleared his throat and tried again. 'What I mean is, I was told to expect someone called Admiral Taksin.'

Taksin frowned. 'I am he.'

Group Captain Tyson looked horrified. 'You are? Good grief.' He dropped his arms to his sides, spun round and called his men to attention, then turned back to salute Taksin. 'I beg your pardon, sir, I didn't realise. I was expecting someone else.'

'Really?' responded Taksin. 'Anyone in particular?'

'Erm, no sir, I guess not. I was just expecting someone who looked . . . well, different, that's all.'

'Do you have a problem with me because of the way I look?'

'Um, no. Not at all, sir. Quite the opposite.' He felt himself blushing as Taksin's eyes bored down into him. 'I just thought you'd be . . . older . . . being an admiral.'

'I see,' replied Taksin nonplussed. 'Right. Well, let's move on. And please call me Admiral rather than sir.'

'Yes, Admiral.'

'Okay, then. Let's get on with things. If you'll all follow me please, we'll go aboard.'

As he watched Taksin turn and set off back towards the ship, Group Captain Tyson caught the eye of his number two and made a discouraging face. As introductions to a senior officer go, it hadn't been the smoothest. And as introductions to an alien go, it had been positively bizarre. In fact, he had to admit to himself it had been a disaster although, he reckoned, he'd recovered well. Quite what he'd been expecting Admiral Taksin to look like, he wasn't sure. A handsome giant of a man with just one pair of arms and legs certainly wasn't up there with the rest of the guesses he and his men had been joking about the night before. Not wishing to appear rude, however, he ran a few steps to catch up with Taksin. 'My apologies for getting off on the wrong foot, Admiral. I was taken by surprise, without a schedule.'

'Schedule?' Taksin queried. 'There's been no request for a schedule. There are far too many variables to begin thinking about such a thing. However, if you need one, I'll ask Commander Collins to look into it.'

'That won't be necessary, Admiral. I see now this program is simply going to evolve as it goes.'

Taksin turned to Group Captain Tyson and gave a curt smile. 'Indeed, it is.'

Group Captain Tyson smiled in response, relieved he might just have managed to get out of an awkward spot, and vowed to keep his mouth firmly shut for the rest of the morning unless the Admiral spoke first. As he stepped on board the ship, he gasped at the sight of the alien engineering. 'Christ Almighty,' he muttered.

'Impressed?'

'How could one not be, Admiral. This . . . this surpasses anything we imagined. It beats the imaginations of Hollywood.'

'I'll take that as a compliment,' responded Taksin, as he led the men to the bank of lifts. 'Now then, you should get about fifty men in each carriage. I'll show your men which button to press for Flight Deck Control Room and I'll see you up there.'

Group Captain Tyson tried his best to exert a degree of command over his two hundred men as they scrambled to get inside four of the lifts, but the ensuing confusion made the episode look like a scene from a Keystone Cops film and Group Captain Tyson soon found himself snapping like a bear with a sore head. The morning's proceedings were not going as he would have liked; so far, they were distinctly amateurish.

The mass exit from the lifts into the Flight Deck Control Room passed with a similar lack of decorum, testing Group Captain Tyson's patience to the limit. He was therefore pleased to finally find himself up against a long pane of what appeared to be Perspex glass, looking down on to the magnificent sight of more than one hundred starfighters parked out on the Flight Deck.

'Right then, gentlemen,' Taksin called out. 'We've got a lot to get through. My plan is to teach you individually. I want to make absolutely sure you're capable of this task. We've got limited resources at our hands and I don't want to lose any of these starfighters in an unnecessary accident. My guess is you'll take at least two hours to grasp the basics of operational flight, so it's going to take a while to get through this preliminary stage. Let's get one thing straight, right from the start. No one, repeat, no one, flies without my express approval. Is that understood?'

'Yes, Admiral,' came the chorus.

'Right. Well, let's make a start. Who will go first?'

'I will, Admiral,' responded Group Captain Tyson.

'Fine. We'll get going immediately. Just before I go though, if you'll let me pass through, gentlemen,' Taksin moved towards a row of instruments. He pressed a button and a ten-foot high screen came to life. 'You can watch the training session on this screen. There are a variety of cameras installed in all starfighters, including three in the cockpit. Just flick this switch to change views,' he said, indicating towards a panel. 'And this knob adjusts the sound. Do you understand?'

'Yes, Admiral,' came the response from several nearby pilots.

Taksin pressed another button and a huge gate that formed the outer wall of the cavernous Flight Deck began a slow ascent back into the ceiling. 'You might as well leave the gate open, but if it rains I would be obliged if you would press it again to close it.'

'Yes, Admiral.'

'Very well, I shall be back with Group Captain Tyson in two hours. I'll then break for lunch for an hour. Hopefully, we can get through three more sessions this afternoon.' And with that, Taksin strode off towards Flight Deck accompanied by Group Captain Tyson in tow.

Before boarding, Taksin turned and said, 'We can start the lesson with me in control and you watching until you've seen enough to take over, or you can be in control from the start with me guiding you. Your choice.'

Group Captain Tyson replied confidently, 'I'd like to assume control from the start, if you don't mind, Admiral.'

'Good. Now, place your left hand up against this panel and say your name in your normal voice. The computer will store your identity.'

Group Captain Tyson did as he was told. The door to the starfighter opened smoothly and they stepped in.

'Hit the yellow button on the wall to your left; that closes the outer door. Pressing it again will open it. Keep the safety latch down on it during flight.'

'Check.'

As they took their seats in the cockpit, two hundred pairs of eyes back in the Flight Deck Control Room followed their every movement on screen.

'Strap your belt on, like so.'

'Check.'

'First, fire up the engine. Press the green button, top left on the control panel. Pressing the red button adjacent to it will shut it off.'

'Check,' said Group Captain and a quiet background purr of an engine began.

'This is your control stick,' Taksin explained. 'That's your accelerator on the right; de-accelerate with it as well. The button on the top is a gun trigger, we'll come to that later. Now then, pull the control stick back a little to raise us up a few feet, turn the stick slowly to the left, round we go. Align with the rear gate. Good, now, turn the accelerator, quite hard.'

'Check.' The starfighter shot off down Flight Deck and out into the open sky. Within seconds the speed was close to five hundred miles an hour.

'Pull the stick back towards you, let's get up high.'

For the next hour, Group Captain Tyson was put through a series of turns, loops, flying upside down, flying sideways, flying up into the stratosphere and hovering over mountain peaks. He took it all in his stride. Nothing fazed him. No words passed his lips except for the occasional "Check", and by the end of an hour's flight he was pretty confident that he and his men would be able to handle themselves well.

'We have an hour left, Group Captain. Would you care to fly in space?'

'Yes please, Admiral.'

'Right, let's get you used to flying in an unfamiliar environment.'

For fifteen minutes, Group Captain Tyson followed Taksin's orders to the letter, repeating the basic operations covered during the previous hour but in space instead. Throughout the experience he kept the same unfazed look on his face, though inside he possessed a smug feeling of satisfaction. The machine had been far easier to master than he'd expected.

'Let's try a new manoeuvre,' said Taksin. 'Pilots are expected to engage in search and rescue. That means putting on a suit and climbing out. Are you up for that?'

'Yes, Admiral.'

'Check out your screen. We're coming up to a redundant satellite, one of the many pieces of junk left floating around up here. Pull up alongside it. We'll attempt to board it.'

Group Captain Tyson felt rather alarmed. 'Are you sure about this, Admiral?'

'Of course I am. Right, press the black button to your right, that will fix our flight path and put us on autopilot. Let's get some suits on.'

Somewhat warily, Group Captain Tyson followed Taksin out of

the cockpit and up a flight of stairs to a chamber in which twenty odd space suits hung from a rack. He donned the gear quickly and nodded his understanding at Taksin's explanation of the controls for the propulsion unit.

As they left the chamber to venture out into the black void of space, Group Captain Tyson could hear Taksin say, through the intercom, 'Don't worry about drifting. These safety lines will withstand the impact of a meteor shower.'

'That's very comforting, Admiral,' replied Group Captain Tyson in a tone devoid of feeling. Seconds later he was circling the abandoned satellite.

'Be careful, Group Captain, it's rotating. Don't want anything to hit . . . Ahh!'

Group Captain Tyson looked around to see Taksin's body limp and drifting. 'Shit,' he swore, as Taksin's body began to spin. 'Admiral? Can you hear me, Admiral?' He pressed the control buttons on his sleeve and set off after Taksin. He caught his body and stared through the visor to see a lifeless face. Holding the body close, he set off back to the starfighter, eased Taksin through the outer door into the chamber and laid him on the floor.

'Admiral? Can you hear me?' There was no response. Without hesitation, he pressed the button he'd seen Taksin touch earlier and seconds later the outer door closed and he turned his attention to the inner door. There was only one obvious button; he pressed it and the chamber filled with air. He removed Taksin's helmet, went downstairs to the cockpit, strapped himself into the pilot's chair, depressed the autopilot button and set a course back to base.

Ten minutes later, just after the starfighter broke through the Earth's atmosphere, a noise behind Group Captain Tyson made him jump.

'Well done,' said Taksin softly.

'Jesus! Sorry, Admiral, you spooked me. Are you okay?'

'I'm fine, thank you. You did well back there. Passed with flying colours in fact.'

Group Captain Tyson frowned. 'Excuse me?'

'You just passed your first major test.'

'Test? You mean you faked that incident?'

'I needed to know how you would respond.'

'You what?' Group Captain Tyson's face flushed. 'You set me up?'

'A test, Group Captain. I needed to know if you could cope with an emergency; whether you'd panic, or call base for assistance or deal with the situation yourself. As I said, you passed with flying colours.'

'Why you . . . you're out of order there, Admiral!'

Taksin's frowned. 'Excuse me?'

'You heard me, Admiral,' Group Captain Tyson exploded. 'That sort of trick is out of order. It's unprofessional and highly dangerous.'

'I told you at the start,' Taksin snapped. 'I make up the rules. This is my program.'

'In that case, Admiral, I'm not sure whether I care for your damn program.'

A smirk appeared on Taksin's face. 'You want to pull out?'

Group Captain Tyson took a moment to compose himself. 'No, Admiral. I have no intention of pulling out. I'm here to the end. My intention is to get this program running smoothly and to get my men trained, as instructed by the Prime Minister. That means I must work with you, Admiral, whether I like it or not.'

'You have no problem with me?'

'No problem, Admiral,' responded Group Captain Tyson sharply. 'None whatsoever.'

'Good. Time for lunch I think.'

'Yes, Admiral. With your permission,' Group Captain Tyson hissed, 'I'll take the starfighter back to base.'

Chapter Thirty

Tension

'He did what?' asked Jennifer, her jaw dropping. 'You're joking?'

'No joke, Commander, that's how it was.'

Jennifer had been queuing for lunch in the canteen aboard the Endeavour when Group Captain Tyson had discreetly approached and told her of Taksin's exploits in space. She chanced a look over at the table where Taksin was sitting on his own looking morose. 'Why would he pull a stunt like that?'

'I really can't say, Commander,' responded Group Captain Tyson curtly.

Jennifer turned to her side and asked, 'What do you make of it, General?'

General Wilson, standing in the queue behind her, looked as though he wished he hadn't been asked the question. He looked for guidance at the other Chiefs of Staff next to him. None came. 'Who knows? He's miffed, that's pretty obvious from the way he's sulking over his lunch.'

The Prime Minister leaned in towards Jennifer and said, 'What do we do then? Do we go over and apologize to him?'

'For what, sir?' responded Group Captain Tyson. 'We did nothing wrong.'

Jennifer stared hard into Group Captain Tyson's eyes. 'You think not? Have you never seen that look before? What about your wife, does she ever look like that?'

Group Captain Tyson shrugged. 'Well, yes, but that's different. She gets that way when she doesn't understand me.'

'Exactly,' Jennifer snapped. 'How right you are Group Captain. It's called male bullshit. I'd bet serious money you and your pilots gave him a hard time. Am I right?'

Group Captain Tyson looked hurt. 'No, Commander. We didn't do anything like that.'

'Really? Tell me, when he greeted you, were the men more shocked to see a normal looking man rather than a grotesque alien with tentacles instead of limbs?'

Group Captain Tyson bristled. 'Well, someone should have warned us.'

Jennifer sighed. 'Oh, for Christ's sake, you know how you fast-jet pilots are always made out to be bunch of arrogant male chauvinists. You've just proved it to be true.'

The Group Captain looked appropriately chided. 'What do you want us to do?'

'Nothing. Absolutely nothing,' replied Jennifer sharply. 'Just treat him like a person, damn it. Treat him like a man, like you would with any officer of a superior rank.'

'Yes, Commander,' said Group Captain Tyson with a degree of bitterness in his voice and walked off to join his colleagues.

'Come on, sir,' said Jennifer to the Prime Minister. 'The least we can do is to be sociable. No one bring this issue up though.'

Jennifer, the Prime Minister and the Chiefs of Staff finished filling their plates and took their trays over to Taksin's table. 'May we join you, Admiral?'

'Of course.'

'Thank you.' They all sat down and began eating.

'So,' Jennifer ventured after a thoughtful few mouthfuls of food. 'What do you make of our pilots' skills, sir? How do they match up with . . . our competitors?'

Taksin reflected on the question a few seconds. 'I've only trained the one so far, but if they're all at that same level, then, well, I suppose, in time, there's hope.'

'Hope? You mean they might come up to scratch?'

'Eventually,' replied Taksin, shifting uneasily in his chair. 'Given the right level of teaching, that is.'

Jennifer quickly stifled a grin that fought to appear on her face. Taksin's discomfort was all too apparent. 'Well, it will take as long as it takes, I guess. Two hundred lessons at two hours each, at the rate of, what, four pilots per day? You'll be finished in two or three months, sir. We really do appreciate your commitment to this program. And your patience.'

'Yes, well, needs must, as you say.'

'Indeed so, sir.' replied Jennifer softly. 'By the way, none of us wish to appear to be pushy, but with nearly five hundred men sitting around on this base, do you have any idea yet for a timetable to get the ship up and running?'

Taksin took his time to wipe his mouth with a paper napkin. 'Not yet, no. I appreciate you're keen to get things rolling, but . . .'

'That's okay, Admiral,' Jennifer interrupted with a pleasant smile. 'All in good time. As I say, none of us want to push things too fast.'

'Thank you for that, Jennifer.' replied Taksin, and turned to the Prime Minister. 'But what about you, Prime Minister, you must have affairs of state to attend to. Are you intending to stay here throughout the training session?'

'Well, if you have no objection, Admiral,' the Prime Minister replied, 'I'd like to stay around for the next day or so, to get accustomed to the operations here. After that, I guess I'd better get back to doing my normal job.'

'Of course. I'll ask Prasert to train a pilot for that executive jet I mentioned, so you can come and go at your will.'

The Prime Minister looked elated. 'That's very kind of you, Admiral.'

'Now, if you'll excuse me, gentlemen,' said Taksin as he rose from his chair. 'I'd better get on with the training program.'

Jennifer looked at the four men sitting around the table with despair. 'You see, all you have to do is treat him as an equal, but with a great deal of respect.'

Chapter Thirty-One

Moodiness

After his lunch, Taksin returned to the flight deck in a less than enthusiastic mood and asked who would be the next pilot for a training session.

'That's me, Admiral. Wing Commander Praed. Second in command.'

'Right. Good afternoon, Wing Commander. Let's get straight to it then, shall we?'

Taksin was treated to a near perfect take-off and an effortless flight performance. The ease at which Wing Commander Praed put instructions into practice flabbergasted him. The pilot not only appeared comfortably in control of the starfighter, but he seemed to be able to anticipate commands before they had been spoken. The more at ease Wing Commander Praed grew, the less so Taksin became. Even the experience of piercing the Earth's atmosphere and shooting off into space didn't stir any emotion on the Wing Commander's face.

'Back to base, please,' Taksin commanded. They'd been flying less than an hour.

'Check.'

The comment rattled Taksin. 'Don't you pilots say anything other than "check"?'

'No, Admiral. Not when training.'

'Tell me something, why have you not asked me any questions?'

Wing Commander Praed shrugged. 'We all watched Group Captain Tyson on the monitor you set up for us. When he got back, he explained a bit more, such as the feel of the craft compared to our own jets.'

'He taught you over lunch?'

'To be honest, Admiral, flying this thing is very comparable to flying a Tornado. The hardest thing is to learn where all the buttons and switches are. We've used very few of them so far, though I appreciate that the ones we haven't used are likely to be for technology that's new to us.'

'Just a matter of learning where a few buttons are?' muttered Taksin. 'Really?'

'Yes, sir.'

Taksin tutted.

On arrival back at base, Taksin was greeted by a worried looking Group Captain Tyson. 'Is everything alright, Admiral?'

'Yes. Why wouldn't it be?'

'It's just you're back much earlier than expected.'

'A change of plan, Group Captain,' muttered Taksin.

Group Captain Tyson gulped.

'I want you and Wing Commander Praed to help teach the basics. I want you to train each man for at least an hour. Feel free to take a small group with you in the cockpit to watch and get a feel for the craft. It seems your men can learn from observation quite efficiently. I'll spend a shorter period with each pilot after they've had an hour with you on the basics.'

'Yes, Admiral.'

'Let's get to it, then. We can train another twelve this afternoon, at least.'

'Yes, sir!' A broad grin appeared on Group Captain Tyson's face as he rushed to organize training teams.

Chapter Thirty-Two

Change of plan

Taksin endured a miserable evening at the end of the first day of training. He had not expected the pilots to be so capable, and took no pleasure explaining that fact to his two compatriots. He went to bed in a huff, slept fitfully and staggered to breakfast feeling uneasy about the coming day's events. It was with a heavy heart that he reappeared on the flight deck where he was given a list of fourteen pilots who'd each had an hour of basic training.

'Right, I take it you know everything already,' said Taksin to his first trainee pilot of the day as he strapped himself in.

The pilot looked hurt by the obvious tone of sarcasm. 'No, sir, I do not.'

'Really? Oh, well, never mind, let's get going.' Without any further instructions or advice, the pilot took off smoothly into the skies. Taksin sighed deeply. He really hadn't expected the pilots to take to the task so easily. 'Tell me,' he said after a few minutes, 'What do you normally do for a training session with your Tornadoes?'

'Well, sir, typically, we'd take a route through the Great Glen.'

'What's that?'

'Mountains, sir. In Scotland. Very beautiful, they are.'

'Show me.'

'Yes, sir. May I inform the Group Captain first? We'll need to get clearance.'

'By all means.'

The pilot pressed the intercom button. 'Group Captain Tyson. Do you read me?'

'Check,' came the response.

'Flight Lieutenant Jensen requesting permission to fly through the Great Glen.'

'Jensen? Aren't you with Admiral Taksin?'

'Yes, sir. I am.'

'And Admiral Taksin has asked you to go through the Great Glen?'

'Yes, sir.'

'Permission granted, but don't fly too fast.'

'Yes, sir. Over and out.'

For twenty minutes, Flight Lieutenant Jensen flew the starfighter through a carefully selected low level course winding past dead ends and high cliffs of mountain ranges causing Taksin to take a firm grip on the arm of his chair.

'Interesting,' Taksin commented at the end of the route, his fingers white from the restriction of blood. 'How many of your Tornadoes have been lost in these mountains?'

'None, sir. Only qualified pilots are allowed to fly this route.'

The absurdity of the answer seemed to be lost on the Flight Lieutenant. Taksin decided not to pursue the point. 'Right, then. I think we've covered that, let's try open space.'

'Yes, Admiral.'

By twelve o'clock, Taksin had had enough. Three training sessions that morning had made his head spin sufficiently to develop a headache. Having asked each trainee to choose a different course, he found each route to have been scarier than the previous, and he really did not want to see another range of mountains. He collapsed in a canteen chair, rather shaken, hopelessly at a loss over what to do next.

'Are you alright, sir?' asked Jennifer as she approached Taksin's table. 'You look as though you've seen a ghost.' She sat down and placed a mug of coffee in front of her.

'Have you any idea what those crazy pilots do in training?'

Jennifer smiled wearily. 'Are they better than you thought?'

'I wouldn't say that,' Taksin snapped.

'No, I guess you wouldn't, sir.'

'And what's that supposed to mean?'

'I'm sorry, sir, I don't mean to be rude, but you are, how can I put it, stubborn at times?'

Taksin looked aghast. 'Stubborn? Me?'

'As I said, sir, I don't wish to be rude.'

'Is that how I come across? Stubborn?'

Jennifer took a sip of coffee while she reflected on an answer. 'Would it pain you too much to delegate power to where the skills lie, sir? We might never fulfil this task otherwise.'

Taksin looked shocked. 'I can't. I just can't accept that they're any good. They're just not the same.'

'You mean they're not the same as your people in Surithani?' Jennifer interrupted. 'No, sir, they're not. These pilots, they're free-thinking people from a democratic country, they seek adventure, they're highly skilled, highly devoted, they want to learn fast and conquer this challenge. They're the very opposite of your people in Surithani.'

Taksin sighed. 'It's so depressing, to find out I've been so wrong all these years.'

Jennifer shook her head. 'I wouldn't say that, sir. In the West, most of our technological development has been crammed into just one century. It's all happened really fast. In the space of one lifetime, we've gone from man's first flight to landing on the moon. Go out into the countryside, talk to the older generation and they'll tell you their grandparents travelled by horse and cart. We're still a backward people really, underneath.'

Taksin picked up a teaspoon and stirred a mug of coffee that had gone cold. 'That's no consolation. It's the same on my own planet. Was, I should say.'

Jennifer was about to say something, but cut short on seeing the Prime Minister, the Chiefs of Staff, General Narai and Admiral Prasert heading their way in a cluster. 'Time to put on your happy face, sir.'

Taksin gave Jennifer a curious look. 'My what?'

As the Prime Minister sat down with his tray of food next to Jennifer, she noticed he appeared to have a few trickles of sweat running down the back of his neck.

The Prime Minister caught Taksin's eye and said, 'I trust you've had a good day so far, Admiral?'

'So-so,' was all Taksin would commit to. Jennifer gave him an admonishing look.

A period of peace was observed for lunch. During coffee, Taksin turned to the Prime Minister and said, 'Forgive me for being rude, but there's something I must discuss with my colleagues.' He then turned and spoke a few words in his native tongue. Narai and Prasert listened and nodded their heads.

'Sorry about that,' said Taksin at length. 'Just some domestics. Now then, Air Chief Marshall, I want a meeting with all Flight Crew at one thirty-five. I have something important to discuss. I would like you and the rest of Star Fleet Command to be there.'

'As you wish,' replied the Air Chief Marshall. He caught the eye of a passing pilot and asked for the message to be passed to Group Captain Tyson.

'And I must leave you,' said Admiral Prasert as he rose from the table.

'Me too, work to be done,' said General Narai leaving with his son.

The Prime Minister looked concerned. 'Is there anything wrong, Admiral?'

'No, not at all,' replied Taksin with a mutter, and passed a few moments in small talk before the tannoy burst into life.

'Attention please. Attention please. This is Captain Mandrake. This ship is scheduled to depart at fourteen hundred hours. All ground staff currently on board must leave the ship at least ten minutes prior to departure.'

Jennifer noted the look of concern on the faces of the pilots a few tables away. She turned to Taksin and frowned. 'A change of plan, sir?'

'Yes, indeed. Come, let's get to it.'

By one thirty-five, two hundred pairs of eyes were looking anxiously around the Flight Deck Control Room amid a humdrum of gossip.

'Ten-shun!'

Taksin strode in to Flight Deck Control Room accompanied by the Prime Minister, Jennifer and the three Chiefs of Staff, stood in front, faced the pilots and took a deep breath. 'Gentlemen, as you've heard, this ship is setting off on its first training session at two o'clock. I therefore need to be quick as my presence is required elsewhere.'

Jennifer caught Group Captain Tyson's questioning eyes. She shrugged her shoulders in response.

'During this last twenty-four hours,' said Taksin, 'I have come to realize that your flying skills far exceed my expectations. I have therefore decided to revise my training plan. With immediate effect, I would like Group Captain Tyson to assume complete control of Flight Command. That means he will take over the administration, planning and organization of the basic training sessions.'

Group Captain Tyson's jaw dropped.

'I hereby give Group Captain Tyson his wings, as I believe you call them. Once a pilot has been granted his wings, he will be authorised to fly solo. Group Captain Tyson will be responsible for the granting of wings to other pilots. How he chooses to do so will be entirely up to him.'

A flicker of a smile appeared on Group Captain Tyson's face.

'I would suggest that the focus remains on basic training for the next few weeks. Once Group Captain Tyson believes his unit is fully competent on the basics, then we shall move on to further stages which I would like to quickly run through with you right now. Stage Two of training will be weapons training. Obviously, we shall need to be proficient at air-to-air, air-to-ground and in-space combat. As soon as everyone here has mastered the basics, we must make weapons a priority. Stage Three of training is what I'd like to refer to as Search and Rescue. I trust the title is self-explanatory, but I'd like to widen the brief of this mission to include non-military, humanitarian action as well. We need to develop a wide range of skills, not just how to shoot, and, just as with your Coastguard service, much can be learnt by pitting yourselves against the forces of nature. Included within this stage, I think it appropriate to clear up all the millions of pieces of junk that have been left orbiting the planet. They'll be a danger to us.'

Jennifer noticed a look of total bewilderment on the Prime Minister's face. It reflected her own.

'Stage Four will be War Games,' Taksin continued. 'Again, I trust the phrase is self-explanatory. By that time, I'm sure General Wilson will be keen to kit out his troops for manoeuvres, and I suggest the Moon would be a good location to start with.'

Judging by the smile on General Wilson's face, Jennifer reckoned he was liking what he was hearing.

'Stage Five I've termed Exploration. We will be flying the Endeavour around the solar system and I'm sure your scientists are eager to visit each of your planets. During this period, you will experience the drudgery of acting as an armed escort, but you should be able to get actively involved in ferrying around scientists, their equipment and provisions. Now then, gentlemen, any questions before I leave you?'

The atmosphere in the room was of stunned silence. No one knew what to say.

'Right then, I'll be going. Group Captain, I will be available at any time for any query or any assistance you may need. Feel free to seek my advice whenever necessary. If you can't find me, ask Commander Collins as she will know where to locate me. And congratulations on your wings.'

Somewhat surprising Jennifer, Group Captain Tyson snapped to attention, saluted Taksin, and said, 'Thank you, Admiral, sir.'

Surprising Jennifer even more, Taksin held out his hand in a gesture she had never expected to see. As the men shook hands with each other, she smiled as the scene unfolded and muttered quietly under her breath, 'Thank god for that.'

Chapter Thirty-Three

Lift off

The atmosphere in Endeavour's Flight Control Room intensified as twenty-five flight personnel gathered, waiting nervously for instruction in the knowledge that they were about to assume control of the multi-million-ton monster of alien technology.

Jennifer stood bouncing on the balls of her feet, as though ready to leap into action if called upon. Taksin appeared calm, she thought, but then he must have undergone take-off hundreds of times before, if not thousands. He stood in the centre of the room, for all the world looking like a conductor readying his orchestra to strike the first chord.

'Are we all ready?' asked Taksin.

'Yes, Admiral,' came the resounding reply.

'Right, let's dispense with lectures, we'll just learn as we go. Captain Mandrake, take the chair, please.' Taksin waited until the man had sat down. 'You have control, Captain, you have a list of instructions. Read them off slowly, please.'

Captain Mandrake nodded. 'Outer doors sealed?'

Prasert nudged one of the crew in from of him. 'That means you. Confirm that blue light is lit up.'

'Check.'

'Engine speed for lift off?'

Taksin grabbed the hand of a crew member sitting nearby which had already been gripping a lever and eased it forward. 'Bring it forward until that needle moves up into the yellow zone. Hold that position.'

'Check.'

'Course set?'

'Check,' replied Taksin himself. 'Hopefully upwards.' He received a few nervous grunts in response.

'Clearance from Tower?'

'Check,' replied the radio operator.

'Then let's take her up.'

Taksin, Prasert and Narai guided the operators' hands over the instruments and seconds later Endeavour lifted off and soared into the skies. Jennifer gave an audible sigh, a mixture of pleasure and relief. She caught the Prime Minister's eye and said, 'I reckon the whole world will be watching our progress tonight.'

'I'm sure they will. It's big news,' replied the Prime Minister. 'Let's hope it doesn't start another world-wide panic.'

'Me too, I don't think I could take any more canned peas.'

The Prime Minister looked nonplussed. 'Canned peas?'

Jennifer smiled. 'It's a long story.'

For an hour the crew was put through its paces as Taksin guided the ship through a series of flying, hovering and landing exercises. By mid-afternoon, Jennifer could tell Taksin was happy. She hadn't seen him so relaxed since the venture started.

'Great work, crew,' said Taksin. 'Let's take her into space and go around the Earth a few times. I guess you've all been waiting for that.'

Jennifer grinned from ear to ear. Things were going well.

Three hours later, having orbited the world four times and allowing everyone the opportunity to take selfies against the backdrop of Earth below, Jennifer yawned, rubbed her eyes and looked at her watch. She went over to where Taksin was sitting studying a screen and whispered into his ear.

Taksin nodded. 'Okay people,' he said to the crew. 'It's six o'clock. Let's break for the day. We'll set the ship in orbit and let you get some rest. If anyone wants to disembark, let Captain Mandrake know and he'll liaise with Group Captain Tyson for transport. We'll resume training tomorrow at, say, nine o'clock.'

The Prime Minister went up to Taksin and said, 'Admiral, I can't begin to describe how happy you've made me today. I never thought I'd live to see this day.'

Taksin grinned. 'Nor did I. You've no idea what I've had to

sacrifice to get this far.'

'I can imagine. We really are terribly grateful for your assistance.'

'So you keep telling me.'

'I do, don't I,' replied the Prime Minister. 'But it's true nevertheless. We'll be fighting-fit fairly soon, won't we, at the rate we're going now?'

'We will indeed. If it makes you sleep easier, remember that we can identify anything as big as a ship entering our galaxy at least a month before it could actually arrive here. If we detected a ship tonight, we'd be ready to fight by the time it got here.'

The Prime Minister offered a warm smile. 'That is indeed very comforting. On that note, though, I will leave you. I must return to matters of state, as well as to my family.'

'Then I shall say goodnight,' said Taksin.

The Prime Minister turned to Jennifer. 'Are you staying?'

'No, sir. Admiral Prasert is kindly giving me a lift to my parents' home tonight. I'm having a break tomorrow.'

'The beach calls,' said Taksin enigmatically. 'As do the horses, no doubt.'

Jennifer gave Taksin a curious look.

Chapter Thirty-Four

Grounded

Dongtan Beach was deserted. Jennifer had the bay to herself. As far as the eye could see, there was nothing but fine white sand, Hoo Kwang trees and the clear blue tropical sea. Leaving Surachai to tether the horses in the corral, she ran down to the shoreline, kicked off her shoes, stripped naked and dived headlong into the calm, warm waters. As she surfaced, she turned to the shoreline and shouted, 'Come on in, Surachai, it's beautiful. Don't be shy.'

Surachai took a furtive look behind him, appearing to wrestle with his conscience for a few moments, then, with a broad grin on his face, eagerly followed suit.

After a couple of minutes larking around in the water, Jennifer found herself standing waist-deep, closer to Surachai than she had anticipated. Her arms lifted, as though they had a mind of their own, and wound themselves around his neck. She inched forward until their noses touched, until their lips touched. Surachai laid his hands gently on her hips, drew her closer until they were entwined in a passionate kiss.

After a hectic and intense few days of meetings, discussions, training sessions and peace-keeping between senior officers, Jennifer had been relieved to be given the opportunity of a well-deserved rest. A moment of unplanned, unexpected intimacy with Surachai was exactly what she needed to boost her spirits. It was a stolen moment; one she hoped would help give her strength to battle through the next week.

Unfortunately, a moment was all it was going to be. For just as she became aware of quite how eager Surachai was for her attention, she also became aware of a buzzing noise coming from the pile of clothes she'd abandoned on the beach. She broke from Surachai's embrace and said, 'Sorry. Duty calls.' She waded back to shore, rummaged in the pockets of her shorts and brought out the communication device making the offensive racket. She depressed a button and said, 'Jennifer Collins speaking.'

'Commander Collins? It's Captain Mandrake. I'm sorry to bother you on your day off.'

Jennifer drew a deep breath. 'That's alright, Captain. How can I help?'

'Well, if you'll forgive me for stooping to a much over-used quote, I'd say Houston, we have a problem.'

'Which is?'

'We've been grounded.'

'I beg your pardon?'

'General Narai instructed us to cease operations. We're back in Brize Norton, on the ground, with strict orders not to attempt flight.'

'What? Why, what's happened?'

'There was a bit of ding-dong earlier. Admiral Taksin got into this terrible row with General Narai and Admiral Prasert. It wasn't a pretty sight, I can tell you. Anyway, the result was that Admiral Taksin flung off in a huff.'

'What were they rowing about?'

'That I can't say, Commander. They weren't speaking any type of language I'm familiar with. However, judging by the body language, I'd say Admiral Taksin is as pissed-off as is possible to get, if you'll excuse my French.'

'And the other two?'

'Well, General Narai appeared to be calm, rational and determined. Admiral Prasert seemed indifferent but I'd say he was on General Narai's side. They both seem okay, it's Admiral Taksin that's got the hump.'

'You think Admiral Taksin is upset?'

'Aye, Commander. Very upset. Distressed, if you will. Whatever they were rowing about, I'd say it was two against one. I'd also say that part of Admiral Taksin's anger arose because he was getting no support from General Narai or Admiral Prasert on whatever issue he had. That's just my take on it, mind.'

Jennifer tried to imagine such a scenario. 'I see. Do you know of anything that may have occurred to trigger off this outburst?'

There was a pause before Captain Mandrake spoke. 'Well, yes, something odd did happen about half an hour before the row. And this is just speculation Commander, mind, but if the incident concerns what I think it did then, yes, it may well have caused the row.'

Jennifer turned to see Surachai emerging from the sea, both hands cupped in front of him in an attempt at modesty. She fell silent, enjoying the sight of his nakedness as he wondered off to retrieve his clothes. 'Sorry, Captain, what was the incident?'

'Admiral Prasert had been giving a lecture in the engine room. I'm told he caught sight of a glass monitor, tapped it a couple of times, then fell silent whilst appearing distracted. Without further explanation, he cut short his lecture, came up to the bridge and talked quietly to General Narai. The two of them disappeared back down to the engine room together, came back up after a few minutes and spent a long time glued to a screen ploughing through technical stuff from what I could see. When Admiral Taksin joined them, that's when all hell broke loose.'

'What do you make of the incident?'

'Well, I talked to a couple of people who had been in that lecture. They say Admiral Prasert was talking about the nature of propulsion at the time, so they got the impression the glass monitor might have had something to do with fuel, although he never got that far in his explanations. It's that tapping that worries me, Commander. I remember, as a lad, watching my father do that to the fuel gauge on his old Morris Minor Traveller, as though hoping it had got stuck.'

Jennifer was shocked. 'You're saying we're out of fuel?'

'That's anyone's guess, Commander.'

'But it's your guess?'

'Aye, it is. Not just mine either. I've had several of the crew come back from the canteen in the last half-hour asking if the rumour's true. News has spread fast and it's not going down well, Commander, people are questioning the competency of those three gentlemen. Checking there was enough fuel at the outset of this operation would seem to have been a pretty basic requirement.'

Jennifer sighed. 'Oh, god.'

'I'm with you there, Commander.'

'Have you talked this through with anyone else?'

'I have, yes, Commander. Admiral Dickens told me to call you. He said you're the only one who knows where Admiral Taksin lives.'

Jennifer turned her attention back to Surachai, amused as he struggled to get his sarong to fit in a way that could mask a rather prominent protrusion. Jennifer said, 'Look, Captain, something's come up this end that I need to deal with right now, but please tell Admiral Dickens I'll deal with it as soon as I can.' With that, she ended the call, picked up her clothes, wondered over to Surachai, took his hand and led him up to the privacy of the communal beach hut.

Chapter Thirty-Five

To know a king

Freshly showered, wearing leather sandals, a light summery knee-length dress and a flowery hat, Jennifer hoped her demure look would help placate an angry king.

His Majesty King Taksin The Great was not receiving visitors today, Jennifer was informed as she approached a clerk in the grand entrance hall of the royal palace. She smiled sweetly and handed over a document for the clerk to read. She'd been told that it would guarantee immediate access, day or night, and was pleased but slightly surprised when the clerk jumped up out of his seat, bowed deeply and asked her to follow him. She let the eager clerk guide her through the main stateroom, up the stairs, into the anteroom where she and the Prime Minister had confronted Taksin a few weeks earlier, and out onto the balcony.

Taksin was sitting alone on a wicker chair, a glass tumbler in hand, a bottle of brandy on a table at his side, looking morose. She said, 'I beg your pardon for the intrusion, sir.'

Taksin turned his head and cast her an appreciative eye. 'You look nice, Jennifer. I've become so used to your usual austere look, dressed in uniform, I forget just how pretty you are.'

'Uniforms have their place, sir. I'm off duty at the moment. May I join you?'

'Of course you may.' Taksin gestured towards a spare chair. 'Would you like a drink? Iced tea perhaps?'

Jennifer looked at her watch and pointed to the brandy bottle. 'It's after six o'clock, so I'll join you in a glass of whatever your having, if

I may.'

Surprise registered on Taksin's face. 'Really? This is strong stuff, I'll have you know. Good quality though, Churchill introduced me to it.'

Astonished, Jennifer asked, 'As in Winston Churchill? The wartime prime minister?'

'That's the one.' Taksin grunted and said, 'Dear god that man could drink.'

'I had no idea you two had met.'

Taksin nodded. 'Several times actually. The last time was in nineteen forty-one when he was up to his neck in problems emanating from the war, and drinking far too heavily. I went to see him at his home, Chartwell I think his house was called, along with Prasert, and before we knew it, we were both legless. He seemed quite alright though.'

'You got drunk with Churchill?'

Taksin shrugged. 'I'm not proud of it. He kept refilling our glasses. Eventually, he had to get a couple of soldiers to help us get back to Prasert's home.'

Jennifer laughed. 'That must have been a sight. But why did you go there, I didn't think you got involved with other country's affairs.'

'I don't as a rule, but I needed his consent to help me with a domestic matter.'

Jennifer laughed again. 'Don't tell me that domestic matter was something to do with a certain Mrs Maud Comyns?'

Taksin's eyebrows raised. 'How on earth do you know about her?'

'I interviewed an old soldier recently, Private Alfred Fry. You may remember him; Mrs Comyns' insisted you should give him his leg back. He also mentioned Mrs Comyns had been instrumental in getting you to give him and his two mates a lift back to England, although he did say you gave him a really rough ride home.'

Taksin snorted, picked the brandy bottle up, poured half an inch into a spare glass, handed it to Jennifer, then topped up his own glass. 'I let that woman take advantage of my good nature once. Bad mistake. She wouldn't let go after that; she got her hooks right into me. I vowed never to show such weakness again.'

'Rubbish, sir. Your good nature comes out often. And it's not a weakness; it's actually a strength.' She picked the glass up, said 'Cheers' and knocked the contents back in one gulp.

Taksin stared in astonishment at Jennifer's empty glass. 'Good grief, Jennifer. I didn't have you down as a hard drinker.'

'I was a university student for six years; I've had plenty of practice.' She helped herself to a refill.

'That will do your liver no end of damage.'

'You mean it won't to yours?'

Taksin stared into his empty glass. 'Touché.'

Emboldened by the alcohol, Jennifer plucked up the courage to say, 'May I ask you a question, sir? I'd like to clear something up, something that's intrigued me.'

Taksin grunted. 'Why not. As long as it doesn't cause me too much grief, that is. I'm not sure I could handle any more of that today.'

Jennifer took a gulp of brandy. 'Back in the nineteen sixties, when the Americans unwisely sent a submarine here, President Burford came to see you didn't he?'

Taksin appeared to reflect on the matter. 'Yes, he did. He came to ask for the return of his ships and men.'

'And you just gave them to him?'

'Well, yes. I did. Eventually.'

'I find that odd, sir, if you don't mind me saying so. From the research I did on the incident, it appears you were demanding a ransom for the safe return of his men. A very large one. But I found no mention of any payment. I was curious to know if President Burford managed to persuade you to do the honourable thing.'

'Pray on my weaknesses, you mean? Like Mrs Comyns used to?'

Jennifer shook her head and took another gulp of brandy. 'No, sir, that's not what I meant. My academic training has been in social anthropology. I'm interested in human behaviour. I don't see any weakness in you. But I would like to get to know your kind side.'

'So you can manipulate me?'

'Again, that's not what I meant, sir. I think there's a caring side to you. I'd like to meet it, that's all.'

Taksin starred into the glass in his hand. 'He offered me a bar of chocolate in return.'

Jennifer's eyes opened wide. 'I beg your pardon?'

'President Burford. He offered me a bar of chocolate. A Hershey Bar, I think it was called. He brought it with him in an ice-box so it wouldn't melt. Said he knew I could have had the whole of his country if I'd wanted to, by force. Said that the chocolate bar typified America, the American spirit, the American dream, that the country was mine to take, to destroy or leave to flourish.'

'And you fell for that flannel?'

Taksin snorted. 'If you mean did I fall for the bullshit, no of course not. He'd apologised profusely by that stage. He knew I wasn't interested in money. There was little room for him to manoeuvre. The offering of a ten-cent bar of chocolate was just the right level of gesture. I took a piece, offered it back to him. That broke the tension.'

'Wow! I'm impressed.'

'At the chocolate? It was disgusting. I hate the stuff. So did Burford. But we ate it, sealing the deal as it were.'

'I meant I was impressed by the sheer nerve of President Burford.'

Taksin grinned. 'I suppose I can be nice occasionally.'

Jennifer reached for the brandy bottle, helped herself to another large measure and knocked it back in one. 'Are we out of fuel?' she asked suddenly. 'Is that the problem, why you've grounded Endeavour?'

Taksin contemplated the bottom of his empty glass in silence for a few moments, before pouring himself a refill. 'You know what I used to be, before I came to this planet? A ship's captain. A commercial ship that is, not a military one. I had command of the biggest ship ever built, with a capacity for a couple of billion cubic metres of freight in the hold, along with a million passengers. Most of my former life was spent in deep space, travelling from one planet to another, transporting provisions, raw materials, or whole populations for colonisation of new planets.' He stood up, stepped forward, leant over the balustrades and stared down at the formal gardens below. 'Life was simple then, I just had to pick up and deliver, keep harmony amongst the crew. Sometimes I feel I'd just like to pack up here, fly off back to that way of life.'

Jennifer sat patiently while Taksin appeared to be reminiscing.

'Before we arrived here, there was another planet we stopped at. It was much bigger than this one, about three times the size, I guess, but similar in atmosphere and climate. It was wild, raw, untamed, perhaps like it may have been here on Earth a hundred thousand years ago or so. That planet had it all; snow-capped mountains, huge forests, savannah as far as the eye could see. Crystal clear waters in the rivers and seas. And, of course, absolutely no pollution. It was one of the most beautiful places I have ever visited.'

Jennifer asked, 'Why didn't you stay there?'

Taksin shrugged. 'After travelling with the same two faces for so many years, I guess we were ready for some fresh company. There's only so much loneliness one can take. So we didn't stay long. Just long enough to re-stock on dilithium, take on fresh water and food.'

Jennifer picked up on a word she'd never heard before. 'Dilithium? Is that your source of power?'

Taksin shook his head. 'Not by itself, no, but it's needed in the nuclear fusion process. Sorry, we haven't covered that subject yet, have we?'

'No. So, Endeavour is running low on this dilithium stuff?'

'I'm afraid so, yes. There's only about six months' supply left, which is nothing really. Perilously close to empty. Normally there'd be enough dilithium on board for hundreds of years of travelling, if not thousands. I didn't think to check; one rarely has to. It's utter madness, if not downright dangerous, to run it down to such low levels, but the last crew were pretty dim. Dimmer than I imagined possible. They were just a bunch of thugs on the run.'

'Can't we just fill up again, here?'

'There's very little dilithium occurring naturally on this planet, and I'm not sure we could manufacture it. I'm a ship's captain, not a scientist.'

'Our scientists could help, couldn't they?'

Taksin shrugged. 'It's an idea. Prasert looked into it earlier today, but he's not hopeful. Says it would take too long and use up too much energy to make its manufacture feasible.'

'Can't we borrow some from one of the other craft?'

Taksin shook his head. 'My ship has plenty, but it's far too dangerous to attempt to extract it.'

'But this other planet you mentioned, does that have any?'

Taksin sighed, returned to his chair and poured out another glass of brandy. 'There's an abundant supply of naturally occurring heavy metals and isotopes on that planet.'

'Then let's go there, as quick as we can.'

Taksin shook his head. 'It's not that simple, Jennifer.'

'Technically?'

'No, I meant socially, politically, morally.'

Jennifer looked puzzled. 'You've lost me.'

'Two problems exist. First, as I just said, there's an abundant natural supply of heavy metals on that planet.'

'Sorry, you'll have to excuse me, I'm a bit thick in science.'

'Gold, Jennifer. It's everywhere. You can kick lumps of it on the ground like you would with flint or chalk on this planet.'

Jennifer swallowed another large gulp of brandy. 'And that's a problem is it?'

'You're the expert in social anthropology. Think about it. We go there with a full crew. What would they do on discovering an abundant supply of gold? Personally, I imagine they'd go berserk with greed, thinking they were entitled to whatever they found. And if we tried to stop them, they'd probably mutiny, thinking we were the greedy ones denying them their fortunes.'

'We could devise a plan to cope with that. We could restrict their entitlement for instance; make that part of the conditions before we went there.'

Taksin gave Jennifer a weary look. 'That's as maybe, Jennifer, but what would happen to the financial stability of this world if it was flooded with a new, abundant source of gold. Gold prices would crash. Remember that gold supports the underlying value of most currencies on this planet. Imagine currencies collapsing all around the globe. There would be mass unemployment, bankruptcies, poverty, complete worldwide mayhem.'

Jennifer frowned. 'Just how much gold are you talking about?'

'Millions if not billions of tons, I should say. Compare that to the fact that all the gold ever mined on this planet comes to less than two hundred thousand tons. Mind you, that's not counting what I've got in store, obviously.'

Jennifer's jaw dropped. 'I beg your pardon?'

'Well, as I was saying, we stocked up on dilithium before moving on. Then we discovered this planet and realised it would suit our purposes just fine. So we decided to stay, but given the advanced stage of civilisation here, we couldn't just impose ourselves by force and expect the locals to accept our presence. We needed money to win over the locals, to buy our acceptance, as it were. So, realising that gold was a precious commodity here, we flew back to the other planet and loaded up with a pile of the stuff.'

Jennifer was gawking at Taksin, open-mouthed. 'You did what?'

Taksin gestured to the roof above him. 'Where do you think the gold came from to furnish this palace so lavishly?'

Jennifer took a sharp intake of breath. 'You mean you looted another planet to finance your lavish lifestyle here?'

Taksin looked pained. 'No one owns that planet, Jennifer.'

'How much did you take?'

'Well, we didn't take that much, maybe three or four hundred thousand tons of ore. We used most of it in construction and decoration over the years, especially in temples, and to pay for setting up the administration of this country, but once the country's agriculture system was running efficiently, we didn't need to use anymore because of the receipt of export duties. Fortunately, our neighbours have always needed as much rice and spice as they can get their hands on.'

'Is there much left? Of your gold, I mean.'

'There's still quite a bit in store; I suppose about half of the original amount.'

'Which is worth, how much?'

'The amount left? If the ore was refined, I suppose it would be worth, what five hundred billion pounds sterling, something like that?'

Jennifer spluttered. 'Five hundred billion pounds' worth of gold. Just sitting in store? Unused?'

'We have no use for it, other than for financial security of course.'

'Financial security,' Jennifer repeated woodenly. 'And what gives you the right to take it but deny it to others?'

Taksin looked hard at Jennifer. 'Are you judging me?'

Jennifer flushed, realised she'd been far too familiar. 'I'm sorry, your majesty. The brandy loosened my tongue. I should not have spoken to you in that tone. I apologise unreservedly.'

Taksin sighed, and rubbed his face. 'No, Jennifer, don't apologise to me and please don't call me your majesty.'

Jennifer's head dropped.

Taksin looked grieved. He placed a hand on Jennifer's arm. 'Jennifer, please, it's me who should apologise. I told you a while ago I have no human friends. I can't, not here, not with the way the people in this country hold me in awe. You know how they prostrate themselves at my feet. They venerate me so much. Too much, truth be told. It would be impossible to enter the level of intimacy needed for friendship to blossom. So, I have no friends to talk to like this, as we are now. If you felt anger towards me a moment ago, then I must have deserved it, from a human perspective, that is.'

Jennifer looked up; her eyes moist. 'Thank you, sir.'

'There's so much you don't know about me, Jennifer, so much I shall never be able to explain, but I'm not a bad guy at heart. And I really do value your opinion, even if it doesn't sit well with me at times. Please don't try to be anything other than yourself in my company.'

Jennifer forced a smile. 'There you go, Mrs Comyns was right, you do have a good nature behind that hard-face mask of yours.'

Taksin smiled. 'Very occasionally, maybe. Look, I've had far too much to drink. Let's meet up in a day or two, on board Endeavour, and talk through how we can manage a visit to this infamous planet I've mentioned without me losing my temper.'

Jennifer nodded.

'I just don't want to see that planet destroyed by humans colonising it, pillaging, stripping out its resources, cutting down its forests, dumping toxic rubbish everywhere. It would break my heart, yet Narai can't see that, he just shrugs and says planetary development is the way of life.'

'I'll come up with something, sir. A compromise somehow.'

'Thank you. Would you like a lift home? I can get someone to escort you if you like?'

'Thank you, sir, I think I may be a bit unsteady on my feet tonight, especially as I haven't had the chance to eat much today.'

'I could send a message to Surachai to come and rescue you. He should be rested enough by now.'

Jennifer blushed. 'What's that supposed to mean?' After a cursory pause she added, 'Have you been spying on me?'

Taksin broke into a wide grin. 'Me? No, never. Wouldn't dream of it. I just like to know that people living in my country are happy, that's all. You and Surachai look very happy together. Look, why don't you stay for a meal. It won't be private, I'm afraid, as it's customary for me to dine with a host of ministers and others vying for my attention, but at least you'll get something solid inside you quick. I'll send word to Surachai to meet you here. He can join us for the meal. It's time I had a talk with him, find out whether his intentions towards you are honourable. He'll be chuffed.'

Jennifer looked aghast. 'Chuffed? Mortified, more like, just like I'd be if I found out you were spying on us at the beach this afternoon.'

Taksin reached for the brandy bottle and grinned. 'Another top up for you, perhaps?'

Jennifer let out a sigh of exasperation. 'You were spying on us, weren't you? I don't believe it.'

'Jennifer, you are a very beautiful woman. Men are bound to look at you, it's in their nature.'

'That's as maybe, sir. But there's a fine line between happening to catch a look and voyeurism.'

Taksin nodded. 'I apologise profusely, of course, but how was I to know you were going to strip off on the beach which, after all, is a public place?'

Jennifer sat in silence for a moment, trying to think of an appropriate retort. None came to her that wouldn't involve straying into areas she wasn't too comfortable with. 'You said there were two problems?'

'I beg your pardon?'

'With that other planet you mentioned just now. You said two problems exist. Gold's the first. What's the second.'

'Ah, yes. That problem. Well . . .' Taksin stood up again, stepped forward to the balcony, leant over and stared vacantly at the gardens below.

'Come on,' Jennifer said. 'Don't keep me on tenterhooks, spill the beans.'

Taksin shook his head in apparent bemusement. 'You do utter some odd idioms at times, Jennifer.'

'It's the brandy, sir.'

'Indeed. Very well, let's hope the brandy will make you forget what I'm about to say. This other planet, it's teeming with life, both in the oceans and across the land.'

'Life?' Jennifer responded sharply. 'On a planet that's close to us? How far away?'

'A couple of months, or so, by the short route, if I remember correctly. Well within range of the current fuel capacity.'

'I was thinking more of the threat from other lifeforms. Is it one of the planets you've helped populate?'

Taksin sighed deeply and sat back down. 'We were fleeing our civilisation, not helping to expand it.'

'There's none of your race there?'

Taksin shifted uncomfortably, took a swig of brandy. 'I might as well tell you now, you'll work it out in time. There are lifeforms there that originated here on Earth.'

Jennifer's face registered the shock she felt inside. 'Like what?'

'Well, a huge range from your animal kingdom, really. Especially useful lifeforms that one would take on a planetary population mission.'

'Such as?'

'Well, food-fish like cod, salmon and trout to fill the seas and rivers; boar, oxen and chickens on the land. Plus the cute ones and those of scientific interest. I imagine some of those taken may be extinct on this planet by now.'

'And these animals came from Earth? Did you take them there?'

'No, we did not. They were there already.'

'You mean it was populated by someone else before you got there?'

'So it seems. When we arrived here on Earth, we took DNA samples from your species and soon realised we weren't the first visitors to this planet. We searched, but never found any physical trace, either here or on that other planet, of anyone from our corner of the galaxy. However, there is definite evidence of genetic engineering in your species. The greatest extent of genetic interference seems to have occurred about two hundred and fifty thousand years ago. It's why the three of us look so similar to you.'

Jennifer gasped. Of all the things she imagined Taksin might have said, that was not one of them. 'Are you saying you're the missing link?'

'Well, not me personally,' Taksin replied with a curt smile. 'But yes, it seems someone from my race manipulated the DNA of primitive human ancestors. Some crossbreeds were successful, others not and so died out.'

The stunning revelation left Jennifer's head spinning. 'Why would they do that?'

'It's what scientists do, I suppose. Push the boundaries.'

'But the morality of it? They're playing god. What right have they got to do that?'

'Exactly, Jennifer. And I'm not defending them. The facts are that a long time ago my people got involved with genetic engineering.

Inevitably, scientists were soon able to offer stronger, disease-resistant babies with prolonged life spans, which the richer members of society eagerly bought into. The consequences were predictable; our population expanded at an unsustainable rate and colonisation of other planets was the only answer to meet the demand for resources. We were therefore compelled to build huge transporter ships and resettle vast numbers of workers on other planets to produce food and materials for the home planet. In time, however, the colonies grew to despise the home planet, especially because the resettled workers, most of which were from the poorer sections of society, were denied the benefits of expensive gene-manipulation.'

Jennifer could well see where such a situation would head. 'War would be inevitable, I imagine.'

'Indeed. Which is why our government decided to ban any further genetic engineering on people. To try to reduce the level of tension. Unfortunately, a lot of scientists were displeased and the war, as such, developed between science and morality. Many scientists fled as far away as they could, to pursue their experiments and ambitions.'

'And some came here?'

'I believe so. Though as I say, we found no physical evidence of settlement.'

'And they would have taken the animals to the other planet? For what purpose?'

Taksin shrugged. 'I can only speculate. Maybe there was an impending natural disaster that caused them to relocate. Maybe some of the scientists had a disagreement, split from the main party and decided to rebuild their version of a perfect world somewhere else. Took all the animals they wanted.'

Jennifer gasped. 'And the animals went in two by two! Oh my god, you're describing an ark. You're not suggesting that was the basis for the story of Noah's Ark, are you?'

Taksin shrugged again. 'Who knows? It's a possibility, I guess. Noah was reputed to have lived until he was nine-hundred and fifty years old, an age well beyond a normal human range. I don't know how long folk-tales can be passed down, orally, amongst human societies.'

Jennifer sat ogling at Taksin for a while. 'This speculation mustn't get into the public domain.'

'I agree. Wholeheartedly.'

'Exactly where is this planet?'

'The planet is close to what you call the Dog Star, in the constellation Canis Major.'

Jennifer's jaw dropped. 'Not Serius A. Don't tell me that.'

'Why ever not?'

'Because of the Dogon Tribe. I couldn't bear having to tell one of my more flippant colleagues he was right after all.'

Taksin looked non-plussed. 'You've lost me.'

Jennifer took a deep breath. 'The Dogon Tribe live in Mali, West Africa. They have an ancient legend that they were visited by people called the Nommos from the Sirius system thousands of years ago. Some of their ancient artefacts depict drawings of the Serius configuration, including Serius B, a white dwarf that wasn't discovered until relatively recently.'

Taksin sucked in air through his teeth. 'Right. Okay. I wasn't aware of them. That's going to make matters even more complicated, having to explain that away.'

Jennifer rubbed her chin. 'Not necessarily,' she replied cryptically.

'Meaning?'

'Meaning, I need to think about it. After some food, that is, and after the effects of this brandy have worn off.'

Chapter Thirty-Six

Altruism

Endeavour had been parked up, idle, in Brize Norton for three full days. Alone by herself, back in uniform and feeling very isolated, Jennifer sat at a table in the ship's canteen with a lukewarm cup of coffee between her hands, surreptitiously eavesdropping on the vexed conversations at nearby tables. It didn't take a doctorate in social anthropology to interpret the restless and demoralised mood of the room.

The canteen fell silent. Jennifer looked up to see all eyes had turned towards the entrance. She noticed Taksin, standing still, scanning the room. She got up, walked towards him, tried to ignore the barrage of hostile looks from the tables she passed, hoping to god no one would vent their anger openly.

'Is everything set?' asked Taksin.

'Yes, sir. Star Fleet Council is all present, waiting for your arrival.'

'Good,' Taksin nodded. 'We'd better get on with it then.'

Jennifer walked with Taksin in silence along a corridor, through an empty Flight Control Room and into an adjacent spacious room which normally served as part of the captain's quarters. As she made her way to the table around which the Prime Minister, Chiefs of Staff and Taksin's two compatriots were already sitting, she noticed Taksin appeared to be doing his best to avoid catching anyone's eye. As she sat down, she said, 'May I start the meeting?'

'By all means,' responded Taksin without lifting his eyes off the table.

Jennifer waited until all other eyes were focused on her. 'The situation is that the rumours of a lack of fuel are true. There's about six months' worth of fuel left on this ship, which is why Endeavour was grounded. Admiral Taksin was concerned that fuel should be conserved before any decision is made on how to re-fuel. Unfortunately, that has led to unforeseen consequences. I'm sure no one here needs to be appraised of the feelings of the crew. They feel upset, angry, like a child having been given a new toy only to see it snatched away before getting to play with it.'

Taksin opened his mouth to speak, but Jennifer cut him off. 'Sir, no one is blaming you for the situation we find ourselves in. Well, at least not openly. Not yet anyway.'

Taksin raised an eyebrow.

'I have a solution,' Jennifer continued. 'One that I think may be acceptable to all parties, although I doubt it will fully satisfy everyone's hopes. It is, therefore, somewhat of a compromise, which will require a bit of give or take on all sides to make it work. However, I believe it is the best way forward.'

Taksin caught Jennifer's eye. 'Will I like it?'

'I doubt it, sir. The best I am hoping for is that you will not reject it out of hand.'

Taksin sighed. 'As good as that, is it?'

'Yes, sir. And I'd like to add that it is probably the only practical way forward.'

Taksin asked, 'Does everyone around the table know the details?'

'No, sir. I've been gathering my thoughts this last couple of days. This is the first opportunity I've had of expressing them openly.'

'Then please feel free to go ahead.'

Jennifer took a deep breath. 'We need the original planned venture to continue and succeed. To do that, we need to re-fuel this ship. The only viable source of fuel is on another planet which, for the sake of a name, I shall call Voltaris. Now, obviously we need to send Endeavour there as soon as possible before the fuel tanks are completely empty, preferably within this week.'

All eyes turned to Taksin hoping for a sign of consent. It was given.

'Admiral Taksin,' Jennifer continued, 'has expressed his concern about human intervention on Voltaris because it is rich in resources and is one of the most beautiful planets he's ever visited, and I think we all know just how badly man can destroy the environment in search of wealth. Of particular concern to Admiral Taksin is that Voltaris possesses huge reserves of heavy metals, especially gold which, he says, is as common as flint on Earth. He feels the reaction to finding an abundant supply of gold will bring out the worst aspects of man's nature. Furthermore, he feels bringing huge amounts of gold back to this planet will undermine the entire world's financial systems. I believe he is correct in this matter. We therefore need to tackle this issue up front.' Jennifer paused to allow her message to sink in.

'Nevertheless, Jennifer,' interrupted the Prime Minister. 'Our budget is rather stretched at the moment. A few tons of gold would come in handy.'

'Again, I agree with that, sir.'

'So?'

'So, sir, I have a plan. We must accept that some colonisation and exploitation of Voltaris is inevitable, but we must guard against the worse aspects arising. Fortunately, we have hundreds of years of history upon which to draw experience. One thing humans know is how to get it badly wrong. So, my plan is, to avoid destroying the beauty of Voltaris, we must exert strict control over who lives there, how they live, what they mine, what they grow, what they cut down, what they fish and what they do with their waste.'

General Wilson interrupted by asking, 'You propose to impose an authoritarian regime on any people living and working there? May I remind you what happened to the Americas. The British government's handling of those colonies, especially the imposition of taxes, led to disaster, in terms of its empire, that is.'

'I couldn't agree more, General, which is why the British government should go nowhere near the planet. I propose that Voltaris is placed under Star Fleet Council's sole ownership and control so that we are responsible for the government of that planet, including setting policies on residency, housing, mining, agriculture, fishing and managing woodland. Naturally, I would not expect any of us to be involved on a day-to-day basis, so I propose recruiting the necessary specialists and bureaucrats to man the entire operation on our behalf.'

Taksin rubbed his jaw thoughtfully. 'Am I right in thinking you would model the administration of Voltaris on Surithani?'

'Indeed I would, sir. The freedom of unfettered exploitation of resources granted to commercial enterprises under capitalism leads to greed, political corruption, destruction of nature, pollution and a loss of humanity. On the other hand, the lack of personal freedom and central control exerted on a population under communism causes no fewer problems. A resource-controlled system based on benevolent dictatorship has its merits and works well in Surithani. I don't see why it can't be applied equally well to Voltaris.'

Taksin raised an eyebrow again. 'I see. Well, I suppose that would be difficult for me to argue against.'

'One moment, Jennifer,' said the Prime Minister. 'It sounds as though you're expecting Voltaris to have a large population. Just how many people do you expect to go there?'

'Millions, sir.'

The Prime Minister looked aghast. 'Millions! Dear god, really? What are they going to be doing with themselves?'

'As I just alluded to, sir, there would be farming, mining, tree felling, fishing and construction communities. The idea would be to replicate communities as we find them here on Earth, minus the pollution, poverty and social injustices.'

The Prime Minister gave Jennifer a puzzled look. 'With what aim? Merely for the sake of colonisation?'

'Oh, no, sir. The aim would be to save Planet Earth.' Jennifer now had seven pairs of eyes staring at her in bewilderment. 'Sorry, gentlemen,' she said. 'I haven't got that far yet, have I?'

The Prime Minister chuckled. 'No, Jennifer. I don't think you have. Pray continue.'

'Well, sir, I view this as an altruistic opportunity to help save this world. By utilising the natural resources of Voltaris wisely, we can call a halt to much of the harmful exploitation and environmental damage being done here.'

Taksin perked up. 'That sounds noble, Jennifer, but how would you propose to achieve that goal?'

'By trading materials like wood, grains, meat, fish and minerals from Voltaris on favourable terms with governments on Earth, provided those governments enforce strict environmental controls in their own countries. Our seas and forests need a break; the resources from Voltaris will enable that break to happen.'

'Whoa, Jennifer,' General Wilson interrupted. 'One moment, please. Just who exactly is going to be on Voltaris to do all this farming and mining?'

'Well, I suggest we throw the suggestion open to the public. Advertise in the newspapers and on television. Offer a new life to volunteers; give them all a plot of land each on which they can build a family home and live a better life in tune with nature.'

General Wilson winced. 'You really think anyone would go? It would be like turning the clocks back five hundred years for them.'

'Exactly, General. That's the attraction. Millions of people are disillusioned with the corruption, greed and inhumanity found on this world. It would be a fresh start for them. The venture would be as thrilling as it was for the pioneers and frontiersmen who headed off into the American wildness a couple of hundred years ago.'

'Millions though?' General Wilson continued in attack. 'You think millions would want to go?'

'Absolutely, General. Think of the fifteen million refugees we have at the moment trapped in appalling unsanitary conditions because of wars. This scheme would provide hope for them. They could rebuild their communities without fear of armed soldiers, religious fanaticism, terrorists or corrupt politicians.'

'Refugees?' The Prime Minister put in. 'You see this as a solution to the world's refugee problem?'

'It could one of the benefits, yes.'

'Interesting idea,' responded the Prime Minister. 'But just a second, Jennifer, before you get carried away, Endeavour can carry, what, fifty-thousand people perhaps? How long will it take to travel to Voltaris?'

Jennifer looked at Taksin for an answer. He answered, 'About five or six weeks in this ship.'

The Prime Minister looked puzzled. 'Five or six weeks? But I thought the nearest solar system was several light years away. Are you saying you can travel faster than the speed of light?'

'No, of course not,' responded Taksin. 'That's science fiction fantasy.'

'Then how?'

'Well, I'll spare you some of the physics, but, basically when you travel at very fast speeds, like a sizeable fraction of the speed of light, then, well, you can get space to bend between two points, to become closer to each other. Provided, that is, that you've laid a trail beforehand. Remember the meeting we had last week, where you could see me through a wall in your office? It's a similar principle with flight. Our first flight from Voltaris to here took twenty years, but we set up a portal both ends, so the trip can now be done much quicker.'

'A bit like using a stargate, in your Hollywood films,' Prasert interjected.

'Okay, thank you, I think I can understand that in very simplistic terms,' the Prime Minister continued. 'So, what with stocking up and unloading, the journey there and back would take four months or so. Moving a million refugees would take, what, six or seven years at the rate of two or three trips per year? And another point, Jennifer, how much produce do you think this ship can bring back from Voltaris, it's a war machine not a transporter.'

In answer, Jennifer turned to Taksin and said, 'I was hoping you may help me out here, sir.'

Taksin looked bewildered. 'I beg your pardon?'

'We have a logistics problem, sir.'

The look on Taksin's face didn't change. 'Sorry, you've lost me.'

'We need a way of moving vast populations and cargo. I was hoping you might be able to come up with a solution.'

'A solution?' Taksin stared at Jennifer for a moment, then his jaw dropped. 'What? No!' Taksin looked horrified. 'You've got to be joking!'

'No, sir. I said at the beginning of this meeting there had to be give-and-take on both sides. Now's your opportunity to give.'

'But . . .'

'Please, sir.'

Taksin looked devastated. 'But that was never the plan.'

'No sir, it wasn't. It was glossed over. We felt it would be pushing you too hard.'

'But not now?'

'We're more desperate now. Please, sir. Please think about it. You still have your ultimate sanction against us. You said before that if things go wrong with Endeavour, you can obliterate everything that offends you. That still holds true with anything else you bring to the table, surely?'

Taksin sat gawking at Jennifer for a few seconds before composing himself. 'I thought you were on my side, Jennifer?'

'I am, sir. But I am also on the side of this planet. It needs saving and you have the means to do so.' She delved into her handbag, pulled out a bar of chocolate and broke a couple of lines into separate squares. 'Would anyone care for a piece of chocolate?' She proffered it to the Prime Minister who shook his head, then to Taksin. 'What about you, sir. I believe you like chocolate.'

Taksin looked confused. 'What?'

'It's Cadbury's chocolate, sir. Britain's finest. Are you sure you don't want a piece? It's not like you to turn down an offer of such a delicacy.'

A startled look appeared on Taksin's face. 'Who told you about the chocolate?'

Prasert laughed and said, 'Jennifer, you really are wicked. I didn't think you had it in you.'

'I fight dirty,' she responded, 'when I'm in the right.'

Taksin's head sunk into his hands. 'Oh, god, I had a feeling this morning it was going to be one of those days. I'm beginning to miss Mrs Comyns, her demands were quite reasonable by comparison.'

'Excuse me,' the Prime Minister interjected. 'What is going on here exactly, and who is Mrs Comyns?'

Jennifer grinned. 'Just a private joke, sir. And Mrs Comyns, I would say, is the original Mrs Bossy Boots. It's a shame we haven't got her here now, she could help immensely. Mind you, I doubt whether she's still alive, though maybe she has a daughter who inherited her determination. I could check on that, I suppose.'

'No!' Taksin pleaded. 'Alright, Jennifer. You can have what you want, just don't mention that woman's name in my presence.'

The Prime Minister caught Jennifer's eye and said, 'You've lost me too, Jennifer, I really don't understand what's going on here.'

'Admiral Taksin,' Jennifer continued, 'has just volunteered us the use of his own ship, a container ship that is big enough to transport one million people as well as a billion tons of cargo. The plan I outlined just now is viable.'

As Taksin buried his head in his hands again, there were gasps around the table.

'But what about the cost, Jennifer?' asked the Prime Minister. 'To provide food for the journey, clothes, tools, temporary shelter on arrival, medicine, doctors, dentists, builders, administrators and god knows what else. You're talking about billions of pounds of investment; we can't possibly afford that.'

'No, sir, I agree we can't. But I do know someone who could stump up enough unrefined gold ore to secure what, say, a hundred billion pounds loan to fund the operation. Naturally, that amount of gold ore would be replaced in due course from the gold mined on Voltaris.' She turned and caught Taksin's eye. 'Well, sir?'

'Excuse me?'

'May we borrow sufficient gold ore to secure a hundred billion pounds of finance?'

Taksin looked aghast. 'A hundred billion pounds? You want a hundred billion pounds off me as well as my ship?'

'Well, yes, sir, but technically we'll just be borrowing some of your gold which we'll replace later.'

Taksin screwed his eyes tight. 'Can I go home please; this day just gets worse.'

Jennifer held Taksin's glare and continued, 'I propose, sir, that the only gold taken off Voltaris would be the amount needed to replace that initial hundred billion pounds worth loaned by yourself. Plus, say, five billion pounds' worth of gold per year for the British government in reimbursement of our costs of this venture. Plus, say, a half kilogram of unrefined ore as a bonus souvenir for each crew member making the journey.'

Taksin winced. 'Is that it? No more demands?'

Jennifer smiled sweetly. 'They are not demands, sir. I'm sure you would have offered us all those things out of your own good heart, in time.'

Taksin grimaced. 'Don't you believe it,' he muttered. A cough made Taksin turn to his right. Admiral Prasert was trying to get his attention.

'There is just one other thing,' said Admiral Prasert.

'Yes?'

'You may need to do some spring cleaning if you intend to use the cargo area.'

Taksin groaned, placed his head in his hands and mumbled, 'Oh, god. I hadn't thought of that.'

Jennifer looked at Admiral Prasert, who was grinning, and said, 'Can we help?'

'I doubt it,' responded Admiral Prasert with a twinkle in his eye. 'Taksin has a lot of clutter in his cargo area.'

Jennifer waited patiently for Taksin to lower his hands.

Taksin squirmed. 'Over the years,' he explained, 'I have been repeatedly attacked by expansionist powers seeking to extend their empires. Whenever an army or navy attacks my country, my policy has been to confiscate weapons of war and to impose fines as a means of punishment in the hope that such aggressive behaviour will be curtailed in the future. These . . . objects . . . that I've amassed are stored in my cargo area.'

Jennifer grinned. 'May I ask for an example?'

'Well, there are several piles of Chinese army uniforms and weapons from the third century.'

'How many?' Jennifer pursued.

'They attacked me with a force of ten thousand men. I made them lay down their weapons and strip their armoury before I let them go. I couldn't just leave the stuff where it was in the fields, some child might have cut themselves on the knives.'

Jennifer laughed. 'You have ten thousand third century Chinese military uniforms lying around. Have you any idea of their historic value?'

Taksin shrugged. 'They're not historic for me. That particular attack is still very clear in my mind. Facing down ten thousand soldiers armed to the teeth is not my idea of a fun day out.'

'What else is there?' asked Jennifer.

'Ships, trebuchets, guns, crossbows, spears, longbows, it's amazing what armies take into battle. Then of course there are piles of gold and silver coins, several cases of jewels . . .'

'Okay, okay,' said Jennifer. 'We get the picture. Do you know where it all came from?'

'I think so, yes. I would have made notes in my journals at the time.'

'Good, so you could return it easily?'

'Easily?' Taksin blanched. 'Maybe. But what about an explanation to go with it? I can see I'd get some flack if I just hand back the stuff.'

Jennifer fell silent while she pondered the issue. 'Wormholes,' she said at length.

Taksin replied, 'I beg your pardon?'

'We need to announce to the world the imminent arrival of a huge transporter ship. We'll tell them it's arriving via a wormhole, and that the forces involved may well pull through clutter that disappeared in mysterious circumstances over the centuries at times of intense disturbance in the space-time continuum.'

Taksin blinked heavily. 'Can I have that again, please, in plain English?'

'Sorry, Admiral, I'm a Doctor Who fan. So is half the world. I'll release some details to the press that might be rebutted by scientists but will play nicely into the hands of conspiracy theorists. Fake news can be useful at times, by completely drowning out reality. If you could just return the articles to their country of origin, in public places but under stealth, like under cover of your fog, I'll deal with the fallout.'

Taksin smiled. 'Jennifer, I'm shocked at your deviousness.'

'Thank you, sir,' replied Jennifer with a nod. 'If that's all, I'd better go and draft my press release.' She started to rise from the table.

Admiral Prasert coughed again.

Jennifer sat down. 'Is there something else, Admiral?'

'It's just that Taksin's not himself today, Jennifer, he seems to have forgotten Cargo Hold B.'

Taksin looked askew at Prasert. 'Cargo Hold B? What's that?'

Prasert replied in his native tongue.

Taksin blanched. 'Oh Christ,' he muttered, as his shoulders sagged heavily.

'Sir?' asked Jennifer. 'Is everything alright?'

Taksin took a moment to compose himself. 'All those years ago, when we left, we were in a hurry. We had no time to offload the cargo I had been carrying.'

'That's understandable, sir. May I ask what sort of cargo you were carrying?'

'Um, I'm not too sure to be honest. I think there was a consignment for the military.'

'Weapons?'

'Um, more likely to have been aircraft.'

'You mean starfighters?'

'A few, maybe. Not all of them though.'

'Sorry, sir, when you say not all of them, just how many are your talking about?'

Taksin winced. 'Difficult to say, really. It's been such a long time since I've inspected the cargo lists. To be honest, I'd completely forgotten about them.'

'Any idea, in terms of numbers?'

'A hundred or so, I suppose.'

'A hundred starfighters?'

'Something like that, I'm not altogether that sure.'

'Are you saying you have another hundred starfighters in your cargo hold?'

'No, he's not,' said Prasert assertively. 'There are ten thousand.'

The gasps around the table were loud and deep.

Jennifer gawked at Taksin. 'Ten thousand starfighters! And you forgot about them?'

'It's been more than three thousand years, Jennifer. It's easy to lose track of things after that length of time.'

'That's as maybe, sir, but ten thousand starfighters! I don't believe it! Were you planning to ever tell us about them?'

'No, I wasn't, to be honest,' said Taksin in a matter of fact tone. 'There didn't seem to be any need. You got all the starfighters you asked for, from this ship. You didn't ask if I had any more.'

Jennifer's jaw dropped. Then she broke out laughing.

Taksin frowned. 'Jennifer?'

'Sorry, sir, I'm not laughing at you. I'm laughing at the situation. If I didn't laugh at it, I'd cry.'

'Really? I don't see how the two are linked.'

'Never mind, sir. What's important is, may we borrow some to use on Voltaris? It's going to be a huge logistical exercise to move people, tents and equipment around the planet without any existing transport infrastructure. It would make a big difference to the success of the project if we could move everyone quickly to their allotted lands.'

Taksin shrugged. 'I guess so. You might want to keep a few thousand here I suppose, but take the rest if it helps. However, I do insist on placing restrictions on their weapon systems. They're to be used for civilian and humanitarian purposes, not for settling wars between refugee communities.'

'Of course, sir. Thank you.'

'One moment,' said Air Chief Marshall Grantham. 'There's just one small problem with that. We don't have ten thousand pilots to offer. We only had a hundred fast-jet pilots to offer at the start. Even with all our other pilots, plus those operating commercially or hobbyists, we still can't make up anything like that number.'

Taksin turned to Jennifer. 'I told you this wouldn't be easy.'

Jennifer fixed Taksin with a glare. 'It's just another recruitment exercise. I'll handle it, although we might have to accept other nationalities, like Americans.'

Taksin grimaced. 'Must you?'

Jennifer returned the sweetest of smiles she could muster. 'Yes,' she replied. 'The future of this world depends upon it. Unless, of course, you allow some of the civilians going to Voltaris to be trained to fly starfighters.'

Taksin sighed. 'Alright, I give in, do as you wish.' He stood up and said, 'Right then. Unless my dear nephew has any other revelations to make on my behalf, I'll leave you to it.'

Prasert winked at Jennifer. 'No, I'm done.'

'Thank god for that,' muttered Taksin. 'Right, if anyone wants me, I'll be down in the engine room rechecking the levels of dilithium.' As he was leaving the room, he turned, shook his head and said, 'You know something Jennifer, I preferred it when you were just the girl on the horse. God help Surachai. I don't think he has any idea of what he's taking on.'

Jennifer blushed.

The Prime Minister gave Jennifer a sideways look. 'Surachai? That name's familiar. Was he referring to the young man with the horses?'

'Possibly, I really wouldn't know,' said Jennifer, grabbing her notes together. 'Now, if you'll excuse me, gentlemen, I have work to do.' She left the room flustered and in rather a hurry. If she had turned around, she'd have seen the Prime Minister grinning.

Chapter Thirty-Seven

A public relations opportunity

John Pierrepoint was a man on a mission. Tall, portly and well into his seventies, this, he hoped, was going to be his day of reckoning. For months he'd endured unbearable frustration watching one annoying program after another on television, listening to so-called expert opinion on spaceships, where the aliens came from and whether they were hostile or not. Worst of all, in his opinion, was the discussion over whether the recent announcement of training on the captured ship was wise. His blood had boiled on many an occasion as he had sat, in silence, fuming at the rubbish he heard from people who didn't know what they were talking about. For he knew better. Much better. And it was high time he acted upon it.

Having served twenty-five years in the Royal Navy, it had been relatively easy for him to pull a few strings, beg a favour from old comrades, and get himself invited on a tour of Endeavour along with thirty other veterans. It hadn't been a hard task, it wasn't as though the ship was going anywhere soon, not with it being grounded. He just prayed an opportunity would arise to enable him to strike.

To his delight, and complete shock, the opportunity presented itself an hour into the tour as his group were being shown around the engine room. His party, dressed in civilian clothes and all sporting white hair, if indeed they had any hair at all, were facing a technician as he was giving a short talk on the machinery surrounding them when suddenly the technician's eyes nearly popped out of his head.

'Attention!' shouted the technician. 'Officer on deck.'

In unison, John Pierrepoint and the rest of the tour group

snapped their feet together as Taksin, looking rather bemused, walked to the front of the group and caught the eye of the technician.

'Begging your pardon, sir,' said the technician to Taksin. 'Commander Collins said it would be okay to show a few old-timers around.'

John Pierrepoint saw Taksin nod in response and make to walk past the group. His moment of opportunity had arrived. With a racing heart, he steeled himself and lurched forward into Taksin's path.

Although Taksin was a man of considerable size, he was nevertheless able to move with lightning speed. The sudden movement of a man stepping out from the crowd caused him to momentarily flinch. He checked his pace, gave the man a harsh look as he made to step past. But then he stopped dead, turned back to face the man and gave him a hard, penetrating stare, as if probing the man's soul. After a moment he said, 'Good god, you've got to be joking.'

'A pleasure to see you again, sir,' said John Pierrepoint.

Taksin grinned. 'I don't believe it. NASA's famous engineer, John Pierrepoint, isn't it?'

The old man's shoulders visibly sagged. 'You remember me then, sir? I thought you'd have forgotten me after all this time.'

'Of course I remember you, John,' responded Taksin kindly. 'Why would I not? After all it's only been a few years.'

'Forty-nine, to be precise, sir.'

'Forty-nine years? Good grief! How time flies.' Taksin rubbed his hand over the back of his head and asked, 'But what on earth are you doing here? You're not working here are you?'

'No, sir,' replied John Pierrepoint. 'I retired five years ago. Us veterans, we managed to pull a few strings and got this tour set up today. I hope you don't mind.'

'Um, no,' said Taksin. 'Not at all. Although I hope no one's charging you a fee to look around.'

'No, sir. It's a free day out for us old troopers.'

Taksin held the old man's gaze a few more seconds before saying, 'So, are you part of the tour agenda? Do you get to tell them your story at the end?'

The old man shook his head. 'No, sir. Of course not.'

Taksin looked mildly confused. 'But why not? I would have

thought it'd be a fascinating note to end the tour on.'

'I can't, sir. I was made to promise not to say anything.'

Taksin appeared to deliberate over the old man's choice of words. 'You were made to promise? You mean you were silenced?'

'Yes, sir.'

Taksin grimaced. 'I'm sorry. I had no idea. Who put you up to that?'

'President Burford, sir. Moments after we returned that day.'

Taksin was incredulous. 'You mean you've never said anything to anyone? In forty-six years? Not one word?'

The old man's voice faltered. 'No, sir. Never. It's been hard though, particularly now that I've got grandchildren. I'd love to be able to get it off my chest, to tell them their granddad had an adventure when he was young.'

Taksin shook his head woefully. 'I'm so sorry, John. That must have been difficult.'

The old man nodded. 'Sometimes I have doubts whether it actually happened. At times I think I might have just dreamt it.'

Taksin scoffed. 'You most certainly did not dream it. And this situation needs rectifying immediately.' At this, Taksin stepped back a few paces and addressed the rest of the visitors who were, by now, looking utterly bewildered. 'Ladies and gentlemen, for those that do not know me, my name is Admiral Taksin, and standing in your midst is a hero. If you will indulge me, that man's story needs to be told.' He took his communicator out of a pocket and pressed a button. 'Ladies and gentlemen of Endeavour,' his voice boomed out over the ship's tannoy, 'This is Admiral Taksin. May I have your attention, please?'

The old man took a handkerchief out of his pocket and wiped his eyes.

'In December nineteen seventy, I was contacted by President Burford of the United States of America. He told me that an Apollo rocket had suffered irreparable damage and that the impending loss of the mission was likely to be too much of a burden for his country to bear. He therefore begged me for any help I could give. Now, some of you, those keen on history, may be aware that particular Apollo lost an oxygen tank in a meteor shower which incapacitated the crew as well as their vehicle. So, although I agreed to help, I insisted on taking two people with me. One of those was a medical doctor, the other, an engineer by the name of John Pierrepoint. The three of us flew from Cape Canaveral in a starfighter to rendezvous with the stricken rocket. We docked and, whilst the doctor went inside to resuscitate the crew, John Pierrepoint and I donned spacesuits. He took a spare oxygen tank he'd brought along with him and I grabbed his tool bag. May I just say that John is one of the bravest men I have ever had the honour to meet, for not only did he readily agree to fly into space with me in a machine the like of which had never been seen by man before, but he undertook a spacewalk at a time when such a thing was considered highly dangerous. Furthermore, whilst I could do little but watch in admiration, John battled for an hour, wrenching away the old tank, welding damaged pipes and embedding the new tank.'

Taksin paused as the crowd around John Pierrepoint gaped in astonishment.

'John Pierrepoint's story has never been told because he was asked by President Burford to keep silent. I can understand why that decision may have been made, but it is now time for that decision to be overruled. As I speak, John Pierrepoint is standing in front of me, down in the engine room. My hope is that you will listen to his story, for every word of it is true. I also hope you'll let him talk to the media, for the world should know about his unstinting and unselfish act of bravery.'

In front of a stunned audience, Taksin lowered his communicator and said, 'There, that should do it. Mind you, it wouldn't surprise me if some people refuse to believe it. They'll think it's just me pulling a media stunt.'

'No doubt, sir,' responded John Pierrepoint. 'But it will be difficult to refute with the evidence you've got.'

Taksin looked blank. 'Evidence? What do you mean?'

'The damaged oxygen tank, sir. It had a part number on it. It can be matched to the original parts listing.'

Taksin blinked. 'Sorry, you've lost me.'

'I took the damaged tank back to your starfighter, sir.'

'You did?' Taksin scratched the back of his head. 'I don't remember seeing it. Where did you put it?'

'In a cupboard, sir. Just to the left of where I hung up the spacesuit. I didn't want to leave it on the floor where it could roll around.'

'In a cupboard?' repeated Taksin. 'But then it should still be there.' He chuckled and added, 'Would you like it as a souvenir?'

John Pierrepoint's face lit up. 'You have no idea how much I've dreamt of getting my hands back on that tank, sir.'

Taksin raised his hand and pressed a button on his communicator. 'Ladies and gentlemen. This is Admiral Taksin again. Further to what I was saying a few moments ago, it appears John Pierrepoint placed the damaged oxygen tank from the Apollo rocket into a cupboard on my starfighter. Given that I've done no cleaning in that vehicle for the last forty-nine years, there is no reason why it should not still be there. For those interested in this matter, John and I shall be up on fight deck in about ten minutes to look for it. The curious amongst you are welcome to join us there.'

Taksin put his communicator away in a pocket, looked around at the people in the tour group and said, 'Right then, who wants a visit to flight deck?'

And so, to the amusement of the odd onlooker, Taksin led the group of thirty retired engineers, technicians and military servicemen along several corridors, up a lift and onto the flight deck where his starfighter was parked. With much flamboyancy, he opened the vehicle and ushered everyone inside.

Jennifer, along with the Prime Minister and three Chiefs of Staff, beat Taksin to the flight deck. As did a hundred other people. She stood well back from Taksin's starfighter, taking in the absurd sight of a group of old people accepting Taksin's hand as he helped them board. She gave a laugh. 'This is surreal. Taksin the Great has become Taksin the Tour Guide. I never dreamt he would allow something like this to happen. It's so unlike him.'

'Making amends, do you think?' asked the Prime Minister.

'I doubt it. Not his style. But I'm sure he can spot a good public relations opportunity when it arises.'

'It would be a gift, if it were true.'

'I guess we'll know in a minute.'

'Something's not quite right though,' said the Prime Minister, rubbing his chin. 'What's this "President Burford asked me to help, and so I did" nonsense. Taksin's made it clear he's never interfered with man's destiny.'

Jennifer shrugged. 'Who knows? Maybe he was just feeling in a good mood that day. I'll try to get to the bottom of it sometime. Perhaps there's something in President Burford's diaries about it.'

'Talking of President Burford, how did we miss the link?'

'If I heard him right, just now, the mission appears to have been covered up and our mysterious Mr Pierrepoint kept schtum.'

'Yes, I'd like to have a chat with Mr Pierrepoint, if you'd arrange it, please, Jennifer. He's English, isn't he? He must be, we haven't let any other nationality on board, so how come he was working in Cape Canaveral?'

'Mmm, the plot thickens,' said Jennifer.

Two minutes later John Pierrepoint appeared at the doorway of the starfighter and raised his prized trophy high in the air. Taksin clapped a hand on the man's shoulder and smiled as dozens of mobile phone cameras clicked away.

Jennifer laughed. 'Oh my god. This is incredible.'

The Prime Minister broke into a grin. 'This really is a gift,' he said. 'Think what it will do to the crew's attitude towards him. They'll think he's human.' He caught Jennifer's eye and added, 'Well, almost.'

Chapter Thirty-Eight

Artefacts

For Nick Ohlson, the BBC's current affairs editor, the day seemed to be getting weirder by the minute as he sat at his desk in Broadcasting House, London, carrying out his morning routine of casting an eye over the unfolding stories on the BBC's website.

Bewildered, he beckoned John Coussens, one of the BBC's top science correspondents to join him.

'What's up, Nick?'

Nick pointed to the computer screen. 'Have you seen these stories?'

'Which ones?'

'Which ones, you ask? The weird ones, of course. It's worse than All Fool's Day out there. Here, grab a seat and I'll show you.' He clicked on the Asia section and opened a news item headed "Chinese Army Artefacts dumped". 'Go on, read this.'

A large pile of ancient artefacts, including thousands of daggers, spears, helmets and armoured chest plates, were found dumped in the central courtyard of the Military Museum of the Chinese People's Revolution in Beijing this morning by staff as they arrived for work.

'It's really weird,' said visiting Canadian tourist Oswald Green. 'There's this huge pile of weapons and uniforms. And I mean huge, like a twenty-foot rubbish mountain. It looks as though the museum's had a clear out and chucked all this military stuff in a gigantic heap.'

A member of the museum's staff, who refused to be identified, would not comment on why the artefacts had been placed outside, insisting 'This has nothing to do with our museum.'

John Coussens scanned the article, shrugged his shoulders and said, 'So? I can't say I'm surprised at anything that emerges from Beijing.'

Nick Ohlson nodded his acceptance of the comment. 'Fair enough, but bear it in mind as you read this next one.' He clicked on a local news item.

As dawn broke over London, the Marine Policing Unit were called out to investigate what appeared to be an eighteenth-century sailing frigate, deserted yet anchored in the middle of the Thames river near Greenwich.

'It's astonishing,' said local resident Gerald Somersby. 'I was out walking the dog when this thick fog bank appeared out of nowhere. It was really frightening, I had to grab hold of these here railings because I couldn't see further than my outstretched hands. Then the fog lifted, just as quick as it had arrived, and there was the ship right there, where nothing had been seconds beforehand. It's a beautiful ship I don't doubt, but I could swear I heard the crew's voices shouting through the mist, words like "Ahoy, there". Jesus, it gave me the creeps.'

John Coussens wiped his hand over his mouth. 'Ancient artefacts spookily appearing out of the blue. Is that what you're getting at?'

'More than that, John. There are a dozen others like this emerging today. Here read this one, it's more revealing.'

Staff at the Royal Palace in Madrid woke to an unusual booming noise at the crack of dawn this morning. On peering out the windows, they were confronted by the sight of a fifty-foot high vortex of swirling grey cloud which lasted some three minutes before fizzling out and leaving, in its wake, a stash of thousands of eighteenth-century gold doubloons.

'Okay, Nick, you've got me hooked. What's going on?'

Nick Ohlson laughed. 'That's what I was hoping you'd be able to tell me.'

'Ah, ha. Okay, I'd be interested in your thoughts first.'

'Well, it's not just that ancient artefacts are appearing out of the blue, it's the way it's happening. All in one night, from east to west as the sun rises. There's a pattern emerging. There's a fog, a mist, a cloud or a vortex appearing over and over again, leaving artefacts in its wake. What does that sound like to you?'

'Erm, as a science reporter, I'm not sure. Maybe you'd be better off talking to someone from the meteorological department.'

Nick Ohlson scoffed. 'Thanks, but no thanks. What about looking at it from a science fiction angle?'

John Coussens fell silent for a moment. He rubbed his eyes and said, 'Are you trying to suggest these events are connected?'

'There's a definite pattern, you have to admit that.'

'And? You think the pattern shows, well, what precisely?'

'What can you tell me about wormholes?'

John Coussens returned a bewildered stare. 'As in space travel or the common garden variety?'

'Space travel, of course.'

'Um, I'm not sure they exist. Outside science fiction that is. They've been postulated, but there's no empirical evidence for them.'

'But if they existed, and one was being used to get here, what would one expect to see?'

John Coussens' bewilderment intensified. 'Um, Nick, you're thinking too hard. Maybe it would be best for you to stick to current affairs.'

'But this is about current affairs, John. I got this strange telephone call late last night on my mobile phone from an untraceable number, telling me to expect the imminent arrival of a huge spaceship that's travelling here through a wormhole which wouldn't be seen by NASA. I assumed it was a hoax call at first, but now I'm not sure. I think that's why all these artefacts are being thrown up around the world. I reckon this new spaceship has visited us before; all this stuff got sucked up into the wormhole hundreds of years ago and is now being discharged on its way through again.'

'Right. Would you excuse me for a minute, Nick?' said John Coussens as he rose from his chair. 'I've got an urgent piece to write for the one o'clock broadcast.'

Nick Ohlson nodded indifferently. 'Sure, thanks for your help. It's set my mind clear at least.' As he watched John Coussens walk away shaking his head, he muttered, 'I'll show you.' He reached for his computer mouse and began a search on Google. Twenty minutes later he was scrolling down the address book on his mobile phone, trying to remember the name of the young lady who had made him feel welcome at Brize Norton a short while ago. He pressed the green call icon. It was answered on the fourth ring.

'Good morning, Jennifer Collins speaking.'

'Commander Collins? It's Nick Ohlson from the BBC.'

'Oh, hi Nick. Nice report you did on the Brize Norton event. I meant to phone and congratulate you about it.'

'Thank you, Commander. I still haven't got over the wonder of it. It's both terrifying and fascinating at the same time.'

'I know what you mean.'

Nick Ohlson paused for a moment before saying. 'Look, Commander . . .'

'Jennifer, please.'

'Thank you. Jennifer, look, I'm sorry to bother you, but something important has come up and I need help clarifying it.'

'Oh yes? Just a second, let me find a chair.' There was a pause for a couple of seconds. 'Right, Nick, fire away. What's the problem?'

Nick Ohlson inhaled deeply. 'If I remember correctly, you've got a seat on what's been termed Star Fleet Council. Is that right?'

'That's correct.'

'And there's only seven other members?'

'Again, you're quite correct.'

'You're pretty clued up with what's going on with Endeavour?'

'I can't deny that.'

Nick Ohlson took a deep breath. 'Are you aware of the strange events happening around the world today? For instance, the eighteenth-century frigate turning up, abandoned, in the Thames; a pile of ancient Chinese military weapons dumped outside a museum in Beijing; a pile of several thousand eighteenth century gold doubloons appearing in a courtyard of the Royal Palace in Madrid?'

There was silence on the phone for five seconds before Jennifer responded. 'Umm, that's a lot of events you're putting into one sentence, Nick. Are you suggesting they're connected somehow?'

'I am, yes.'

'And the reason for that would be, what exactly?'

'A wormhole.'

'I beg your pardon. Did you just say "wormhole"?'

'I did. I've just been googling them.'

'That sounds weird, Nick. Googling wormholes, that is.'

'It is, but the search results are weirder, especially if you look into the storylines of science fiction films. Did you know that when a spaceship enters a wormhole it can pull other objects into it? It's what got me thinking, what with these strange happenings today, what if there's another spaceship on its way? What if all these old things are being dumped as a result of being pushed out of a wormhole by another spaceship on its way to us?'

There was silence on the phone.

'Jennifer? Are you still there?'

'Nick, I can't say anything on this matter.'

Nick Ohlson drew in his breath. 'I'm right, aren't I?'

'Nick, please. Something very big is about to happen. I can't talk about it right now.'

'So, you admit there's another spaceship on its way?'

A sound came through the phone as though Jennifer was sucking on a lemon. 'These matters are very delicate, Nick. A lot of diplomacy is needed. You're the BBC's current affairs editor, you must know I couldn't possibly comment on the possible arrival of another ship.'

'You're denying it?'

'I'm denying nothing.'

'Can I quote you on that?'

'No. Sorry, Nick.'

'People need to be told the truth.'

'I'm sure they do, Nick. But they also need protection from the hysteria that media hype sometimes fosters upon them.'

'Granted. Look, how about a deal here, Jennifer. Let me have an exclusive on this. I'll put together a short report today based entirely on my own thoughts, a bit of a teaser as it were, just to set the scene. Then perhaps we could meet up, and you can give me the official version of what's going on, and I'll report on that without resorting to hyperbole. How's that?'

It sounded as though Jennifer was sucking lemons again. 'I don't know, Nick. It may be a bit early to announce our plans.'

'Plans?'

'Sorry. Forget what I just said.'

'Good plans or bad plans?'

'Good plans, Nick. Very good plans, indeed. And very secretive at the moment, so I would appreciate your confidence in the matter.'

'Of course. When can we meet? How about tomorrow morning?'

After a couple more seconds with a fresh lemon, Jennifer replied, 'Very well. I'll pick you up at London Heliport in Battersea at ten o'clock tomorrow morning. I'll take you up to Endeavour, we can talk there.'

'Thank you, Jennifer. See you then. Bye.' He pressed the red end call button and punched a clenched fist into the air.

Fifty miles south of Nick Ohlson's desk at the BBC, Jennifer got up off her beloved old sofa, pocketed her mobile phone and went to the kitchen to fill the kettle. Five minutes later she sat back down with a steaming cup of black coffee and a smug look on her face. This was going to be an easier sell to the media than she imagined. With that thought in mind, and with renewed vigour, she turned her attention to packing the last few vestiges of her life in her flat in Lewes High Street. She glanced at her watch, just ten minutes to go before her lift was due. She wandered around the flat, now empty of all her personal items. She looked out the back window and absorbed the view down the Ouse Valley to the sea at Newhaven for one last time. She'd miss the flat. It was the end of an era, an end to her academic career. Hopefully it heralded the start of a new life, a better one; one that would include Surachai as a permanent fixture.

She was roused from her reverie by the sound of the front door bell. She checked her watch. Good, that should be her lift. She scrabbled downstairs and opened the front door to find two men standing outside on the pavement. One extremely tall and lean, dressed in black, one rather short and chubby, dressed in a suit.

'Charles,' she addressed the shorter one. 'Sorry, I wasn't expecting you.'

'I've just come for the keys, that's all. Are you all done?'

'Yes, thank you,' she responded. 'My friend Prasert is here to give me a lift. I've just got to bring down two suitcases . . .'

'I'll get them,' said Prasert and he bounded up the stairs.

Jennifer stood on the pavement patiently waiting. She became aware of a hullabaloo down the road, people running, sirens shrieking in the distance. 'What's up, any idea?'

Charles Seymour, the landlord's agent, shrugged. 'No idea. Ah, here we go, your suitcases. Shall I take the keys now?'

'Yes, of course.' She handed two sets of door keys over. 'Bye then, Charles.' She turned her attention to Prasert. 'Thanks for doing this. Did you manage to park discretely somewhere out of town?'

'Out of town? No one said anything about that.'

Jennifer frowned. 'Then, where . . .?'

'As close as I could get. Up by the castle. Or what's left of it, I should say, I had trouble recognising it just now. Mind you I suppose my last visit must have been quite a few years ago. It enveloped the whole town then, and there was this really good battle brewing. The barons against the king. Great fun it was. King John was useless though, as a tactician, and we won easily.'

'You fought in the Battle of Lewes? Really?'

'I never miss the opportunity for a good fight. Unless my dear uncle has his way and puts the dampeners on it, he can be a miserable git at times.'

As a police car came fast up the High Street and turned into Castle Precincts, Jennifer asked, 'So, erm, where exactly did you park?'

'Oh, on the old jousting ground. It's the nearest piece of open land I could find. A bit of a squeeze though.'

'Ah, that could be the problem. I was wondering what the commotion was about. We'd better get up there quick.'

A minute later, as Jennifer neared the castle precincts, her way was blocked by a traffic warden. 'Can't go up there, Miss,' he said. 'There's a major incident going on.'

'Are you by any chance referring to the starfighter my friend here parked on the jousting grounds?'

The Traffic Warden glared up at Prasert. 'That vehicle belongs to you, does it, sir?'

Prasert put the suitcases down and replied, 'Well, yes, where else was I supposed to park. This town is a nightmare for parking.'

'That's as maybe, sir,' said the Traffic Warden coolly. 'But you have no right to park where you did. There were some people playing bowls there, they're rather upset you've ruined their game.'

Prasert shrugged. 'I did ask them if it was alright, I said I'd only be two minutes.'

The Traffic warden looked at his watch. 'It's been five minutes at least, sir.'

Jennifer tutted. 'Then give him a ticket. In the meantime, if you'll excuse us, we've got work to do.' She strode off purposefully.

'Just a minute, Miss,' the Traffic warden called out. 'What shall I do with this ticket?'

Jennifer's response made a handful of bystanders blush.

Chapter Thirty-Nine

The colonisation program

'Finish your coffee,' said Jennifer in the canteen onboard Endeavour, pointing across the table to an untouched cup. 'I'm told a warm drink helps with shock.'

Nick Ohlson's face had turned a ghastly pale colour. 'A million people at a time,' he said woodenly. 'Two trips a year. This is planetary colonisation on a massive scale. You're taking the human race into a new phase, a new dimension almost. It's the stuff of science fiction novels.'

'There are sixteen million refugees, Nick. Their plight is horrific. They're forced by the Western World to live in squalor; no sanitation, no clean water, starvation rations, doctors have to choose which babies are given medicine and which are left to die. You know what it's like, the West has a moral conscience but it's simply impossible to take them all in. A few hundred refugees are given residence in some Western countries, as a token gesture, but most governments simply can't afford to do more than that.'

'I know . . . but . . . a million at a time . . . to another planet. It's mind-blowing. And the logistics are staggering.'

Jennifer grunted. 'Tell me about it, I've got a team of a hundred staff working on ordering and taking delivery of sufficient provisions for a million people to survive a year. I think we've cornered the world's market in tents, prefabricated buildings, solar panel equipment, sawmill machinery, farming tools, clothes, mattresses, sleeping bags, medicine, tinned food, rice, toothpaste. The list goes on and on. Then there's the recruitment program; we need doctors, dentists, forestry and farming experts, engineers, carpenters, fishermen, cooks . . .'

'But the cost of all this, Jennifer, it must run to billions.'

'It does.'

'But we're not officially out of austerity yet, how can the Prime Minister justify the expense? He gets enough flack with his generous commitment to foreign aid as it is.'

Jennifer broke into a smile. 'There's good news on that one, Nick. It won't cost the British taxpayer a penny.'

'Really? Who's footing the bill then, the IMF?'

'Nope. It's private finance.'

Nick Ohlson looked incredulous. 'You're kidding me.'

'Not at all. I've set up a charitable organisation with the objective of helping out humanitarian crises, and I've got one hundred billion pounds sterling to fund it.'

Nick coughed. 'Holy Moses! One hundred billion? And which politician has got his hands on that little pot?'

'None of them. At the moment I'm the organisation's only bank signatory.'

'You? Alone?'

'Yep. It makes me break out in a cold sweat at times, but someone has to take responsibility. I guess that's my punishment for proposing this venture in the first place.'

Nick threw Jennifer a curious look. 'Punishment?'

Jennifer broke into a wry smile. 'Sorry, Nick. A private joke. I've been told the donation is in lieu of my wedding present.'

'You're getting married?'

'So it seems, though I didn't know about it.'

'And the ship? The new ship that's coming through the wormhole, is that being given to you as a wedding present as well as the hundred billion pounds?'

'Yep.'

'Wow! That's impressive. Just who are you, exactly?'

Jennifer snorted. 'Just a girl on a horse, apparently.'

'I beg your pardon?'

'Sorry, Nick, that was another private joke.'

'You must have some very rich and powerful friends indeed. And very interesting ones at that. There can't be too many people who can gift a spaceship.'

'True. But I would have settled for a pair of shoes as a present instead. Much more practical than a bank balance so big it won't fit on to the bank statement.' Jennifer fell silent, a faraway look descended upon her face.

'Jennifer?'

'Sorry, Nick, my mind was drifting. Look, I have to confess I could do with your help. Endeavour will be flying to this new planet, Voltaris, in three days' time. We've located a hundred refugee families on the Syrian border who are willing to give it a go, become our test group. I'd like a team from the BBC to go with them, to record their experiences, to put a documentary together, perhaps, about Voltaris, what new settlers may find waiting for them, how they can expect a life of freedom without fear of war or terror. The team will get full unrestricted access at all times during the flight there and back, and will have transport at their disposal to fly around Voltaris at their convenience. If funding is an issue for the BBC, I'll happily authorise reimbursement of all costs associated with the trip.'

Nick's jaw dropped. 'Wow!'

'I must explain that there will be another film crew travelling to Voltaris, to make television adverts for promoting jobs and settlement. But their task is defined, the crew come from a marketing company, their objective is to sell the product, to sell the idea of a new life. The BBC's role would be different; you will be completely independent, serving no one else's agenda. Obviously, this would be an exclusive deal for the BBC. And an exclusive for you, of course, Nick, in that I'll leave it to you to pitch it to the powers that be. Naturally, we would hope that the documentary would promote the positive aspects of settlement by refugees there, but I wouldn't dream of imposing restrictions on the documentary's content or storyline. If the team took the right equipment with them, I'm sure the documentary could be ready for broadcasting the moment they return, and I guess the audience for it would be huge, maybe the biggest in recent broadcasting history. And if you wish to imply that it was your idea, your baby as it were, well, who am I to say it wasn't?'

An ear-to-ear grin appeared on Nick Ohlson's face. 'That's very generous of you, Jennifer. Before I leave, though, there are just a few points I'd like to get clear.' He reached for his cold coffee cup. 'Any chance of a refill?'

Chapter Forty

Voltaris

Perhaps due to Taksin's display of generosity over John Pierrepoint's story or, more likely, to the human spirit of adventure, the six-week trip to Voltaris was destined to be a success from the moment of its announcement. One hundred and fifty people who had worked as crew on board Endeavour in its first short period of training signed up for the mission. History was in the making; man's first flight to another planet. Few wanted to miss out on this once-in-a-lifetime opportunity.

It took two days to load food, equipment and personnel, and another four hours to fly to Jordan and locate the volunteer refugees in their camp. But then Endeavour was off, engines at full thrust, heading for the stars with Prasert at the helm beguiling the crew with descriptions of the natural beauty awaiting them on Voltaris.

The trip lasted five weeks and three days. For some that meant five weeks of boredom with nothing to do except sit around, chat, read a book or watch a film. For others, it meant five weeks of anxiety, being kept on tenterhooks, forever wondering when they were going to get there. Yet the time did pass and, eventually, Prasert announced to the passengers that they had arrived and if they would care to look out of a porthole, they could catch sight of the blue planet in the distance as the ship began its deceleration.

Endeavour orbited the planet once, as though flying a victory lap, with Prasert giving a running commentary on the extent of continents, mountain ranges, waterfalls, seas, ice caps, equatorial jungles, deserts and savannah. It was like Planet Earth, he told them, only three times as big, far more beautiful and suffered no pollution. It was as Earth might have been if man had never evolved.

On landing, five hundred people disembarked awestruck in their moment of historic glory. This was it, the first steps taken by a human being on another planet. Human life would never be the same again. They had entered a new era. They were the first explorers, the first settlers. Their names would enter history books, alongside the like of Neil Armstrong and Buzz Aldrin. Emotions ran high. Prasert, not wishing to spoil their moment, wisely kept his mouth shut.

Excitement was allowed to run its course, but then the crew were reminded that they'd come to work. And so the task of setting up tents for refugees started, as did the establishment of a small town of prefabricated buildings to house the hundreds of scientists, administrators, surveyors, doctors, dentists, nurses, cooks, lumberjacks, plumbers and carpenters who had signed a two-year contract to construct the first colony.

It wasn't long before someone stooped to pick up a shiny stone off the ground, realised what they were looking at and yelled, 'Gold!' Others followed swiftly. Within minutes, hundreds of people had abandoned their tasks and were running amok, scrabbling for ever-larger chunks of gold ore. As the weight of gold bore heavily on arms and in pockets, the practical problem of where and how to store it became an issue. Those on two-year contracts came to their senses quickly and abandoned their hoards with a reluctant shrug. Those on short-term mission-specific contracts returned wide-eyed to Endeavour, only to be met by security guards with metal scanners, a set of scales and a log book. To howls of protest, the security guards calmly went about their duty of confiscating any gold ore in excess of half a kilogram per person. For the most vociferous of complainants, a copy of a standard mission contract was shown to them in which Clause 57 (f) had been highlighted in red: *no person shall remove more than half a kilogram of material from Voltaris*. Protestations that no one had read their contract before signing were given short shrift.

Gold fever lasted an hour. Contemptuous mutterings continued for several days.

By the end of the third day, tent city had been well and truly established, with each refugee family given a deluxe model four-room cabin tent, mattresses, sleeping bags, kitchen cutlery, an ensemble of farming hoes, spades, forks, saws, hammers, nails, fishing rods, knife sharpeners, buckets, balls of string, clothes, a sufficient quantity of cans of meat and sacks of rice to survive a year and, finally, several bags of vegetable seeds. All of which had been provided free, courtesy of Jennifer's charitable organisation.

While scientists set off to explore the planet, and surveyors to mark out promising areas for new settlements, the BBC film crew set about filming how humans coped with mundane matters such as a different sun and moon in the sky, a twenty-seven hour day, and the knowledge that the inhabitants couldn't simply telephone home to check on their relatives. Another film crew focused on the more positive aspects of being a pioneer.

After three weeks, the film crews declared they had sufficient footage. The news was welcome to Prasert, for the hundred and fifty core crew had been showing a growing displeasure of their life since it had turned into one long tedious camping holiday. With uncharacteristic wisdom, Prasert announced it was time to depart and made a note to keep mission-specific crew to a bare minimum in the future.

As Prasert bade farewell to a small gathering of administrators and scientists who were staying on, someone asked him why the grasses, plants, trees, wildlife, insects and birds were so similar to those found on God's Earth. Avoiding controversy, he offered Jennifer's pre-discussed answer, by way of explanation, 'What would you expect to evolve with such similar environmental conditions?'

Chapter Forty-One

The Sprit Of Freedom

Low level grey clouds hung over Brize Norton creating a depressive atmosphere so typical of a dull English November day. Inside the airbase canteen, the atmosphere couldn't have been more different as a hundred pairs of eyes stared out the windows, excitedly scanning the skies in anticipation of the arrival of the promised new ship. Jennifer checked her watch: nine twenty-eight. Taksin was due any second, but there had been no word from the tower. Given Taksin's description of his freighter, she wondered how something so large in the skies could possibly avoid radar detection. Yet he'd managed it with Endeavour. She vaguely remembered he'd once said something about using a veil to hide his starfighter from radar, perhaps it was possible to veil a whole ship. If so, that was something that had yet to be explained.

Out of nowhere, a shape appeared less than a mile away, breaching the clouds; the dark underbelly of an intergalactic monster. Jennifer gasped as the realisation of Taksin's claims about his ship dawned upon her. It was gigantic. Twelve thousand feet long, five thousand feet wide and almost the same in height. Not that she could see its top, since that part of the ship remained shrouded by clouds as it came to a terrifying ground-shuddering rest.

'Oh, dear god,' Nick Ohlson sighed as he took in the size of the ship. It looked like a sea-going oil tanker magnified several thousand times over. 'That is a truly awesome sight.'

'We'll need to give it a name. Something appropriate to reflect this moment, I think. Any thoughts?'

'How about the HMS I-think-I've-just-wet-myself?'

Jennifer gave a brief laugh. 'That's quite apt, Nick, but hardly noteworthy. I was thinking more along the lines of Spirit Of Freedom. I'm told that's what its original name actually translates as.'

Nick Ohlson tutted. 'Very sensible, I'm sure. Can we get aboard right away, start filming, get a piece together for today's broadcasts?'

'Sure,' responded Jennifer, and with none of the pomp and ceremony that had been laid on for the arrival of Endeavour, she boarded her own craft along with Nick Ohlson's television crew and flew up in to the clouds to locate the flight deck's doors.

Chapter Forty-Two

A familiar voice

It had been a week since Endeavour had returned from Voltaris and Jennifer found herself sitting in the office of an advertising company in Soho, in quiet anticipation as an image of a forested mountainside burst onto a large television screen. It was a perfect scene, one of paradise; still mist, early morning sun, backlit trees, decaying bracken. The drone camera zoomed in to a stream gushing down the mountainside into a lake, at the side of which a man battled to reel in a fish the size cod used to be in the Atlantic Ocean in the nineteenth century. Then it zoomed away, to the edge of the lake, downstream into the rich pastures of a valley floor, and on towards sandy beaches and a deep blue sea.

'This is Voltaris,' a familiar voice spoke. 'It is a planet rich in beauty and natural resources, unspoilt by commercial exploitation, government corruption or war.'

'John Hurt?' blurted Jennifer. 'You managed to sign up John Hurt for the voice-over?'

'Who better?' an advertising account manager responded. 'His voice is well known in our sitting rooms.'

'So is the scene with an alien bursting out of his chest! I trust the irony wasn't intended.'

'No, it wasn't. Polls show his voice is trusted.'

'But he's dead, isn't he?'

'A mere technicality these days. We had sufficient voice recordings from previous sessions to patch together what we needed, along with some digital wizardry, that is.'

'I hope you're right,' muttered Jennifer, turning her attention back to the screen.

The scene changed to an encampment of a hundred or so tents, spread at twenty-metre intervals, olive skinned children running and playing happily in the sun, women hanging out clothes to dry, men chopping wood. The scene moved on to a river a hundred metres away, smiling teenagers casting nets and hauling in dozens of fish. 'These are the first inhabitants of Voltaris,' the presenter's voice continued. 'They have been here just six days. In another week, work will begin on constructing timber framed houses for them to use instead of tents. Then they can begin reconstruction of their original community. Each family has an allotted half-acre space for a house and a garden to cultivate vegetables and small livestock and a thousand acres are earmarked as communal farmland.'

Jennifer read the translated text at the bottom of the screen as a family were being interviewed.

'Over the coming years,' the presenter's voice continued, 'Voltaris will become home to many of the world's sixteen million refugees. Each one of them will be given a new life, a house, land, hope and a means to sustain independent lives. This is our commitment to the world; our way of responding to humanitarian crises in war torn countries. We need doctors, nurses, dentists, engineers and a host of other skilled workers to help reconstruct communities for these people who have been displaced by the misery of war. If you are interested, please visit the website displayed at the bottom of your screen and register your interest now.'

'Impressive,' Jennifer proclaimed as the advert finished. 'Let's hope it goes down well.'

'We've made several alternatives. Here, let me show you,' said the advertising account manager as he pressed a button on his remote control.

A second advert came on. The opening shots showed depressing scenes of run-down housing estates, boarded up properties, people sleeping rough, piles of garbage on streets, communities in decay, people living in misery.

A voice proclaimed, 'Social deprivation, despair, a lack of hope. Is this how you want to live? Is this really where you want to raise your family?' The scene changed to the mountain, stream, lake and beaches of the first advert. 'There is an alternative. It's called Voltaris.

It's a planet rich in beauty and natural resources, a planet waiting for the adventurous to start a new life; a natural, rich life, rewarding in a way last known only to the pioneers that headed out across the plains of America a hundred and fifty years ago, fleeing from persecution and eager to claim a stake in the new lands. Now you too have that same opportunity.'

The scene changed to workers constructing buildings made from wood.

'Voltaris needs skilled workers, people who can hew trees, saw timber, build houses from natural products and fence farmland. If this is you, please register your interest on our website now.'

The advertising account manager paused the tape and said, 'We have a few other takes, aimed at professionals.' He pressed a button on his remote to reveal scenes of inner-city strife, pollution, commuters in overpacked trains and traffic jams.

The same voice proclaimed, 'Do you want a better life? Do you dream of having a job without a commute, where there is no rent to pay, no taxes on your income? Where you keep all of what you earn? Would you like to escape cramped cities, move to a life with no stress and no social problems? Well, this is Voltaris,' continued the voice as the scenes of human misery cut away to a backdrop of unspoilt wilderness. 'There are no cars here; no unsightly tarmacadam roads. There are no guns. This is where you can raise a family in peace, where your children can play without fear. We are currently recruiting doctors, nurses, administrators, carpenters, plumbers, fishermen, lumberjacks, farm managers. So, if you want a better work-life balance, pick up the phone and call us now or visit our website and register your interest.'

'I'm sold,' said Jennifer. 'Get them all aired as soon as possible, preferably between nine and ten o'clock in the evening when parents are resting at the end of a hard day.'

'We've provisionally booked the first broadcast to go out just before the ten o'clock news on Monday night.'

Jennifer smiled. 'Excellent. Nothing like being hit hard on the first day of the week.'

'May I ask what the budget is, for airing on the television that is?'

'Ten million for the first week. Go for saturation. Let's see what the response rate is.'

'Very good. And our fees?'

'You've earned it in spades. Get your accountant to email me your invoice as soon as you can. I'll get the ten million pounds for the advertising transferred to your company's account this afternoon, along with another ten million to cover your fees.'

The public's response to Jennifer's advertising campaign was of far greater magnitude than she could possibly have imagined. The airing of the three adverts on television followed an earlier Panorama Special that evening in which Nick Ohlson introduced the world to the delights of intergalactic travel arrangements aboard Spirit Of Freedom, from its spacious family apartments to leisure parks, gymnasiums and canteens.

By eleven o'clock in the evening, Jennifer's office had reported a hundred thousand website hits. By the end of the next day, the number of hits exceeded half a million. By the end of the second day, Jennifer realised the enormity of the task facing her team in sifting through the applicants, separating the good from the bad, the genuine from the disaffected, the hard worker from the opportunistic.

It took two months of round-the-clock work for Jennifer's team to put together the crew and passengers for the maiden flight of Spirit Of Freedom. But, eventually, nine hundred and eighty-seven thousand three hundred and six souls set off for Voltaris, with an elated Admiral Prasert at the helm.

Chapter Forty-Three

Unwanted attention

As a boy, Prasert had grown up on a space station. Not the small, gravity-free, claustrophobic type that orbited Earth manned by a handful of dedicated astronauts, but an immense station the size of a moon, highly sophisticated and home to ten million inhabitants.

Orbus was its name. Home to an administrative power that controlled trade and colonisation throughout the union of civilisations that sought to benefit from undertaking business with their intragalactic neighbours.

The top half of Orbus was covered by a transparent but protective dome that housed its own atmosphere, and contained a thriving city, farmland, lakes, beach resorts and palatial houses for the elite to escape the unsightly aspects of a so-called advanced civilisation.

The bottom half of Orbus was devoted to docking facilities for some sixteen hundred interplanetary freighters and warships that were in service. Repairs, maintenance, changing of crew and cargo, and construction of new ships could all be handled efficiently and in the comfort and safety of what was effectively a huge port.

Orbus had been on Prasert's mind a lot this last year. It had been his home. He had attended school there, lived well, spent weekends at the family villa near the beach. He had felt alive there, in tune with his surroundings, able to blend in well with his social peers. There, he had had hopes and dreams. The arrival of the rogue spaceship some eighteen months ago, the presence of an active squadron of starfighters and the re-emergence of Spirit Of Freedom had brought back fond memories of a different life. And now, after a six-week flight to Voltaris, not just aboard Spirit Of Freedom, but in charge of the ship, its crew and passengers, he felt the years of frustration suffered since leaving Orbus may at last be over. For, finally, he had a proper job. One with never-ending activity; decisions to be taken, orders to be given, responsibility to be accepted.

It was therefore with disbelief and considerable distress that, as he toured the Flight Control Room, checking instruments before commencing the ship's return voyage from Voltaris back to Earth, a klaxon sounded. Momentarily stunned, he stood stock-still, staring at a screen on which he would have sworn a blip had been visible a few seconds ago.

'Anything wrong, sir?' an operative asked.

Prasert's mind raced. What he had just seen, if indeed he had not imagined it, would jeopardise everything he held dear right now. He flipped a switch and the klaxon stopped its wailing. 'Umm, I think we have a situation developing,' he said at length. 'We appear to have attracted unwanted attention. But as your dearly beloved Corporal Jones is wont to say, don't panic. Let's just carry on as though nothing out of the ordinary has happened.'

Chapter Forty-Four

Message in a bottle

'That dress may be a little too hot for a wedding out here, don't you think dear?'

Jennifer glanced up from a wedding dress brochure and smiled at her mother as she sat down at the veranda table. 'Just looking for inspiration, Mum, that's all.'

'You're planning a traditional wedding here, in St Barnabas' church, I assume?'

Jennifer shrugged, 'I'm not sure, I haven't discussed it with Surachai yet.'

Judith Collins raised an eyebrow and reached across the table for a pitcher of water, 'Do you mean you haven't discussed whether to have a Buddhist or Christian wedding, or do you mean you haven't discussed the idea of marriage with him?'

'Both,' replied Jennifer. 'I thought I'd investigate the options first.'

'And what if Surachai says no?'

Jennifer returned a smile. 'He won't. He hasn't plucked up the courage to ask yet, but I'm working on that. He knows what's best for him, I just need to create the right situation for him to feel comfortable with a proposal, to make it seem as though it was his idea.'

Judith Collins raised an eyebrow again as she took a sip of cool water. 'Well, I'm not sure I approve of your methods, my girl, but I can't say your father won't be pleased. He's got you down for supplying us with six grandchildren at least. We could do with the sound of more young feet running around the place, Marcus and

Gerry are growing up far too fast. I hope you'll be letting me babysit whilst you're off gallivanting around the world?'

'Of course I will, Mum.' She looked up from the brochure and said, 'Hopefully, things will settle down soon. Then I'll be able to focus better on my future, get the new house decorated . . .' She broke off at the intrusive sound of her communicator buzzing in her pocket. She took it out, apologised to her mother, and said 'Jennifer Collins speaking.'

'Commander Collins? It's Captain Mandrake, onboard Endeavour. Sorry to bother you, but we've got a bit of a crisis going on at the moment. There's a klaxon ringing quite loudly in the Flight Control Room and no one has the remotest idea how to turn it off. It's pretty deafening, as you may be able to hear in the background.'

'That's okay, captain, I'll deal with it. I'll speak to Admiral Taksin.'

'I'd be much obliged.'

Jennifer ended the call and pressed another button on her communicator. After relaying the message to Taksin, she blanched on receiving his response. She lowered the communicator and said to her mother, 'Sorry, Mum, I shall have to go.'

'Can't you stay until your father gets back for lunch, dear? He'll be sorry he missed you.'

'I'll pop in to his office on my way and say hello.' She checked her watch and let out a deep sigh. 'My life seems to be one crisis after another these days.' She stood up and stretched. 'I'd better go and see Surachai up at the stables; we were supposed to be eating at his mother's tonight, celebrating one of his sisters' birthday. I doubt if I'll get back in time for that. I'll have to sweeten him up somehow, soften the blow.'

It took Jennifer longer than she'd anticipated to complete her sweetening up exercise on Surachai. It was all of three hours later when, having showered, brushed straw out of her hair, donned her tunic and said her farewells to her father, that she set off for to join Taksin.

As she entered the Flight Control Room aboard Endeavour, she was greeted by a sea of anxious stares from the Prime Minister, the three Chiefs of Staff, Colonel Travis and at least fifteen others, all of whom had gathered around the central figure that was Group Captain Tyson. She glanced at Taksin and Narai sitting at the other end of the room, huddled in front of a monitor, but knew better than to interfere. She wandered over to join the main group.

'Did you catch it?' she asked Group Captain Tyson.

'We did.'

'What was it?'

Group Captain Tyson shrugged. 'I've no idea. Some sort of bullet shaped capsule thing, about the size of a washing machine. Flying like the clappers though, it took us quite a few attempts to net it.'

'Didn't Admiral Taksin say anything about it? What it was, for instance? Where it came from? How come it was flying almost direct at us?'

Group Captain Tyson shook his head. 'No, not really. Nothing beyond that it was desperately important for us to catch it, intact.' He indicated in the direction of Taksin and Narai. 'Those two have been hunkered down like that for twenty minutes now, and not one word of English spoken. It's unnerving. And the suspense is killing me.'

'We'll know in good time, I guess.' At the sound of her name being called out from across the room, Jennifer turned, responded, 'Coming, sir,' and set off towards Taksin.

Taksin looked up from his chair and said, 'We need a meeting of Star Fleet Council immediately, Jennifer. And could you ask Colonel Travis and Group Captain Tyson to join us, please? Tell them they're welcome to bring along their second in commands. Captain Mandrake better join us too.'

'Will do, sir. Is there anywhere in particular you wish to meet?'

'No, just so long as there's a table. I need to lay out some models.'

Ten minutes later, Jennifer ushered Taksin, Narai, the Prime Minister and the requested officers into a quiet room away from the superfluous prying eyes that had gathered in the Flight Control Room.

'Okay gentlemen, and Jennifer of course,' said Taksin. 'I'm sure you're dying to know what's going on, so I'll get straight down to it. Take a seat if you wish.' No one did. 'Very well, let's start with the klaxon that sounded a few hours ago. As you may have guessed, it was triggered by the capsule that Group Captain Tyson and his team kindly managed to retrieve. That capsule was a communication device, a sort of distress flare, rarely used and rather archaic in nature.

I suppose you could compare it to a message placed in a bottle and thrown into the sea. Now, as I'm sure you'll appreciate, one would need to be in rather a desperate situation to resort to such an unreliable form of communication.'

Jennifer's heart skipped a beat. 'It contained a message? Like an SOS?'

'It did.'

Jennifer sighed. 'Not from Admiral Prasert, please say not from him.'

'I'm afraid so, Jennifer, yes.'

Jennifer gave a very audible gasp.

'It seems that Spirit Of Freedom came under surveillance whilst visiting Voltaris. By another ship, that is. And ever since Spirit Of Freedom departed Voltaris, this other ship has been close on its tail.'

Taksin's words brought forth a collective gasp.

'As you are aware, Spirit Of Freedom was due to return in the next few days but, fortunately, Admiral Prasert has had the sense to fly home as slow as practically possible. Spirit Of Freedom should take another six months to arrive here on the trajectory Prasert has indicated. This, I believe, is good news for us.'

General Wilson snorted. 'Really? I don't see how.'

'Well, it makes me realise Prasert is being rather smart. And rather brave, I have to add. Protocol would demand he investigate the other ship, send it a signal, demand the captain reveal his identity and intention, or face aggressive action. But Prasert's message in that capsule says he's ignoring protocol. He's pretending he doesn't know the other ship is there. He's carrying on flying without deviation from course, without taking defensive action.'

'And why would he do that?'

'As I said, he's being brave.'

'How so?'

'Prasert's action, or rather lack of action, will have aroused the curiosity of the captain of the other ship. I think Prasert's got the other captain believing his ship has remained unnoticed.'

'To what objective?'

'I believe Prasert is leading the other ship straight to us, as slow as he dare go without raising suspicion.'

General Wilson grunted. 'That's great. Just what we wanted. Another bloody alien ship coming to attack us.'

'Actually, General,' said Taksin firmly, 'that is exactly what we should want. I can't believe Prasert has thought this through so well.'

General Wilson vented another grunt. 'Thought it through so well? Sorry, Admiral, that needs some explaining.'

Taksin rubbed his chin. 'The other ship is unlikely to be friendly. You'll have to take my word on that. If Prasert attacked the other ship, he could well lose the battle, especially with so few tactically experienced, weapons-trained crew aboard. However, if he did win a battle, it would have probably meant blowing the other ship up and that would mean there would be debris scattered everywhere, leaving a trace of what happened. That is a situation we really do not want.'

'Okay. I get that.' General Wilson conceded. 'But how does that make Admiral Prasert brave?'

Taksin grinned. 'Imagine you're in a war, General, in the battlefield. You're walking back to your camp, a secret camp, unknown to the enemy. You hear someone move behind you. Your instinct is to turn around and challenge them, but you worry that the enemy behind you is stronger, can outgun you. You continue to walk, relaxed, never turning your head, not for the merest glimpse because that would be sufficient for the enemy to realise they'd been noticed. Ahead, you know your mates in camp are expecting you, that they'll be watching out for you. You put your full trust in your mates, that they will be on the alert, that they'll see the enemy behind you. That's a very unnerving strategy to play.'

General Wilson grimaced. 'OK. I'm with you now. You're saying his best strategy is simply to continue his course, pretending ignorance of the other ship's existence, and trust that we will resolve the problem in due course.'

Jennifer interrupted and said, 'Sorry, but how can he do that, Admiral, pretend he doesn't know of the other ship's existence, that is. Wouldn't it be obvious to the other ship that they had been detected?'

Taksin tweaked an earlobe. 'Well, not necessarily, no. Let me explain.' He placed two scale models of spaceships on the table, one in front of the other, and covered the rear one with a cloth. 'Our intruder is hiding, coming into view for no more than twenty seconds once every ninety-three minutes.'

'You mean the intruder is cloaked?'

'Yes, Jennifer,' replied Taksin. 'I believe that is a term familiar to you all here, one used in your science fiction movies?'

'You can cloak something as big as that?' asked Jennifer. 'You never told us that.'

'Indeed you can,' responded Taksin. 'And I make no apologies for not telling you earlier. It wasn't relevant to any conversation we've had to date. Anyway, the ninety-three-minute interval between appearances is revealing in itself. It's very suggestive of the origins of the crew and is why I say they won't be friendly towards us.'

The Prime Minister rubbed his jaw and said, 'Admiral Prasert is taking a huge gamble. Spirit Of Freedom could be blown to bits any second. Wouldn't it have been better for him to try to fight it out? At least he would have had a chance.'

'No,' said Taksin emphatically. 'That would be a last resort, and Prasert would know that. We don't want to leave any trace of our involvement. We don't know who might also be out there. We don't want anyone to come looking for a ship that's disappeared.'

The Prime Minister nodded. 'Fair enough, but if they're not friendly, as you suggest, then why haven't they blasted Spirit Of Freedom already?'

Taksin hesitated before offering a response. 'Spirit Of Freedom was a well-known freighter in its day and this part of the galaxy is uncharted. The captain of the other ship probably observed Voltaris sufficiently to understand that a colonisation program was in progress. That would beg the question where did the people originate. I imagine that curiosity has got the better of him. The discovery of a new planet, one with vast resources, would earn him a good bonus. Not forgetting there's also the salvage value for finding Spirit Of Freedom. It's been missing for a long time.'

'They're playing a waiting game,' Jennifer clarified. 'Waiting to see where Spirit Of Freedom takes them. And then what? Attack us then?'

Taksin took another moment before responding. 'Possibly. But there are other scenarios to consider. With far more disastrous consequences.' Taksin fell silent, adding to the already tense atmosphere.

Jennifer realised several eyes were on her, as if urging her to respond. 'May we have your thoughts on that matter then, sir?'

Taksin caught Jennifer's eyes fleetingly. 'Yes. Sorry, I was miles away for a moment. I've mentioned before that the original crew of this ship, Endeavour, were a bunch of uncouth thugs who'd managed to take over the ship and were seeking a place to lay low. It's quite likely that this new ship was searching for them. What concerns me is that a search would normally be undertaken by a search party.'

'By a posse, you mean?' asked Jennifer.

Taksin nodded. 'Exactly. As I've said, this new ship is reappearing regularly every ninety-three minutes. I'm concerned it's not just checking on the location of Spirit Of Freedom but also sending a communication back to the main posse, as you call it. If that is happening, there'll be many more ships heading this way in the very near future.'

Jennifer gulped. 'Oh Christ! How many?'

Taksin shrugged. 'Ten? Twenty? It's difficult to say. But if word gets even further back than the posse, then the answer is likely to be hundreds.'

'Shit!'

'Precisely,' responded Taksin. 'My thoughts exactly, Jennifer. Which is why we need to capture this new ship intact and look at the captain's log.'

Jennifer looked aghast. 'Capture it? How can you possibly do that?'

Taksin broke into a smile. 'That's why I've asked Colonel Travis and Group Captain Tyson to attend this meeting. To ask if they're willing to give it a go.'

Colonel Travis gave Group Captain Tyson a sideways look before saying, 'Could you explain, sir.'

Taksin picked up a model of a third spaceship and placed it on the table. 'This is us, on board Endeavour. We fly out to intercept the new ship. We have the advantage of surprise; we know the course the new ship is on, its speed, when it is visible and when it is not, and we'll be cloaked. Whilst cloaked, we get behind it, draw up alongside, then we'll tell Prasert to divert Spirit Of Freedom and let loose a thousand starfighters under Group Captain Tyson's command to await its reappearance. When it does uncloak, they won't find Spirit Of Freedom in the position they're expecting. They'll be caught off-guard, and the starfighters strike at that precise moment, stunning the ship. The nearest starfighter then zooms in to the back of the stunned ship and a handful of Colonel Travis's men jump out of that starfighter onto a maintenance platform and key a code into a panel which will raise the Flight Deck Gate. The rest of the starfighters fly in to Flight Deck and Colonel Travis and his men overpower the ship.'

The stunned silence lasted a full ten seconds. The Prime Minister broke the silence with a nervous laugh. 'And this will work? This plan of yours?'

'Prasert's slow voyage has given us a few months to prepare. The closer he gets, the more obvious his trajectory becomes, and therefore Earth's location becomes known to the enemy. I suggest we take the battle to them, but we'll still have a few weeks to practice the manoeuvre, on the way there. And let me say I have the greatest confidence that Colonel Travis and Group Captain Tyson will make it work.'

Jennifer exchanged a glance with the Prime Minister. Taksin caught it and smiled. 'Yes, Prime Minister, I did indeed just say that I have the greatest confidence in your men.'

'I'm sorry, Admiral,' responded the Prime Minister. 'I didn't mean any offence.'

'None taken,' replied Taksin. 'But it's the very nature of Colonel Travis and Group Captain Tyson that make me say with confidence that they will succeed.'

'How so, may I ask?'

Taksin grinned. 'Because, Prime Minister, the procedure I just outlined is exactly how I overpowered this very ship last year. Admittedly, it was going slower, and the thugs on board were idiots, but I did it alone, all by myself. And that, Prime Minister, is why Colonel Travis and Group Captain Tyson will succeed, because they refuse to accept I could better them.'

Colonel Travis caught Group Captain Tyson's eye, gave him a wry smile, before turning his attention to Taksin. 'About this panel and code, sir. How do you know it will work?'

'A factory default setting, Colonel. My people make all the ships, and they let home-grown ship captains know the code. However, its existence is considered a National Security issue, so it's not in the manual and buyers from other planets are not informed about it. This new ship, the interval of ninety-three minutes, it's a familiar unit of time, similar to the hour in use here. Only it's not the unit in use on my home planet. I'm pretty certain, therefore, that the captain will not know of its existence.'

Colonel Travis smiled. 'You're saying we have an edge?'

Taksin returned the smile. 'We do indeed, Colonel. We'll take the fight to them, that will give us another advantage. We can attack them in our own good time, catch them off guard with any luck.'

'Then what are waiting for, sir?' said Colonel Tyson. 'Let's get the show on the road.'

'Right, yes indeed,' Taksin turned to Captain Mandrake and said, 'We'll need to take on provisions for a year for at least three thousand people. You'd better liaise with Jennifer for that, she's got staff who are well used to such logistical exercises.' Taksin turned to Jennifer and said, 'Will you stay and take charge of things this end?'

Jennifer snorted. 'Like hell I will, sir, I'm coming with you.'

Taksin frowned. 'We're going to war, Jennifer. It's going to get violent, and very unpleasant things can happen in the heat of the moment in war.'

'I don't doubt that, sir. I'm going with you to help sort out any mess that may arise. I'm not going for the fun of it.'

Taksin looked afresh at Jennifer. 'Very well, if you insist, I won't argue.' He looked at the men around the table. 'Group Captain, we'll need the full complement of a thousand of your Starfighters. Colonel, we'll need, say, two of your men on each Starfighter, that's two thousand men. Let's aim to leave one week from now.'

Chapter Forty-Five

An edge

Jennifer stared out of a starfighter's cockpit window in awe as a thousand similar craft quickly came into position in a well-rehearsed rolling tank-track formation. Deep in space, hundreds of millions of miles from Earth, a battle with an alien spaceship was about to commence and she was more terrified than she could possibly have imagined.

'Two minutes to go. Time to cross your fingers.'

Jennifer turned to face Taksin, who was sitting in the adjacent pilot's seat, and returned a weak grin. 'You've picked up some interesting idioms yourself, sir. I'm not sure that one's exactly what I want to hear at the moment.'

'Nervous?'

'I think I'm going to vomit.'

'You don't have to be doing this, Jennifer,' said Taksin kindly. 'You could have chosen to remain on board Endeavour.' He paused for a moment then continued, 'Do you want me to take you back?'

Jennifer shook her head vigorously. 'No, sir. I have a duty to do this. Same as everyone else out here. It's just . . . it's just so terrifying now that we're here, actually about to do it rather than rehearsing.' She took a deep breath and peered out the window into the depths of space. Any second now a monstrous alien ship was expected to appear out of nowhere, and they were going to attack it, capture it with luck, blow it to smithereens if not. She gave a burst of nervous laughter.

'It will work out okay. I promise,' replied Taksin, as if trying to calm her. 'Everything has gone according to plan. We've practised this attack procedure non-stop for ten days, the crews can do it in their sleep. Spirit Of Freedom has been steered well out of the way. The crew of the enemy ship will be well and truly baffled when they next reappear. We have our edge, as Colonel Travis called it. And, as a bonus, we now even have Prasert and forty other starfighters on the side-lines.'

'I know, sir, it's just . . . oh, I don't know. Nerves, I suppose.'

The communications system crackled and a voice exploded, 'There it is!'

Jennifer leaned forward trying to see where it was.

'Stun it for Christ's sake!' shouted Taksin.

'I've hit it!' another shout came. 'I've hit it! I've hit it! I've hit it!'

Jennifer pointed to a source of light in the far distance. 'There, sir. It's de-cloaked.'

'Stun it again!' Taksin screamed into the coms. 'Stun it again! And again! And again! Keep stunning the bloody thing!'

As Taksin turned his Starfighter in the direction of the newly-appeared ship, Jennifer took long deep breaths in an attempt to calm her racing heart. She shuddered at the thought that every one of the three thousand crew in the other Starfighters would be on an adrenaline-induced high by now, actually loving every second of the action.

'Look out, sir!' cried Jennifer, as a body in a space suit flew past the window so fast she scarcely recognised what it was. 'Oh my god, there's another one! And another! Oh my god,' she cried, 'we've got casualties!'

'No! Don't think like that, Jennifer,' snapped Taksin. 'They're probably okay, just drifting. The rescue team will pick them up.'

Jennifer looked puzzled. 'I thought they were going to be roped?'

Taksin winced. 'Sorry, I didn't want to tell you. Last minute change of plan. Colonel Travis said the ropes got in the way, held his men back, he said.'

Jennifer looked at Taksin in horror. 'They're jumping on to a moving ship, unharnessed? And you agreed?'

Taksin shrugged. 'His men are incredibly brave. If they choose to hurl themselves at a moving ship with no safety ropes, who am I to disapprove?'

Jennifer was astonished. 'You've changed your tune.'

Taksin smiled. 'Have I? And you think that's wrong of me?'

Jennifer shook her head. 'No, sir. It's just unexpected. You, adapting to us, that is.'

Taksin chuckled. 'Come on, let's go see how they're doing.'

As they drew nearer the alien ship, Jennifer could tell it was an almost identical model of Endeavour. Surrounding it buzzed hundreds of Starfighters like wasps, ready to strike if anyone tried to make a getaway. At the back of the ship, to the bottom left of the entrance gate she could see a suited soldier on the maintenance platform, punching the air, performing his own little victory dance. Jennifer gave a grunt at the recognition of testosterone at work. 'Well, he's happy at least. Mind you, I guess he deserves a medal.'

'Indeed,' said Taksin as he looked around the ship's flight deck for somewhere to land. Hundreds of armed soldiers were disembarking from Starfighters, running towards doorways into the interior of the ship. 'I think all three thousand deserve a campaign medal. Maybe a few special ones as well, for bravery over and above the call of duty. They really are doing extraordinarily well.'

Jennifer took stock of the scene. 'Organised chaos, if you ask me.'

'All in accordance with procedure,' said Taksin. 'Colonel Travis should have control of the ship by now. Come on,' he said as he set the starfighter down, 'let's get to Flight Control, it's been twenty-five minutes, the crew are likely to be recovering from the shock of being stunned.'

'What will we do with them?'

Taksin paused for thought. 'I'm not too sure. It largely depends upon who they are. We need to interrogate them if possible.'

Jennifer tentatively made her way towards Flight Control, two steps behind Taksin, and dodging Colonel Travis's armed men running through the corridors. As she stepped into the Flight Control room General Narai and Admiral Prasert rushed up from behind and spoke sharply to Taksin. Huddled to one side of the room lay a group of fifteen members of the crew, appearing groggy and disorientated, surrounded by armed soldiers. Narai walked over to them, bent down and uttered a few words. A moment later Jennifer froze in horror as one of the crew shouted loudly, prompting his comrades to spring off the floor and launch a frenzied attack.

As Narai fought bare handed with four attackers, he shouted to Prasert as two others ran towards the communications desk. Quite calmly, Prasert shot the first in his stride, shot the second as his hand slammed down on the communications console. In a rage, Narai made short work of the attackers, smashing bodies against furniture, twisting necks, breaking spines.

Incapacitated by shock, Jennifer could only watch in horror as Taksin raised his gun, pointed it at Narai, and screamed like an animal in pain.

Chapter Forty-Six

A moment of madness

'What did you say?' shouted Taksin.

Narai stared across the room at the gun in Taksin's hand, grunted and said, 'You heard him just then. They know about the Fist Of God and its connection to you.'

Taksin took a tighter grip on his gun. 'And you know about that too?'

'Of course I do,' replied Narai sharply and walked a few steps towards Taksin. He knelt down on the floor and stared up into Taksin's eyes. 'Go on, shoot me,' he said.

'How long have you known?' Taksin snapped back.

'Since the beginning,' said Narai calmly. 'Go on, shoot. Please, relieve me of the burden.' He bent his head in supplication.

Taksin's voice grew tenser. 'You've known all along?'

'Since we left.'

'But it was supposed to be a secret! No one else could possibly know.'

'That was the plan. For you to think no one else knew.'

Taksin looked confused. 'Plan? What plan?'

'The President's plan, of course.'

Taksin gasped. 'And he told you?'

Narai shrugged. 'Of course he did.'

'Why?'

Narai wiped a hand across his face. 'The Fist Of God was my project. It was me who ordered its construction.'

Taksin drew in a sharp breath. 'Then you're responsible for the death of my wife.'

Narai lifted his head, jerked it towards his son, 'And the death of Prasert's mother.'

Taksin threw Prasert a look. 'He knows too?'

'I told him a few months ago.'

Prasert came alongside his father, knelt down. 'You can shoot me too,' he said. 'It has to be done. I understand.'

Taksin tightened his hold on the gun. 'I trusted you,' he cried.

'And I pledged my allegiance to you,' replied Narai. 'Dying will be a relief. Please, do it. Put me out my misery.'

Taksin's finger quivered on the trigger. A tear ran down his face. He wiped the sweat from his brow. After a tense few seconds he loosened the grip on his gun, his arm falling to his side. 'No, not yet. There's work to be done here.' He wandered over to the communications console, jabbed at a button and data came up on a large screen on the wall. Taksin stared at it in horror.

Narai got off the floor, looked up at the screen and said quietly, 'No, don't do this to yourself. Please.'

'A traitor!' Taksin screamed. 'You see what they say about me? A traitor, a war criminal! Sentenced to death in absentia! Reward for information! Orders to kill on sight!'

Narai sighed. 'Please, Taksin, this is not helping. Don't read any more of this rubbish. It's just propaganda. We need to know their strength, who's out there, where they are.'

Taksin laughed hysterically. 'You think so, well let's see then.' He tapped violently at a keyboard. 'Oh, look. I guess you're right. Fifty-three other ships, all soon to be heading this way hell bent on revenge, thanks to that last signal being dispatched. Sorry, Prasert, but you weren't quite quick enough there.'

'Please,' said Narai. 'Let's deal with this calmly, in good time.'

Taksin laughed shrilly again. 'Calmly! Fifty-three ships coming for us, and you want me to remain calm?'

Narai looked around at the stunned faces of the humans in the room, frozen in shock, unable to understand the scene unfolding in front of them. 'This is doing us no favours.'

Taksin followed Narai's eyes, registered the look of shock on Jennifer's face. 'You know, something, you're right. I'll do this in private.' He bashed away at the keyboard again.

Narai looked at the screen, at a mass of pictures and writing flashing by. He sagged in despair and said, 'No! Don't transfer the data. Don't do this to yourself.'

But it was too late. Taksin stormed out the room.

Chapter Forty-Seven

Playing god

Jennifer had watched the scene in abject fear. Though not understanding a word of their tongue, the body language was enough to convince her something very serious had just occurred to their relationship. As she stood in stunned silence, Narai came over to her and said, 'I'm sorry you had to witness that.'

'Is he okay?' asked Jennifer. 'I thought he was going to kill you.'

Narai grunted. 'I was hoping he would.'

Jennifer was shocked. 'I beg your pardon?'

'Sorry, Jennifer, but that's the way it is.'

Jennifer waited a few seconds in the hope that more would be forthcoming. 'May I ask what all that was about?'

Narai sighed, 'Another day perhaps, Jennifer, but not now.'

'May I ask where he's gone?'

Narai rubbed his chin. 'I imagine he's gone to Spirit Of Freedom, back to his old quarters. He'll be comfortable there.'

Jennifer frowned. 'Comfortable?'

'He's got a lot of things on his mind. He's just caught up with rather a lot of history, written in a very uncomplimentary way about him. He's gone off to read it in peace, so it'll be best not to disturb him on the way back to Earth.'

'But that's a couple of weeks away.'

'It is, yes. But I imagine he'll need several months of quiet solitude to digest the data he's just downloaded. And to decide what to do.'

'What to do? What do you mean by that?'

'Well, I don't wish to unduly scare you but, as we feared, this ship was just a scout, part of a posse on the trail of Endeavour. There are fifty-three other ships in the main group. They would have been in regular contact, which has now been broken, so it won't be long before they'll be heading this way to work out where this one has got to.'

Jennifer's jaw dropped. 'Fifty-three ships, warships like Endeavour? We haven't a chance in hell.'

'Well,' said Narai rubbing his jaw again, 'Technically speaking, it may actually be them that don't have a chance in hell.'

Jennifer grunted. 'You're saying we can take on fifty-three warships with the resources we have, and win? Even without the advantage of surprise, which I assume we won't have?'

Narai grimaced. 'It sounds worse than it is.'

'Care to explain, sir?'

'No, sorry Jennifer. I wouldn't.'

'You're serious though, aren't you? You really think we can defeat such a force.'

'Yes, I do. But it depends on whether Taksin wants to save Earth or not.'

Jennifer was gob-smacked. 'I don't understand. Why wouldn't he?'

Narai sighed heavily. 'It's hard playing god, Jennifer. Especially for an ordinary man. Give him time, and plenty of space. That means staying away from him. Everyone that is, including me and you. He's got a lot to think through, and he won't take kindly to unwanted interruptions.'

'So it's simply back home, keep out of Taksin's way?'

Narai nodded.

'How long for?'

'A few months perhaps. Give him time, there's no need to hurry. Those ships are far off at the moment. They won't pose any serious level of threat for a couple of years or so.'

Jennifer sighed. 'So, what do you want us to do in the meantime?'

'Well, we need to get back to Earth immediately. Prasert will return to Spirit Of Freedom. Captain Mandrake should be okay with Endeavour. I'll oversee this one being taken back. I want to make sure the mess is cleaned up properly.'

Jennifer frowned. 'You mean the bodies?'

Narai nodded. 'I don't want your scientists carving them up, trying to find what makes them tick.'

'I see. Yes, of course. I understand.'

'There is one thing you can do though.'

'Yes?'

'Well, if all goes well with Taksin, and we can capture those fifty-three ships, then we'll need fifty-three recovery teams. Say six personnel to a team. They'll need training how to fly, use the communication systems and survive in space for a year or so. And there'll be a lot of organisation in respect of their provisions. There's no time like the present to get started on that exercise. You'll want to be ready to move as soon as Taksin makes his mind up.'

Jennifer nodded. 'Okay. I can get on with that. Seems pointless though, if you reckon Taksin might not want to save Earth.'

Narai sighed. 'He's in a complicated situation.'

Jennifer snorted. 'Complicated? Sorry, sir, but it seems very uncomplicated to me. We're under threat of a mass invasion, an impending war of Extinction Level Event proportions, and you believe Taksin has the power to prevent it. I see no complication with that scenario. Not if he's on our side, on Planet Earth's side that is. Are you suggesting he's not?'

Narai shook his head. 'It doesn't come down to an equation as simple as that, Jennifer. There are other factors to take into consideration. What's needed is for Taksin to decide that saving your species is the better alternative. It's a route our people have been down before and I can't say I'm in agreement with the choice we made. It didn't work out well for us. But I really don't know whether Taksin would choose a different route.'

'And this choice you mention, it's his to take, is it?'

'It is indeed.'

'And you or Prasert can't influence him?'

Narai shook his head. 'No.'

'Can we influence him?'

Narai took a moment to reply. 'Maybe.'

Jennifer perked up. 'How?'

Narai rubbed his chin and spoke softly. 'Taksin likes you, Jennifer. You remind him of his wife, when she was young. You possess many similar characteristics. If I would suggest anything, I would say go home, spend as much time with your young man. Surachai, isn't it? Taksin's mentioned him several times, how the pair of you ride through the woods, gallop along the shoreline, play about in the sea, sit on the sand staring at the horizon, embracing, talking about plans for a future life together. Continue to do all those things now, in the hope that Taksin sees you. When he does watch you, he doesn't mean to spy, not in a weird way. He watches you when he's down, feeling sad and miserable. For him, watching you is like watching a favourite romantic movie on a cold, wet, depressing winter's afternoon, curled up on a sofa with a box of chocolates and a glass of wine.'

'He said all that about me? Really?'

'He did. He has an immense fondness for you.'

Jennifer wiped tears from her eyes. 'And in the meantime, Taksin's simply not to be contacted?'

'I would not advise it. It would be detrimental. At the risk of sounding corny, may I remind you of that old saying, "love conquers all". It might actually be appropriate here.'

Jennifer took a tissue from a pocket and wiped at her wet eyes.

'Taksin's a good man with a fine history,' continued Narai. 'There's a good chance he'll make the right decision.' As Jennifer turned to leave the room, he added, 'Oh, I nearly forgot. You'll need to put together an extra team. A special one. Five people should do it, I'll give you my thoughts on that later.'

Chapter Forty-Eight

A new life on its way

The house in the foreign enclave that Jennifer had chosen to live in was a well-proportioned villa three doors down from her parents, constructed in the late Victoria era and typical of the grand English colonial style of those times. Five bedrooms upstairs, three reception rooms downstairs, a large central hallway with an impressive staircase, rooms for staff under the attic eaves. It had been empty for eight years following the previous occupier's demise at the grand age of one hundred and two and, judging by the pink bathroom suite, had probably last been updated in the early nineteen sixties. With a major refurbishment necessary, and an extraordinarily limited market of eligible buyers, Jennifer had offered twenty-five thousand pounds sterling for the leasehold interest, inclusive of all furniture and effects.

The executor and heir of the previous owner's estate, a grandson living in a council flat in Portsmouth, England, found Jennifer's offer particularly galling since old family photographs showing his father growing up in a house of manorial proportions, and waited upon by servants, had left him with an unrealistic expectation of the value of his grandmother's villa. However, after an eight year wait for an offer, and having received regular bills from the Consular for not just garden maintenance but also a local community service charge, as per the property's lease, the executor accepted Jennifer's offer, though with little thanks and even less grace.

Three months had passed since Jennifer had last seen Taksin. She assumed he'd been holed up in his palace mulling life over, giving thought as to whether saving the human species was a better alternative, as Narai had put it. An alternative to what, she had wondered a thousand times. It was a dilemma she could not fathom.

And each afternoon during that three-month period, she'd followed Narai's suggestion to the letter, throwing herself wholeheartedly into a regime of horse riding, swimming, walking the shoreline with Surachai and sitting on the beach staring at the horizon, Surachai talking of wanting babies, she of her aspirations and plans for the house.

Never had Jennifer felt so fit and tanned. Yet never had she felt such despair. In the smallest bedroom, a nursery it would be, she found herself alone one Sunday afternoon, sitting on an ancient metal bed, a white dust-sheet thrown over it, crying to herself, her hand held against her stomach feeling for signs of the new life within, not yet two months old. For what was the point of bringing a new baby into the world if it might all end in a matter of a year or two. And she had no one to blame other than herself for the mess, for it was she that had helped push Taksin to accept the whole space-exploration venture, especially the colonisation program. And if Voltaris had not been colonised, then maybe the alien ship would have merely passed by. Now though, the one million refugees she had convinced to start a new life on that distant planet had been abandoned, left vulnerable, left to face a terrifying fate.

A war was brewing, of that she was certain. A galactic war with fifty-three alien ships as powerful as Endeavour on their way to Earth for their day of revenge. Would life exist on Earth afterwards? But if she and her baby did manage to survive, did she really want to raise children in a post-apocalyptic world where survivors would have to rebuild civilisation? These were fears she had hidden from Surachai, and they had increasingly eaten away at her soul.

A loud knock, reverberating around the house, brought Jennifer out of her reverie. She wiped away her tears and made her way downstairs to find a palace official standing outside the front door. The man bowed and proffered her a scrolled parchment. She thanked him and stared at the royal seal on the scroll in trepidation.

To her disappointment, the letter from Taksin said little, other than requesting her to arrange a meeting of Starfleet Council on board Spirit Of Freedom later that afternoon. She looked at her watch; breakfast time in London. Her starfighter was parked in a warehouse down at the port. There was no time to lose, she would have to put on her happy face and get on with the task.

Chapter Forty-Nine

Fist Of God

As quiet as a mouse, Jennifer eased open the door to Taksin's private quarters aboard Spirit Of Freedom and tentatively poked her head around. In the centre of the plushly furnished room lay a round table at which she could see the three Chiefs of Staff and the Prime Minister sitting alongside General Narai and Admiral Prasert. Admiral Taksin was standing off to one side at a kitchenette, filling up a glass jug with water.

'Come in, Jennifer. Do please take a seat. We haven't started yet.'

'Thank you, sir,' replied Jennifer sheepishly. She shut the door, walked self-consciously across the room to the far end of the table to a vacant chair. She sat down, drew a notepad and pen out of her bag and acknowledged the others with a curt nod.

'Very well, I shall begin,' said Taksin as he returned to the table. 'You will know by now that there are fifty-three hostile ships out there, probably not too far away and in all likelihood heading this way. And I'm in no doubt you're expecting me to set out a plan to resolve the situation, to neutralise that threat.'

General Wilson grunted. 'You haven't disappointed us yet, Admiral. But I'm certainly interested to see what kind of rabbit you could pull out of the hat now. The way I see it, we're completely outnumbered.'

Taksin took a moment before continuing. 'Before I do so, pull the proverbial rabbit out of the hat, that is, I need to tell you something about myself. Something very private, something that I had never expected to share with anyone. Not even with Narai and Prasert. It's been my guilty secret, I suppose you could call it. I've been hiding it for a long time, bottled up inside. But I recently discovered that my compatriots knew about it after all, and that's a matter I've been reflecting on this last three months. Given that the cat's out the bag, as it were, with my secret, I've come to the conclusion that I should share it with you too. In fact, it will be absolutely necessary to tell you, in order to gain your trust for what I propose to do about those fifty-three hostile ships. However, I must warn you that once you know of my secret, our relationship will change. Life will never be the same for you again, nor for me.'

'You don't need to do this, sir,' Jennifer protested.

Taksin flashed a false smile. 'Actually, I do, Jennifer. You can't have the current threat resolved without knowing my story, my history, the reason I'm here on Planet Earth.'

Jennifer blushed and lowered her head.

It was a few seconds before Taksin resumed. 'Sorry,' he said. 'This is not easy for me.' he reached for the water jug and a glass, poured a full measure and took a sip. 'I have mentioned in the past that I used to be a ship's captain. The captain of this ship, the Spirit Of Freedom, to be precise. My life consisted of commuting between planets, transporting people and goods. It was a simple life, one that I felt comfortable with. On long journeys, my wife would often join me, in these very quarters. She was always worried I wouldn't look after myself properly. She was my rock. She was my world. My life was nothing without her. My kids would come along too; a boy and two girls, no more than toddlers.' He paused, rubbed his eyes. 'I'm sorry. Remembering them hurts deep.' He took another sip of water. 'Many of the political elite on my planet were what you might term liberal socialists. We were an advanced race, in comparison to your own, that is, both in terms of technology and society. But there was always a minority who disagreed with the political majority's staunch ideological beliefs. Typically, it was the military hawks, always warning of the threat from other planets, of the jealousy and hatred of our ideals.' He turned his head and nodded in Narai's direction before continuing, 'General Narai is a good example. He was the third highest ranking officer in our army, forever warning of impending war, how we were about to be attacked and needed to be prepared, to be able to strike back. And he was very vocal about it. I'm sure you can imagine how his views went down with a government committed to peace through political persuasion, with politicians who refuse to believe anything but good intentions from neighbours.'

Narai's shoulders sagged. 'They were fools,' he muttered. 'Bloody wishy-washy, woolly minded do-gooders . . .'

Taksin held up a hand. 'Thank you, Narai. I'm sure everyone gets the picture. I'm sure everyone at this table can readily see comparisons on this planet.' He turned to face Jennifer and continued, 'We had a strong army. Very strong indeed, and very well resourced. Our government gave them a good budget because the army policed the interplanetary trade routes and they needed hundreds of ships like Endeavour to enforce peaceful trade and cooperation. But, over the years, strains appeared. People from other planets who we traded with resented our presence, resented the imposition of our laws on the way they could trade, use the transporters that we built and sold to them, resented paying duties to us. Although my people colonised other planets, we never invaded already established colonies, never sought domination over others; we just wanted trade to flourish in a fair way. I suppose it was naïve of our politicians, a far too simplistic model of the politics of trade relations between communities of differing cultures. But the army were aware of the tensions building up and were determined to have the upper hand if and when war broke out.' He stood, picked up the empty water jug and walked to the kitchenette. 'Then some bright spark turned an obscure piece of quantum theory into practice and designed a propulsion system that would enable a ship to travel faster than light. Much faster.'

Jennifer drew a breath in sharply and uttered, 'But that's not possible!'

'No, it shouldn't be, I grant you that,' responded Taksin as he refilled the jug. 'But odd things happen when you travel at speeds approaching that of light. Variables that may have been thought insignificant can become dominant, new particles can emerge altogether. And as for things like entangled photon particles, their nature goes beyond weird. To be honest, the science is a little beyond me. All I know is that it was proved possible to effectively jump across space in a very short time.' He sat back down at the table, poured a fresh glass of water.

'Jump?' Jennifer interposed. 'As in disappearing from one place and instantly appearing in another?'

Taksin drew a deep breath. 'Effectively, yes, as I just said. However, understanding the concept is as hard as trying to understand things like Herr Schrödinger with his cat that's both alive and dead at the same time. However, I'm led to believe that, in practice, it may actually take a while to do so.'

'In practice?' Jennifer spluttered. 'You mean it's been done? There are ships out there that can do it?'

Taksin held up an admonishing hand. 'Not so fast, Jennifer, you're getting ahead of the story.' He crossed his arms, leaned back in his chair and said, 'About the same time, some other bright spark designed a weapon that could wipe out a whole planet with one press of a button. As you can imagine, it wasn't long before the army decided to combine the two new technologies to achieve the ultimate weapon; one that allowed a ship to travel anywhere in our galaxy in an extraordinary short time, undetected, appear in the skies out of nowhere and obliterate an entire dissident people. It was named Fist Of God. Unfortunately, like any other expensive military project, even one conducted in the utmost secrecy, it needed government approval. That meant involving politicians, defence committees, budget committees and so on. And I'm sure you can understand how the project was perceived by most of those politicians whom, I must stress, were ideologically opposed to weapons.'

General Wilson grunted. 'Sounds familiar,' he said and threw the Prime Minister a look of disdain.

'I'm sure it does, General,' said Taksin. 'I expect you can guess what happened next.'

'Oh, let's think hard on that one,' said General Wilson with as much sarcasm as he could muster. 'If the army wanted it kept secret, some asshole politician would have leaked its existence to the press.'

Taksin nodded. 'Got it in one, General. And within what seemed a matter of weeks our army's secret was known about by everyone, including all our trading partners, many of whom didn't like us or didn't trust us. I imagine they saw Fist Of God as such a terrifying weapon they simply couldn't allow us to possess it.'

General Wilson sighed. 'Don't tell me, your enemies launched a pre-emptive strike?'

'Very good, General. That's exactly what happened. All our enemies joined together to attack us. However, our army led a pretty good intelligence operation, and saw it coming. That gave our government a short period of time to consider how they would respond to it.'

Narai slammed his fist on the table. 'We should have counter-attacked,' he said. 'Bloody pacifist politicians chose not to fight.'

Taksin waited a moment. 'My wife and her sister, that's Narai's wife, Prasert's mother, were off visiting their parents. My kids had gone along with their mother. They were in the city that was hit first in the pre-emptive strike.'

The ensuing silence was broken by the sound of Narai sobbing.

'You'll have to forgive Narai,' said Taksin soothingly. 'Fist Of God was his project. He's never got over the loss of his wife, never forgiven himself for the billions of people that were killed. He's still bitter, still angry, still wants to fight. Despite his vow.'

'Vow?' asked Jennifer.

Taksin stood up, walked a few paces in thought, returned, stood behind his chair, rested his arms on the head-rest. 'Fist Of God was due to undergo initial trials, in secret. I was in charge of transporting it well out of the way of prying eyes. It was during that journey, before the trials began, that the war commenced. The first I knew of it was when I received a message broadcast by the President of my people instructing me to offload the crew on the nearest inhabited planet and await the arrival of Narai. The following day Narai arrived, along with Prasert, and gave me a sealed note from the President outlining his government's wishes. Fist Of God, it seemed, was not to be used in retaliation, but to be entrusted to me to do with as I saw fit. And Narai was to guard me, having made a vow to the President to protect me, unconditionally, without knowing for what purpose. At the time, despite our family connection, I had no idea that Narai knew anything about the Fist Of God project. The scenario presented to me by the President was that Narai had no idea of the special cargo I was carrying. I was therefore the only person in the universe who would know the fate of Fist Of God.' Taksin paused a moment before adding, 'I just wish it had stayed that way.'

Jennifer drew in a sharp breath, caught Taksin's eye and said, 'Oh my god!'

Taksin smiled at Jennifer. 'You're a clever girl, Jennifer. You can see where this story is going can't you?'

A shocked Jennifer said, 'I'm so sorry, sir. We assumed the worse about you, that you were on the run, that you were a war criminal or something awful like that. Nothing else fitted the profile.'

'Jennifer!' snapped the Prime Minister. 'Please mind your language.'

'But he'd prefer us to think like that,' Jennifer retorted. She caught Taksin's eye and said, 'You'd prefer us to think you might be one of the bad guys.'

Taksin smiled. 'Infinitely preferably to the truth.'

Jennifer wiped away a tear trickling down the side of her face. 'I'm so sorry, sir. I wouldn't have been so mean to you if I'd known.'

The Prime Minister caught Jennifer's attention and said, 'Do you mind telling me what's going on here?'

Jennifer caught Taksin's eye again and said, 'May I tell them, sir?'

Taksin nodded and responded, 'Be my guest.'

'Thank you, sir,' said Jennifer. She took a moment to compose herself. 'This Fist Of God, this foulest of weapons ever created, destroyed the liberal civilisation it was built to protect. Ultimately, the politicians knew that it should never have been built, that it's dreadful power would be too much for any civilisation to hold. They knew that to use it would be like opening Pandora's Box, setting them on the road to hell. So they decided to get rid of it by giving it to the one person who could see things clearer than any politician, the one person who knew what would be best to do with such an evil thing.' She fumbled in her bag for a tissue.

'And that person was?' The Prime Minister interjected.

'Just a humble, ordinary man, sir,' replied Jennifer wiping away a flood of tears. 'The bravest, most courageous ordinary man I've ever known.'

The Prime Minister threw a look at the chiefs of staff and received looks of blank detachment in response. 'I'm sorry, Jennifer, you've lost us.'

Jennifer snuffled. 'Of course, sir, you're all politicians. And most politicians, being vain, would have used this weapon to establish their own empire. But only an ordinary man, free from the corruption of politics, would realise that the best thing to do with this weapon would be to fly to the end of the galaxy, dig a big hole, bury it, sit on top of it and keep it a secret.'

The Prime Minister's jaw dropped as he took in the news. 'Are you saying what I think you're saying?' He caught Taksin's eye and said, 'You have this Fist Of God, Admiral? Here on Earth?'

Taksin sighed. 'I do indeed.'

'Then we can use it to defend ourselves,' said an elated Prime Minister. 'We can fly out to meet the fifty-three alien ships, attack them before they know what's happening.'

'Not so fast, sir,' responded Jennifer sharply. 'It's not that simple.'

'Why not?' demanded the Prime Minister.

'Because of Pandora's Box, sir. Once the evil is out of the box, there's no putting it back in.'

The Prime Minister waved his hand in a dismissive gesture. 'Rubbish! We're talking about saving the entire human race.'

'Indeed we are, sir,' said Jennifer forcefully. 'History is repeating itself, if you hadn't noticed. Once the rest of the world know about Fist Of God, we're going to face the same dilemma as Admiral Taksin's people faced.'

The Prime Minister gave a nonchalant shrug. 'Then we must maintain secrecy, prevent leaks, not tell anyone about it.'

'Indeed, sir, I agree wholeheartedly,' responded Jennifer. 'But think of the logical progression of that statement. The only way to maintain complete and utter secrecy, after we've used it, is to kill everyone that knows about it. And that means us, all of us around this table.'

After a few seconds of stunned silence, the Prime Minister said, 'And who would actually do that, Jennifer? Who would kill me, who would kill you?'

Jennifer looked at Narai. 'You would, General, wouldn't you? It's part of your vow, isn't it? To keep the secret safe? For Admiral Taksin to maintain his sanity, you've been assigned the task of killing anyone that learns of it.' She paused as a thought came to mind. 'Oh! Of course, Admiral Taksin would have needed to believe you and Admiral Prasert knew nothing about Fist Of God, that's why he got so upset with you three months ago when we captured that last ship, why I actually thought he was going to kill you.'

'I begged him to,' responded Narai. 'To release me from this burden I've been carrying for so long. I lost everything in that war, I have been dead since then. No offence, Jennifer, but killing you all here, right now if it comes to it, would raise no more emotion in me than swatting a fly.'

Jennifer gulped. 'But you won't, will you, General, because things have changed. Admiral Taksin thought no one knew about Fist Of God, but for the last three months he's known that you actually knew about it from the beginning. And you're still alive today, so I imagine Admiral Taksin has made some compromises.'

Taksin grunted. 'You're good at this, Jennifer.'

'It's my subject, sir. I'm a social anthropologist, it's what I do for a living.'

'Right,' replied Taksin. 'So, you now know the dilemma I've been in recently. To save the human race I've needed to tell you my secret. Now it's out, I have to say I feel a slight sense of relief. Apprehension as well, of course. But I'm hoping we can find a way of working this out for the best. I have no wish to see Narai or Prasert fall victim to the curse placed on this secret. They are likely to live a long time, so the shared nature of this secret is something I'm going to have to get used to. Fortunately for me, you humans don't live that long, so I'm keen to find a way to limit the number of people that need to know about it as they'll need monitoring for the rest of their lives. No loose talk, no chat-show revelations, no mention of it in any memoir. Any remark about it will result in a visit by Narai in the dead of night. Everyone understand?'

A general murmur of agreement rumbled around the table.

'Good,' said Taksin. 'Right then, enough of these cat and rabbit analogies, when do you wish to leave?'

'We're ready to go now,' responded Jennifer. 'I suggest we give everyone forty-eight hours' notice so they can say their farewells.'

Chapter Fifty

The special team

When Endeavour had landed at Brize Norton just over a year ago, it had been greeted by an awestruck crowd and given full press coverage. When Spirit Of Freedom had landed in the same place five months later, it had been greeted by a handful of less than enthusiastic workers on a miserable, damp winter's day. When Fist Of God landed, it did so without ceremony, under tight security and under cover of a moonless night.

Three hundred and twenty-three personnel, with bulging packs hoisted upon their backs, marched quietly out of one of the air base's sheds and headed into darkness towards the windowless, bullet shaped ship that sat quietly on the airstrip. Behind them came an orderly line of cargo carriers and forklift trucks.

At the head of the marchers, Jennifer signalled for the convoy to halt. She dug her hand into a pocket, pulled out her communicator and held it to an ear. 'Admiral? We're ready for loading.' A few moments later a rumble emanated from the belly of the ship, a gate opened in its side and bright interior lights revealed a cargo bay. 'Okay people, let's get aboard as quick as we can. Please enter single file, to your immediate left. You'll find cabins down the corridor. Make yourself comfy.' She turned to a face a group of three men, clipboards in hand. 'Okay guys. Get the containers on board. I'll come back and check with you shortly.' She then turned to a group of four men and said, 'Please follow me.'

Jennifer led the group of four to an elevator in which they travelled way up high above the cargo deck, along a corridor that ended up facing a sealed doorway. She placed the palm of her right hand against a panel to the side of the door and was pleasantly surprised to find that it opened instantly. She stepped into the flight control room, in the middle of which stood a stern looking Admiral Taksin dressed head to toe in his usual black clothes. She cleared her throat and said, 'Admiral, may I present four of our finest, ready to serve on this flight.'

Taksin surveyed the familiar faces of the four men walking into the room behind Jennifer; Captain Mandrake, Colonel Travis, Group Captain Tyson and John Pierrepoint. 'You're kidding me,' he muttered.

Jennifer was stung by the rebuke. 'No, sir, not at all. I kid you not. As you know, Captain Mandrake has served on Endeavour since it was brought into commission. Colonel Travis and Group Captain Tyson have not only been dedicated to our program from the start but have spent the last three months undergoing intensive training on flight control and weapons systems aboard Endeavour, under General Narai's personal instruction. As for John Pierrepoint, he spent twenty years as a radar operative on submarines, after his adventure with you, and has spent the last couple of months aboard Endeavour brushing up those skills. You won't find four other people so committed to this mission.'

Taksin held up a placatory hand. 'That's not quite what I was getting at, Jennifer. I'm just surprised . . . that's all.'

Jennifer stared hard at Taksin, waiting for an explanation. It wasn't offered.

'Very well,' said Taksin with a deep sigh. 'No doubt you've made the right choice, being the world's leading social anthropologist that you are.'

'Thank you, sir,' said Jennifer tersely. 'I'll ignore your sarcasm and take that as a compliment.'

'If you must,' muttered Taksin. 'Right then. We need to move fast. So, if I may, I'll take you gentlemen straight through to the crew quarters where you can offload your luggage. I'm hoping to leave within the hour, so I'd be grateful if you would kindly return here promptly and familiarise yourself with your stations. You'll find the systems very similar to those on Endeavour. Obviously, I shall offer you as much help as you need, but experience tells me you probably won't ask.'

Each of the four-man crew offered the merest of conciliatory nods towards Taksin.

'Just as I feared,' muttered Taksin, but nevertheless gave a grunt of approval. 'Right, Jennifer, I'd be grateful if you'd oversee boarding.'

'Yes, sir,' came Jennifer's curt response. She slid off her backpack, dumped it in a corner and left the room.

Fist Of God was by far the smallest of the four spaceships Jennifer had travelled on, at barely three thousand feet in length. Walking briskly back along the corridor that led to the elevator, she was reminded the ship looked the meanest of those she'd seen, no doubt built to foment fear in the mind of its enemies. The brutality of its power seemed to emanate from its very walls. It was not a happy ship, she concluded, as she exited the elevator on the way to check progress with the men with the clipboards.

Forty-three minutes later, with everyone aboard, Jennifer returned, exhausted, to the flight control room. 'That's it, sir. Gates are closed. Everyone aboard.'

'Excellent,' replied Taksin. 'Then we'll get going without further ado.' He turned to Captain Mandrake and said, 'You know the drill well, I believe?'

'Yes, Admiral.'

'Jennifer, please inform our passengers that we'll be taking off immediately. They need to sit down somewhere safe, preferably holding on to something secure to avoid injury.'

'Yes, sir,' responded Jennifer and conveyed the order via the ship's tannoy.

'All yours, Captain,' said Taksin. 'Let's get her up. Head for Voltaris and beyond. In your own time.'

'Aye, aye, sir.'

As Jennifer crossed the room to retrieve her backpack, the sudden force of take-off took her by surprise. Stumbling over, she gave vent to a shriek.

'Sorry, Jennifer,' Taksin called over from across the room. 'I did try to warn you. The engine's rather too powerful for the gravity-equalisation system to react fast enough.'

'Now you tell me,' muttered Jennifer as she picked herself off the floor. With a flushed face, she sat down hard on a spare chair and said, 'Don't worry about me, no bones broken.' She caught Taksin's eye and noticed a grin break out on his face. Despite her momentary loss of dignity, she couldn't help but return the smile.

Whilst the others in the room busied themselves with controlling the flight, Jennifer took a moment to take in her surroundings. There were no windows, but there was a large screen projecting the forward view of the ship's course, alongside of which were smaller screens projecting side and rear views. Trying to work out the ship's progress, it seemed no more than a minute before the ship was out of the Earth's atmosphere and flying past the moon. Another minute later, she could no longer make out Planet Earth on the rear-projection screen. The ship certainly appeared to be going extraordinarily fast. Taksin, she noticed, looked unfazed as he rose from his chair and came alongside Group Captain Tyson.

'Keep your hand steady on the accelerator, as it is, Group Captain.' He then caught Colonel Travis's attention, pointed to a small dial on the console and said, 'In a moment, the number on this display will move upwards from the current display of zero point zero zero. When it does, please read the numbers out, aloud, so I can hear, if you don't mind.'

'Yes, sir,' responded Colonel Travis.

Taksin sat back down and busied himself reading information on a screen.

After a few seconds, Colonel Travis said, 'Admiral, the numbers on the display are moving. It's showing zero point zero one . . . zero point zero two . . . zero point zero three . . .'

'Increase acceleration, Group Captain, please,' replied Taksin without taking his eyes off his console screen.

'Zero point zero five . . . zero point zero six. . . zero point zero seven . . .'

Taksin continued studying information on his console.

'Zero point two zero . . . zero point two five . . . zero point three zero . . .'

'A bit more acceleration, please, Group Captain.'

'Zero point three five . . . zero point four zero . . . zero point four five . . .'

Taksin rose from his chair, stepped towards Colonel Travis and watched the numbers increase. 'Jennifer,' he called out, 'Please announce to our passengers that we shall shortly be passing into . . . into . . . what did you call it, a wormhole? There is likely to be turbulence, so would they please ensure they are sitting down somewhere safe again for the next five minutes or so.'

'Will do, sir.'

'Zero point five zero,' Colonel Travis said loudly as his eyes flicked back and forwards between the large forward-projection screen and the numbers on the display screen on his console. 'Zero point five five . . . zero point six zero . . .'

'You won't be able to see a wormhole, Colonel, if that's what you're looking for,' said Taksin.

'That's not what was concerning me, Admiral, it's those odd patterns on the screen up there.'

Taksin took a moment to observe what Colonel Travis had pointed out. 'Indeed. Odd isn't it. It's just light, seen from a position itself travelling at a relatively fast speed, that's all. The computer will adjust for the effect in a moment.'

The explanation appeared to give Colonel Travis little comfort. 'May I be bold, Admiral, and ask a question?'

'By all means, Colonel.'

'It's these numbers I'm reading out, sir. The display seems to cater for numbers above one.' He paused momentarily and then continued, 'Will we be entering such territory?'

Taksin offered the briefest of smiles. 'A very good question, Colonel, and one that I cannot answer in the definitive. The technical manual I've been reading says yes, but I am unaware of any direct observational evidence to suggest one way or the other.'

Colonel Travis blinked hard. 'No direct observational evidence,' he repeated woodenly. 'You mean no one's tested it yet?'

'Quite right, Colonel. This will be the ship's maiden voyage.'

Colonel Travis' face fell. 'Maiden voyage? Just how old is this ship, sir?'

'About seven thousand years, I suppose, give or take a few centuries. Almost brand new. Why?'

Colonel Travis caught the eye of Group Captain Tyson sitting alongside and mumbled, 'Maiden voyage for a seven-thousand-year-old crate? That wasn't in the briefing.'

Group Captain Tyson wiped a bead of sweat from his forehead. 'Admiral, are you suggesting this ship is supposed to travel at a speed faster than that of light?'

'You have the correct operative word there, Group Captain. Supposed to, is an expression that sums it up well. We're here to try it out.' He reached for a chain under his shirt collar, pulled out what looked like a large key made of diamond shaped crystals and gave it considerable study.

Colonel Travis kept one eye on the key, one eye on the numbers, 'Zero point eight zero . . . zero point eight five . . . zero point nine zero . . .'

Taksin leaned over Colonel Travis's shoulder and inserted the crystal key into a slot.

'Zero point nine six . . . zero point nine seven . . . zero point nine eight . . .'

Taksin wiped a hand across his mouth.

'Zero point nine nine.'

'Time to test the theory,' said Taksin and turned the key.

Simultaneously, Colonel Travis and Group Captain Tyson screwed their eyes shut.

'Oh, ye of such little faith,' muttered Taksin.

Ten seconds later the ship gave a shudder and Colonel Travis opened his eyes wide. With a nervous yelp he shouted, 'One point zero five, Admiral, and rising fast!'

Taksin vented a sigh of relief. 'Well, well, it actually works. I am amazed.' He stepped to one side and said, 'Right then, to business.'

Colonel Travis's jaw dropped in astonishment. 'And there was I,' he muttered to Group Captain Tyson, 'thinking this would be a well-honed operation.'

Jennifer crept up to Colonel Travis and said quietly, 'Please remember the terms of your engagement, Colonel. What you see, what you experience on this ship, must stay a secret, it must never be revealed.'

Colonel Travis nodded meekly. 'No one would believe me anyway, would they? Einstein proved nothing could travel faster than light, didn't he?'

Jennifer placed a hand on Colonel Travis's shoulder. 'That's the spirit, Colonel, whatever your thoughts, best keep them unsaid. You too Group Captain.'

Group Captain Tyson nodded. 'Sure, but think what a squadron of jets like this could achieve. We could master the universe.'

Jennifer gave Group Captain Tyson a hard stare. 'Exactly. And I'm sure you can see the issues we'd have with a ship so powerful. Fortunately, this is the only one in the universe.'

'That's a shame.'

'That's as maybe, but who would you trust to hold the key to control a ship like this? Yourself?'

'Well . . .'

'And if you held the key, who would you trust to act as your crew. Who would you trust to have around you, knowing they might seek to steal the key from you for their own interests? It would be as toxic as possessing the Elder Wand.'

The analogy was lost on Group Captain Tyson. 'The what?'

'Harry had the right idea; bury the damn thing and don't tell a living soul about it. That's something to think about during this voyage, gentlemen,' said Jennifer, and she wandered over to stand behind Taksin who was talking with John Pierrepoint, leaving both Group Captain Tyson and Colonel Travis thoroughly befuddled.

'Right then, John,' Taksin was saying. 'Let me explain your mission. We're searching for a large group of enemy ships. They are what I believe you call a posse, their original mission being to search for the renegade ship that came to Earth a year ago. We captured one of the posse's ships three months ago when it stumbled across Spirit Of Freedom near Voltaris. Unfortunately, Spirit Of Freedom would have proved a far more interesting find than the renegade ship, so they stalked Spirit Of Freedom half way back to Earth and sent signals back to the main posse informing them of what they were doing.'

'Wow! You think this posse might be heading for Earth in search of Spirit Of Freedom?'

'Almost certainly. There are fifty-three ships similar to Endeavour in that posse. We need to find them and neutralise them.'

John Pierrepoint gasped. 'Fifty-three! But we haven't a chance against such a force!'

'Well, actually, we do,' Taksin responded. 'If we find them first, we have every chance of stopping them dead. We have the element of surprise on our side, and this ship contains a very powerful weapon system.'

'You think we can find them?'

'I'm hoping you'll find them, John. That's why you're here, to show off your radar skills.'

John Pierrepoint looked blank. 'Right.'

Taksin smiled. 'Cheer up. It'll be a doddle compared to that spacewalk you did fifty years ago.'

'I'm no spring chicken these days, sir.'

'That's as maybe, but you've got experience. Now, hopefully all fifty-three ships will be in a close group, so I expect them to appear as a neat cluster on the radar. They may well even be in formation which should aid identification considerably. Unfortunately, the ships could be anywhere, so it may take us a while to pinpoint them. Got that?'

'Yes, sir,' responded John Pierrepoint, though he looked rather bemused.

'Good. Right, let me show you how to operate this piece of equipment. It may take a while to get used to, as I assume you've realised the computer has to extrapolate data backwards to guess the location of objects out there.'

John Pierrepoint's facial expression turned to one of complete confusion. 'Right.'

It took less than an hour for John Pierrepoint to grasp the dynamics of what he stubbornly called the radar. Pleased with his pupil's progress, Taksin sat back at his console and stared at the screen.

As the hours passed, Jennifer busied herself making coffee and sandwiches for the crew, and watching Taksin as he sat studiously in front of a monitor occasionally pressing a button. Gradually, she noticed his expression changed to one of apparent frustration. Eventually, curiosity got the better of her, she wandered over to Taksin and peered over his shoulder. 'You've been staring at the screen for the best part of this trip, sir,' she asked. 'Is something the matter?'

Taksin looked up at Jennifer and replied, 'No. Not really. It's the instruction manual, that's all. I've read it thoroughly except for the last chapter. I can't access it and that worries me because it may hold vital information.'

'Corrupted data?'

'No, it's password protected.'

'And that's stumped you? With all your technical know-how?'

Taksin made a face. 'I'm not an expert on everything. But this should be accessible to those that need to know, like the ship's captain. The codes I know about, that work on other ships, don't work here. I can't think what else the manufacturer is expecting.'

'Just a second. Why is it password protected, with all the palm-print and eye-scanning identification systems in place elsewhere?'

Taksin appeared to reflect on the matter. 'I'm not sure, to be honest. It does seem odd now you come to mention it. It's not a usual method used by manufacturers, I must admit. Though I can't imagine why anyone else would get involved.'

'I use my mother's name and birthday. Have you tried that?'

'It's a long shot, but I'll give it a go,' said Taksin, smiling, and poised a finger over the keyboard. 'So, what's your mother's name?'

Jennifer gave Taksin a rebuking slap on the shoulder. 'That's not what I meant.'

Taksin gave Jennifer a broad grin. 'I know, but it was worth it to see your reaction.'

Jennifer gave Taksin a rebuking glare as he turned around and stabbed at the keyboard again.

After a few moments of watching Taksin's unsuccessful attempts, Jennifer said, 'Did you just say that password protection was not usual for manufacturers.'

'I did indeed. Why?'

'Well, you said the other day that this ship was Narai's project. Is it possible he was involved with this instruction manual?'

'The last chapter, you mean?'

'Yes. It could be something he didn't want others to know. Wanted it kept a secret. Wanted it accessible to a limited number of people?'

'Possible, I suppose, but then if he wanted me to know, he could have told me before we left.'

'Perhaps. It was just a thought . . . do you know his mother's name?'

'Narai's? Yes, I do. But I don't know her birthday. Anyway, we don't go in for those sorts of passwords. We go for complex algorithmic stuff.'

'Which could not be guessed by anyone else?'

'Exactly.'

'But a mother's name and birthday would be known to those close to him, like Prasert. And he would have been a boy when this was set up, maybe unfamiliar with algorithms?'

Taksin gave Jennifer a long stare. 'Prasert! The natural inheritor. Of course, not Narai's mother, but Prasert's mother.' He pressed hard at a few keys and the screen unlocked to reveal an array of data. Taksin's jaw dropped as he read. 'Oh, dear god!'

'What is it?'

'It's . . . It's nothing, Jennifer. Just stuff.'

But Jennifer could sense the lie. 'Right, well, I'll leave you to it,' and she drifted away knowing from the intense look on Taksin's face that something was very wrong indeed.

It took twelve hours of searching the emptiness of deep space before John Pierrepoint called Taksin's attention to a blob on his screen. Another three hours later, after skirting around it from different angles, the computer had managed to identify fifty-three individual components to the blob.

'I'm a little surprised,' said Taksin to Jennifer as she peered at the screen. 'At maximum speed, they're almost seven years distance from Voltaris. I didn't think the stray ship we picked up would have wandered more than two years distance from the main posse. I'd have left later if I'd known.'

Jennifer shrugged. 'Well, we're here now.'

'Hmm,' muttered Taksin. 'Are there enough provisions for the crews for seven years?'

'Five years only. They'll have to manage on mushrooms, or whatever else they can grow on-board. Of course, we could always take more provisions to them on this ship half way through their journey.'

'We could abort, come back in a couple of years.'

Jennifer was horrified at the suggestion. 'Abort? No way, sir. The program for colonising Voltaris has been suspended for the last three months already, we can't afford any more delays.'

Taksin studied Jennifer's face. 'Very well, then. Captain Mandrake,' he called out, 'Let's bring the ship around behind them. Jennifer, if you would, please announce to our passengers that their voyage is coming to an end. Tell them we'll shortly be coming out of that wormhole and that they should stay seated for the next few minutes.'

Whilst Jennifer did as instructed, Taksin busied himself with keying in data at his console and moments later the large forward-looking screen showed a computer-generated ring encircling an area in the far distance. Caressing the surface of a red button, he said, 'Group Captain Tyson, on my order please decelerate rapidly, we need to get the speed well below one point zero zero before I fire this thing.'

'Yes, Admiral,' responded Group Captain Tyson. 'Upon your order.'

As the target approached, Taksin's finger continued to caress the button surface. Moments later, the ship was well passed its target. Taksin's finger had not moved. A bead of sweat had broken out on his forehead. 'Go around again please, Captain Mandrake.'

'Is everything alright, sir,' asked Jennifer.

'Yes, thank you, Jennifer. A minor hitch I wasn't expecting, that's all.'

'Can we help?'

Taksin pondered a while. 'Yes, indeed. Colonel Travis, may I ask you to undertake a task for me over here?'

'If I can, Admiral, yes of course.' He stood up and wandered over to join Taksin.

'Thank you, Colonel. I have set the weapon system controls to fire a pulse that will obliterate all life forms on those fifty-three ships. The pulse brings about instantaneous death by causing a body to implode at the molecular level, leaving little more than a pile of dust. I thought pushing this button would be an easy matter. However, I have to confess I am finding the idea of it more difficult than I had expected.'

'Would you like me to do it instead, sir?'

'That would be a great relief. Thank you.'

Colonel Travis caught Taksin's eye and said in a kind manner, 'The crews of these ships, sir, are they your people?'

Taksin nodded. 'Yes, Colonel. They are. Genetically, that is. But they're from a colony set up a hundred thousand years ago; a colony that went rogue and chose to annihilate the majority of people on my own planet.'

'I see,' responded Colonel Travis. After a few seconds he said, 'Please tell me when to press the button.'

Taksin called across the room, 'Decelerate now, please, Group Captain'.

'Yes, sir,' came the response.

Taksin looked up at the screen and waited as the computerised monitors adjusted for the change from theoretical position to actuality. After a few moments he said, 'Any time now, Colonel.'

Colonel Travis pressed the button without batting an eyelid.

'Thank you, Colonel.'

'Will one shot be enough, Admiral?'

Taksin considered the matter. 'Quite right, Colonel. Another one, just in case, then.'

Colonel Travis pressed the button again.

'Right,' said Taksin. 'That's that, then. Captain Mandrake, please steer the ship as close behind as possible and we'll begin disembarking. Jennifer, if you wouldn't mind, I'll leave the organisation of that to your good self.'

Jennifer nodded and disappeared down to the cargo bay. It was another twenty-six hours before she was able to report that all three hundred and eighteen personnel and their containers had been offloaded and transferred to the fifty-three ships, safely and without incident.

'That's it, sir. All finished,' she was pleased to tell Taksin as she found him again sitting at his console. 'Ready to head home.'

Taksin stood up calmly and said, 'Then it is time for you, along with Captain Mandrake, Group Captain Tyson, Colonel Travis and John, to leave. You should join one of the other ships. I have to go somewhere else by myself.'

Stunned, Jennifer said, 'I beg your pardon, sir.'

Taksin drew a gun and pointed it at Jennifer. 'I said, Jennifer, it's time for you to leave this ship. Now, go, if you would, please.'

Chapter Fifty-One

Orbus

Jennifer stared incredulously at the gun in Taksin's hand. 'Are you serious, sir? Are you really going to use that thing?'

'Don't push me,' responded Taksin.

Jennifer laughed. 'We're in the middle of nowhere, sir. Trillions of miles from anywhere, and you say you have to go somewhere? Like where, may I ask?'

'Never you mind,' responded Taksin sharply. 'I have matters to attend to, that's all you need know.'

'Meaning what?'

'Meaning I need to take this ship somewhere else. On my own.'

Jennifer stared at Taksin in confusion. 'To do what?'

'I'd rather not say. Where I'm going, I can't guarantee your safety and I know you're with child. That's why I want you off this ship.'

'What exactly are you planning to do?'

'I'd rather keep that to myself.'

'Is this thing you've got to do a personal matter, involving family for instance, or does it involve the security of Earth?'

Taksin blinked. 'It's for the good of your planet, if that's what concerns you.'

'Well yes, that does indeed concern me. Which is precisely why I can't let you go off alone, anywhere.'

'It's far too dangerous for . . . '

'For a woman? Is that what you were going to say?'

'You can't deny you are a woman, Jennifer. Some things are simply not fit for a woman.'

Fuming, Jennifer crossed her arms. 'Really? Like what?'

'I'm not getting into an argument with you Jennifer. Where I'm intending to go is dangerous, so please just do as I ask for once.'

'Dangerous is it? Well that settles it. It's even more imperative for me to go with you. All of us, in fact. You need a crew.'

Taksin took a firm grip on his gun. 'I'm ordering you to leave, Jennifer.'

'I am not leaving you.'

'I said leave. All of you. Right now.'

'Or what,' Jennifer demanded. 'You're going to shoot me, are you, in cold blood?'

'Don't tempt me. Now, do as I say and leave.'

'To hell with your orders, sir. I am not getting off this ship.'

'Jennifer. For god's sake, just do as you're told. Is it really so hard?'

'Sod you!'

'I beg your pardon?'

Tears ran down Jennifer's face 'I am not leaving you. Shoot me if you must, but I am not leaving you.'

'Jennifer, please, be sensible. Just do as I say.'

'No.'

'Then I'll shoot.'

'Go on, then, shoot me dead, right now.'

Taksin wavered. 'Jennifer, please. Look, where I'm going, what I hope to do, not only is it going to be really dangerous, I have no idea whether it will work. I can't guarantee being able to return.'

'I don't care,' shouted Jennifer. 'I am not leaving you. I am not going to leave you to face danger alone. Damn it, I can't abandon you. Don't you understand . . . I love you too much.'

Taksin's face dropped, though his hand remained tightly gripped around the gun. 'Oh,' he said meekly. 'I see. I didn't think you felt the same.' After a few awkward seconds, he added, 'But what about Surachai? I thought you wanted to marry him?'

Jennifer blushed. 'I didn't mean that I loved you in quite that sense, sir.'

'Ah,' responded Taksin, 'Sorry, I thought you meant . . .'

Jennifer wiped away the tears from her face. 'Oh, don't apologise, you idiot.'

Taksin looked taken aback. 'Idiot?'

Jennifer laughed. 'Oh, for god's sake, put that damn gun down, won't you?' She crossed the floor space to Taksin, put her hand on the gun and pushed it downwards. 'Now, tell us what this mission is you're planning.'

Taksin looked down into Jennifer's eyes, sighed and relented. 'Orbus,' he replied. 'It's a space station. It's enormous, the size of a small moon. Part of it serves as a dock. It's where container ships unload, where materials are stored, where repairs are undertaken, where fuel components are stored. It's where populations in transit gather, change ships. The systems on it control the entire trade in my part of the galaxy. There's a fully functioning city on it too; offices, shopping malls, houses, blocks of apartments, and it can certainly accommodate ten million people. Then there's the countryside; farmlands, forests, a sea, well, a giant freshwater lake to be precise, surrounded by beautiful beaches, hotels and villas for the rich. There's an entire self-sustaining ecosystem in operation here, powered by sunlight, creating its own weather.'

'And this Orbus is important to you?'

'It's the heart of my civilisation. Our pride and joy.'

'And you want to visit it?'

'I want to neutralise it. I want to rip the heart out of that part of the galaxy, make sure no further attacks from there are possible.'

'I see,' responded Jennifer. 'Well, I'm all for destroying the enemy's base, so it sounds like a good idea. How long does it take to get there?'

'Normally? About four thousand years. In this ship, maybe a week.'

Jennifer gasped. 'A week, is that all? Wow! I didn't realise we could be so close, time-wise, that is. That's really quite unsettling.' She reflected on the scenario for a moment and continued, 'If the technology on this ship had been put into commercial operation, Earth would have been discovered and exploited long ago, wouldn't it?'

'Exactly. This ship is too dangerous to exist, and that's part of the reason I need to get to Orbus.'

'Right. But we're all coming with you. Like it or not.' She turned to face the others. 'Isn't that right guys?'

'That's right,' responded Colonel Travis.

'I'm up for it too,' said Group Captain Tyson.

Captain Mandrake nodded. 'Aye, sir.'

John Pierrepoint shrugged. 'Well, I've got nothing else on at the moment. I guess my wife will enjoy the break without me hanging around the house.'

Jennifer turned to Taksin and gave him a glare.

'Oh, all right then, but don't blame me if things go wrong. Captain Mandrake, please set a course for Orbus.'

'Coordinates, sir?'

'All the zeros should do it.'

Jennifer had never imagined quite how dull life aboard a ship travelling into the depths of space could be. Hour upon hour passed at a pace slower than she'd ever experienced in her life, with little to occupy her mind other than reading a book, making meals for the crew or dwelling upon what fate lay ahead at the end of their journey.

Having flown on countless long-haul flights from London to Singapore, on her way to Surithani, she knew just how much of a relief it always was to finally hear the captain say that he was starting the plane's descent, that they would be landing shortly. After six days, eleven hours and thirty-seven minutes of mind-boggling boredom, it was with a similar feeling of relief that Jennifer greeted Taksin's announcement that their destination would be reached within a few minutes. She wandered over to stand near Taksin, all the better to observe the action.

'Very well, gentlemen,' said Taksin to all. 'Let us commence battle. Group Captain Tyson?'

'Yes, sir?'

'We need to get our speed down rapidly. Please decelerate, as sharp as possible.'

'Yes, sir. Decelerating now.'

As Fist Of God shuddered in its deceleration, screens flickered as images adjusted from those based on predictive data to those based on actuality. Twenty minutes later, the ship's speed was down to a level that enabled clearly defined images to be seen on the forward projection screen. In the far distance, a blue dot appeared, growing larger by the second.

Jennifer pointed at it and said, 'I take it that's your planet, sir.'

'Indeed it is. But I can't say I'm pleased to see it, not in its current state of hostile occupation. There must be unbearable suffering on it.'

'Do I see three moons shining?'

'Two, Jennifer. The light you see reflected from the one on the left is bouncing off Orbus.'

'Wow, that must be some space station.'

'It is. Just a second . . .' Taksin turned from the screen, sat down and made a slight adjustment to one of his controls. 'Colonel Travis,' he said, 'We need to give Orbus a neutralising blast. Could I impose upon you again?'

'Of course, sir.' replied Colonel Travis. He crossed the room and assumed a position near the firing button. 'But I thought you were going to blast it to kingdom come.'

'Those were Jennifer's sentiments, Colonel, not mine.'

'I see,' responded Colonel Travis, although the frown on his face appeared to contradict that statement. He threw Jennifer a quizzical look, received a shrug in response, then said to Taksin, 'As before, sir, may I ask if any of your people are on this Orbus?'

Taksin nodded his head. 'Almost certainly, Colonel. The thugs that took control of my planet and people would have delighted in using them as slave labour.'

'You accept there will be collateral damage?'

Taksin nodded his head again. 'It's unavoidable. However, at least this will put them out of their misery. And it's quick, they won't know what's happening.'

'Very well, sir.'

'Are you ready, Colonel?'

'Yes, sir.'

'On three then, please. One . . . Two . . . Three!'

Colonel Travis depressed the button and a narrow beam of bright orange light left the ship. Taksin waited a few seconds, checked his controls and said, 'Again please, Colonel.'

'Yes, sir.'

'Thank you.'

'Sir!' shouted John Pierrepoint. 'My screen's showing four ships in the vicinity. They'll know now that we're hostile.'

'Yes, thank you, John,' responded Taksin calmly.

Jennifer placed her hand on Taksin's arm. 'Then let's get out of here fast, sir, before they retaliate.'

'Not yet, Jennifer. We've far from finished our work here,' replied Taksin. 'I need to dock with Orbus.'

Jennifer was left dumbfounded.

'Colonel Travis,' said Taksin, 'May I prevail upon you to press the button again a few times, I'll just line up the four targets John has mentioned.'

'Can't we just blast them to smithereens instead, sir? Make sure they're properly inoperable?'

Taksin shook his head. 'I understand where you're coming from, Colonel, but I don't want to risk damaging Orbus. I need it intact. Any explosion out here would send shrapnel flying for millions of miles.'

Colonel Travis looked a little peeved.

'Don't worry, Colonel, you'll get your chance to shine in about half an hour.'

Colonel Travis frowned. 'Oh, yes? May I ask for details?'

'Certainly not, Colonel, not with Commander Collins standing behind me intent on taking issue with my every word.'

Jennifer gave vent to a gasp. 'I heard that, sir.'

'I'm well aware of that,' muttered Taksin, and gave Colonel Tyson a wink. 'Now then, Colonel, four ships, two shots each should do it. On three, one . . . two . . . three.' Within thirty seconds all four ships had been neutralised. 'Good, thank you Colonel. Now then, as I said, give it about half an hour and I'll have need of your services again. You'd better get Group Captain Tyson ready for action too. I think the action out there is going to become pretty intense very soon.'

Colonel Tyson walked off with a smile on his face.

'What are you up to, sir?' asked Jennifer.

Taksin put on his best attempt at an innocent face. 'Making sure Earth is safe, of course.'

Jennifer wasn't convinced at the attempt.

'Captain Mandrake,' Taksin called across the room. 'I want to get inside Orbus. Please continue on the same course, it should take you inside, into a docking area. Keep the speed low, please.'

'Aye, aye, sir.'

Orbus was bullet shaped, a hundred miles long, thirty-five miles in diameter, a glassy dome on its topside reflecting sunlight, a dark underbelly beneath. All eyes stared at the forward projection screen as the ship drew closer, as the sheer size of the space station became apparent. Once past the entrance, an array of docked ships could be seen, stacked up well into the distance as though on a giant shelving unit.

'Oh, wow!' said Jennifer. 'There must be hundreds of ships in here.'

Taksin looked up from his monitor. 'One thousand three hundred and twenty-seven, to be precise, according to on-board records. That's rather more than I expected, they represent about ninety percent of the entire fleet.'

'Are these all transport ships?'

'About half. The other half are military, similar to Endeavour. And there'll probably be hundreds of smaller craft on aboard each of them.'

'So, you're saying there'll be hundreds of thousands of starfighters amongst this lot?'

'I do, yes.'

'Dear god! But we can't leave them here, they're too much of a threat.'

Taksin nodded. 'I agree with you, Jennifer.'

'We must blow them up then.'

'We could, yes. That's Plan B, though.'

'Plan B? You mean you have another plan?'

'Your logic is impeccable, Jennifer.'

'So, you're going to do, what exactly?'

'Well,' Taksin smiled. 'How about stealing them?'

'Stealing them? Sorry, but I don't understand. We couldn't possibly put any into this ship, the cargo bay is too small.'

'They already have a home, Jennifer. We just need to steal their home.'

Jennifer looked aghast. 'You mean steal the space station?'

Taksin smiled again. 'You catch on quick at times.'

Jennifer looked flabbergasted.

'Captain Mandrake,' Taksin called out. 'I'm taking control of the ship,' he said, pressed another button and stood up to look at the screens.

Jennifer followed suit, turning to the rear projection screen and seeing an enormous circular, spiral gate close behind them. 'Oh, dear god,' she muttered. 'You've got to be kidding.'

'I most certainly am not,' responded Taksin. 'I had no idea until I managed to read that last chapter of the instruction manual. It seems Narai had plans for Fist Of God well beyond those I'd been told about. I've just switched control to something a little more than automatic pilot. The ship should now be drawn into a chamber in which it will become absorbed as an auxiliary engine.'

It took Jennifer a moment to catch on. 'You mean this space station will effectively become a ship powered by Fist Of God? We'll be able to fly it back to Earth?'

'Apparently. But it hasn't been tested, of course. Narai was keeping that one quiet, didn't want the politicians to know about it. This whole space station was run by the military, so I guess it wasn't too hard to keep the adaption work secret.'

'Why would he do it though?'

'Why?' Taksin reflected on the issue. 'Well, simply because he's military, I suppose. He doesn't trust politicians, always wants the upper hand, always wants a Plan B. I guess this was his backup plan, for the military to be able to escape a war, to be able to survive, to be able to fight another day.' The ship suddenly shuddered as it came to a halt. Taksin sat down, interrogated his monitor and said, 'That's it. We're connected. We have control of Orbus. Captain Mandrake,' he called out. 'You're back in control, we need to turn around and head back the way we came. Please bear in mind that the ship has grown somewhat, we're several hundred thousand times the size and mass.'

'Aye, aye, sir, I'll take it slowly.'

'Now, if you'll excuse me Jennifer, there's something very important I have to do.' And with that, he pressed another button and spoke in his native tongue for the best part of three minutes. 'There, that should do it,' he said at length, catching Jennifer's attention.

'Do what, sir?'

'I've just broadcast on every communication channel down on the planet, letting them all know who I am and what I'm doing.'

Jennifer gasped. 'You've done what?'

'I need my people, or what remains of them, to understand the implications of what I'm doing. I'm giving them the chance of freeing themselves from the thugs controlling them, to be able to restart their civilisation.'

'But won't those same thugs have heard?'

Taksin grinned. 'I do hope so.'

A shout came from a few feet away. 'Sir!'

'Yes, John?'

'All hell's breaking out on my screen. There are thousands of blips rising from the planet. The computer is identifying them all as starfighters.'

'Good,' responded Taksin.

'Good?' Jennifer snapped at him. 'What the hell have you done?'

'Colonel Travis, Group Captain Tyson,' Taksin called over to them. 'To action, if you please. It seems there are several thousand starfighters heading this way. It will take them an hour to reach us. I hope you are able to pick them all off by then. You have my permission to fire at will, weapons set for blasting to smithereens, as you called it. Try not to hit the planet, please.'

For a couple of seconds, the two officers looked stunned. Then with a joint yelp of excitement they rushed across the room to the firing stations and began their biggest, deadliest war game yet.

Jennifer gave a grunt. 'Very clever, sir. You've drawn the enemy away from the planet. Freeing your people.'

Taksin smiled. 'That's the plan, yes. I'm hoping every ship on the planet has been sent up here to stop us leaving.' He cast an eye in the direction of Colonel Travis and Group Captain Tyson. 'Judging by the delighted expressions on their faces, I can't imagine there will be any left.'

'So, home now?'

'Yes indeed.'

'I was wondering,' said Jennifer, 'whether, um . . .'

'Whether what, Jennifer?'

'Well, instead of going straight home, I was wondering whether we could stop off on the way, pick up the fifty-three ships. I know the crews signed up for the trip, but seven years is going to be a hell of a long time for them.'

Taksin sighed. 'Captain Mandrake,' he called across the room. 'Did you hear that? New orders from Commander Collins. Seems she's the one wearing the trousers around here.' He neatly sidestepped the swipe aimed at him.

Epilogue

Jennifer's marriage took place in St Barnabas' church just three weeks after returning safely to Earth. The small church at the heart of the Foreign Enclave in Surithani had never been host to so many people, for not only was the country's ruler present but so too was the British Prime Minister. Fortunately, the white wedding dress she had ordered two months beforehand still fitted, despite the obvious signs of a baby-bump.

Taksin, dressed in a black satin outfit with a splendid gold badge pinned to a white sash, towered proudly, though rather ungainly, over the congregation at the alter and had to be prompted rather loudly by Jennifer to hand the ring to the groom.

Surachai, dressed in a formal suit, looked even more handsome than he did bare-chested on a horse. As happy as a man could possibly be, his face nevertheless showed signs of confusion, caught between a look of pride at having such an esteemed personage as his best man and the desire to prostrate himself at the king's feet.

Prasert was the first to throw confetti as the happy couple emerged from the church, though did so by way of upending a large bucket of dried rose petals over the bride's head. Taksin apologised profusely for his nephew's boorish manners, as Jennifer fought to extract any dignity from the situation.

Orbus had been placed in permanent orbit around the Earth and, after granting a long lease of his manor house, grounds and historical collections in Holtye to the National Trust, Prasert had relocated to the space station to take charge of running it. Taksin had hoped the responsibility of such a demanding job would be the making of his nephew, though clearly the incident with the confetti proved he may have been a little too optimistic.

Jennifer's plan to save Planet Earth's resources, cut carbon emissions and reduce pollution went into overdrive once Taksin had been browbeaten into allowing the newly captured ships to be used to fulfil her ambitions; Orbus was destined to become a major passenger transportation hub and the new go-to choice of holiday resort; Voltaris would be provided with a weekly ferry service; plastic in the oceans would be cleared; and fossil-fuelled long-haul flights would be reduced dramatically.

Narai abandoned his Caribbean island of Cunera and resettled in his old villa on Orbus. On the day of the wedding, he sent a last-minute message to Jennifer, wishing her all the best but also expressing his regret at not being able to attend on account of sudden illness. As the wedding ceremony was in progress, he stood in front of a life size painting of his wife hanging in his villa, vengeance darkening his mood, and hoped Taksin and Prasert would be far too distracted to question his excuse. He took hold of the painting, slipped a catch embedded in the frame, swivelled it forward and cautiously manoeuvred down a concealed flight of steps, at the bottom of which lay a formidable looking door. Placing his hand on a security panel, the door yielded to reveal an enormous hanger where a hundred craft lay parked, each a starfighter-sized mini-version of Fist Of God. Two minutes later, a portal opened in the outer wall of Orbus and one of those craft shot out, disappearing from sight within seconds.

Printed in Poland
by Amazon Fulfillment
Poland Sp. z o.o., Wrocław